MELODY FROM THE DEAD

DETECTIVE INSPECTOR MARC FAGAN

JASON CHAPMAN

OFFWORLD
PUBLICATIONS

i

Author's notes

This novel is a work of complete fiction. The names, characters and incidents portrayed in it are the work of the author's imagination. Any resemblance to actual persons, living or dead, events or localities is entirely coincidental.

Graphic content warning

This story contains language that some will find offensive. Also references to sexual abuse some will find upsetting.

It comes down to two simple choices.
Chase the dream, or give up.

C H A P T E R   1

DAY 1

Vine Road music studios – Monmouthshire – 2:54pm

Detective Inspector Marc Fagan glanced up at the crystal clear blue sky, smiling to himself.

'Something you want to share, boss.' Detective Sergeant Sean Watkins remarked.

'I was just thinking. We used to ride our bikes all the way from Abergavenny. Hoping to catch a glimmer of the artists that played here. Some of the biggest musicians have recorded albums at these studios. This place was buzzing back in the day.'

The two detectives trudged up a gravel track towards a series of converted barns. A crime scene investigator was unloading equipment from the back of a van.

'Afternoon Dia.' Fagan greeted. 'What have you got for us?'

'You're going to want to see this, Fagan.'

Fagan and Watkins followed the CSI through what appeared to be a courtyard. A man was unloading a guitar from the back of a top of the range 4X4 Mercedes.

'There's a lot of construction work going on. They're expanding their sound studios.' The CSI explained.

Finally, they reached their destination, which was a field at the back of the studios. Builders were laying the foundations for a series of buildings. Police cordons were in place. A police officer stood guard at the entrance to the field. Fagan and Watkins slipped into some PPE before entering the field.

A CSI tent had been erected over a trench that had been dug to lay electrical cables.

1

'Glad it's dry,' Fagan remarked. 'I bet this ditch fills with water. When it's pissing it down.'

Both detectives jumped down into the trench.

A CSI was kneeling, brushing loose soil off what appeared to be human remains.

Fagan looked back towards the studio buildings. 'So, one body found at the back of a famous music studio.'

The CSI looked up. 'Yeah, the shit is really going to hit the fan when this gets out. This studio has always relied on anonymity. It's one of the most famous recording studios in the country. Easily as famous as Abbey Road. But you wouldn't know it was here. There's no signpost on the road or anything.' The CSI looked down at the remains. 'What do you see, Inspector Fagan?'

Fagan examined the remains before realising why the CSI had asked the question. 'Where's the head?' He paused. 'Come to think of it, where are the hands?'

'Exactly.' The CSI said. 'What we have is one dead body missing head and hands.'

'Obviously to prevent identification, should the remains ever be found.' Watkins suggested.

Fagan glanced towards the studio building. 'Those buildings are quite a distance away.' He glanced at the surrounding fields. 'We're in open countryside out here.'

'What's your thinking, Boss?'

'Whoever dumped this body didn't expect it to be found. However, they weren't taking any chances either.'

'So they remove the head and the hands to prevent any form of identification?' Watkins added.

Fagan puffed out his cheeks. 'Any idea how long these remains have been in the ground?'

'Thirty years. The body is well preserved. This field used to be a peat bog, but the builders have drained the field so they can start construction. Whoever this is, she's female.'

'Any clothing?'

'No.'

Fagan nodded. 'Ok, so we have a naked Jane Doe, minus head and hands. How are you able to be so precise about how long the body has been here?'

The CSI pointed to another forensic tent. 'Go take a look.'

Fagan and Watkins hauled themselves out of the trench and walked over to the other tent.

A statue sat on an evidence table. Along with a watch.

Fagan studied the statue of a woman wearing a helmet, clutching a shield with the union jack etched on to it. A brass plate was visible on the wooden base. He suddenly realised what he was looking at. 'Wow, it's a Brit award.'

'And it's genuine.' The CSI said.

Fagan picked up the award and read from the plaque. 'Awarded to Alexandrea Xavier for best album. 25th June 1993.' Fagan searched his memory.

'I know her,' Watkins said. 'The missus is a huge fan.'

'Yeah.' Fagan nodded. 'I was seeing a WPC in the early 90s. She used to have all her albums. What did they call her? Alex X.'

'They're always playing her songs on the radio.' The CSI said.

'Hang on.' Fagan pointed back towards the trench. 'Headless body over there.' He looked down at the award. 'Found with a Brit award belonging to Alexandrea Xavier.' He glanced at Watkins. 'But she isn't dead, is she?'

Watkins yanked his phone from his pocket and googled her name. 'Nope, according to her Twitter feed, she's still alive and kicking. Been a while since she posted anything. Last post, December last year. Wishing her fans a merry Christmas.' Watkins thumbed through her Twitter page. Loads of videos from her younger days when she topped the charts. She has ninety-two thousand followers.' Watkins returned to Google and punched in her name again. 'According to Wikipedia, she was born on May 20th 1970. Original name, Alexandrea Price.

Had a younger sister, Abbey.' Watkins paused. 'It says here she committed suicide in 1993.'

'Suicide?' Fagan questioned.

'This Wiki page is vague. It doesn't give any details.'

'Does it give a date of death?'

'No.'

Fagan glanced at the award. 'This was awarded to Alex X in June 1993. The month before that, her sister commits suicide.' He looked at the watch on the table. The CSI had wiped the dirt away from the face. 'It's a Rolex watch.' Fagan could just about make out the branding on the face. He turned the watch over, spotting an inscription on the back. 'I can't make it out.' Fagan squinted at the back of the watch. 'Labs will have to clean this up.'

'Whoever this is, boss, liked a bit of bling.'

Fagan processed the information available to him. 'Ok, so we have one headless corpse, one Brit award belonging to a 90s pop icon. Plus a Rolex watch. Her sister commits suicide a month before this award is handed out. What's the connection?'

Watkins tried his best to summon an explanation.

Fagan looked at the CSI. 'I take it the manager of the studio is available to talk to?'

'Yeah, he's in the main farmhouse.' The CSI pointed back towards the studios.

Michael Banks sat in a spacious farmhouse kitchen, staring out of the window. He spotted two men walking towards the back door.

Fagan tapped on the open door.

'Come in and sit down.' Banks invited with a solemn tone.

Fagan produced his ID. 'DI Fagan, this is DS Watkins. Are you the manager of this place?'

'I'm the manager and owner.' Banks sighed, staring out of the window towards where the CSI team was working.

4

'Not the best publicity for you, Mr Banks. A body being found at the back of your property. This being a prestigious recording studio and all.'

'This place has been one big headache since I brought it.' Banks grumbled.

'When was that exactly?'

'November 2019.'

'Shit timing.'

'Yeah.' Banks sighed. 'When covid kicked off, the country went into lockdown. I was stuck with this white elephant. All my backers pulled out. Couldn't find one musician who was interested in recording here. Thought I was going to have to sell it at a loss.'

'Looks like you've changed your mind. There's a lot of construction work going on at the back of the studios. What are you building?'

'Three new studios and luxury accommodation. Before I bought this place, all the artists stayed at the Agincourt hotel just up the road.'

Fagan and Watkins glanced at each other.

'They're still using it at the moment. But within a year, we'll have four new bungalows with five bedrooms each. We'll probably use the hotel still. But it will just be for entourage staff. The musicians will stay within the studio complex.' Banks frowned. 'But now we've discovered a body in the field out back. It's just another bloody setback. I've already spent a fortune on this project. It took three years to convince the local council to let me drain a peat bog so that I can build. They finally granted me permission last year. How long until you remove whoever it is you found out there?'

'CSI officers will stay on and check they haven't missed anything. It shouldn't be too long. What made you change your mind about selling the studio?'

'Last October I got a call from Netflix of all people. Totally out of the blue. They told me they were looking at establishing a series of sound studios in the UK. To produce soundtracks for movies and films. They said this place was high on their list because of its rural location. I had a meeting with them last November and we got the ball rolling. There's a public footpath that runs through this land. Local ramblers were kicking off big time when I closed it off. Eventually, the council gave me permission to drain the peat bog. They were going to turn me down. I contacted Netflix about the issue.' Banks smiled. 'Netflix contacted the council and twisted their arm. If you know what I mean. The council even marked out a new footpath for the ramblers to use. I have had lots of flak over the draining of the peat bog from the local press. Some la de da Lord up the road. Having a go at me for desecrating ancient land'

Fagan smiled. 'I take it that would be Lord Barry?'

Banks nodded. 'I had a big write up in the local press about what I was planning. That's when all the country bumpkins kicked off.'

'How much land does this studio occupy?' Watkins asked.

'Approximately eighty acres. It is a large piece of real estate. Definitely worth the investment. After Netflix contacted me, Amazon got in touch. Also wanting to build sound studios. But it was in January I really hit the jackpot. Disney came calling, looking to set up recording studios for an orchestra. Last week, I was in London and had a meeting with them. They plan to record soundtracks for a new *Star Wars* series and a couple of *Marvel* films.'

Fagan smiled, imagining how excited Jamie Evans was going to be when he got the chance to tell him.

'When it's all finished, this place will be buzzing again. It'll be like a mini Hollywood in the middle of rural Monmouthshire. All the major artists are coming back. Got a lot of big names lining up to use this place again. But I cannot mention any of them because of privacy concerns.'

'Of course.' Fagan said, jotting down notes.

'The problem lockdown caused, was these pop stars with big houses built studios in their back gardens. This place really took a hit during the pandemic. I put the staff on furlough, hoping things would bounce back. But by the end of 2021, it wasn't happening, so I had to let them go. I felt shitty about it. I spent most of last year deciding if I was going to sell the studio. By October, I'd made up my mind. I was about to put it on the market. Then Netflix got in touch. I started getting phone calls from new artists wanting to record here. Then Amazon called. It's really turned around for me this year. Now that the artists are returning, I thought about taking on new staff. But most of the major recording artists have their own sound engineers. I suppose it cuts down on the cost of hiring new staff. I pay for a security company to monitor things. We had a major theft last November.'

'What was stolen?' Fagan asked.

'Everything from studio one.' Banks explained. 'It's our oldest studio. It was quite a professional job. The thieves broke in and stripped the studio bare. Even the sound insulation panels off the walls. Some panels had been there since they first set up the studio in the seventies.'

'Do you have much knowledge regarding the history of this studio?' Fagan asked.

'Not really.' Banks admitted. 'One of the blokes I used to employ told me the history of this studio when I bought it.'

'Have you always been in the music industry, Mr Banks?'

Banks shook his head. 'Before I bought this place, I was an investment banker. Had enough of London and wanted the quiet life. It's been hard going over the past few years. I have had my difficulties with this place. But now things are looking up, I can look forward to retirement.'

'Not looking at keeping this place, then?'

'No. As soon as construction is completed and I've secured contracts with Disney, Netflix and Amazon, I'll give it a couple of years. Make sure the business is turning over a healthy profit, then sell it on for a mint.'

'I've thought you said Netflix and the other businesses have signed to record here?'

'It's not as simple as you might think. There's still a lot of paperwork to sort out. My solicitors are handling that.'

'How much do you plan to sell the studio for?'

'I have already had an evaluation. After the work is complete and things are up and running, I'll be able to sell this place for twenty-five million.'

'Nice.' Fagan stated.

'If it's studio history you're interested in. There's a hall of fame corridor at the main entrance to the studio. Lots of pictures of former artists that have recorded albums here.'

'Mind if we have a look?' Fagan asked.

'Knock yourselves out. I have to make a phone call. Feel to have a wander.'

Fagan and Watkins entered the main studio entrance.

'Bloody hell, they've had some giants record albums here.' Fagan remarked, walking by dozens of photographs that lined the corridor wall.

Watkins spotted a framed photo which had a signature scrawled on it. 'Boss.' He pointed.

Fagan stared at the image of a famous glam rock artist with band members. 'Not this studio's finest moment, considering what he is.' He looked further on down the corridor 'Here we go.'

Watkins stared at a framed photograph of Alexandrea Xavier. He glanced at Fagan. 'Smart looking piece, Boss.'

'She was.' Fagan inhaled, rubbing his hands together. 'This is what we're going to do. We're going to head back to Newport central. You're going to get the Greggs in and we'll grab Brooks for a briefing.' He checked his watch. 'Then we'll call it a day. Our friend in the ditch at the back of the studio isn't in a position to tell us what happened.' Fagan lifted the framed photo off Alex off the wall.

8

Newport central police station - 4:23pm

Fagan stared at the mug of coffee Constable Brooks held out. 'That's not Aldi's shit again, is it?'

'No.' Brooks sighed. 'It's Asda gold roast shit.'

'Can't you get decent coffee once in a while, inste cheap crap?' Fagan grumbled.

'There was only four quid in the tea, coffee and bis kitty. Maxwell House is almost nine quid a jar. I'm thinkin, giving up coffee all together.'

Watkins breezed into the room with an open box confectionaries from Greggs.

Fagan grabbed a doughnut as he walked by. He brace himself before sipping the cheap coffee. 'Ok then you two.' He glanced at the clock. 'We knock off at five, so let's get as much in as possible. We have the headless remains of a female. Discovered at the back of Vine Road Music studios. Located just outside Monmouth on the old Abergavenny road.' Fagan pointed to a plastic bag containing the statue. 'We have one Brit award. According to the plaque, the award was given to Alexandrea Xavier in June 1993. We also have the remains of a Rolex watch.' Fagan looked at the photo he had taken from the studio. 'We know Alex was one of their recording artists back in the 90s.' Fagan glanced at Brooks. 'What have you got?'

Brooks looked down at his tablet. 'Alexandrea Xavier, born May 20th 1970. She was a local girl. Born just up the road in the Royal Gwent. Had a sister called Abbey. Daughter of a steel worker called Simon Xavier, formally known at Simon Price.

9

ccording to her Wiki bio, her father had an accident while working at Llanwern steelworks in 1982. Nearly killed him. He had over sixty percent burns.'

'No mention of who mam is?' Fagan asked.

'There's no mention of any mother.' Brooks explained, staring at the information on the screen. 'In 1986, Price encouraged his daughter to join a band. After hearing her singing in her bedroom.'

'Name of the band?'

Brooks scanned the Wiki page. 'They're called Lead from the Back. The frontman guitarist was called Steve Wakeman.'

Fagan walked over to a large whiteboard and wrote a list of names.

Watkins tapped the name out on his laptop. 'Lead from the Back is still going. They have a website and the usual social media pages.' He paused, reading a brief bio. 'Wakeman is the only original member of the band left.'

'How long did she spend in the band?'

Brooks continued to read through the Wiki page. 'Just over three years. Apparently, Alex and her band mates auditioned for a talent show in Cardiff in October 1989. A record producer, called Frankie Jordan, spotted them.'

Watkins tapped in the name to Google. 'Here we go, found him. Frankie Jordan was born in Monmouth in 1950. He was one of two men who set up Vine Road music studios.'

Fagan finished the last of his doughnut. 'Who was the other bloke?'

Watkins scanned the text. 'Someone called Mickey Mercury. Formally known as Michael Spencer. Born in Coleford on the Monmouthshire and Gloucestershire border in 1949. They set up the studio in 1973. Rented space in the farmhouse attic at the current location. In 1977, they made enough money to buy an old barn and convert it into a studio. Following the launch a group called the Antagonists.'

'I remember them. They were a punk band.' Fagan

recalled.

'That's what it says here. They went on tour with The Sex Pistols and the Clash. The Antagonists have sold thirty million albums worldwide.'

'Are they still about?'

Watkins took a moment to answer. 'No. They're all dead. Two died in the 80s from drug overdoses. One died in the 90s from alcohol addiction and the last band member died of a stroke ten years ago.'

'I'm surprised anyone from those punk era bands is still alive. They were into some serious drugs back then. Sid Vicious and his girlfriend Nancy both died of overdoses.' Fagan wrote Jane Doe on a whiteboard. 'Right, getting back to the remains found in that field. The CSI said the victim is female.' He wrote Alex X under Jane Doe's name. 'Our priority is to track down Miss Xavier.' He looked at the statue. 'The Brit award found with the remains belongs to Alex. CSI also found a Rolex watch with the body. There's no sign of any clothing. So our murderer stripped the body naked before dumping her. This raises two questions. Number one, who is our headless victim? Number two, what is Alex's connection?'

'According to an article I just found, Alex Xavier is retired and the living the dream in Spain.' Watkins revealed. 'This article is nine years old.'

'What's the source?'

'An online Welsh music magazine called Word on the street. They're Cardiff based, so they're not too far away.'

'Does it say where in Spain she's living?'

'Yeah, she's in a place called Tarragona.'

Brooks carried out a quick map check. 'It's about sixty miles south of Barcelona. Doesn't look like there's a lot there. Not the resort kind of place you'd go on holiday to.'

'Quiet and secluded.' Fagan glanced at Watkins. 'Does it say why she's out there?'

Watkins studied the article. 'Ah, here we go. Let me read

from the article from when Frankie Jordan signed her up.' Watkins cleared his throat. 'They were glorious years, recalls Alex, speaking from her Spanish villa in Tarragona. When I first joined the band, Lead from the Back, we'd tour all over south Wales. Mostly university campuses. We'd do a regular gig at Bristol University. It was so much fun. We'd do a lot of the pubs in Cardiff and the surrounding valleys. My dad would accompany us on our gigs. You know, just to make sure I wasn't getting into any trouble. When I first joined the band, dad changed our surnames names to Xavier. Back then, we were writing our own music. The lead guitarist, Steve Wakeman, helped me develop my skill as a lyricist. He taught me that music comes from the soul.'

'Very poetic.' Fagan interrupted.

Watkins carried on reading. 'In September 1989, a music scout spotted us and invited along to a talent show in Cardiff. A major music producer was in town looking for unknown groups to sign. I just treated it as another gig. I didn't really pay it much attention. But then everything changed when I saw that Frankie Jordan himself was on the selection panel. I just looked at him and thought, wow, one of the biggest promoters in the music industry is about to hear me sing. I belted out a few of the songs me and Steve had co-written. Later that evening, Frankie called us all over to his table. We were there until six o'clock in the morning talking about our hopes and dreams. Frankie snapped us up straight away. I remember me and Steve being over excited. At last, we were on our way. We were like children on Christmas morning.'

'It says here in this article I found. Frankie Jordan was the Simon Cowell of the late eighties.' Brooks mentioned.

'Watkins continued.' I guess from the start, I was too blind to see the cracks in our relationship. Me and Steve had been an item for just over two years. When we first signed with Frankie, he promised us we'd stay together. But, six months down the line, he changed his mind. It's only now, with hindsight, I can see Frankie was never interested in Steve and his band. It was me he was interested in. Frankie told me to concentrate on my own lyrics and forget what me and Steve had written together.'

'Ok. So trouble in paradise.' Fagan speculated. 'Frankie signs up the band, but in reality, all he's interested in is Alex. So he causes friction between Alex and her bandmates.'

'This is interesting.' Watkins said. 'Alex complained to Jordan about how he had treated her bandmates. But then Frankie booked her to be one of Madonna's supporting acts when she did her world tour in 1990. I actually got to sit down with my idol after the concert and had a heart to heart. Madonna advised me, never let any man hold you back. It was then I knew I had to turn my back on Steve.'

'Hang on.' Brooks interrupted. 'I just got a ping on Steve Wakeman. According to our police database he's got form for GBH.'

'Who did he smack?'

'In March 1990, South Wales police charged with assault against Frankie Jordan. Almost six months later, he was convicted again for harassment.'

'Against Frankie Jordan?' Fagan guessed.

Brooks shook his head. 'No, Wakeman was convicted of harassment against Alex X. But she didn't file the complaint against him.'

'Let me guess, Frankie Jordan filed the complaint.'

Brooks nodded. 'When he was convicted of assault, Wakeman was given a three month suspended sentence and ordered to pay two grand in court costs.'

Fagan looked at Watkins 'Does it say why Alex X dropped out of the show business scene?'

'The long hours finally got to me.' Watkins kept reading. 'That's when the drug abuse started. At first it was a pick me up to boost my confidence before a gig. Then I started taking them after a concert to keep me high. When I used to do the encore at the end of a gig, I would walk off stage where no one could see me. Do a line of coke and then go back on stage. It was kind of like a mental orgasm. Always being in euphoria, never wanting to come down from the ceiling.'

'And the truth comes out.' Fagan said, finishing a second doughnut. 'It's always about the drugs. Save that article and we'll come back to it. Right now we have to concentrate on the remains found at the studio.'

'But it always goes back to Alex, doesn't it, boss?' Watkins said. 'The Brit award found has her name on it.'

Fagan stared at the lack of information on the whiteboard. 'Yeah, it does, shit.' Fagan stepped back from the whiteboard. 'Ok, consider this. We have one body in a ditch, minus a head. Alex's award is present. We know she's still alive and now living in Spain. Did Alex murder somebody?'

Watkins and Brooks exchanged glances.

'Look, I know how it sounds. But Alex dropped off the face of the earth overnight. One minute she's on top of her game. Then the next minute she was at rock bottom.'

'But they still play her hits on the radio. So she hasn't totally dropped off the face of the earth.'

'What was the last hit she had?'

Brooks carried out a quick search. 'March 1994. She had a number one called Last Chance.'

'Interesting choice of song title. Considering she just upped and left the pop industry.' Fagan scrawled the words on the whiteboard.

'The nineties produced a long line of pop sensations.' Watkins said. 'Think about it. Alex was top of the charts from 1990 to 1993. What came after that?'

Fagan shrugged.

'Come on Boss. Who burst onto the music scene in the mid-nineties?'

Fagan returned Watkins' question with a blank stare.

'The Spice Girls. Bloody hell, don't say you don't

remember them.'

'Of course I know who the Spice Girls are. I just didn't take any notice of them. I was more of an Oasis fan. They were constantly feuding with Coldplay. Liam Gallagher and Chris Martin had some brilliant bust ups.'

'The Spice Girls dominated the charts with a string of hits and a crappy film. I still haven't forgiven my sister for dragging me to the cinema to watch *Spice World*.'

'Before we go off track here, let's consider who our murderer is.' Fagan circled Alex's name.

'Going out on a limb with that assumption, boss.'

'CSI found the remains with Alex's Brit award, which puts her at the top of our suspect list. Any guesses on who our headless victim is?'

'A groupie.' Brooks suggested.

'Good guess.' Fagan replied. 'These popstars have legions of fans. People who latch onto them, hoping to be part of their lives. That means we have to question everyone who was close to Alex. We'll draw up a list of names. I wouldn't mind talking to her former bandmate, Steve Wakeman. I bet he's got an interesting story to tell.'

Watkins glanced at his laptop. 'Lead from the Back is based in Chepstow. They have a jamming session every Tuesday night in the Boat Inn.'

Fagan's phone buzzed. He looked at the screen. 'looks like we'll have to cut this short. The chief wants a word with me. Let's meet up first thing in the morning and try to piece all this together.'

CHAPTER 3

4:56pm

'Take a seat Detective Inspector Fagan.' Chief Constable Paul Griffiths instructed.

Fagan sat, but could feel his nerves kicking in. The fact that Griffiths sounded official and unemotional gave Fagen cause for concern.

Griffiths seemed to take forever to say something. 'Listen Marc, there's no easy way to say this but you're under investigation regarding your actions towards Benny Nelson.'

'My actions towards Benny Nelson, sir,' Fagan repeated. 'I haven't done anything to him. If anything, he's taunted me. All the TV and radio interviews he's given. Accusing him of crimes he never committed. If you ask me, we've been falsely implicated. Then there's that ridiculous petition he's got running to sack me. It's a bloody circus, sir.'

'The Independent office for police conduct doesn't think so.'

'I have done nothing wrong. Nelson is playing us like a fiddle. Jesus, he's even written a book that's being released in the next few days. He's set to make a small fortune off the lies he's about to spin.'

'I can't stop him from writing a book.'

'No, but you can stop him from appearing on every TV show and slagging the police off for doing their job.'

'Did you?'

'What's that supposed to mean?'

'Do your job. You have a history with Benny Nelson. You assaulted him on more than one occasion.'

16

'I can't believe I am hearing this bullshit from you.'

'Watch your tone, Detective Inspector Fagan.' Griffiths warned.

'Alright then. I can't believe I'm hearing this bullshit from you, *sir*. That was *forty* years ago. I have paid my dues since then.'

'What do you mean?'

'Are you really that naïve, sir?'

'Hey, I'm on your side.' Griffith stated. 'I was on the phone to the commissioner earlier trying to convince him to call off the IOPC.'

'I served two years in prison for my past crimes. One of which I deeply regret.' Fagan's mind was thrust back forty years earlier to the night outside the Farmers Arms.

Griffiths looked down at a document in front of him. 'It says here you had many disputes while you served time at Usk young offenders institute.'

'Jesus Christ, it was prison. What do you expect? It was no picnic in Usk, I can tell you that. I defended vulnerable prisoners from being abused by other prisoners and serving prison guards. At no time did I just beat anyone up for the sake of it. When it was a young offenders institute, Usk made the film Scum look like a Disney film.' Fagan stared at Griffiths. 'Why are you doing this? Why are you allowing Benny Nelson to get the upper hand on us? We should be looking into the crimes he's been accused of committing in the past. The endless sexual abuse allegations. One woman committed suicide because she was raped by Nelson when she was just fourteen. She had to endure years of ridicule. Being accused of being the local bike. Why has Benny Nelson got away with so much over the years?'

Griffiths remained silent.

'When we arrested him in connection with the murder of Rebecca Jenkins, he could take the piss with that fancy lawyer of his. And then it was followed by some bullshit report about

Nelson suffering from mental health issues and could be a danger to himself if arrested again. Tell me how he could afford a lawyer that would cost the rest of us the price of a house in this town.'

'Benny Nelson has been the victim of a vicious bullying campaign in this town for the past five decades.' Griffiths pointed out.

Fagan stared back in disbelief. 'I cannot understand why you defend that dickhead. The man has been a thorn in this town's side for decades. Allegations of rape and abuse. Being arrested again and again, only to be released. Now that I've come back to town, the focus of attention seems to be on me.'

'And why do you think that is DI Fagan?'

'You tell me.' Fagan shot back.

'Look, I'm not happy with the situation myself.' He paused. 'You seem to be a good officer. Your skills as a detective are invaluable. But you must understand there are rules that need to be followed.'

'What rules have I broken exactly?'

'You arrested a vulnerable man and subjected him to an interview he wasn't fit to hold.'

'Jesus, Nelson has really done a Jedi mind trick on you, hasn't he. The man is playing you. He's playing all of us, including the victims in Abergavenny. You would have thought, in the light of the Jimmy Savile scandal, the police would be open to the possibility that sex offenders don't have to be dirty old men in raincoats. They can be celebrities, football stars, TV stars.' Fagan paused. 'Serving police officers, judges, doctors. People from all walks of life.'

'I'm afraid it's out of my hands.'

'And what exactly am I to expect? A roasting from a woke committee. More concerned with media relations than catching criminals. Jesus, look at what the police have become over the past few years, will you? We have to look after the wellbeing of those who seek to eat away at law enforcement.

Those idiots who throw statues into the sea because they think it's their moral obligation. Those morons who sit in the middle of motorways pretending they care about the environment. While all the time gaining popularity on social media. When will it end? When the police force is disbanded, allowing the criminal element to take over. Do you have any idea what it's been like during the past few years? Struggling through this bloody pandemic while criminals roam free. Benny Nelson is an example of that. He's using mental health issues and his popularity on social media as a weapon against us.'

Like I said, it's out of my hands.'

'Have you not listened to anything I have just said?'

'Look, my hands are tied, DI Fagan.' Griffith said sternly. 'Like you, I have superiors who do not want to rock the boat. Benny Nelson is that boat.'

'There is no boat to rock. When we arrested Nelson, we had reason to suspect that he was a lead suspect in the murder of Rebecca Jenkins. He even sat there and confessed to her murder.'

'Even though he didn't murder her.' Griffiths pointed out. 'Can you see what we are up against? Nelson is mentally unstable. The fact he tried to take his own life is proof of that. We have to tread carefully.'

Fagan massaged his forehead.

Griffiths took a deep breath. 'The committee is deciding whether to take you off active duty. Don't worry, it doesn't look like they're in a rush to make any decision soon.'

'So what, you're suspending me until whenever this committee wants to see me?'

'No.' Griffiths shook his head. 'You are to take a back seat from all leading investigations.'

'You're grounding me?'

'In a way, yes.'

'What am I supposed to do until I have to face this

committee?'

'I understand you are investigating a cold case regarding a body found at the back of Vine Road music studios.'

'I still need a team.'

'You can keep Watkins and Brooks. We're not exactly chock-a-block. We need to keep you out of trouble for the time being.'

'Is that what you see me as, trouble?'

'No, I don't but you have to keep a low profile. I have had a few national newspapers wanting the scoop on you'

Fagan glared back at Griffiths. 'Fine sir, if that's the way you want to play this game.'

'I can assure you, DI Fagan, this is no game.'

Fagan stood. 'Is that all, sir?'

Griffiths hesitated. 'Dismissed DI Fagan.'

C H A P T E R 4

The Cantreff Inn – Abergavenny – 7:23pm

'Fagan, my old mucker.' Jamie Evans called out from the corner of the bar.

'The usual, is it Fagan?' Jackie Mills asked, grabbing a pint glass.

Fagan plonked himself on a barstool, pointing to a bottle of brandy. 'I'll have a double one of those, please, Jacks.'

'Are you working?' Jackie asked, glancing at the bottle.

'No, I got off over an hour ago.' Fagan paused. 'Just had a barmy with my superior. I've been put on the back burner.'

'The back burner?'

'I am under investigation concerning my conduct as a police officer.'

'Let me guess.' Jackie sighed. 'That twat Nelson.'

Fagan nodded.

Jackie poured the brandy. 'Just this one. I don't want you in here drowning your sorrows. It's exactly what that prick wants.'

Evans joined him at the bar. 'So what has that fat bastard done now?'

'He's brainwashed that dick of a chief constable, that's what. Then there's that online petition. It has over sixty thousand signatures. I was on it the other day. Jesus, I was tempted to sign it.'

'Fagan, listen to me. He's just trying to pile the pressure on.' Jackie said. 'We all know what he's like He's being fucking people over all his life. All those girls who have tried to have him locked up. Michelle Pike committing suicide, because of what he did to her when she was fourteen.'

'Well, he's doing a good job. The chief constable of South Wales police seems to think the sun shines out of Nelson's arse. We've got to treat him with kid gloves because of his delicate mental health issues.'

'He's playing the system.' Evans said. 'Besides, we all know who the grandfather of that chief constable was.'

'Bob Benson.'

'When Nelson got me done for harassment a few years back, he made up a load of shit about me. It really tore me up. Tyler and Evans had to stop me from going round Benny's house and killing him.'

'You need to move off that shitbox of an estate.' Jackie advised. 'You're not short of a few bob, Jamie. Daisy deserves better than where you're living.'

'When we first moved there, it was ok. Now over half the people are on the dole.'

'Not everyone who's on the dole is a twat.' Jackie argued. 'Don't be such a snob.'

'To be honest, I was thinking of selling the taxis.'

'Can you afford it?' Fagan asked.

'Course I can. I'm turning a tidy profit at the moment. Kids are not living with us anymore. We were thinking of buying a bungalow with a nice garden and drive. A couple of spare rooms for a man cave and when the kids come to stay. Me and Daisy can look forward to a nice early retirement. She's looking at finishing early from the bank.'

'Sounds like you got it all planned out. What about you Jacks? Would you ever let this place go?'

Jackie shook her head. 'They'll be carrying me out in a box. I promised our nan I'll be here until the end.'

Fagan knocked back the shot glass. 'Nelson will be releasing his book later this week. There was big write up about him in the Argus.'

'I read it. Made me sick to my stomach.' Jackie said. 'He'll

22

slip up one of these days, Fagan. You coming back to town has really spooked him.'

'How do you mean?'

'Think about it. He's been a blot on Abergavenny's landscape for decades. You suddenly turning up after forty years has rattled him. What do you think that petition is all about? He clearly wants you out of the way.'

'Why?' Fagan asked, staring at the shot glass.

'You put him in the hospital twice.' Evans said.

'That was forty years ago.'

'You'll be surprised how many people still hold on to grudges,' Evans shrugged. 'Perhaps he sees you as a threat. The man has been untouchable for most of his life. Now that you're living back in town, he's got something to fear. Look at Jimmy Savile.'

Fagan glanced at Evans. 'What about him?'

'He got away with everything. Right until he died, how?'

'He knew people.'

Evans shook his head. 'No Fagan, he knew everyone. Royalty, prime ministers, MPs, music stars, TV stars, film stars. The man reached the top of everything. He ran Broadmoor hospital for Christ's sake. So he knew everyone's dirty little secrets.'

'So, what, you're saying Benny might know secrets?' Fagan shrugged. 'What exactly?'

'When you arrested him for Becky's murder, you opened a can of worms. A paedophile ring that could have been in this town decades ago. Perhaps there's someone still around who doesn't want to spend the rest of their lives in jail.'

'It's not exactly something I can investigate, is it? I'm being watched from above.'

'Can we talk about something else?' Jackie said. 'Otherwise, that twat Nelson is going to wind us all up. How was your day, Fagan?'

Fagan looked about, noting the pub was empty. 'Are you

expecting many customers tonight?'

'No, my usual crowd of ramblers were here at lunchtime. The only reason I opened the door was to let some fresh air in. Then Evans walked in. I was going to chuck him out, then you waltzed in.'

'Close the door. I have something to show you.'

Jackie locked the main entrance.

Fagan called up a picture on his phone. 'What do you reckon this is?'

Evans peered over Fagan's shoulder, studying the images. 'That's a Brit award, ain't it?'

Fagan nodded, and zoomed in on the plaque. He handed his phone to Jackie.

'Alexandrea Xavier.' Jackie squinted at the screen before glancing at Fagan. 'As in Alex X?'

'The very same.'

'I loved her back in the day. I bought all her albums.' Jackie pointed towards the corner of the bar where a classic 1950s style jukebox stood. 'I got her albums on the jukebox. They played one of her songs on the radio earlier.'

'Where did you find that?' Evans asked.

'In a field at the back of Vine Road Music Studios just outside Monmouth.'

'Wait, you're talking about *the* Vine Road studios. Where shit loads of top bands have recorded albums.'

Jackie handed back Fagan's phone.

'We found this award with a Rolex.' Fagan paused. 'And human remains, missing both the head and hands.'

Jackie and Evans exchanged shocked expressions.

'Since this is a cold case, Griffiths is assigning me.'

'Well, it's not Alex X she isn't dead.' Jackie picked up her phone. 'I follow her on Twitter. She doesn't post a lot. She's one of those reclusive pop stars.'

'Like Kate Bush.' Evans said. 'She keeps herself to herself. But last year there was a revival in her music. Thanks to

24

Stranger Things. They used one of her tracks, *Running up that Hill*.'

'So what's the story then, Fagan?' Jackie asked.

'That's what we're trying to figure out.'

Evans stared at the image of the plaque. 'This Brit award was handed out in 1993. Hang on, you've just jogged a memory.'

'What memory?'

'I've met Charlotte W and Dillon P.'

'Who?'

'Charlotte West and Dillon Powell. They were both massive back in the nineties. I remember them releasing a track with Alex X for charity. It's one of my famous people taxi stories. I started Skywalker Taxis in 1990. I used to work all hours. I used to leaflet my business.'

'You mean Daisy used to.' Jackie remarked. 'I remember her moaning to me one day that you had her delivering leaflets all over Monmouthshire'

Evans smiled. 'Daisy really helped me launch my taxi business. Anyway, I had a call out of the blue from Vine Road studios. I remember, because they phoned me at three in the morning. They wanted me to drive Charlotte and Dillon down to London. Along with a few other people. It was definitely the night of the Brit awards. Daisy taped it off the telly. We watched it a few days later. I remember yapping away about it. I told everyone who I had in the back of my van.'

'Did they talk much on the way down to London?' Fagan asked.

'No, and that's the thing. I remember it being really frosty in the minibus. None of them uttered a word. I even tried to start up a conversation. One of the blokes who was with them told me to shut the fuck up and just drive. When we got down to London, they paid me five hundred quid. That's why I remember it so well. But I never kept my mouth shut about it. When I got back home, I told everyone. I didn't recognise there three blokes in the back. But it was definitely Charlotte and Dillon with them.'

'I remember watching the Brit Awards on the telly that year.' Jackie said. 'That was the time Alex had a massive punch up with Charlotte W, her so-called bestie. It was also Alex's last appearance on TV.'

'Were Alex, Charlotte and Dillon a group?' Fagan quizzed.

'No. At first they were rivals, sort of. Alex and Charlotte sang a couple of hits together. Sold a lot of songs.' Jackie smiled. 'I remember the year before. They teamed up with Charlotte's boyfriend, Dillon P.'

'Dillon was a cross between Rick Astley and Jason Donavon.' Evans said.

'They were all Welsh. Alex was from Newport. Charlotte was a Swansea girl and Dillon was born and bred Gurnos estate in Merthyr.'

'Why did Alex and this Charlotte have a punch up?' Fagan asked.

'Alex was shagging Dillon behind Charlotte's back. It was just a rumour at first. But looking back, it was obvious. Alex, Charlotte and Dillon performed together on Children in Need. It was the year before the Brits.' Jackie smiled. 'Alex wrote the song they performed together. It stayed at number one for six weeks. Raised a lot of money for Children in Need. The single was called Love is a triangle.' Jackie signed into her YouTube account and located the video. 'I have played this hundreds of times.' She scrolled through the video before stopping at a certain point, before handing it to Fagan. 'There, you can see the expression on Charlotte's face when Alex and Dillon are giving each other suggestive looks. There'd been rumours in the press for months that Alex and Dillon were seeing each other. It wasn't until the Brit Awards when the shit really hit the fan. According to the News of the World, one of their journalists had caught Alex and Dillon together. On the night of the awards he handed Charlotte a picture of Alex and Dillon snogging. Charlotte went ballistic.' Jackie took the phone from Fagan and called up another video. 'This is the only video on YouTube of the fight. I remember watching it live on ITV. Never understood why the video isn't available.' Jackie pointed at the screen. 'The person who took this video was sitting at the back. There's a gap in the audience, with a view of the stage.'

Fagan studied the video, straining to hear what Alexandrea was saying.

'To this day, no one knows what she said.' Jackie remarked. 'They reckon she was completely off her face that night. This is the part where Charlotte flies on stage.'

Fagan could barely make out what was going on. The video's poor quality made it impossible to make anything out.

'It's a shame what happened to her. Alex was talented. But in the end, the drugs won. She released one more hit and then vanished into obscurity.'

'What happened to Charlotte and Dillon?'

'By the time the Brit awards happened in 1993, Charlotte's career was already on the slide. Her manager Mickey Mercury had a reputation for dropping stars the minute they started to lose the popularity. He dumped her at the end of 1993. The next thing anyone knew, the pop world was knee deep in the Spice Girls.'

'Christ.' Evans cursed. 'You couldn't turn on the radio or open a newspaper without seeing them plastered all over the place. Mind you, I had a thing for Sporty Spice.'

'Where are they now?' Fagan asked.

'I think Charlotte is still singing.' Jackie did a quick google search. 'Yeah, she runs her own recording studio in Cardiff. According to this she's also a promoter, though nowhere near as big as her former manager.'

'Did the papers mention anything about an after party? They always have those following an award ceremony.'

'That, I couldn't tell you.'

'What about Dillan? What happened to him?'

Jackie carried out another search. 'He dropped out of the music scene in 1997 after a string of disastrous flops. According to this he runs a mind sanctuary just outside Llandovery in mid Wales.'

'Mind sanctuary?' Fagan questioned.

'It looks like one of those new age spiritual enlightenment places.'

'Everything regarding Alex's demise seems to revolve around that one particular night, at the Brit awards.'

'What's your thinking, Fagan?'

'The CSI claimed the remains they found had been in the ground for thirty years. The date on the Brit award proved that.'

'So who's the stiff?' Evans said.

'That's the mystery here. Everyone is still alive, so it just going to be a matter of interviewing them.'

'Hold on, boys.' Jackie interrupted, holding up her phone. 'Alex, just put out a tweet, and she's posted a picture.'

'Jesus, she doesn't look well, does she. The years haven't been kind to her,' Evans remarked.

'Oh no.' Jackie pointed at the screen. 'Hi Guys, will be making a major announcement tomorrow. I'm afraid cancer has finally caught up with me.'

Fagan stared at the picture. Alex was wearing a purple headscarf. Her face was gaunt and pale.

'Look at all the likes it's getting.' Jackie tapped the heart icon.

'You don't look very convinced, Fagan.' Evans said.

'Something isn't right here.'

'Yeah, the poor girl has got cancer. That's never right, is it.' Jackie said. 'Looks like she hasn't got long either.'

'I didn't mean it like that, Jacks. What I meant was we find human remains at the back of Vine Road music studios. The evidence we have suggests that Alex X is involved because of the Brit award found with the remains. And now literally hours after the discovery, Alex X puts out a tweet saying she's got cancer.' Fagan stared at the photo. 'Something doesn't sit right here. I'll start tracing her whereabouts tomorrow. I'm also going to contact the former owner of the music studio.'

'You know who you should talk to.' Evans said.

'Who?'

'Eddie Falcon.'

Fagan searched his memory before smiling. 'Bloody hell, Eddie the Falcon. I remember him from school. Used dress in that leather jacket with fuck you, spelt out on the back with studs. Had bleached blonde hair. Looked a bit like Billy idol.'

'That's the one.'

'What did they call him at school?'

'Spliff.'

'Yeah, used to smoke a lot of weed.'

'I remember when he was rushed to Nevil Hall. The silly twat sat in the middle of the Mardy playing field, eating magic mushrooms. He didn't realise he was eating deathcaps.'

'He wasn't the sharpest tool in the shed, was he.' Fagan chuckled.

'I went on a couple of dates with Eddie,' Jackie admitted. 'We had a bit of fun, you know.'

'Where is he now?' Fagan looked at Evans.

'He runs Falcon Vinyls on Whitehorse Lane.'

'I've walked past there a few times, never clocked it was him running the shop.'

'Eddie worked out Vine Road studios for a few years in the eighties.'

'I remember the time he gave Benny Nelson a good hiding for eyeing up his younger sister, Samantha.' Jackie recalled.

Fagan nodded. 'She was a good-looking girl, very tall, had jet black hair down to her arse.'

'Well, looks like you've got another mystery on your hands, DI Fagan. If you need the Scooby gang to help, you know where we are,' Evans said.

CHAPTER 5

Day 2
Newport Central police station – 9 36am

'Morning boss.' Watkins greeted.

Brooks walked up to Fagan, holding a mug of coffee and a croissant in a paper bag.

Fagan glared at the coffee mug.

'Don't worry, it's Nescafe gold roast,' Brooks assured him.

'Finally, you're learning how to suck up to me.' Fagan winked at him. He bit into the pastry. 'Ok then. Did anyone catch the tweet that Alex X put out last night?'

'Yeah, I spotted it about ten o'clock, just before I went to bed,' Watkins said. 'The missus was going wild. She told me that Alex hardly puts out a tweet.'

'I thought it was too much of a coincidence she put out that tweet hours after we find a body at her old recording studio. With a Brit award with her name on it.'

'That was my thinking, boss. Do you think Alex might know something?'

'It's something we have to consider. Someone is still working at the studio. Someone who has a long history.' Perhaps they alerted Alex and forced her to break cover after so long.'

'Bit of a long shot, boss. Could be just a coincidence.'

'Maybe, but the manager told us he had to fire everyone yesterday when lockdown happened.'

Brooks handed Fagan his tablet. 'Actually, there is someone with a connection to that studio that goes back a few decades. I phoned the studio owner and asked him who ran security at the studio. It's a company called Mitchell security solutions. They have a website, loads of high-profile clients, including pop stars. The bloke who started the company is called Alun Mitchell.'

Fagan stared at a man on the screen.

'He's been in the security business since 1989. Scroll down.' Brooks instructed.

Fagan swiped the screen. 'Well, well, the plot thickens.' He handed the tablet to Watkins. 'That's Mitchell stood next to Alex X.'

Watkins read the information underneath the photograph. 'It says here Mitchell was her bodyguard from 1990 to 1993.'

'Until 1993, the year she dropped out of show business.' Fagan said. 'It all seems to revolve around that year, doesn't it?'

Watkins handed back the tablet.

Fagan swiped back up the screen, spotting a photograph. 'Hang on.' He stared at the photo. 'That's Rocky Richard Bishop standing next to Mitchell.'

'Who's the hell is that?' Brooks asked.

'He was a Welsh featherweight boxing champion. World champion in 1989. I remember him spending time inside for GBH. It made national headlines. He left a bloke in a coma for six weeks. The result of a fight in a Swansea nightclub.'

Watkins tapped away on his keyboard. 'Bishop spent nine months in Cardiff clink in 1987.'

'Sean, run a check on Alun Mitchell.' Fagan instructed.

'Bingo.' Watkins declared after a few minutes. 'Alun Mitchell spent nine years in prison. From 1979 to 1988.'

'What for?'

'Attempted murder.'

'You're joking. And he got a job as a bodyguard. I take it he served time in Cardiff clink.'

'Yess boss.' Watkins spotted something else. 'Mitchell was also a person of interest regarding the disappearance of a

31

young girl back in 1978. Police questioned Mitchell in relation to the disappearance of sixteen year old Dorothy Morris.'

'I'm guessing Mitchell and Richard Bishop crossed paths while they served time in Cardiff. So what has all this got to do with our headless victim from the music studio?'

'It's definitely not Alex. That much is obvious.' Brooks pointed out.

Fagan scrolled through the picture on his phone, looking for the plaque. 'The inscription on this plaque is dated 25th June 1993.'

'Which was on a Firday,' Watkins said, looking at a calendar on his laptop.

Fagan nodded. 'So, our murderer dumped the body on the night of the Brit Awards. Sean, call up that article you were reading yesterday.'

Watkins clicked on his mouse. 'Let me see, where was I yesterday? Alex started on the drugs. She was doing a line of coke before and after a gig. Here we go. In September 1991, Frankie got together with Mickey Mercury. At the time Mercury was managing two of the top 90s pop sensations, Charlotte W and Dillon P.'

'That's Jordan's partner from the music studio.' Fagan walked over to the whiteboard and scribbled Mercury's name.

Watkins carried on reading. 'I remember when me and Charlotte co-wrote our first song, Girls get it Together. Frankie and Mickey rushed us to the studio to record the single. It smashed the charts in the UK and the US. We did this whirlwind tour of both the UK and America. That's when I met Charlotte's boyfriend, Dillon Powell. He was already a pop sensation. You know, the boy next door look. Blue eyes, gorgeous blonde hair. He was on the cover of just about every glossy magazine. We seemed to click straight away. He'd been dating Charlotte several months. They had a couple of hits together. Dillon confided in me that Charlotte treated him like shit. She was the more ambitious one. They had a string of very public bust ups. Papers like the News of the World would follow them everywhere, just to see them have one of their fights. Then one night after a gig Dillon came to see me. He'd had this massive bust up with Charlotte. We talked for hours before we fell into each other's arms. That's when our affair started. It was near impossible to get any time together. The press were hounding me all the time. They followed Dillon around. He had to deal with hordes of screaming teenagers.'

'So she's admitting she was seeing Dillon behind Charlotte's back?' Fagan stated. 'They carried on with their affair. A friend of mine, who's a fan, said that Charlotte found out about their affair on the night of the Brit awards. She reckons a journalist from the News of the World snapped a picture of them having a snog. He then gave a picture to Charlotte. That's why she stormed onto the stage at the Brit awards and gave her a good slapping. The video on YouTube is shit.' Fagan glanced at Brooks. 'Get hold of someone from ITV. See if they have archive with footage of the Brit awards from 1993.'

'This is where it gets juicy.' Watkins said, scanning the article. 'Alex claims she was totally in love with Dillon. He was also doing drugs. She says here that the sex was out of this world.'

Fagan clapped his hands loudly before rubbing them together. 'It's a classic combination. Sex, drugs and rock and roll.'

'What's this got to do with the headless corpse?' Brooks asked.

Fagan took a deep breath. 'That's the big question here. It seems like an impossible case. A body without a head and hands. Whoever murdered the poor wretch before dumping them at the back of Vine Road studios was worried police could identify the body if it was ever found.'

'So they removed the head and the hands to make it impossible to identify the body.' Watkins finished.

'Exactly.' Fagan glanced at Watkins' laptop. 'What else does that article say?'

Watkins scanned the text. 'When 1993 arrived, the hits continued. But I was struggling. My manager let my younger sister accompany me on tour, which helped enormously.'

'This is the sister that committed suicide.'

'Must be,' Watkins guessed, before continuing. 'She tried her best to get me off the drugs. But by then I was a total mess. When the 1993 Brit Awards nominated me as pop sensation of the year, I was euphoric. And that's when it all came crashing down. I can't even remember the Brit Awards that year. But the press made sure they detailed every slurred word I blurted out when I accepted the award. The TV cameras caught it all. Charlotte rushing at me, punching me. Dillon then punching Charlotte.'

'Which is why we need to get hold of ITV.'

Watkins carried on reading. 'My promoter, Frankie, decided it was time for rehab. He booked me in the day after the Brits. I spent nearly eighteen months in the clinic. But that was just the start of my nightmares. In August 1993, Frankie visited me at the rehab centre. He told me that my sister had taken her own life two days before his visit. That's when I decided to quit the music industry for good.'

'Hang on a sec.' Fagan interrupted. 'Frankie Jordan booked Alex into rehab the day after the Brits. Which proves our victim was murdered on the 25th of June 1993. Think about it. There's a punch up at the Brits between Alex, Charlotte and Dillon. Alex didn't attend any Brit Awards after party.'

'Not in London anyway.' Brooks pointed out.

Fagan pointed at him. 'Nice deducing Andrew. What if the after party was at Vine Road Studios?'

'Bit of a trek, from London to Monmouth, boss.' Watkins mused.

'Not really. Late Friday night, straight up the M4, then up the A449. Two and a half hours tops if they travelled back late

34

at night. If there was an after party, then it couldn't have been at the studio. It didn't look like the kind of place where you'd hold a party after an event like the Brit Awards. Perhaps there was one at the Agincourt hotel. That's just down the road, less than a mile.'

'But how did the body end up at the back of the music studio, if the party was at the hotel?'

'That's what we need to find out. Our victim is female. She's murdered. Head and hands removed. Our murderer buries the rest in the field at the back of the studio. With the Brit award and an expensive watch.' Fagan glanced at the award in the plastic evidence bag. 'That needs to go down to the labs ASAP.'

'You think it could be the murder weapon?' Watkins asked.

'It's possible the Brit award could be the murder weapon.' Fagan walked over to the table and picked up the bag. 'Definitely heavy enough to give someone a good smash over the head. What about the parents of Alex and her sister?'

'The father died in 2019. No luck finding the mother.' Brooks revealed.

'She could have remarried, which means a name change. Didn't Alex's Wiki page mention Alex's dad worked at Llanwern steelworks?'

Watkins scanned the article. 'Yeah.'

Fagan looked at Brooks. 'I know it's a longshot, but give Llanwern a bell. Find out if there is someone still working there who might know Simon Xavier, or Price.'

'Going off track a bit, boss.'

'Not really. If we can build a picture of family life, then it might prove useful.' Fagan glanced at the whiteboard. 'So there's an after party at the studio or the hotel. Our victim is murdered. Alex either witnessed the murder or she's number one on our suspect list. It's possible the Brit award could be the murder weapon. We won't know until it comes back from the labs.' Fagan wrote Frankie Jordan's name. 'Jordan was probably at the party because he owned the studio. Then we have the bodyguard, Alun Mitchell, ex-con. jailed for attempted murder. Served time with a well-known boxer. That's four people who were at the after party.'

'There's no way there would have just been four people at the after party.' Watkins said.

'How the hell are we going to find out who was at that party?' Fagan sensed the frustration mounting.

'We need a guest list.' Brooks remarked.

Fagan stared at him, repeating his words. 'Guest list.' He broke out into a smile, looking at Watkins. 'What did the manager of the studio say they were building in that field?'

'New recording studios and luxury accommodation for the artists.'

'Right, and before now, all the artists stayed at the Agincourt hotel, just down the road. When we went out there investigating that murder at Skenfrith castle, the hotel manager said they liked to keep things old school. In fact, he said the hotel's guests insisted on it. He showed us the guestbook that Professor Turner had signed. That's how we knew he had been staying there. So in theory, they might keep the guestbooks. Think about it. Some very famous musicians have used that recording studio over the years. So its stands to reason they'll have all the guestbooks. You know, something to show off. Oh look, Bob Dillon stayed her once, or Elvis. Providing there was an after party at the Agincourt. Alex and the others must have stayed at the hotel? She would have signed the guestbook. Along with other guests at the party.'

'So it's just a case of calling at the Agincourt.' Watkins said.

Fagan nodded. 'Right, this is what we're going to do. Brooks will do all the groundwork. Contact ITV, find out if they have a tape of the Brit from 1993. Also contact Llanwern. See if anyone is still there who may have known the father. I also want you to track down everyone who would have been at the

Brit awards with Alex that evening. Her manager, the bodyguard, everyone. I also want a list of the groups that Frankie Jordan managed at the time of the Brit awards in 1993.' He looked at Watkins. 'Contact the foreign office and get hold of a list of expats living in Tarragona.'

'You flying out there, are you, boss?' Watkins questioned.

'No, you are. I'm in the middle of renewing my passport.'

'What.' Watkins moaned.

'It's only a two-hour flight, and Tarragona is only an hour's drive from Barcelona.' Fagan glanced at the clock on the wall. 'You can get a priority booking within a few hours. Get hold of the local Spanish plod before you fly out. They should give you an assist on this.'

'What are you going to do?'

'I'm going to have a chat with someone who used to work at the studio. Then I'm going to have a talk with that boxer. I'm then going out to the Agincourt hotel to see if our theory on the guestbook is correct. Later on I am going to have a chat with Alex's former bandmate and boyfriend.' Fagan clapped his hands. 'Come on, heads down and arses up.' He looked at Watkins. 'You should be back by late this evening.'

'Do you want me to arrest Alex?'

'No, of course not. That's way too much paperwork. Just ask her about events after the Brit awards that night.'

CHAPTER 6

Falcon Vinyls – Abergavenny – 10:56am

'Marc Fagan, as I live and breathe.' Eddie Falcon smiled broadly, offering his hand. 'I was wondering when we'd bump into each other. I heard you'd moved back to Abergavenny.'

Fagan smiled back. 'How you doing, Spliff?'

'Christ, no one has called be that in an age.' Falcon burst out laughing.

'What happened to all that long hair?'

Falcon rubbed his bald head. 'It's called getting old, mate.'

Fagan glanced around the shop. 'You've done well for yourself. I always thought vinyl was dead.'

'Vinyl is far from dead. This place is rammed every Saturday morning. A lot of youngers come here with their parents and grandparents. More artists are releasing their tracks onto vinyl. The technology has come a long way. No more scratchy sound anymore.'

'This takes me back to Kestrel records that used to be just down from Barclays bank.' Fagan remarked.

'I spent a fortune in there. The place used to be buzzing. It's why I set up this shop. I remember bring furious when it shut down. Had to rely on Woolworths for my music. I was never a fan of CDs when they first came out. Most of the older ones who come in here mention Kestrel records from the old days. So, are you looking for anything in particular? Got some classic stuff from our more youthful days.'

'Sorry, no, I'm here on business.' Fagan pulled his ID from his pocket.

Falcon put his hands up. 'Listen, if this is about that time I graffitied the town hall in 1982, I was just expressing myself artistically.'

Fagan chuckled. 'No mate. I was talking to Jamie Evans last night in the Cantreff. He said you used to work at Vine Road Music studios just outside Monmouth.'

Falcon puffed out his cheeks. 'That takes me back a few decades.'

'I don't suppose you have time to have a chat about your time there?'

'Yeah, sure.' Falcon nodded. 'Lindsey.' He called out.

A young woman with jet black hair appeared from the back of the shop.

'This is my niece, Lindsey.'

Fagan glanced at Falcon. 'Sam's daughter?'

Falcon nodded.

'Where is she these days?'

'In London, married to a millionaire art dealer.' Falcon said proudly. 'Lindsey is at Cardiff university studying journalism. When she's got free time, she comes up here to give me a hand.'

'You never married then?'

Falcon nodded. 'Yeah, got four brilliant kids, spread all over, Australia, Canada, Scotland and New Zealand. I lost my wife to covid back in 2020.'

'So sorry mate.'

'Yeah.' Falcon sighed. 'The pandemic was shit for everyone.' He looked at his niece. 'Me and Detective Inspector Fagan here are off to Coffee Lab. Take care of the place while we're gone.'

Falcon stared at the image of the Brit award on Fagan's phone. 'Let me get this straight. You found this award, with a headless corpse at the back of Vine Road Music studios.'

Fagan nodded, sipping from his latte cup. 'Along with a Rolex watch.'

Falcon placed the phone on the table.

'How long did you work for Vine Road Studios?'

Falcon considered the question. 'About five years. I started there in 1983 until 1988. Just before Alex X hit the charts. She was massive.'

'So you got to know Frankie Jordan and Mickey Mercury very well.'

'Oh yeah.' Falcon sipped from his cup. 'Good times back then. The place was buzzing. I met so many famous artists out there. I used to get invited to the Agincourt hotel all the time for drinks. Met some massive stars.'

'Anything used to go on out there, you know, illegal?'

'Where do I begin?' Flacon chuckled. 'It was the eighties. Everyone was doing something.' Falcon paused. 'Including myself. I am ashamed to admit it. I'm completely clean now, don't even drink.'

'But you liked a spliff back then.'

Falcon waved away the comment. 'Yeah, but that was just weed I used to grow in my dad's greenhouse. Unless you count that incident with the magic mushrooms. I used to hang out with all the heavy metal bands that recorded albums out there.' Falcon recalled some names. 'Let me see, there was Molten Fury. They were a wild bunch. Massive back in the late seventies and early eighties. Then there were the Savage Demons. They were off their heads most of the time. I used to get wasted with the lead singer of Crimson Wraith. He overdosed in 1987. What was his name? Andrew White. He used to be covered with tattoos. You couldn't see one patch of skin. When I was at the studio, I saw all kinds of shit going on.'

'Did Jordan and Mercury know what was going on?'

'Good grief, yes. I went down to Newport with Jordan once. He went down there specifically to pick up a shitload of coke from a dealer. Brazen as hell they were. Talking about how high the artists would get.'

40

'What were they like, Jordan and Mercury, to work with?'

'Jordan was a right dick. He'd fly off the handle when something went tits up. Which was literally every day. Bit of a control freak, if you ask me. Some bands that recorded at the studio would cause all kinds of problems. Especially the metal bands. Most wanting to do things their own way. Jordan was already making connections with all kinds of people. Johnny Baron, the American music mogul, would visit us now and then.'

'What was your job there?'

'I was just a lowly sound mixer. Jordan was always on my back. He was never happy with anything I did. I really enjoyed that job. It didn't pay much. But to be amongst all the musical greats was payment enough. I worked with the metal bands. Mostly in studio three. Jordan used to run studio one, while Mercury ran studio two'

'What was Mercury like?'

'As queer as they came.' Falcon replied. 'These days he's out and proud now. But in the eighties, he was firmly locked in the closet. AIDS was just gaining notoriety from the press. During the eighties, gay people were getting a lot of bad publicity. I heard he changed his name to Mercury when Freddie died. I remember the studio being plastered with Queen posters. A lot of bands with gay members used to record at the studio. Namely studio two. I remember a regular group called Capture. Whenever they'd turn up, Mercury would book the Agincourt hotel. He'd vanish for a few days at a time.'

'Mercury told you this?'

'Yeah. I got on with him better than Jordan. I was straight. But Mickey used to confide in me a lot. Mickey lost a lot of friends to AIDS. Including the lead singer of Capture. Not a month went by where he didn't go to a funeral of someone who had died from the disease. Johnny Baron was gay. Whenever he used to visit, him and Mickey used to retire to the Agincourt. It used to wind Jordan up big time.'

'Jordan was homophobic then?'

'Big time.' Falcon revealed. 'He used to call Mickey every name under the sun. Queer, arse bandit, shirt lifter, poofter. But Jordan was no angel himself.'

'How do you mean?'

'A lot of bands used to turn up with groupies. You know, young girls along for the ride, in more ways than one. The Agincourt hotel was a paradise for those who liked that kind of thing. I remember when *a certain glam rock artist* turned up at the studio. Fuck me, Jordan used to treat him like royalty. He would turn up with a bunch of girls in his limousine. Not one of them used to look older than sixteen. They booked a suit at the Agincourt. Whenever he turned up at the studio, the girls used to look really excited about being there. But then the next day, they looked as miserable as sin. Jordan and his *glam rock pal* used to look so pleased with themselves.'

'Did you ever question anything regarding the underage girls that used to go to the studio?'

'Once, and I got my head chewed off. A group called the Paraphernalia used to record at the studio. They were massive in Australia. Jordan used to love them. They were big money spinners for him. One day, they turned up with an entire entourage of young girls. And when I mean young, I mean some of them didn't look much older than fifteen. Jordan was like a kid on Christmas day. I heard him on the phone to the manager at the Agincourt, reserving a couple of rooms. I remarked to Jordan they were too young to be hanging around at the studio. Jordan told me to fuck off and mind my own business.'

'How come you quit in 1988?'

'I didn't quit. I was bloody sacked.' Falcon revealed.

'Why?'

Falcon let out a snort of derision. 'Jordan was having one of his off days. We were short on staff so I lent a hand in studio one. This band called Retrospect came in to record an album. They were superb. Just emerging from the new romantic era that had been dominating the charts for the past decade. Two female lead vocals and backing. Anyway, Jordan wasn't happy with the way I was mixing a track. The guys from Retrospect didn't have a problem. We got on really well. But Jordan exploded for no apparent reason. He fired me on the spot. I tried to argue that he was in the wrong, but he wasn't having any of it. The lead drummer from Retrospect had a right go at him. Jordan told him if he didn't like the way he did things, then he could fuck off. It really pissed me off when I lost that job. My wife Jo had already had our first kid and was working on the second. I had to get myself a job at this chicken factory in Hereford. I endured ten years in that shithole before quitting. Jo was brilliant, she was so supportive. We scraped the money together to start up the record shop and have been doing it ever since. It's not been easy, but it's been worth it. I thought the pandemic would finish us. But it proved to be a boost. I have a thriving online trade.' Falcon inhaled. 'When Covid hit, Jo became ill. They rushed her to Nevil Hall. She clung on for two weeks. Enough time for the kids to come home and say goodbye to their mam.'

'A lot of good people were lost to the pandemic.' Fagan remarked.

Falcon drank from his cup. 'So, you have a headless corpse at the back of Vine Road studios. That's going to cause a lot of commotion when it hits the media. Speaking of which.' Falcon produced his smartphone. 'I see Alex X tweeted a short message and a picture last night. She's also got a countdown timer on her Twitter feed. She's posting a video at eight o'clock tonight. The news media is going into meltdown over it. No one has heard from this woman in thirty years. And now she just turns up out of the blue. Announcing that she has cancer. Me and Lindsey were looking at the picture she posted last night. She doesn't look like she got long left. Looks like someone from the *Walking Dead*. There are loads of people gossiping this morning about what she's going to announce tonight.'

'One of my officers is flying out to Spain to track her down.' Fagan revealed.

'Good luck there, mate. Alex X hasn't been seen in thirty years. Strange thing is, she surfaces now and then. Literally every ten years.'

'We came across an article yesterday. That was at nine years old.'

'Is that the article published in the online magazine, Word on the Street?'

'Yeah.' Fagan replied.

'I know the editor, Eric Tone. He promotes a lot of my stuff.'

'How did he get the interview with her?'

'I don't know, but I can give him a ring later on and find out.'

'That would be brilliant.'

'Alex was a good-looking girl, wasn't she? She turned some heads. But the drugs finally got to her. I remember the year of the Brit Awards. When Charlotte West burst on stage and gave Alex a hammering. Then Dillon Powell jumped up and punched Charlotte. Dillon P, he was a boy and half wasn't he. He was screwing both Alex and Charlotte at the same time. After Alex went into rehab, Charlotte's career took a nosedive. Dillon kept going for a few years. He was around to see the emergence of the Spice girls. Then his career crashed. Oasis, Coldplay, Take That, Stereophonics, the Manic streets Preachers were on their way up.' Falcon stopped. 'Just a second. Show me the picture of that award again.'

Fagan called up the picture and handed his phone over.

'A couple of months after the Brit awards, I remember one of the sound editors from the studio knocking on my door. Apparently, Jordan had fired all the staff the day after the Brits.'

'Did Jordan mention why he fired them?'

'No. But they closed the studio for two weeks. That's what the sound engineer told me, anyway.'

Fagan considered the new information.

'You think it's possible they were covering their tracks?'

Fagan nodded. 'It's possible.'

'I bumped into Frankie Jordan about six months ago.'

'Where?'

'In Crickhowell. I was at a book reading session at a place called Book-ish. The lead singer of a band that used to record at the studio was reading from his biography. I was sitting in the audience, looked across the room and there was Frankie Jordan, sat on his own. After the reading, I walked over to say hello. Ignorant fucker blanked me. He's a recluse just like Alex. Lives on the other side of Crickhowell. He's been spotted at The Green Man festival over the years.'

'Did you ever keep in touch with Mickey Mercury?'

'No, but he was another one I bumped into last year. He actually spoke to me and apologised for what Jordan did in 1988.'

'What's he doing these days?'

'He's still well known in the music industry. Runs a big effects studio in Cardiff Bay. It's where the old Doctor Who exhibition used to be. He boasted that he'd just finished a project with Taylor Swift.' Falcon smiled. 'Still as camp as ever.'

Fagan jotted down notes.

'I see those two years of porridge you did at Usk sobered you up.' Falcon changed the subject.

'They did.' Fagan said.

'I was in the Black Lion the night you had that fight with Tim. When you smashed his head up against the wall, the blood sprayed everywhere. Jackie Mills was screaming at you. Then you punched that copper. The rest of them just piled onto you.'

Fagan recalled that night as if it were yesterday.

'That twat Nelson is releasing a book at the end of the week. He's been bragging about it all over social media.'

'Didn't you give him a hammering once?'

Falcon nodded. 'Sam was only thirteen, but she was a tall girl for her age. Had jet black hair. I was very protective back then. Nelson came up to me one day and said, your sister is lush isn't she. Would mind giving her minge a good licking. I went apeshit. Kicked the fuck out of him.' Falcon suddenly recalled a memory. 'I just remembered. Benny used to hang around the studio. He gave me a wide berth because of the hammering I gave him.'

'Benny hung around the studio?'

'Yeah. He was there all the time I was there. He was definitely still there when I got fired.'

'Did he work there?'

'No, he just used to hang out. Nelson always had a camera with him. Whenever the Paraphernalia would turn up, Nelson would photograph them. Plus the young girls that used to accompany them. I remember having a go at him. It was just before I got fired. Told him he shouldn't be at the studio if he didn't work there. That fucker was probably the one of the reasons I got fired. Him and Jordan used to be as thick as thieves.'

Fagan's phone buzzed. 'Listen, I have to go. It's been nice catching up, Eddie. I'd appreciated if you'd get back to me regarding that interview in that magazine.' Fagan handed Falcon a card. 'Call me when you have something.'

CHAPTER 7

Blaina -12:23pm

'Keep your fucking guard up, will you!' Richard Bishop growled. 'For fuck's sake. If you fight like that on Saturday in Cardiff, then your opponent is going to take full advantage.'

The young boxer raised his gloves.

'Right, from the top, start again.' Bishop looked towards the entrance to his gym. A man in a Barbour jacket and blue shirt strolled towards him. 'Can I help you, mate?'

'Rocky Richard Bishop, I take it.' The man smiled.

'Yeah, that's me.'

'Mind if I have a quick chat?'

'Have you bought a copy of my book?'

The man looked back. 'Uh, no. I was just hoping for a few minutes of your time.'

'Then fuck off. I don't need any ageing fanboys in here, wanting a *chat.*'

The smile quickly vanished from the man's face. He pulled an ID from an inside pocket. 'DI Fagan with Gwent police. And until five seconds ago, I was a fan.'

'Shit. I'm sorry, ok.' He glanced at the young boxer. 'I'm trying to teach the boy how to fight.' Bishop climbed over the ropes. 'What can I do for you, DI Fagan?'

'I was wondering if you remember the time you spent in Cardiff prison.'

'Like it was yesterday.' Bishop smiled. 'Believe it or not, I enjoyed my stint in Cardiff. Made me see life from a different perspective. That's why I set this place up. It helps the local kids stay off the streets.'

'Is that where you met Alun Mitchell?' Fagan called up the photograph he had grabbed off the internet.

Bishop frowned. 'Come on, we better talk in the office.' He looked back at the ring. 'And you, keep your bloody guard up.' They walked towards the office door. 'Jesus, that boy is going to get a clobbering on Saturday.'

Fagan took stock of all the photographs on Bishop's office wall. 'I see you've met all the greats.'

Bishop glanced at the pictures. 'Yeah, my promoter used to drag me all over the world.' He looked at a photo of him standing next to Muhammad Ali. 'That bloke was a diamond. You couldn't have met a nicer man.' He set a cup of coffee down in front of Fagan. 'So what's that twat Mitchell been up to now?'

'I'm just looking into his background. He served time in Cardiff.'

'Yeah, I only did nine months. He introduced himself the moment I showed up. He'd already served a few years inside. Established himself as the alpha male on the block. I reckon I put the willies up him a little. Me being a boxer and all.'

'Why did you call him a twat just now?'

'Because he owes me ten grand. I was the reason he was able to set up that security company of his. Now he'd bodyguard to the rich and famous. Well, he used to be. He hires out muscle now. But I was there in the early days. Bit of a psycho, if you ask me.'

'How so?'

'The other prisoners on the block used to be terrified of him. I'm surprised he got out of prison. He was always taunting the prison guards.'

'You were out years before he was.'

Bishop nodded. 'We kept in touch, or rather he kept in touch, bordering on stalking me. When he was released, he turned up at the gym where I used to train. By then, my best years were behind me. My former promoter had already

48

dumped me. But I was still doing ok in the UK boxing circuit. The money was still coming in. Mitchell knew this, which is why he asked me for money.'

'And you just handed over the ten grand?'

Bishop nodded. 'I know what you're thinking. I'm a boxer and all. Able to take care of myself. What people don't understand is that most boxers just fight. Outside the ring, we're just like anyone else. Boxing was a job, not something I took everywhere with me.'

'What about the bloke you put in a coma for six weeks?'

'A lucky punch. The fall put him in a coma. Not me punching him. The press had field day. Accusing me of being some kind of animal.'

Fagan pulled out his notepad. 'So Mitchell still owes you the ten grand you lent him over thirty years ago?'

'Yeah, I bumped into his last year at a charity event. I confronted him about the money he owed me. The next thing I know, I was being manhandled out of the door by some of his security staff.'

'When you gave him the money, did he leave you alone straight away, or did he stick with you?'

'He stuck to me for several months. I used to ask how the security company project of his was coming along. He would say he was working on things. Looking back, I reckon he asked for the money because he was fresh out of prison and knew he wouldn't have been able to get a job. My wife would complain. He'd constantly turn up at our house. Hang around the gym intimidating the boys that used to train here. I remember having to face off against him once. He even put the shits up me. I was so glad he lost interested in me when he met Frankie Jordan.'

Fagan glanced up from his notepad. 'Frankie Jordan, as in the music promoter?'

Bishop nodded.

'How did that happen?'

'Jordan used to watch me fight. He used to bet a lot of money on me. Jordan watched my last professional fight in London. He congratulated me for winning after it was over. He was with that Alexandrea Xavier.'

'So you introduced them?'

'More like Mitchell introduced himself. I remember he couldn't take his eyes off Alex. Mind you, she was a stunning-looking girl. Until she went on the drugs. She's back in the news. Something about a message on social media last night.'

'And you never saw Mitchell after that?'

'For a few weeks. Then he turned around and said he was going into the music business. To be honest, it was a release. Me and the wife were glad to be rid of him. When I was in prison, he used to boast about all kinds of things he'd done. This one time, he told me he'd murdered someone.'

'He admitted this to you?'

Bishop nodded. 'I thought he was full of it. Until he described what he did to the poor girl after he had murdered her.'

'What did he tell you?'

'He said he'd removed the woman's head and threw the rest of the body in the Usk.'

'Jesus.'

'Mind you, he was full of himself. Half the time I didn't know whether he was spouting a bunch of bullshit or actually telling the truth. He once told me he was in the SAS and trained to kill. I was so glad to be rid of that psycho.'

Fagan finished jotting down notes and snapped his notebook shut. 'Well, thanks for your time.'

Bishop picked up a copy of his biography and scribbled his signature before handing it to Fagan. 'For being a twat when you first walked in.'

Fagan took the book.

CHAPTER 8

The Agincourt hotel – 1:56pm

Fagan waited for Brooks outside the main entrance. He had messaged him an hour earlier requesting they meet up at the Agincourt. Watkins had also messaged Fagan, saying that he had boarded a plane and was on his way out to Barcelona.

A police car rolled into the courtyard of the hotel. Brooks climbed out of the passenger seat.

'I hope you've been a busy bee over the last few hours, Andrew.'

'Yes, sir. First off, I contacted the ITV archives. They said it would be some time before they could release any footage of that Brit award ceremony. They claimed it has something to do with copyright. I gave Llanwern steelworks a call. The factory manager has been there forty-three years, just about to retire. He's not available to talk until tomorrow. I have the contact details of people who may have been with Alex after the Brit awards ceremony. Her manager, the bodyguard, Dillon P and Charlotte W. I thought I'd leave it to you to contact them sir.'

'Good work.' Fagan complimented. 'Still no luck in tracking down the mother of Alex?'

'No, sir. My guessing is she doesn't want to be found or, like Alex's father, she's dead. I'll get hold of a list of artists Jordan managed as soon as we get back to Newport central.'

'I appreciate the hard work you are putting Andrew. I've never been any good at research.'

The manager of the hotel spotted Fagan and Brooks walking through the door. It took him a few moments to remember where he had seen Fagan before. 'Detective Inspector Fagan. I hope you're not here regarding another murder enquiry.'

Fagan approached the front desk, smiling. 'Of sorts?'

The manager stared back. 'Of sorts?' He looked towards the doorway. 'Someone has informed there me was a large police presence at the music studio yesterday. Is everything okay?'

Fagan dodged the question. 'You obviously remember the last time I was here. Can you recall telling me you're a traditional hotel? And your guests prefer it that way.'

'I vaguely remember having that conversation. What is it you wish to know today, Inspector?'

'I notice you haven't got a computer at the front desk.'

'Well spotted Mr Holmes.' The manager couldn't have sounded more sarcastic if he tried.

'Do you keep all your guestbooks?' Brooks asked before Fagan had the chance to let off an equally cutting remark. 'As in going back years.'

'We keep all our guestbooks, yes.'

'We need to see a guestbook from June 1993.' Fagan requested.

'Why do you need to see a guestbook from that particular time?'

'We are trying to determine if a certain person was staying here.'

'I take it this person is someone famous, connected with the studio just up the road?'

'We're not at liberty to say at this moment.' Fagan said.

'I'm only asking because we have two types of guestbooks here. One for our ordinary clients and another guestbook for our better known clients.'

'Why two guestbooks?' Brooks asked.

'Our more well-known clients prefer the public didn't know they were staying here.'

'So, why not just sign in as Mr or Mrs Smith?'

The manager shook his head. 'We have had this tradition for centuries. Some of our oldest guestbooks date back to the thirteenth century.'

'And you keep them on premises?' Fagan remarked.

'Yes, we have an exclusive library in our cellar.'

'You have a library in a hotel?'

'This hotel dates back to 1415 DI Fagan.'

'Well, we'd like to see your guestbook famous people sign.'

The manager disappeared into the office for a few moments before returning and placing the guestbook on the counter. 'This is our most recent guestbook.'

Fagan opened the first page and ran his finger down the list of name. 'No way, Tom Cruise has been here in the last three months.'

'You'll be surprised the number of celebrities that visit Monmouthshire Inspector Fagan. Anthony Hopkins has been spotted a few times at the market in Abergavenny.'

'What about guestbooks that go back to the 90s?'

The manager picked up the guestbook. 'For that, we'll have to take a trip to the library.'

'How many rooms does this hotel have?' Brooks asked as they made their way towards the library.

'The Agincourt Hotel has seventy rooms. Sixty rooms for our general guests and ten rooms reserved for our more exclusive clientele.'

When they reached the cellar, Fagan took stock of the considerably large wine racks. He stopped to read a price label on one of the bottles. 'Twenty-five grand for a bottle of wine! Are you taking the piss or something?'

The hotel manager seemed unphased by Fagan's shock. He glanced at the bottle. 'It's a 1912 vintage Inspector Fagan. Created on April 12th, the day the Titanic sank.'

'Lots of money to be made from wine, is there?' Brooks questioned.

'A great deal of money, if you operate in the right circles. Most of these bottles will never be opened.'

'Seems like a waste of you ask me.' Fagan said, looking at the price tag of another bottle. 'I like a nice bottle of red.'

The manager produced a key as they approached a door.

Fagan noticed how big the room beyond was. 'I never expected to see a library in a hotel.'

'The Agincourt hasn't always been a hotel.'

'It's very cool in here.' Brooks remarked.

'Yes, we have a climate control system. This room has to have a constant ambient temperature. Some of these books date back a thousand years. The more valued books in our collection are kept under lock and key.'

'Who comes in here to read?' Fagan enquired.

'We get a lot of academics who visit the hotel for research. That poor chap murdered at Skenfrith castle a while back, came in here the day before he met his ghastly end. Here we go.' The manager pointed to a bookshelf. 'This is our nineties section. What year did you say you wanted to look at?'

'1993, June to be exact.'

The manager ran his hand along the collection of guestbooks before plucking one off the shelf and handing it to Fagan. 'I'll see if there are more from that year.'

Fagan walked over to a table and sat down. He flicked through the pages, scanning the names that guests had signed. 'There she is.' He announced. 'Alexandrea Xavier signed this guestbook. The writing is scruffy, but it's definitely her. They said she was off her face on the night of the Brit awards so she could barely scribble her name.'

Brooks pointed at the time she signed in. 'You were right, sir. They did travel from London after the Brit awards. Looks like they arrived before midnight.'

Fagan smiled as he read down the list. 'Everyone was here that night. Alex, her manager, the bodyguard, Mickey Mercury, Charlotte West, Dillon Powell.' Fagan continued down the list. 'There's at least twenty people here who accompanied them. Our victim has got to be someone on this list.'

'That's quite a few people to track down, sir.' Brooks jotted down the names.

'Get on to the labs after. Find out if they've had any luck cleaning off that inscription on the back of the watch.'

'Will do.'

'So they get back here before midnight. Some kind of fight breaks out. Resulting in a headless corpse being dumped with the Brit award and a Rolex. The murder must have taken place at the music studio. So our victim must have gone back to the studio with her murderer.' Fagan looked over towards the manager, who was sorting through a bookshelf. He clicked his fingers loudly. 'Excuse me, mate.'

The manager walked over.

'What's your name?'

'James Carson.'

'James, do you have any long-term members of staff? Someone who would have been here in June 1993?'

The manager pondered the question. 'That would be Kevin Railson, our head chef.'

'We'd like a word, please.' Fagan smiled.

A few minutes later, Fagan and Brooks were sitting in a large kitchen.

'Please be quick with your interrogation, Inspector Fagan.' The manager grumbled. 'We have a rather important event in a few days. There's a lot to prepare for.'

'Important event?' Fagan asked, looking at the head chef.

'There's a load of bigwigs from the music industry turning up. It's something to do with the reopening of the studio down the road there. It's also their fiftieth year in business.' Railson explained.

'How long have you worked here, Kevin?'

'About thirty-three years now. I started at the bottom as a

waiter and worked my way up.'

'So you've seen a fair few celebrities over the years?'

'Oh yeah, I've seen all the greats. Got quite a big autograph collection. People assume it's just pop stars that come out here. Quite a few actors use this place. They like to go walking around the area. Tom Cruise was out here not long back. This place was popular with a BBC a few years ago. They filmed Doctor Who out this way, at Skenfrith castle.'

'Ever seen anything interesting? Like some of these celebrities having a temper tantrum?' Brooks asked.

'All the time. They're like little children when they don't get their own way. A lot of the guests who stay here expect you to be available twenty-four seven. I remember when Johnny Depp stayed here once. He ordered a roast beef dinner at two o'clock in the morning. Our head chef went apeshit.'

'Are you familiar with Alexandrea Xavier?' Fagan asked.

Raison nodded. 'I was a massive fan. Met her a few times. She recorded her biggest hits at Vine Road Studios during the 90s.' Railson smiled. 'You want to know about the fight, don't you?'

'Fight?' Fagan attempted to sound innocent.

'I remember the last time she was out here. There was a massive fight. It was the night she won a Brit award.'

Fagan threw Brooks a glance. 'Can you recollect who was fighting?'

'Just about everyone. Alex, her music promoter, her bodyguard, Alex's dad. Charlotte W was also there and Dillon P.' Railson paused. 'And another girl, a friend of Alex's but I never knew her name.'

'I know it was thirty years ago, but can you remember what they were arguing about?'

Raising searched the memory of his distant past. 'I was just a waiter. We'd been asked to stay on. There was a late night function going on. Something to do with Dillon Powell. Lots of local bigwigs from the police and government.' Raison focused on a memory. 'It was the night Alex had won the Brit award. I remember it because they flew by helicopter from London and landed in the field at the back of the hotel. There were two helicopters.'

'Can you remember what time this was?' Brooks asked.

'I reckon around eleven o'clock, maybe. I remember this woman getting into the hotel. I saw her talking to Alex at the main door. She looked upset, crying. The doorman kicked her out. After that Alex was fuming about something.'

'Ok, so the doormen chucked this woman out.' Fagan interrupted. 'Then what happened?'

'Um. I remember them all piling into the kitchen. First, it was just Alex and her dad. She was having a right go at him. Calling him all the names under the sun. She screamed at him. You knew, and you didn't fucking tell me. Her friend came into the kitchen and tried to calm her down. Alex then screamed at her friend.'

'He knew what?'

Railson shrugged. 'God knows. But I remember Alex having the Brit award in her hand. She was going to smash him around the head with it. But then her bodyguard stormed into the kitchen and stopped her. That's when she flew at him. We were all standing there, gobsmacked. Then everyone piled into the kitchen. He manager, Charlotte and Dillon. Charlotte's manager was also there. Alex was screaming at all of them. Calling them a bunch of bastards. Saying they were just using her. That's when Gareth, the head chef, at the time chucked them all out of the kitchen.'

'So they went back into the restaurant?' Brooks asked.

'No, they all left through the back door of the kitchen. Gareth locked the door. But the window was open, so we could still hear them arguing. They were there for a good five minutes screaming at each other.'

Fagan scribbled notes on his pad. 'Did you see them after that?'

'No. Gareth was fuming. We'd been told to prepare this celebratory meal. But they ate none of it. They must have gone back to the studio down the road and carried on arguing there.'

'So you don't know if they returned to the hotel?'

'No, they didn't come back. And I know that because I was seeing one of the housekeeping staff. The rooms they booked never got used.'

Fagan snapped his notebook shut. 'Thanks for this information.' He glanced at Brooks. 'We'll head back to Newport and take a stock check of everything.'

CHAPTER 9

Newport Central police station – 3:13pm

Fagan glanced at his phone. 'Looks like it will be a few hours before Watkins has any useful information. So we'll have to manage without him. Ok, let's recap. It's June 1993, the night of the Brit awards. Everyone is super excited. Alex has been nominated for best album. Charlotte's career is on the slide. Alex has been screwing Dillon behind Charlotte's back for several months. Paparazzi get a photo. When they present Alex with her award, Charlotte bursts onto the stage and gives Alex a belting. Dillon then rushes onto the stage and punches Charlotte.' Fagan considered what he had just said. 'Here's my question. If Charlotte hated Alex that much, then why go back to the after party at the Agincourt hotel?'

'It was an act, sir,' Brooks suggested.

'I was thinking the same thing.'

'You know what these celebrities are like. Anything to stay relevant. If Charlotte's pop career was about to take a nosedive, then a stunt like this would have kept her in the news.'

'And kept people buying her records.' Fagan added. 'After the award ceremony, they fly back to the Agincourt by helicopter. That's when all hell breaks loose and they have a massive argument in the hotel's kitchen. The head chef, then a waiter, witnesses it all.' Fagan flipped open his notebook. 'It all started when a mystery woman gained access to the hotel. Railson said that she was upset. After the woman is thrown out, Alex has a massive bust up with her dad. She said.' Fagan checked his notes. 'You knew, and you didn't fucking tell me.'

He tapped his pen on the notepad. 'What did Alex's father know? It was obviously something pretty bad for Alex to fly off the handle. She was going to belt him with her Brit award, but then the bodyguard intervened. Alex then has a go at him.'

'Don't forget Alex also had a go at her friend when she tried to calm her down.'

'After that, everyone piles into the kitchen. Charlotte, Dillon, Jordan and Mercury. Alex accuses them of using her. Then the head chef chucks them all out of the kitchen. They were out the back for several minutes, continuing to scream at each other. They then left. Railson said they didn't come back to the hotel. So they must have gone back to the music studio. Something happened at the music studio, resulting in someone's death.' Fagan checked his notepad again. 'According to the witness, Alex, her dad, the bodyguard, Charlotte and Dillon, and Jordan were there, along with Mercury.'

'Plus that friend of Alex.'

'It has to be her.' Fagan speculated.

'Sir?'

'The body at the back of the music studio.' Fagan said. 'They all went back to the studio. Something happened resulting in Alex's friend being murdered.' Fagan recalled the conversation he had with Evans the day before. He picked up his phone and located Evan's number.

'How's it going, Fagan?' Evans greeted.

'Jamie, do you remember that conversation we were having yesterday? About you meeting Charlotte W and Dillon P.'

'Yeah.'

'You said you drove them down to London. How many people were in the car?'

Evans took a moment to sum up an answer. 'Five. Charlotte, Dillon, and three blokes. I reckon they were their managers and probably a minder.'

60

'And one of them told to shut your gob when you tried to start up a conversation?'

'Yeah, nasty looking bloke. Kept an eye on me all the way to London. I even put my foot down to get there quicker. I couldn't wait to get them out of my minibus.'

'And they paid you five hundred quid?'

'Yeah, that was the only good thing about that fare. I still have a record of the fare.'

'No way!' Fagan exclaimed.

'Yeah. I started Skywalker Taxis in 1990. Used to log everything in notebooks. Then in 1995 I got myself a computer. Dean Tyler helped me digitise everything. I kept records of all my fares because of tax purposes. The reason I still have it is because I got Dillon and Charlotte to autograph it. I still have the carbon copy they signed. It'll take me a while to dig the information out. It's on CD somewhere.'

'Jamie, you would be doing me a huge favour if you could do that.'

'I'll start looking.'

Fagan hung up. 'Right, they go back to the music studio. They continue the argument they had at the Agincourt. For some reason, Alex's friend is murdered. Charlotte, Dillon, and three other blokes jump in a taxi and head back to London.'

'Why didn't Alex travel back with them? Or her dad.'

'Shit, you've got a point there.' Fagan shrugged. 'She could have stayed at the studio with her friend's body. Plus, her dad must have stayed with her. Despite her being really pissed off with him.'

'Who buried the body at the back of the studio?'

'Someone must have travelled back from London to dispose of the body. That someone has to be the bodyguard, Alun Mitchell. Making him our prime suspect in the murder.' Fagan walked over to the whiteboard and scribbled Mitchell's name. 'Mitchell has form. He spent time inside for attempted murder. When I spoke to Richard Bishop earlier, he claimed

61

that while Mitchell was in prison, he confessed he had already killed someone, and that he had cut off their head. He then dumped the remains in the river Usk. Mitchell was inside between 1979 and 1988. If he was telling the truth about a previous murder, then we have to be talking before he went down. Do us a favour, Andrew, run a check to see if there are records regarding headless bodies being found in the Usk. You'll have to go right back to the seventies.'

'Will do.'

'If Mitchell murdered someone prior to him doing time, then he is one of the front runners for the murder. The question is, why did he murder whoever it is in that ditch?'

'An argument that got out of control, maybe.' Brooks considered.

'It all goes back to our mystery woman that showed up at the Agincourt. She's the catalyst. A bodyguard spots her and chucks her out of the hotel. Following that, the first person Alex attacks is her dad. She said he knew something, but he didn't tell her.'

Brooks' phone pinged. 'CSI has cleaned off the watch.' He handed his phone to Fagan.

Fagan read the inscription on the back of the Rolex. 'To Andrea, thank you for always standing by me, friends forever, Alex X. Where's the list of names you copied from the guestbook at the Agincourt hotel?'

Brooks handed Fagan his notebook.

Fagan scanned the list. 'Here she is. Someone called A Jones signed in the night Alex did.' He double checked the list to make sure there was none else with a first name starting the same initial. He returned to the whiteboard and scribbled the name. 'Andrea Jones was present at the music studios. She must have been the friend that entered the kitchen while Alex was having an argument. She goes back to the studio with Alex and the others and is murdered.' Fagan inhaled. 'The question is, why?'

'Think it could have been an accident?'

Fagan puffed through his cheeks. 'It's possible. I've investigated quite a few deaths that have turned out to be an accident.'

'But if it was an accident, why cover the whole thing up? What's the point of burying the body at the back of the music studio? When they could have phoned the police.'

'Fame.' Fagan said. 'Think about it. Alex had just won her first Brit award. She was a cash cow for her manager.' Fagan paused. 'I tell you what, it's looking more likely that Alex was a key player in the murder of Andrea Jones. The Brit award must have been used as a murder weapon.'

'But you just said Alun Mitchell was our lead suspects.'

'Yeah, I know,' Fagan said, staring at the whiteboard. 'Consider this. What if everyone had a role in this Andrea's murder? It could be possible that this Andrea Jones was blackmailing everyone. And they'd had enough.'

Brooks shrugged. 'Why was she blackmailing them?'

'Perhaps Andrea knew something they didn't want getting out. Alex had a very public drug problem. Andrea may have had dirt on any of them.'

'But cutting off the victim's head and hands was extreme.'

'Maybe, but it would have prevented identification. Finding the body has rattled a few cages. Alex hasn't been heard from in nearly thirty years. She has a Twitter page. But just sends out tweets now and then. Hours after the body is discovered, she's put out a tweet with an image saying she's got cancer.'

'A deathbed confession?' Brooks suggested.

Fagan smiled. 'Yeah, and by the by the looks of this recent photograph, she hasn't got long left. When Watkins tracks her down, he'll have to be cautious. From the look of her, I'd say she's only got weeks to live. Which means by the time we get the extradition order from the Spanish authorities, she'll be dead and buried.'

'What about the others? They were obviously witness to the murder of this Andrea Jones.'

Fagan stared at his computer. 'Charlotte and Dillon didn't last long beyond 1993. Charlotte's career was already on the slide. By 1994, the Spice Girls eclipsed her. Dillon has a string of flops and vanished from the pop scene in 1997. That's when he released his last single, Guilty Parties.'

'Interesting choice of song title.'

Fagan tapped away on his keyboard. 'He's now running some kind of new age mental health clinic just outside Llandovery. Dillon's mind crafting.'

Brooks smirked. 'A play on words.'

'Charlotte runs a recording studio in Cardiff.'

'Now that we have a name matching the remains, wouldn't it be a good idea to haul someone in for questioning?'

Fagan shook his head. 'No.'

'How come?'

'The remains have been in the ground for thirty years. Alex is on her last legs, so arresting her would be pointless. Hopefully Watkins might get some information when he locates her.'

'But that still leaves Charlotte, Dillon the minder, plus the two music producers.'

'They'll close ranks on us the moment we pull any of them in. They've had thirty years to cover this up. Whoever murdered Andrea Jones is probably sweating.'

'Do you still think Alex is in the frame for the murder of Andrea Jones?'

'We won't know that until Watkins gets hold of her. I'm going to interview her former bandmate and boyfriend later on in Chepstow. I want to build up a picture of her early career.' Fagan studied the picture of the inscription. 'To Andrea, thank you for always standing by me, friends forever, Alex X. Thank you for always standing by me.' He mulled the words over. 'It's obvious whoever this Andrea Jones is, she was an important part of Alex's life. This message suggests they'd been friends a long time. This Andrea Jones could be a friend from school or a friend of the family.'

'So how did she end up in that ditch?'

'It was definitely because of an argument that started in the kitchen of the Agincourt.' Fagan said. 'The head chef at the Agincourt confirms that. They'd been friends for a long time. Andrea did something to piss Alex off big time.'

'Do you reckon Dillon could have been screwing Andrea?'

'That's a possibility.' Fagan tapped Dillon's name into Google. 'There are loads of articles of him being involved with a string of female popstars in the nineties.' Fagan spotted something that caught his attention. 'Here's something. An article from the Argus published in June 2012 claimed that Dillon was cautioned and questioned by South Wales police. Following a string of allegations in the wake of the Jimmy Savile scandal.' Fagan found himself thrust over forty years into the past. Summer 1980 when Savile visited Abergavenny. The week Danny Llewelyn went missing. The week of the forest coalpit dorms abuse. George Walker's harrowing account of what happened to his son, Graham.

'You ok, sir.' Brooks remarked.

Fagan snapped out of memory lane. 'Yeah, I'm fine. Now the plot thickens. According to this article, Dillon's arrest was part of Operation Yewtree.'

'The investigation into sexual abuse by prominent figures in the entertainment industry.'

Fagan tapped on his keyboard. 'Let's search for Dillon in the police database.' The computer hard drive hummed. 'Bingo.' Fagan smiled. 'Dillon P, or Powell, was arrested in May 2012 after a rape allegations against him. Police released him without charge. It says here, he's been arrested before regarding a similar allegation in June 1993.' Fagan stared at the screen. 'You're kidding!'

'What?' Brooks asked.

65

'In January 1993, Police arrested Dillon for attempted rape. The woman who made the allegation was Andrea Jones.'

'So we have another suspect.'

'We do.' Fagan said, reading the information on the screen. 'The charges were dropped almost immediately after Andrea withdrew her allegations.'

'Sounds like a payoff deal to me, sir,' Brooks said.

'That's exactly what it sounds like. Only whatever amount Dillon paid Andrea wasn't enough for her.'

'Do you think she demanded more money from him?'

'It certainly looks like it. Obviously, Dillon wasn't going to pay her any money. So he murdered her instead.' Fagan paused. 'Hang on, we're going about this arse backwards.' He tapped another name into the search box of the police database before sitting back, clasping his hands behind his head. 'And the plot thickens even more. Alex's manager, Frankie Jordan, has been questioned on fifteen occasions over the past few decades. All on allegations of rape or sexual assault. Jordan was also arrested in the wake of the Jimmy Savile scandal.' Fagan recalled the conversation he had with Eddie Falcon. 'According to my source, Jordan had a taste for young girls.' Fagan remembered the name of a group Falcon mentioned. He tapped their name into Google. 'Paraphernalia are still about.'

'Who?'

'A group my snout mentioned. They have a website. They're a Hereford based group. The lead singer is called John Truman. He runs Hereford Music studios.' Fagan tapped the name into the search bar. 'Police arrested Truman under Operation Yewtree. They also released him without charge.'

'Are we going off track a bit here, sir?' Brooks said. 'Should we be concentrating on the body found at the back of Vine Road Music studios?'

'And that's what we are doing.' Fagan tapped on his keyboard again, searching for Mickey Mercury. 'The other owner of those studios, Mickey Mercury, has an arrest record that stretches back to the sixties.' Fagan sensed a wave of adrenalin cascade over him. 'Jesus.' He gasped.

Brooks got up and walked over to Fagan's desk, peering over his shoulder. 'What have you found?'

Fagan pointed at the screen. 'The first time Mercury was arrested was at the London Hotel in Abergavenny in 1968. But he grew up in Coleford.' Fagan had an idea. He stood up throwing his jacket on. 'Andrew, I want you to call up all the arrest records that Jordan and Mercury have as well as Dillon. I want names of all the women who have made allegations against them. And men who have made allegations against Mercury. I want you to get a list of the band members from the Paraphernalia and run their names off against Operation Yewtree. Also, find out who made the rape claim against Dillon Powell. I've a feeling a very dark picture is being painted here.'

'Where are you off?'

'I'm going to take a stroll down memory lane.'

CHAPTER 10

Abergavenny Museum – 4:06pm

Nigel Thomas smiled at Fagan as he walked through the museum. 'Detective Inspector Fagan, how are you on this fine day?'

Fagan looked around the museum. 'I see you've got the place up and running, Nigel.'

'Just about. I don't suppose I'll be seeing those daggers any time soon, will I?'

'Afraid not, especially since two of them were used as murder weapons.'

'Can't believe that Amanda was some kind of serial killer. I've had Jamie Evans nagging me to collaborate on a book. He wants to call it Murder, mayhem and Monmouthshire.'

'Typical of Evans.' Fagan chuckled.

'So what brings you in today?'

'I've got something I need to discuss.'

Thomas nodded. 'Sure.'

A few minutes later, Fagan and Thomas were sitting in the back office of the museum.

Thomas sipped from a cup of coffee. '*The* Vine Road music studios on the outskirts of Monmouth?'

Fagan nodded.

'Is it me, Fagan, or are you a magnet for dead bodies? Ever since you've returned to Abergavenny, there's been more murders than in your average episode of *Game of Thrones*.'

Fagan smiled. 'You told me a while back you had collected a load of photos from the London Hotel.'

'Yeah, after the incident with Benny Nelson, I went through

all the photos. I discovered quite a few with a much younger Benny in, and his father.'

'How many photos have you got of the London hotel?'

'Over three hundred. I didn't realise I had that many.'

'I came across an arrest record earlier of one of the original studio owners, Mickey Mercury.'

Thomas nodded. 'He managed a few Welsh pop sensations. Tried to poach the Manic Street Preachers away from their manager. Almost ended up being sued by them.'

'Mickey Mercury's first arrest took place at the London Hotel in 1968.'

'Interesting.' Thomas opened up his laptop.

'I couldn't come across any old pictures of Mercury. There are loads of him online with various artists he's been connected with.'

Thomas tapped away on the keyboard.

'I don't suppose you could find out if any of those old pictures you have at the London have Mercury in them.'

'Shouldn't be a problem.'

Fagan stood. 'Well, I won't take up your time. Give me a bell when you have something.'

Thomas looked up at him. 'Where are you going? Sit back down Fagan. This will only take thirty seconds.'

'I thought it would take you hours to sort through all the photos and find a match.'

'Evans' mate, Dean Tyler, gave me some software a few years back. It's a really clever piece of kit. It allows me to take a picture of someone who is old and compare them with other photographs of when they were younger. I'll just grab something off Google images.' Thomas clicked on his mouse. 'I have already imputed my entire picture collection into this software. Here we go. I've got eight matches.'

Fagan looked over Thomas' shoulder. 'Well, well, well, look who we have here. Mercury with Sergeant Bob Benson and Ernie Brown.'

'Now Lord Brown.' Thomas added.

'Hang on.' Fagan pointed at the screen. 'That's also Lord Barry.'

'What exactly are you looking into here, Fagan?'

'I was doing a search earlier and came across Mercury's criminal record. I'm also looking into the background of Alex Xavier's former manager, Frankie Jordan. It's a bit of a jumbled jigsaw at the moment. Alex was having an affair with another 90s pop icon, Dillon P. He's also got a criminal record. Police arrested Jordan and Powell in the wake of the Jimmy Savile scandal. But they were both released without charge.'

'I remember Dillon Powell. My late wife Jane had a crush on him. We watched the Brit awards when Charlotte burst on stage and gave Alex a good old slap.'

'Powell was questioned in 2013 about a rape allegation made against him. Police arrested him under Operation Yewtree.'

Thomas took a moment to register the name. 'Jesus Fagan, what can of worms have you opened now?'

'Operation Yewtree ended in 2015 and was succeeded by Operation Winter Key, now known as operation Hydrant.'

'If you ask me, it's all been swept under the carpet. But the recent death of Rolf Harris has brought everything bubbling to the surface again. I was watching the documentary on ITVX the other night about him. You need to watch that, then watch the two-part documentary on Savile. Both documentaries build a picture. I reckon Yewtree exposed too much for the police to handle. There were dozens of celebrities questioned about their past activities.'

'Including Dillon P.'

'I saw the short video Alex released last night. By the looks of her, she will be dead within the month.'

'She was looking like our prime suspect because of the Brit award found with the body. But there are few other suspects in the frame, including Dillon.'

70

'So this mystery body found at the back of Vine Road studios could have been murdered by Dillon P.'

'We also have another suspect. Alex's bodyguard.'

Thomas clicked on the next photo.

Fagan immediately spotted someone. 'That's Benny Nelson's lawyer, Wilson Fletcher Crawford. With his arm around Mercury.'

'They look like they're close.' Thomas commented. 'They're basically cuddling up to one another.'

'I had a feeling about him when I met him a while back. Benny Nelson's lawyer specialises in sexual misconduct cases. When I arrested Nelson in connection with Rebecca's murder, I did a background check on Crawford. He's the go to lawyer for celebrities who have been accused of sexual assault, rape and any other crime that's classed as a sex crime.'

'How was Nelson able to afford him?'

'That's what I'm still trying to figure out.'

Thomas scrolled to the next photo. 'This is a group photo. There must be fifty people in this photograph. Taken in 1967.' He pointed at the screen. 'There's a very young Benny Nelson.' He studied the image. 'Whoa, hang on a sec.'

'What?' Fagan asked.

Thomas pointed at a man stood on the end of the group. 'That's Charlie Butcher.'

Fagan ran the name through his mind. 'Charlie Butcher, the barber?'

'Yep.' Thomas nodded. 'Funny, he's the last person I'd expect to associate himself with the London.'

'Is he still about?'

'Yeah, Chalie is still kicking about. He still runs His and Hers hairdressers.'

'What, the one opposite the Angel Hotel?'

'That's the one.'

Fagan smiled, recalling a memory. 'I remember our mam taking me there when I was a nipper. She used to drop me in at Charlie's while she went to have her hair done. What was his wife's name?'

'Debbie.' Thomas answered. 'I went for a trim a few weeks back. Your name came up.'

'In what context?'

'In a good way. We were discussing recent events out at Skenfrith castle and Benny Nelson.'

Fagan looked at the image of a younger looking Charlie Butcher. 'Wonder if he knew any of these back in the day.'

'Charlie knows everyone. He'll tell you a story or two when you sit in that barber's chair of his.'

'He's not originally from Abergavenny, is he?'

'No, Charlie's a Londoner. Came to Abergavenny in the late sixties.' Thomas stared at the photo. 'I wouldn't be surprised if this picture was taken not long after Charlie and Debbie moved to Abergavenny. He's a bit of a mystery is our Charlie.'

'Why?'

'My mother used to take me there to get my hair cut. She once said that Charlie could have been part of the Kray twin gang. I have asked him about it a few times, but he's always laughed it off.'

'Might be worth having a word with him about Mickey Mercury.' Fagan mused.

'So, getting back to your mystery. How do you reckon that body ended up at the back of the music studios?'

'We're investigating the possibility that some kind of argument broke out between Alex and several other people. They were staying at the Agincourt hotel on the night of the brit awards. We have a possible name for the victim. We believe they were murdered and dumped on the night of the Brit Awards.'

'The Agincourt hotel. Another establishment that's surrounded by controversy.'

'How do you mean?'

'The Agincourt has been around for centuries. A lot of

72

famous musicians have stayed there who have recorded albums at Vine Road studios. Stories about shenanigans have been filtering out of that place for decades. It's made the national press regularly. So, another day, another mystery for DI Fagan.'

Fagan inhaled, nodding. 'If you ask me, I've kicked over another hornet's nest. We have a body at the back of a well-known music studio and several high-profile figures who've been questioned under Operation Yewtree.'

'And you think you may get into trouble if you dig any deeper?'

Fagan nodded. 'You're right. Operation Yewtree was too big for the police to handle. In the wake of the Savile allegations there were thousands of other reports of sexual misconduct. By major figures in the entertainment industry and other sectors. Following his death Liverpool police received over two thousand complaints from all kinds of people. You could tell who was trying to pull a fast one and who was genuine. We had to assign an entire team to the investigation. Then in 2015 we had to ship everything down to the Met in London.'

'Do you know why?'

'I reckon it was because Yewtree exposed something that was never meant to see the light of day. Rumours had been circulating about Savile for years. But because of his connections, he was untouchable. I remember when he turned up at that sports field in 1980. Everyone wanted a piece of uncle Jimmy. He knew what he was, and he revelled in it.'

'Just like Benny Nelson.' Thomas pointed out. 'The rumours about him have been circulating for decades. There have been claims made from loads of people in Abergavenny. But nothing has ever stuck to him.'

'That's because he's got that expensive solicitor.' Fagan's phone buzzed. 'Andrew, what have you got for me.'

'I got a result from that query, sir. The allegation made against Dillon Powell.'

'Go on, I'm listening.'

'Gwent Police arrested Dillon Powell in March 2013 regarding a sexual assault that allegedly took place in 1991. According to the report, a woman called Amy Lewis said that Dillon assaulted her after a concert in Newport. At the time she was twelve years old. She also claimed they met on a number of other occasions and engaged in sex. This was at the studio and at the Agincourt. The report is quite detailed and graphic.'

Fagan glanced at Thomas. 'Do you have an address for this woman?'

'Yeah, she's a Pontypool girl, or Talywain, to be exact.'

'Text me her address. Thanks for that, Andrew.' Fagan hung up.

'Another piece to add to the puzzle, DI Fagan.' Thomas said.

Fagan nodded, running his hand through his hair. 'I think I need a haircut.'

His & Hers hair salon - Abergavenny

Charlie Butcher looked up from the newspaper he was reading. He took a moment to recognise the man he had last seen over forty years ago. 'Marc Fagan.' Butcher smiled, offering his hand. 'I see the boy I once knew, in the man standing before me.'

'How are you, Charlie?' Fagan smiled.

Butcher tapped his leg. 'Besides a knee replacement at eighty-four, not bad.'

Fagan glanced around the barbershop. 'Nothing has changed. It's just how I remember it.'

'I've given it a few licks of paint over the years. Are you here for a cut?'

'Yeah, why not.' Fagan looked toward the barber's chair.

74

'Take a seat.' Butcher invited.

Fagan stared at his ageing face in the large mirror.

'Everyone gets old Fagan. There's no shame in it.' Butcher said, throwing the cover over. He started trimming away at Fagan's hair. 'A lot has changed over the years. I bet you hardly recognised Abergavenny when you came back.'

'Some things have gone. Other places have sprung up, and there's those things that have stayed the same.'

'Like Benny Nelson.'

Fagan sighed. 'Like Benny Nelson.'

'I know you've been away nearly forty years, Fagan, so I won't nag you about Nelson.'

'He's the talk of the town at the moment.'

'Twat has got a book coming out at the end of the week, hasn't he? Called, Injustices Within. I was talking to the manager at Waterstones the other day. Nelson walked in last week and actually said that he'd be available for a book signing.' Butcher let out a snort of derision. 'The nerve on that bastard!'

'He's playing the system at the moment. There's not a lot we can do about it.'

'I've come close to punching his lights out over the years. Even had a run in with his old man a few times when he was alive. Greasy little toad he was.'

'Did you know him well, Nelson's dad?'

'Everyone knew Bill Nelson, but most people avoided him.'

Fagan shifted in his chair. 'Bill Nelson used to go drinking in the London.'

Butcher glanced at Fagan in the mirror. 'Bend over junction, they called that place. A wide variety of people used to drink at the London. You can't call them the names we used to call them. Nowadays it woke this, woke that. I can't even have a decent fart in front of my customers, just in case I offend someone.'

Fagan chuckled. 'You ever bump into Mickey Mercury?'

Butcher paused, searching his memory before nodding. 'Jesus, that takes me back. Yeah, Mickey Mercury. Went on to become a music producer, didn't he? Used to co-own that music studio just outside Monmouth. Mickey was quite the character. Always dressing for the occasion. Every Saturday night in the London.' Butcher clipped away at Fagan's hair. 'The place was full of characters. Dodgy fuckers, most of them'

Fagan's curiosity kicked into gear. 'Did you know Bob Benson?'

'Everyone knew Bob Benson. And Bob Benson knew everyone else.' Piece of work.' Butcher said with an air of resentment. 'Couldn't believe it when I saw he'd been bumped up to chief constable of South Wales police. The bloke was as bent as they came.' Butcher put the scissors in a tray. 'I think we're done there, Fagan.'

Fagan climbed out of the chair and handed over a ten-pound note. 'You're not native to Abergavenny, are you?'

Butcher smiled. 'How did you guess?'

'Which part of London are you from?'

'The east end.'

'A boom town for the criminal underworld back then.' Fagan remarked.

Butcher stared back. 'One day, Fagan, we'll sit down and have a pint. I'll tell you my life story. But it's not for the faint of hearts.'

C H A P T E R   1 1

Talywain – Pontypool – 5:16pm

Fagan held up his ID badge. 'Are you Amy Lewis?'

'What's this about?' Amy rolled her eyes. 'Jesus, don't say that dick of a son of mine has got himself into trouble again.' She grumbled.

'Actually, Miss Lewis, I was hoping to have a chat with you. It's about Dillon Powell.'

Amy stared back for a few moments before opening the door wider.

Fagan sat down at a kitchen table. 'Lived her long?'

'About three years.' Amy placed a mug of coffee in front of Fagan. 'You said you were here about Dillon Powell. I'm not in more trouble, am I?'

Fagan sipped from his coffee mug. 'Why would you be in trouble?'

'Because that's what happened when I tried to tell you lot about my experiences. That prick got away with everything. Him and that twat of a solicitor of his. Arrogant bastard claimed I was like everyone else. Just out for a cash grab. How could Dillon P be the monster I was making him out to be? I spent six hours in a fucking police station being grilled by a couple of right arseholes. Making out that I was lying. That I had made everything up just to get attention.'

'Which police station did you go to?'

'The main one in Cardiff. They didn't even give me anything to eat.'

'Do you think you could talk about your experience with Dillon?'

Amy shook her head. 'Sorry, but I don't trust the police. Not after what I went through ten years ago. All I wanted to do was get the truth out. The bloody the police didn't want to know. What makes you any different from the rest of them?'

'I can understand your unwillingness to make any further statements. I cannot discuss the details, but I am here in connection to another crime that Dillon Powell may have committed. You're not part of any active investigation into false claims or anything. I'm here voluntarily. If you'd like, I can leave and you won't see me again.'

Amy inhaled, glancing out of the window. 'It's hard to know where to start. I'd won a competition to see Dillon in concert and meet him backstage. At the time he wasn't as famous as he became. But everyone knew who he was around the valleys. A Gurnos boy done good. That's what they used to say about him.'

'When did you win this talent contest?'

'Summer 1990. I'd just turned twelve. I saw Dillon on Wales Today. His manager, or whatever they're called, was doing an interview. Dillon was on the rise and was due to record his first album. His manager used to run a community recording studio on the Gurnos Estate in Merthyr. The day after he was on the TV, our school announced a singing competition, to be judged by Dillon.' Amy smiled. 'I used to have a bit of a voice back then. Fancied myself as Whitney Houston. Dillon travelled all over the south Wales valleys picking out the best singers. When he came to our school, I sang my heart out. I couldn't believe when he picked me as the best singer. We had our photos taken, and he promised me he'd give me advice on the night of the concert.'

'Where was the concert?'

'Newport leisure centre. I know it's not the Albert Hall, but it was everything to me.'

'Were there any other competition winners there on the evening of the concert?'

'No. It was only years later, I realised what Dillon was playing at.'

'What did you mean by that?'

'When the competition was being run, Dillon picked one person from each school. All the competition winners were girls. All of them were about my age.'

Fagan scribbled away furiously in his notebook. 'Were you alone when you turned up at the concert?'

'No, I was with my mam. But she wasn't allowed backstage after the concert finished.'

'Not even at Dillon's dressing room door?'

'You couldn't really call it a dressing room. More like an office for the manager at the leisure centre.'

'You ok carrying on?' Fagan asked.

Amy nodded. 'When the concert was over, I had to wait at least half an hour until I could see Dillon backstage. He was signing autographs for his growing legion of fans..'

'Can you recall the name of the manager?'

Amy took a moment to recall. 'Cole Harris.'

Fagan jotted the name down.

'Looking back, it was weird.'

'How do you mean?'

'Cole escorted me to the dressing room and told me to relax and have fun. It's not every day you get you meet a future popstar.'

'Can I ask what were you wearing that day?'

'A short skirt and a tiny top. My mam encouraged me to dress much older than I actually looked.' Amy glanced down at the garb she was wearing. 'I'm a little more conservative these days with the way I dress. I plastered the makeup on. The heels my mam bought for me made me look five years older.'

'He liked the way you dressed?'

'God yeah. When I walked into that room, his eyes virtually popped out of his head. I remember him saying that he could believe I was twelve. I looked eighteen. What a stupid, impressionable, naïve young girl I was back then. I was tall for my age and I developed early. I started my periods at ten.'

'Amy, listen to me carefully. You were none of those things. That's what sexual predators want. They always make out that you're the one at fault. You're not to blame for anything. Do you understand?'

Amy nodded.

'How old was Dillon at the time?'

'In his twenties, mid-twenties.'

Fagan took his time with his next question. 'Are you able to tell me what happened when you were in the office?'

Amy wiped away tears. 'His, uh, manager showed me to the door. When I entered the office, Dillon was sitting on a sofa. He smiled at me and padded the spot next to him inviting me to sit. *God,* why did I go into that room?' Amy questioned herself. 'Just before I went backstage, I had an attack of stage fright. My mam had a right go at me. I was terrified. But, in a good way. I was one of those girls who had a mad crush on him. I saw him signing autographs earlier on in the night. The girls were tripping over themselves just to get close to him. At one point security had to throw two girls out who started fighting.' Amy composed herself. 'So, he invited me to sit next to him on the sofa. Because of the crush I had, I literally jumped on top of him.'

'What happened next?'

'We talked for a while. He sat there flattering me. Said how impressed he was with my voice. Dillon claimed to know a top singing coach. He promised to get me singing lessons. He reckoned I could be the British version of Whitney Houston.'

'You told him you liked Whitney?'

Amy nodded. 'When I won the school singing competition, I told him everything I wanted to do in life.' Amy became frustrated. 'I wish I could take that *stupid* girl and give her a bloody good slap.'

80

'Why? You weren't to know what was going to happen to you.'

'I suppose not.' Amy massaged her forehead. 'I was just caught up in the excitement.'

'Take your time.'

'He just kept saying over and over he couldn't believe how young I was. Then he said.' Amy inhaled. 'Any boy would be lucky to have a girlfriend like me. I was just in awe of the man, you know. Dillon Powell became one of the biggest popstars of the day. And he was telling me how good looking I was. He moved closer and started stroking my hair. He said that I could go to a party with him the week after if I wanted.'

'What did you say?'

'What do you think I said? Yes, of course. He was about to record his first album. Until then, he'd recorded all his songs on the Gurnos estate. But then his manager booked him into a proper studio. When I was sitting on the sofa next to him, he said that he wanted me to watch him record his first song. He wanted me to be part of his life.'

'Can you remember the name of the studio?'

Amy tried to remember before shaking her head. 'No, sorry, but I know it was just outside Monmouth.'

Fagan stared back at her. 'Vine Road music studios?'

Amy hesitated. 'Yeah, I remember now. Vine Road music studios. Bit of a shabby place back then. A lot of famous bands have made songs there.'

'Ok, so you were sitting on the sofa with him. He was stroking your hair. What happened next?'

Amy gulped from her coffee mug. 'He, uh, moved in closer. He reeked of cigarette smoke. Dillon was a heavy smoker. He said we could sit for a while and kiss. But that's only if I wanted to.' Amy let out a snort of derision. 'I was too in love with him to say no. I'd only ever kissed two boys before that, and that was just a peck on the lips. When we were kids, we'd dare each other to do all kinds of stupid stuff. Dillon moved in. At first, it was just light kissing. He then stopped and said he could teach me to kiss like a real woman. That's when he shoved his tongue into my mouth.' Amy closed her eyes, clasping a hand over her mouth. 'Even today I feel sick just thinking about it. I can still taste the cigarettes as he shoved his tongue down my throat.' She took a deep breath. 'That's when his hands wandered up my skirt. When he reached my knickers, I found the strength to pull away. He apologised straight away. Said that he couldn't help it because I was such a beautiful-looking girl. I said it was ok.' She looked at Fagan. 'But it wasn't ok, was it?'

He shook his head. 'No, it wasn't.'

Amy buried her head in her hands and sobbed.

Fagan slipped his notebook into his pocket. 'I think we can leave it there, Amy.'

Amy shot back a defiant look. 'No, I want to tell you everything. You are the first copper to show any kind of interest.'

Fagan pulled his mobile phone from his pocket. 'Do you mind if I record this?'

'No. I want to get it out of me. I need to let people know.'

Fagan tapped the record icon on the screen. 'Take your time Amy.'

'I can't recall how long I was in that office for. It seemed like hours. When it was over, I scribbled down my phone number I got up to leave. He followed me to the office door. He asked me for one more kiss, so I obliged. That's when he pinned me up against the door, shoving his groin into me. He had a right stiffy.'

'How long did he take to contact you?'

'A few days later. He invited me out to watch him recording his first single for his album at the studio. There were lots of people there, including Alex X.'

'Alexandrea Xavier was there?'

'Along with Charlotte West. It was so chaotic. I remember

82

the two studio owners having a go at Dillon's manager for turning up late. Said they'd booked another band later that day.'

'What happened after Dillon finished recording at the studio?'

'That's when he dropped a bombshell.'

'Which was?'

'I told him I needed to get home. Mam would be worried. He told me he had phoned my mam and explained to her I'd be staying at a hotel just down the road from the studio. I remember being furious with her. When we went back to the hotel, I sneaked away and phoned her. She told they might let me record some songs at the studios. I told her they didn't want to know. It was Dillon they were interested in, not me.'

'Do you think your mam pushed you into a relationship?'

'God yeah. Mam was determined to make some money out of me going out with Dillon. She hoped if I lived the life of a popstar's girlfriend, she would benefit.'

'Is your mam still about?'

'No. She died of cancer in 2015. We hadn't spoken since 2003. I didn't even turn up for her funeral.'

Fagan didn't want to sidetrack. 'The hotel you just mentioned. Was it called the Agincourt?'

'Yeah, I've driven past there a few times over the years. Every time I drive by, my blood freezes. A load of us went back. Alex, Charlotte, Dillon. Plus another band. I remember their lead singer stroking my leg when I sat next to him. God, it made my skin crawl.'

'Do you recall the name of the band?'

Amy massaged her temples. 'The Paraphernalia. I remember them because they always used to turn up with loads of young girls. Makes my stomach churn just thinking about it. Anyway, at the end of the night, when we were all going back to our rooms, Dillon said he'd booked two adjoining rooms. But he was full of it. The only reason he said that was to make me go back to his room with him. When I realised he had lied, I said I wanted to go home. Dillon explained that there were no taxis at the time of night. When I went to leave, he stood in front of the door. He started getting upset. Said that I didn't love him, and that I was just using him. Jesus, I was twelve years old, for Christ's sake. I didn't know what love was. I have spent years going over what he said.'

'Paedophiles often use language to disarm their victims.' Fagan explained.

Amy looked at him. 'That's exactly what Dillon did. He said he'd fallen in love with me the moment he clapped eyes on me at the singing contest at my school. He said that he could give me the life I always dreamt of. Being a singer like Whitney Houston.' She sighed. 'I fell for it, hook, line and sinker. That's when he led me over to the bed.' She swallowed. 'I just lay down and let him get on with it.'

'He raped you?'

Amy barely managed a nod. 'I thought it was the right thing to do. If I let him do whatever he wanted. I would be allowed to sing at the studio.'

'How long did the abuse continue?'

'A year, maybe.'

'Why did it end?'

'He started seeing Charlotte, didn't he.' Amy answered. Resentment was clear in her tone. 'I visited that studio dozens of time over the course of 1990. The owners let me record tracks, but they never saw the light of day. Just before Christmas that year, I turned thirteen.' She paused. 'That's when I confronted Dillon about his relationship with Charlotte.'

'What was his reaction?'

'Sheer rage, He said that I was trying to be controlling.'

'Did you tell your mam what happened that night? The time when he first raped you.'

84

'Yeah, but she didn't give a shit. Mam was born in a rough part of Cardiff. When I told her what had happened, she just said it was one of the harsh lessons of life. She told me she had lost her virginity when she was ten.'

For a moment, Fagan's stomach turned somersaults.

'The last time I turned up at the studio. He didn't want to know. Charlotte was there recording her first album. By then, they were a couple. I remember her telling me I was just a silly little girl trying to play gown up mind games. So I left the studio and walked back to Monmouth. I wasn't living with mam. She was off doing her own thing. I was in foster care. My foster parents were brilliant. They told me to go to the police and tell them what Dillon had done.' Amy hung her head. 'I tried to tell the police everything, but they didn't want to know. Dillon already had his first number one hit.'

'It must have been hard for you.'

Amy nodded.

'That first night at the hotel, when he raped you. Did anyone see you together, or see you go up to the room he had booked?'

'We were all in the bar that night. Charlotte, Alex, Dillon. The two owners of the studio along with Dillon's manager.'

What time did you leave the bar and go up to Dillon's room?'

'I honestly don't recall. It was thirty years ago.'

Fagan nodded.

'When Jimmy Savile died and all the rumours emerged of him being a paedophile, I started doing a little research of my own. I came across an article about people who had met through Friends Reunited. They would talk about their experiences with Savile. So I posted a request for people who had known Dillon in his early years. Within two days, I had thirty responses. All from girls who had encountered Dillon. Some of them knew him from the Gurnos Estate in Merthyr. Another four girls won the singing competition I had taken part in. We met up. There were about six of us. One girl told a really harrowing story. Her name is Vicky. She'd won the competition. Dillon pulled the same trick he pulled on me. He invited her to the studio to watch him record his album. After, he took her back to the hotel and raped her. She was just eleven years old.'

'Jesus.' Fagan gasped.

'That's not the worst of it. Dillon was abusing a few of us at the same time. Vicky told me once that Dillon, Charlotte, and another woman had taken her back to their room and forced her to take part in group sex. They said it was a special birthday present.' Amy paused. 'For her twelfth birthday.'

Fagan inhaled. 'So Charlotte was also involved with sexual abuse?'

Amy nodded. 'That's what Vicky claimed. We decided that one of us should pluck up the courage and go to the police. There were loads of women going to the police and talking about Savile. So we thought we had nothing to lose. I volunteered to speak to the police.'

'What happened?'

'Nothing for quite a while. I remember walking into Cwmbran police station and giving a statement. The officer at the time said they'd look into it. About three months passed before a detective turned up at my door. He said I had to report to Cardiff main police station, the following week. When I turned up, I didn't expect the third degree. They interviewed me for five hours. There were two detectives and one solicitor who said he was representing Dillon. Piece of shit made me feel like I was the one who had carried out the abuse. About two weeks later, I had a letter saying that Dillon was considering taking legal action against me for slander and defamation of character. I sat in that police station for five hours and told them everything. But it didn't make any kind of difference. Dillon is still walking around free. Still making shitloads of money when they play one of his songs on the radio. They said because it was so long ago, there were too many inconsistencies. The police said they had questioned everyone who I claimed was in the bar. My accounts conflicted with everyone else's.'

Fagan tapped the stop icon on the screen.

'So, are you finally going to do something?'

'It's not up to me, I'm afraid, Amy.'

'Huh, typical police response.' She mocked.

'I know it's hard. But I am investigating a separate crime. Dillon is at the centre. If it comes to anything, then your statement will open a door for those who have been the victim of abuse by him and others. I cannot arrest Dillon for an offence he's already been questioned about. Unless fresh evidence comes into play.'

Amy nodded.

'Do you have contact details for this other girl who said she was abused by Dillon and Charlotte?'

'Yeah, but she won't speak to you. None of the other girls will either. When I went to the police and they put me through hell, it put all of them off telling their own stories.'

Fagan handed over his business card. 'It could help us with our investigation. Give her my details and tell her I'd like her to volunteer for an interview. This girl Vicky you just mentioned. She said that both Dillon and Charlotte and another woman abused her. She didn't give a name, did she?'

'No, sorry.'

'Was it just Dillon abusing you? Or was Charlotte involved?'

'It was just Dillon. After he gave me the brush off, I realised he didn't want to know any more. I never returned to the studio after that. That girl I just mentioned said she went there for about two years.' Amy inhaled. 'There is another thing.'

'What's that?'

'There was another bloke there. He took a lot of pictures. Not just me, but loads of young girls.'

Fagan recalled the conversation he had with Eddie Falcon

the day before. 'Can you recall a name?'

Amy took her time answering. I think his name was Ben.'

'Ben, or Benny?'

Amy nodded. 'Yeah, Benny. He made my skin crawl. After Dillon and me used to have sex. Dillon would leave the room and fetch Benny. He'd make me strip and take loads of photographs. He said it was for artistic purposes.'

'Did he ever try anything?'

'No, as far as he was concerned, I belonged to Dillon. He must have taken hundreds of pictures of me.'

Fagan stood. 'Thank you for being so brave. Amy.' He glanced at his phone. 'I have to leave.'

'DI Fagan.' Amy called out as Fagan headed towards the door.

Fagan turned.

'I'm not after money or fame. None of us are. All we want is justice and closure. Is that too much to ask?'

'No, it isn't.' Fagan replied. A thought suddenly popped into his mind. 'When you stayed at the Agincourt, did you sign the guest register?'

Amy took a moment before nodding. 'Yeah, in fact the manager insisted on it every time me and Dillon stayed.'

Fagan smiled back and nodded. 'Thank you. I'll be in touch soon.'

CHAPTER 12

The Boat Inn – Chepstow – 6:34pm

'Steve Wakeman?' Fagan asked.

A bald man in his mid-fifties plucked the strings on his guitar. 'That's me.' He said without looking at Fagan.

Fagan pulled out his badge 'DI Fagan, Gwent police.'

'Something I can help you with, Inspector?' Wakeman continued to strum his guitar.

'I was wondering if we could have a chat. It's about, Alexandrea Xavier.'

Wakeman looked at Fagan, before glancing at the other band members who were staring at him. 'Take five guys.'

Fagan sat at the bar and ordered a glass of coke.

Wakeman heaved himself on the barstool next to Fagan. 'So, what's Alex been up to now? I saw her tweet last night. Poetic justice, if you ask me.'

'Not a fan, then?'

Wakeman grimaced. 'We had a good thing for a few years. Then she dumped me for fame and fortune.'

'Which is why I am here today. You knew Alex in her early days. What was she like?'

The barman placed a pint in front of Wakeman, who pointed at a display cabernet behind the bar. The display case contained a guitar with a blue ribbon draped over it. Alex's autograph was scrawled on the front of the guitar. 'I bought her that guitar when she joined our group. She gave it back to me.'

'Why did you keep it if you have a grudge?'

'It's not Alex I have a grudge against. It's that bloody

manager of hers. Frankie fucking Jordan.'

'I read an article the other day about your early days. You and Alex Were having a relationship?'

Wakeman gulped from his pint glass. 'Yeah, we were an item for a few years. They were the best years.' Wakeman smiled.

'How did you first meet Alex?'

'I put an advertisement in the local rag. Our former lead singer got herself pregnant, silly cow. She didn't want anything to do with the music scene after she had the kid. So we needed a new lead singer. I put the ad out and a few girls replied. Most of them couldn't sing shit.' Wakeman glanced at the guitar case. 'But then Alex blew me away when she auditioned. She could sing, and she was a brilliant guitarist. She was self-taught. Got herself loads of books when she was fourteen and learnt to play. By the time she joined us she was writing her own songs. She was perfect. You could give her something to play and she'd pick up on it straight away. Alex had so much raw talent.' Wakeman looked at the mounted guitar behind the bar.

'Did you know her farther well?'

Wakeman nodded, taking another gulp. 'Simon Price. Yeah, I knew him. Terrible what happened to him at the steelworks.'

'Some kind of accident?'

'Simon was severely burnt.'

'What about Alex's mother?'

'Never met her. Alex hated her for what she did to her father. While he was recovering in hospital, her mother was having an affair. Six months after Alex's father got out of the hospital, their mother upped and fucked off. Alex was twelve and her sister was five. Alex said that her mother couldn't cope with looking after an invalid husband and two girls.'

'Do you know what year this was? When Alex's dad had the accident.'

90

'1982, I think. Alex told me they almost got chucked out of their house because Alex's dad couldn't work. His mate helped them out with money. And he looked after them. The moment that Alex turned sixteen, she got herself a job at a supermarket to help the family. It was a struggle for them. When she was fourteen, her dad's friend gave her an old guitar he got from a charity shop. She once told me that music helped her cope with the anxiety. She would lock herself in her room for hours, learning to play. And play she could. I remember when she auditioned. She bought her battered guitar and sang a number by Suzi Quatro.' Wakeman reminisced. '*You can't give me love*. Alex nailed it. I thought she sang the track better than Suzi. I gave her the gig there and then.'

'What year was this?'

'1986.' 'Wakeman replied. 'Probably about June. She'd just turned sixteen. I was eighteen. He smiled. 'Best time of our lives. When Alex joined the band, we grew in popularity. Weddings were our best gigs. People were getting fed up with hiring a disco. We did the pub circuits and the lager clubs. It was brilliant. We gained notoriety for writing our own songs. Our bookings were through the roof.'

Fagan remembered something from an earlier conversation with Watkins and Brooks. 'You were obviously popular on the student scene then. You know, universities and colleges.'

Wakeman shook his head. 'We never played a gig at a university. I couldn't stand those places. Full of toffs. We'd stay mainly on the pub and club circuit. Played at a few small music festivals.'

Fagan jotted a note on his pad. 'When exactly did you hit the big time?'

'You mean when did Alex hit the big time? Let me think.' Wakeman puffed out his cheeks. 'It was in March 1989. We'd been on the South Wales music scene for around three years.

Alex spotted an article in the Argus several weeks earlier about a talent competition in Cardiff. She nagged me for weeks before I finally said yes.'

'You weren't particularly interest then?'

'Talent competitions weren't my thing. We already had talent. I didn't fancy being paraded in front of some dick of a record producer.'

'But you went anyway.'

Wakeman nodded. 'By then, me and Alex were a full on couple. I was mad about her. She was absolutely stunning. I'm not exactly Brad Pitt. I counted myself lucky to have a girl like that hanging off my arm. We had a fantastic time together.' Wakeman sighed. 'And then we turned up at that talent contest. Frankie Jordan and Mickey Mercury were there. They ran a music studio just outside Monmouth. They were looking to create their own home-grown popstars. Stock Aitken Waterman was struggling with getting their stars to hit the top ten. Unless you count Kylie who topped the charts with everything she sang.'

'Many people at the talent contest?'

'Loads turned up. Wanting to be the next big thing, Including and Charlotte W.'

'Charlotte West was there as well?'

'Yeah.' Wakeman stated. 'Jordan and Mercury really hit the jackpot when they found those two.'

'What happened when Jordan chose you?'

'Alex was on top of the world. She had been working hard for the past year. Writing her own lyrics and producing new music for the band. She did her best to learn to play the keyboard, but she was terrible at it. Sounded like Les Dawson when he played the piano.' Wakeman paused. 'I guess when Alex joined our group in 1986, she was the driving force. Just before she joined us, I was considering breaking up the band. Alex made a difference in all our lives.'

Fagan looked around the bar. 'But you're still here, and she became a pop icon.'

Wakeman nodded. 'When Jordan spoke to us after the show, we talked for hours about our dreams. Alex spoke the most. She was so excited at being picked to record at Vine Road studios. She said it was her dream to go all the way to the top.'

'I remember Jordan saying to her, with a voice like that, you'll got to the top, and further.'

'Weren't you happy about winning the competition?'

'No. I only took part because Alex had been begging for weeks. We were making decent enough money. We were doing five or six gigs a week. It wasn't just a weekend wedding gig. It was a full time living. We could charge up to three hundred quid per gig. We could do whatever we wanted. My dad even converted the garage out our house into a studio so that we could rehearse. The moment we won that talent competition, everything changed.'

Fagan sipped from his glass. 'In what way?'

'Me and Alex started arguing almost immediately. I remember when we first turned up at the studio to have our first recording session. Jordan wasn't happy with anything we played. We had our own style. But Jordan wanted us to be more pop group than the style we were playing. He said pop music made the most money. Not bands trying to be creative and creating their own style. He had a few instrumental soundtracks there. He made me and the boys sit in the next room. I could hear Alex churning out a few songs. She sang Madonna's *Material Girl*, *Saving all my love for you* by Whitney and Kylie's *I should be so lucky*. Jordan ignored us, and just focused on Alex.'

'When did you break away from Alex?'

'Towards the end of 1989. Me and Alex had been arguing for months. The only reason Jordan kept us around was to keep Alex happy. Then he booked her to go on *Top of the Pops*. When he broke the news, she was so excited. She said that she could wait for all of us to play on the BBC. Then Jordan really dropped the bombshell. He told us that Alex would appear without us.'

'What did you do?'

'I hit the fucking roof. I flew at Jordan.'

'Is that when you assaulted him?'

Wakeman nodded. 'Told him I had had enough, and that he was constantly stabbing us in the back. Alex was too full of herself to stand by us. She had stars in her eyes. We had a massive bust up about her appearing on *Top of the Pops*. When that moment came, I knew I had lost her. I was heartbroken. It was such an emotional ordeal. When I saw her getting into the car to go to London, I knew it was finally over.'

Fagan recalled the moment he left Rebecca sobbing at the train station. Begging him not to go. He quickly pulled himself back to the present. 'Did you sign any kind of contract?'

'No, and that's what caused most of the arguments in that first year. Jordan kept fobbing us off. Saying it was a lengthy thing drawing up contracts. A lot of legal people involved. But I knew it was a load of bollocks. It wasn't until later that I found out he had signed Alex within a month of us turning up. Jordan had forbidden her to tell us. I remember having a chat with the rest of the band members at the time and said we should ask Jordan for a payoff.'

'Did you get any kind of payoff?'

'No, but we got a huge fuck off from Jordan. Piece of shit really fucked us over. Do you know what's both ironic and sinister at the same time?'

'What's that?'

'When Alex first appeared on *Top of the Pops,* the main presenter for that show was Jimmy Savile.'

'While at the studio, did you ever see anything out of the ordinary?'

Wakeman threw Fagan a side glance as he gulped down his pint. 'Depends what you mean.' He placed his pint glass on the bar, savouring the beer's taste.

'Did any young girls used to hang out at the studio?'

'Is this what this interview is all about, Inspector Fagan? You didn't even tell me what you're actually here for.'

'We found the remains of a young female individual at the back of the music studio. And that's all I am prepared to say at this moment. But I am not here to question your involvement, Mr Wakeman.'

Wakeman digested Fagan's words before speaking. 'Vine Road studios was a Mecca for young girls and young boys.'

'How young?'

'The boys that used to show up were mostly teenagers, sixteen and up. Mickey Mercury didn't hide the fact he was gay. Used to shout it from the highest rooftops. Most of us got on with Mercury better than Jordan. There was a group that was recording at the studio at the time called The Flamboyant. I didn't hold any kind of grudge toward them because they were gay. I saw all of us as music artists, straight and gay. They were quite a good band. They're still about now. I went to see them last year. They supported The Pet Shop Boys in Nottingham. Mickey would spend a lot of time with them and their entourage at the Agincourt hotel, just up the road.'

'What about young girls?'

'Well, that's where it gets disturbing. And I just want to state for the record that I had no part of anything that went on at that studio. The girls that used to show up at the studio were young.'

'Age range?'

'Nine or ten upwards, maybe. They used to come in with a group call the Paraphernalia. Bunch of arseholes and pervs. Jordan thought the sun shone out of their arses. They were big in Australia. He'd been making a fortune since the late seventies. They were the reason the studios grew in popularity during the eighties. That's what gave him the idea that his studio could launch big popstars in the UK.' Wakeman paused. 'When the Paraphernalia used to show up, they always had a bunch of young girls. Jordan and those pricks and the girls used to disappear into the Agincourt. I never saw the same girl more than three times. It was like a revolving door, so to speak.'

'Ever see any of these girls upset?'

'All the bloody time. Especially when they used to come from Jordan's office. This one time, I remember hearing screaming coming from his office. This girl must have been fourteen.' Wakeman guessed. 'Poor thing looked terrified when she flew out of Jordan's office. I confronted Jordan about it. He told me if I wanted to be part of Alex's life, then I should keep my nose out of his fucking business. They had a saying at that place. What happens in the studio, stays in the studio.'

'Weren't you tempted to report any of it?'

'There was no one to report it to. Besides, I was in love with Alex. I couldn't go to the police and say stuff. It would have totally rocked the boat.'

Fagan drank from his glass. He remembered the reason he had called at the pub. 'Do you know anyone called Andrea Jones?'

Wakeman snorted. 'God, aye. What a piece of work she was.'

'How so?'

'She was the one that got Alex hooked on drugs. She did it just to stay in Alex's life. If she could get drugs, then Alex would depend on her.'

'Did Alex always do drugs?'

'She wasn't into hard drugs. Not at first, anyway. We all used to smoke a bit of weed. The odd Saturday night after a gig, we'd share a joint. But nothing like the shit Alex eventually got into. No thanks to Andrea.'

'How did Andrea come on to the scene?'

'They were schoolmates. Andrea would turn up most

weekends when we were out on a gig. She called it moral support. Andrea was there the night Alex won that talent contest in Cardiff. She was pissed as a fart, and all over Jordan. He didn't mind. They even disappeared for about twenty minutes. Andrea was always copping off with someone when we did a gig. It was her thing, if you catch my drift.'

'When did Alex get into hard drugs?'

'About six months after we started recording at the studio. A lot of bands used to go there and bring all kinds of shit. Andrea, being Andrea, was shagging just about every bloke who walked through the studio door. So she got to know all the dicks bringing shit in. Towards the end of 1989, it at was obvious Jordan was going to tell us to fuck off. The arguments got more intense. He expected more from Alex. So Andrea would offer her a shoulder to cry on. By the time she did that *Top of the Pops* show, Alex was on her way to being addicted to hardcore shit. After her launch on *Top of the Pops* the hits came thick and fast for Alex. One hit record after another. Andrea was there in the background supplying her with uppers, as she called them.'

'Did Alex ever meet Madonna?'

'Not that I recall.' Wakeman paused. 'Wait, you've read that article in Word on the Street magazine.'

Fagan nodded. 'I was looking at it yesterday.'

'Everything in that article was a load of bollocks.'

'What about her dad, Simon Xavier? I take it you knew him well?'

'Yeah, Simon was ok. He'd watch us play when it was just us. He used to drive us to our gigs. He enjoyed being on the road. Gave him a sense of purpose after his accident at the steelworks. He'd turn up at the studio to support Alex. I think he died a few years back. Alex obviously looked after him in his later years. Lived in a nice house on the outskirts of Devauden. Shame about what happened to her sister.'

'Suicide.' Fagan remarked.

97

'Did you ever see Alex after you split?'

'Just once.'

'When?'

Wakeman recalled the moment. 'About a month before her famous bust up with Charlotte at the Brit awards.'

'How did she seem?'

'She was a total mess. Alex told me she had had a guts full of everything. She missed the days when it was just us out on the road. She hated everyone that surrounded her or smothered her. Jordan, Andrea. The legions of fans she had amassed to during her career. That prick of a boyfriend, Dillon.' Wakeman glanced at the guitar. 'She gave me that back. Said she didn't want to destroy everything good in her life.'

'Did you know Dillon Powell at all?'

'Not really. I avoided him. Bit of a dickhead. But's that what you get from the Gurnos Estate. He was another one who liked the young girls. There were plenty of them hanging around the studio for him to *consume*.'

'Did you see Dillon doing anything illegal with young girls?'

'No. Dillon was the cautious and clever one. Because of his good looks and blonde hair, the girls would swarm around him. Jordan, on the other hand, would walk past a young girl and slap her on the arse. A lot like Sid James from the Carry On films. He even laughed like him.'

Fagan drained the last of the Coke from his glass.

'After Alex's famous meltdown at the Brit awards, I tried to contact her. I turned up at the studio one day and confronted Jordan about it. He had me thrown out of the studio.'

'What about security at the studio?'

'It wasn't security, it was a hired thug, Alun Mitchell. What a nasty piece of work he was. Used to have this menacing glare. Everyone was terrified of him. If you crossed Mitchell, you'd spend weeks watching your back.'

'Did Alex say anything else to you the last time you saw

her?'

'She wanted out. She said she'd had enough of the constant bullshit she had to endure. After the fight at the Brit awards they plastered her all over the Sunday papers. The News of the World published several pages. Exposing Alex's life for the world to see. After they threw me out of the studio, I went to see Alex's dad. He told me to fuck off. I didn't understand why he did that. We got along really well when we were out on the road.'

'Why did you just mention the article published nine years ago was a load of bollocks?'

'There were so many inconsistencies. I phoned the editor and having a go at him. First off, we never toured any of the universities, and we'd never done a gig in Bristol. Second, the article made me out to be the controlling one. I wasn't in control of anything. I remember being livid with the article. So I hopped on a plane to Barcelona and drove to Tarragona to confront her.'

'Why did she say to you?'

'She didn't say anything because she wasn't living in Spain. I looked everywhere for her but couldn't find her. I visited her dad just before he died, but couldn't get anything from him. I tried to track down her best mate, Andrea. No joy there. I even went out to see her former manager, Jordan. He told me the usual, fuck off and don't come calling again.' Wakeman finished his pint. 'Just after that article was published, she created her Twitter account. She doesn't post much. Merry Christmas and reminding people what a huge star she was in the early nineties. And now she's put out that tweet about her having cancer.' Wakeman inhaled. 'I'd give anything, just to see her one more time.'

Fagan climbed down from his barstool. 'Thanks for talking to me today, Mr Wakeman. You've been very helpful.' He placed a card on the bar. 'Call me if you can think of anything else.' Fagan headed for the door.

'DI Fagan.' Wakeman called out.

Fagan turned to face him.

'When you find Alex, tell her I'm sorry. I'm sorry for everything that happened to her.'

Fagan nodded and turned.

CHAPTER 13

The Cantreff Inn – Abergavenny – 8:53pm

Jackie placed a pint on the bar as Fagan walked through the door.

'You know me all too well, Jacks.' He winked at her.

'I know most people, Fagan. You, like most of my customers, are a creature of habit.'

'Fagan, over here, mate.' Jamie Evans called out.

Simon Edwards and Eddie Falcon were sitting in the corner of the bar with Evans.

'How goes the big case out at Vine Road Studios?' Edwards asked.

Fagan supped from his pint. 'It's been an interesting day. Found out quite a lot about the place.'

'Who's you been speaking to?' Evans asked.

'I'm can't go into details,' Fagan said.

'You know we're not going to gossip, mate. We haven't blabbed about other stuff like Rebecca or Nelson.'

Fagan savoured the taste of his beer, glancing at Falcon. 'Everything you said about Nelson was true'

'I know it was,' Falcon replied. 'He was always hanging around the studio.'

'I spoke to someone today who said that Nelson took photos of her. And before you ask Jamie, no, I'm not going to name person I spoke to.' He took another swig from his glass. 'I interviewed a woman who said she'd been raped on multiple occasions by Dillon Powell.'

Evans clasped his hand over his mouth, coughing. Trying not to spit beer over everyone.

'Wouldn't surprise me about Powell.' Edwards slapped Evans on the back. 'He used to come across as an arrogant prick when he was famous. Saw an interview with him on *Going Live* many years ago. He was flirting with Sarah Greene.'

'The woman I spoke to today claimed there were loads of young girls abused at the recording studio and the Agincourt hotel. South Wales police arrested Powell under Operation Yewtree in 2013. They also arrested Alex's manager, Frankie Jordan. Both men were released because of lack of evidence.'

Evans cleared his voice. 'The police investigation that followed Saville's death?'

'Yeah.'

'So what does this mean exactly, Fagan? Have you stumbled onto another sex abuse scandal?'

'It's beginning to look like that.'

'What about the body you've discovered?'

'We've identified her as a close friend to Alex..'

'Bloody hell, Fagan. Sounds like you're up to your neck again.'

Falcon looked at his phone. 'We're all dying to know what Alex is about to say in less than ten minutes.'

'They've been playing her songs on the radio all day long.' Jackie sat down next to Edwards.

'Yeah, the news has been talking about her all day.' Evans said. 'They reckon she hasn't got long left. She wants to say goodbye to her fans.'

'It's a shame, really. She was one of those stars that blazed for a few years before fading.'

'Like Amy Winehouse.'

'I loved her.' Jackie said. 'She had one hell of a voice, didn't she. She's another one who was a drug addict. Why are all the best musicians addicted to drugs?'

'Didn't her husband get her hooked on drugs?' Fagan speculated.

Falcon nodded. 'That's the general belief.'

'The person I interviewed earlier said Alex's best mate got her hooked on drugs.'

'It's always like that. Most artists start up their music careers clean. Once they start mingling in certain circles in come the drugs. When I was working at Vine Road studios we'd get a constant stream of hopeful bands coming in to record tracks. Most of them came and went in the blink of an eye. But those who stayed eventually succumbed to the shit Jordan used to bring in. It was a real money spinner for Jordan.'

'Are you saying that there was a drug trade operating out of the studio?'

'Yeah, Jordan knew what he was doing. The studio was in the middle of nowhere. Wasn't like a housing estate, where people could go to the police and complain. No one gave a shit because its wasn't visible. It was the perfect spot. Drugs and the music industry go hand in hand. After a while the studio got a reputation for a place where you could hang out, produce music and get high. There were so many heavy metal bands going out there during my time there. Razor Wire, The Bleak Dead, Black Demons, The Dark Abyss, Cliff Edge. All of them were doing shit.'

'Two minutes, guys,' Evans announced, staring at his phone. 'It's going on YouTube as well.'

'Got any suspects regarding the body at the back of the studio?' Falcon asked.

'We're building our case. There's a growing list. But it's not like we can go out and make an arrest. We have to have probable cause. Evidence has to be gathered.'

'Here we go,' Evans announced.

Everyone armed themselves with a screen.

The ten second countdown displayed on Alex's video.

'Hi Everyone, it's Alex X here. I would just like to thank you for the warm messages that have flooded in over the past twenty-four hours. In a time of such darkness in my life, it's comforting to know there are people who have so many good things to say.'

'Ah, that's lovely, bless her.' Jackie remarked, tapping the heart icon.

'It hasn't been an easy road for me. I know there are so many of you who want to know what I have been up to over the last thirty years. I was in such a dark place for so long. The music industry can be a brutal place. It can consume you and suck you under, like a riptide on the ocean. I would like to express gratitude to my loyal fanbase. Who have remained faithful to the music that I produced. All the letters I have received over the years have given me a source of comfort. They have helped me to rebuild my life. That night at the Brit awards changed me in ways I could never imagine. I knew then I had to get out. I am so grateful for the support I got from my manager, Frankie Jordan. Who has done such a great job over the past thirty years. Keeping my music relevant.'

Evans pointed at his screen. 'Jesus, the hearts are really flowing.'

'But now I have to announce with great sadness, that I have terminal cancer.'

Jackie wiped tears away that trickled down her cheek.

'My doctor has informed me I have weeks left. Therefore, I have decided to share my last moments with you. I have also some exciting news for you. Over the past few years, I have been working with Frankie and we have produced new music for both a new generation and the generation who listened to my music. This new album is due to be released at the end of the week. And is called The Memories We Leave. Another piece of exciting news I have for you is that I have just released a single on the net.'

'On the net?' Evans remarked. 'Bit of an old fashion term.'

'This single is called True To you. I am dedicating this new single to my most loyal fans.'

Falcon thumbed the screen on his phone. 'It's just gone live on Prime Music.' He switched apps. 'Now Spotify has just uploaded. And finally, yep, it's just been uploaded to Apple music.'

Edwards looked up from his screen. 'She's going to make a fortune before the night is out.'

'I've just bought the song.' Jackie revealed.

'Hang on Jacks. Don't start playing it just yet. I want to see what else she has to say.' Fagan said.

'I am donating fifty thousand pounds generated from music sales to Cancer Research UK.'

Jackie smiled. 'That's really thoughtful.'

'I will be making one more appearance this weekend, via Zoom. At the fiftieth anniversary of Vine Road Music Studios. Thank you all so much. I love you all.'

Jackie hit the play icon on her phone screen. For a few minutes everyone listened to Alex's song. 'I really like that song. It's got a really haunting melody to it.'

Evans was staring intensely at his phone screen.

Fagan noticed the bemused look on his face. 'What's the matter, Jamie? You don't look very convinced.'

Evans glanced up. 'I don't know. If you ask me, it's too much of a coincidence. Police find a body at the back of a music studio that Alex recorded he songs at. Then suddenly, she turns up and not only blurts out she has cancer, but she releases an album. Which I'm sure, is going to make a shitload of money for her former record producer.'

Edward rolled his eyes. 'This isn't one of your stupid conspiracy theories, is it, Evans?'

'I'm just saying. It's too much of a coincidence.'

'I'm sure she'll have plenty of trolls running her down.' Jackie remarked. 'You know what those twats are like.'

'Jamie is right.' Fagan said.

'Jesus, not you are well, Fagan.' Edwards chuckled.

'I'm a serving police officer. It's my job to speculate. Even if I have to wander into the conspiracy theory arena.

Sometimes solving crime can involve all kinds of weird speculation.'

'Do you think Alex may have been involved with whoever they found in that field out the back of the studio?'

'Until we get the chance to speak to her, we won't know.' Fagan's phone buzzed. He looked at the screen and stood. 'Watkins, you better not have been lying on a sunbed drinking sangria all afternoon.'

'No, boss.' Watkins replied.

'What have you got?'

'Nothing boss.'

'I take it you've found Alex and spoken to her?'

'No.'

'What do you mean, no?'

'She's not out here, boss. I couldn't find her anywhere.'

'Then what the bloody hell have you been doing all afternoon?'

'Interviewing expats that live out here. I have spoken to about thirty people in all. They have all said the same thing. Alex has never lived in Tarragona. I have spoken to an elderly couple who've been out here for over thirty years. They've never seen anyone matching Alex's description. Local plod also provided me a list of expats living within a fifty-mile radius. There's no sign of Alex anywhere near Tarragona.'

'Where the bloody hell could she be?' Fagan said loudly.

Fagan's friends all looked in his direction.

'I'm at the airport now, boss. It's not worth me hanging around. My flight leaves in an hour.'

'Get back here, get some kip. We'll pick this up tomorrow at Newport central.' Fagan hung up.

'Well?' Evans stated.

'There's no sign of Alex in Spain?'

'Which means she has to be a prime suspect in the murder of Skeletor.'

'Show some bloody respect, Jamie.' Jackie chastised him.

106

'That's a human being.'

'But that has to put Alex in the frame for the murder of the mystery body,' Edwards said.

Fagan looked at Eddie. 'Did you get hold of your mate from that magazine that ran the interview with Alex ten years ago?

'I rang him, but he wasn't available to speak.'

'As soon as he contacts you, let me know.'

'Will do, Fagan.'

'I wonder what poor Dillon P must be thinking? You know, Alex's ex-boyfriend.' Jackie said.

Fagan glared back at her. 'Poor Dillon. Are you having a laugh, Jacks? I interviewed a woman today who described how Dillon raped her when she was twelve.'

Jackie clasped her hand over her mouth. 'Jesus, not Dillon.'

'You missed the conversation we were having before you sat down, love,' Edwards said, cuddling up to her.

'Dillon is no blue-eyed boy, Jacks. Police arrested him arrested in 2013, as part of Operation Yewtree.'

'Operation Yewtree was in response to the allegations made against Jimmy Savile.' Edwards said. 'I watched that documentary on Netflix last week. I've watched it about five times over now.'

'I remember when Savile came to Abergavenny.' Jackie recalled. 'There were hundreds of girls buzzing round him. He was having the time of his life. He wore that hideous red tracksuit. They even bussed kids in from other schools just to meet him.'

'Jesus, I just remembered something.' Falcon announced. 'When I was working at the studio, I knew a sound engineer who had been there since that late seventies. When I first started, he told me about the things that went on. He said that one day in May 1980, Savile turned up at the studio with a load of young girls. Then, a few hours later, *Mr glam Rock* himself arrived. Jordan was there, all excited. The sound engineer reckons there were loads of girls at the studio. The three of them went to the Agincourt hotel with a bunch of girls.'

'I just had a really dark thought.' Evans said, looking at Fagan. 'While Jordan and his paedophile mates were at the Agincourt. Nelson, and Bob Benson, along with the rest of the pervs, were at Forest Coalpit dorms with Graham Walker and the other boys.'

Jackie shuddered. 'Jesus, I think someone is dancing on my grave.'

Falcon stared at his phone. 'I'm just looking at Wikipedia. Some critics labelled Operation Yewtree as a witch hunt.'

'How the fuck can people call it a witch hunt?' Edwards questioned. 'These twats got away with abusing kids for years. They knew they could get away with it because they were famous. Savile rubbed shoulders with some many rich and powerful. It really makes you wonder what else went on.'

'So what's your next move regarding the body at the back of the studio?' Evans asked.

'I'm going to question the former owners and see if it turns up anything.'

CHAPTER 14

Day 3
Newport Central police station – 9:24am

'Morning, boss.' Watkins greeted with a yawn.

Fagan looked back at him. 'Where's your tan?'

'I was only in Spain for an afternoon. I was mostly indoors talking to people.'

Fagan sat down in his chair. 'What did you find out?'

'According to everyone I spoke to, Alexandrea Xavier has never lived in Tarragona. I spoke to one couple, Maggie and Peter Miles. Kept me talking for ages. They have been out there since 1987. They were one of the first couples to move to that area. As far as they're aware, Alex has never as much as set foot in the area. But, and this is where it gets interesting. There have been a few people out there looking for her. Including a journalist from the South Wales Argus.' Watkins checked his notes. 'Someone called Terry Williams.'

'Interesting, the couple you spoke to kept names.' Fagan remarked.

'Here's where it gets really interesting. I checked with the south Wales Argus about an hour ago. He still works there. I spoke with him briefly. He said he flew out to Spain looking for Alex in connection with an article he wrote in the Argus in 2013. The article briefly covered the arrest of Dillon Powell in connection with a rape allegation.'

'So he travelled to Spain to track down Alex. hoping she would dish the dirt on Powell. Might be worth a visit to the South Wales Argus later on today.' Fagan hauled himself out of his chair and walked over to the whiteboard. 'Right, let's recap, shall we. One body found at the back of Vine Road music studios. Believed to be Andrea Jones, close friend to Alex X. She was murdered and buried on the night of the Brit awards.

'Or murdered on the night of the Brit Awards and buried the following day.' Watkins said.

Fagan Nodded. 'We know that Frankie Jordan and Mickey Mercury owned the studio back then. This makes them top on our priority list of significant witnesses.' Fagan looked at Brooks. 'Did you run a full background check on them?'

'I did, sir. First there's Frankie Jordan. Born March 1946 in Monmouth. His birth name was Frankie Marsh. He was an only child. His mother brought him up alone after his father was killed in action during the Suez Crisis in 1956. In the 60s Frankie changed his second name to Jordan. It's where his father died after being wounded in the Suez Crisis. In 1965, Jordan got interested in the music industry. In 1967 – 1969 Jordan did a stint at Radio Caroline before returning home to Monmouthshire. He worked in a music shop for several years. By 1973, Jordan saved enough money to rent out some attic space in an old farmhouse. He put an ad in a paper for a partner. Michael Orchard answered the ad.'

'Anything more recent?'

'We already know Jordan was arrested in 2013 under Operation Yewtree. Police questioned him regarding an allegation from a woman who claimed Jordan raped her back in the eighties. She was just fourteen. She said that Jordan and another man.' Brooks checked his notes. 'John Truman, who was the lead singer of a band called the Paraphernalia, raped her over a course of two nights. At the Agincourt hotel.'

'We're building a rather seedy picture of what went on back then.' Watkins said.

'But what good is it?' Fagan questioned. 'Police released both Jordan and Truman without charge.'

Brooks nodded.

'That's the key problem with Operation Yewtree. So many of the allegations made against the numerous celebrities were decades old. When I was in Liverpool, I spoke to one woman who claimed one of the England squad that won the world cup raped her in 1966. But her story fell apart when she failed to give locations. Then we had a ninety-seven-year-old woman walk into Edge Lane police station, claiming she was raped by a major Hollywood star back in the forties. Her statement was taken, and she described in great detail what happened. But there was nothing we could do about it. Because it happened back during the war. Plus, the Hollywood icon in question died in the sixties. That's the thing with Jimmy Savile. The man travelled all over the country, meeting countless people. There were over six hundred lines of enquiry. And that's the tip of the iceberg. They reckon there could have been ten times that many. He was given the key to the entire country. There wasn't a door that Savile couldn't open. There were so many warning signs in plain sight we should have seen. Including that interview with Andrew Neil. So many times Savile straight up admitted he was someone nobody should trust.' Fagan sighed. 'But we just laughed it off. It's like a serial killer hiding in plain sight.'

'Wire in the Blood.' Watkins said.

'What about it?'

'The missus loves that show. She was watching the first season the other night on ITVX. A former football star, who turns out to be a serial killer.'

'What about Mickey Mercury?'

Brooks continued. 'Formally known as Michael Orchard. Born October 1950 in Coleford on the border between England and Wales. Mercury struggled with his sexuality early in his life. Bullied at school for wearing a skirt. When he became an adult, he found it hard to fit in with society. Often being ridiculed for his femininity. In 1966 Orchard travelled to London and discovered the underground gay movement. He found purpose in his life. Had a string of partners. Mercury was musical minded and could play the piano from an early age. In 1973, he answered an ad in a local paper and partnered up with Frankie Jordan. They started Vine Road music studios and invited local bands to record in their attic studio. Orchard changed his name to Mickey Mercury in 1991 following the death of Freddie Mercury.'

'Arrest sheet?'

'First arrested at the London Hotel in 1968. Then arrested again in 1969 during the Greenwich Riots.'

'What's the Greenwich riots when it's at home?'

Watkins tapped on his keyboard. 'The Greenwich riots happened in London, July 1969. They were apparently in response to an event called the Stonewall Riots that kicked off in June 1969 in New York. Mercury was arrested and charged with disturbing the peace. A year after the event, Mercury organised the first gay pride rally in Cardiff. Arrested during the rally, again for disturbing the peace. He's considered as a pioneer within the LGBT community. Has written several books on gay rights. Last year, he received a lifetime achievement accolade at the Cardiff Gay Pride award ceremony. For representation and promotion of the gay community in the music industry. Mercury has worked with a lot of celebrities who have advocated the LGBT community, including Taylor Swift. For the past fifteen years, he's run a visual effects studio in Cardiff. Still heavily involved with the music industry producing music videos at his studio.'

'Any involvement with Yewtree?'

Watkin stared at the screen. 'No, Mercury is clean, as far as that is concerned.'

Fagan pointed at the whiteboard. 'Next on our list is Alun Mitchell.'

Brooks studied his tablet. 'Not as much as the other two. Alun Mitchell, born in 1957. Served time inside for attempted murder.'

'According to Richard Bishop yesterday, Mitchell confessed to murdering someone and dumping their headless corpse in the Usk. He made the confession while they were in prison. He also boasted that the head is in the one place the police will never think to look.'

'I forgot to mention, sir,' Brooks interrupted.

'What?'

'I got a result of that headless corpse enquiry. Police found the body of a headless female just down from the transporter bridge in Newport, in 1978. Samples were kept and stored away for decades. According to a pathologist's report, she was pregnant at the time of her murder. Then, in 2008, the body was identified after the sister came forward and supplied a DNA sample. An operation was running at the time to identify dead bodies that turned up in Newport in the 70s. The deceased was identified as Sixteen-year-old Dorothy Morris. Her mother and her sister reported her missing, but the police never found her. Following her disappearance police interviewed Alun Mitchell who was supposed to be her boyfriend.'

'Was he arrested in connection with her disappearance?'

'No, he was just a witness and supplied an alibi. According to records, there were nine headless corpses found in the Newport area between 1977 and 1981. They were all female. Police believed that a serial killer may have been stalking local women in that area.'

'Mitchell was in prison in 1979 for attempted murder.' Fagan pointed out. 'So it would have been easy to rule him out of any enquiry if the police thought a serial killer was stalking the Newport area. Right, getting back to our list of suspects. We'll have to rule out Dillon and Charlotte for now. Because the items found with the body have a direct link to Alex. The Brit award and the Rolex. Both items have Alex's name on them. So let's speculate. We know Alex and her entourage turned up at the Agincourt hotel after the Brit awards. They flew from London to Monmouthshire by helicopter. It's too long ago to check for some sort of flight plan. However, we have a witness who saw them all arguing in the in the kitchen. We have the guestbook from the hotel that proves Alex and the others, including our victim, were present at the Agincourt.'

'It's just a simple case of tracking down Alex, boss.' Watkins said.

Fagan nodded. 'Exactly.' He frowned at the whiteboard. 'That's if we can locate Alex. Ok, so let's assume that Alex had a direct involvement with the murder of Andrea Jones.'

'As in murdered her.' Brooks stated.

'Yes, as in murdered her. Question is, why?'

'An argument that got out of hand.' Watkins suggested.

'Yeah, but what?' Fagan glanced at his scribblings on the whiteboard. 'For the moment, let's put the argument at the back of the list. The deed has been done. Andrea has been murdered. We're certain she was murdered at Vine Road music studios. So the crime has taken place. Andrea is lying dead on the floor. The Brit award is our number one candidate as being the murder weapon. A conversation takes place between the guilty party and any witnesses. For all we know they could have considered phoning the police. But the injuries sustained to Andrea Jones would have suggested she suffered more than just a nasty fall.'

'Blunt force trauma.' Watkins said.

'Definitely. So calling the police would have been out of the question. I mean, we are talking about Alex X, one of the biggest pop sensations to come out of the nineties. Frankie Jordan must have been present at the murder scene. There was no way he was going to call the police. Alex had just won the Brit award for best album. The money would have been rolling in. There was no way Jordan was going to sacrifice his number one star.'

'And no one else wanted to take the blame for the murder,

either.' Brooks added.

'So they come up with a plan that involves the decapitation of Andrea's body. My money is on Mitchell for that endeavour. He's got the form for it. To distance themselves from the crime, they all jump into a taxi and head down to London. Alex and her father stay at the studio. With Andrea's body'

'But why?' Watkins quizzed.

'Alex was her best mate. The inscription on the back of the watch proves that. They'd been mates since school. So she's stays with the body out of guilt and waits for her co-conspirators to return and dispose of the body. The deed is done and then she quickly vanishes from the limelight. She could have carried on, but she didn't.' Fagan glanced at Andrea Jones' name. 'I suspect out of guilt. So she goes into pop exile. Retreating from the world of show business. Her manager, Jordan, carries on. Promoting her records and keeping Alex's career alive in the eyes of the pop industry.'

'But why didn't anyone question why Alex had dropped out of the pop scene?' Brooks mentioned.

'They probably did.' Fagan answered, looking at Watkins. 'Didn't you mention there were various attempts to track Alex to Tarragona? '

'Yeah, but now that you mention it, boss, the couple I spoke to yesterday said that people have only been going out there in the last ten years looking for her.'

A notion surged to the forefront of Fagan's thoughts. 'After that article appeared in the music magazine, nobody had a clue about Alex's whereabouts before then. So where was she Between June 1993 and 2014? It's safe to say Spain wasn't in the picture. Perhaps somewhere closer to home?' Another idea dawned on Fagan. 'According to Alex's former bandmate, Steve Wakeman, her father lived just outside Devauden in a large house. Andrew, I need you to contact land registry. Find out when Simon Xavier bought that property and who took it over after his death?'

'Do you believe that will lead us to Alex, boss?' Watkins inquired.

'Not only that,' Fagan continued. 'She might have lived with him, staying under the radar. His death in 2019 could've prompted Alex to sell the house and do a runner for the second time.'

'Sounds like quite a stretch, boss.'

Fagan exhaled slowly. 'It's the best theory we have for now. Our immediate task is to contact the former studio owners, Frankie Jordan and Mickey Mercury. Let's summon them for questioning. I'm guessing they'll both try to stall us. We'll work that to our advantage. The more time we get to gather evidence, the more we can shake the puzzle and hope the right pieces fall into place.' He turned to Brooks. 'I want you to investigate the 1978 headless body case. Check if the sister's still alive. This could finally solve a 45-year-old murder. I'll talk to Alex's father's old colleague. He could be the key in tracing their mother. She seems crucial to the puzzle.' Fagan clapped his hands. 'Right, come on, let's get our arses into gear.'

CHAPTER 15

Llanwern Steelworks – Newport – 10:06am.

Paul Freeman smiled as Fagan entered his spacious office. He stood, offering a handshake.

'Thanks for seeing me.'

'Please sit, DI Fagan.' Freeman gestured to a comfortable chair. 'I have to admit when my HR department contacted me yesterday, I thought they were taking the piss. They said you wanted to talk to someone about Simon Xavier.'

Fagan nodded. 'This isn't directly concerning Simon. It's in connection with another matter I can't discuss. I wanted to talk to someone who knew the family. How long have you worked here?'

'I'm in my forty-third year. Looking forward to retirement next year.'

Fagan nodded. 'How well did you know Simon?'

'We were good mates. Simon was several years older than me. When I started, he took me under his wing. Showed me the ropes. We'd go out on the piss around Newport. Great town back in the early eighties. Most of the pubs have gone now.'

'He was a family man?'

Freeman nodded. 'Thought the world of his girls. Whenever we'd go away on rugby tours, he'd get them something nice.'

'Happily married?'

Freeman inhaled. 'That's what I thought. His wife Jan was a bit of a looker, you know. Simon would bring her to the social club and she get pissed. Had to drag Simon off a colleague one night. Jan had too much to drink. Snogged this bloke on the dance floor in front of him. Simon went ballistic. Nearly put the bloke in the hospital. Got arrested for it. He used to have some massive fights with Jan. I never thought they were suited.' Freeman paused. 'Then everything changed when Simon had his accident.'

'What happened?'

'Hot water pressure heater burst. Two men died straight away. Simon was badly scalded. I didn't think he was going to make it through that first night. I went to see him a week after the accident. Luckily, the scaling hot water didn't touch his face. But just below the chest, it was a total mess. Two years of skin grafts. And then, to top it all off, that twat of a wife buggered off one day. Said she couldn't cope.'

'What about the girls?'

'Social services suggested they should go into fostering. The mother didn't want to know. Simon was three years in and out of rehabilitation.'

'Did he receive any compensation for his injuries?'

Freeman shook his head.

'Why not?'

'My predecessor all those years ago was a bit of a dick. At the enquiry, he claimed he ordered the three men not to start up the equipment because of issues with the pressure system. He was full of shit. He actually told those men to start up the system. Not only that, but he told them not to bother with PPE. It was sweltering that summer. The manager told the men they'd only be running the plant for an hour. To test out the pressure system. So there was no need for full protective clothing. Simon told me this years later. He said he had an argument with the manager over safety concerns. But the twat in change told him that if he didn't do what he was told, then he would sack him. Fortunately, in 2018, there was another investigation into what happened in 1982. The hearing ruled in favour of the families. I testified on behalf of

Simon and told the enquiry everything what Simon had told me. It's the least I could do after what happened to those men. The families received seven million each compensation. They bloody well deserved every penny.'

'You just mentioned social services. Did Alex and Abbey go into foster care?'

'No, me and my wife took them in. We couldn't have children of our own. My wife, Trudy, loved looking after the girls. We had a three-bedroom house, so there was plenty of room. We even converted the back room into a bedroom for Simon. It was a struggle for Simon. He couldn't find work. I was constantly putting my hand in my pocket for the girls. Made sure they never went without at Christmas. When Alex turned fourteen, I brought her this old guitar from a second hand music shop. Alex used to sing in front of the mirror in her bedroom. Trudy loved listening to Alex sing. She had an amazing voice from a young age. When she turned sixteen, Alex got a job in a local supermarket to help with bills. It was a bit of a relief for me. Then, in 1986, she joined a band and went touring around south Wales. She still worked in the supermarket, but she was also making money with this band.' Freeman smiled. 'Simon changed their surname to Xavier. I told him he was off his nut. In 1989, Alex won this talent competition. Simon was over the moon about it. Alex and Simon moved out and were living in a cottage near the studio. The following year, Alex released her first number one. As soon as the money flowed, Simon gave me thirty grand.'

'That's very generous.' Fagan remarked.

'He said it was for all what me and Trudy had done for him and his family after his accident. In 1991, Alex came to visit us at Christmas time. It was brilliant. Alex's younger sister, Abbey, was living with us. But it all changed because of the money Alex was earning.. Me and Trudy were so happy for them all. Especially after what they had been through as a family.' Freeman paused, taking a breath. 'But we lost track of them in 1992. The visits became less frequent. Me and Trudy assumed it was because of their busy lifestyles. Alex was a huge pop star. We knew we'd see them less frequently. Abbey went on tour with her during the summer holiday. She phoned us once and said she was having a whale of a time. She had just met Dillon Powell. The other Welsh pop sensation. She said he was amazing and gave her a load of signed merchandise to give out to her friends. We were so happy for Abbey.'

'What about their mother?'

'Simon once told me she showed up, asking for money. He told her to fuck off. I don't blame him. She didn't want anything to do with those girls. When Jan left Simon to cope with two girls on his own, it almost destroyed him. Simon told me, if it weren't for me and Trudy stepping in and helping out with the girls, he would have taken his own life.'

'You really helped that family when they needed it.' Fagan praised.

'It was the least we could do. Towards the end of 1992, the newspaper articles circulated about Alex having a problem with drugs. The News of the World was constantly hounding Alex. They were like vultures. Abbey came to stay with us for several weeks.'

'How did she seem?'

'Very withdrawn. Not the excited younger sister we assumed she'd be.'

'How old would Abbey have been?'

'Twelve. She was born in 1980.'

'So there was a ten-year gap between Abbey and Alex?'

Freeman nodded. 'Yeah. Simon told me that his wife didn't want to have kids.' Freeman let out a snort of derision. 'All that woman wanted was a good time. I remember Simon having a go at me once when I asked him why he was with her.'

'He obviously loved her.'

'I suppose. You know what they say, love is blind and all

that nonsense.'

'Did you or your wife try to talk to Abbey about why she had become withdrawn?'

'We tried, but Abbey told us she was just tired. Simon had hired private tutors while they were out on the road with Alex. Abbey claimed she missed her friends at Haberdashers in Monmouth. She said her dad promised her she could go back to school in the new year. Abbey even asked if she could come and live back with me and Trudy.'

'I take it you said yes?'

Freeman nodded. 'When Simon showed up to collect her, we spoke to him about what Abbey wanted. Simon jumped down our throats. He said that Abbey would be out on the road with him and Alex on her UK tour until May. She was frequently back and forth the studio recording new songs. It devastated Trudy when Simon refused to let Abbey stay with us. When we first took the girls in, Abbey was only two years old. She'd grown up in our house. So it was natural Trudy thought the world of her. She was the mother Abbey never had.'

Fagan nodded. Imagining the scene. 'So it was 1993 and Alex was on tour until May. Did you see them at all?'

'We saw them once. Alex sent us a couple of VIP tickets to Wembley stadium. The place was rammed. It reminded me and Trudy of the time when we got married. We bought tickets to Live Aid. That was an amazing day.'

'When was Alex's concert?'

Freeman considered the question. 'Late April. I remember Trudy being so excited at being allowed backstage to see Alex and Abbey. But, it wasn't the fairy tale she thought it would be.'

'Why is that?'

'Alex was unrecognisable. I mean, she wasn't the girl we had looked after during the eighties. She could barely utter a word. I'm guessing it was the drugs. We were there for less

121

than five minutes. Trudy didn't like it. She is very outspoken. Not in a gobby way. But if you piss her off, she'll tell you about it. She flew at their manager. Had a right go at him. Said the girls needed to have time off from the constant touring. Next thing we knew, we were being manhandled out of the door by some thug.'

'The manager your wife had an argument with. Would this have been Frankie Jordan?'

'Yeah.' Freman said. 'After the concert, we came back home. Trudy was beside herself with worry.'

'Did you see their dad at the concert, Simon?'

'No, that's what got us thinking. Funny you should mention that. We were at the Boat, in Chepstow last year. Bumped into the band that Alex used to play with. We always thought they'd hit the big time with Alex. But their lead singer said he'd been sidelined. A month after the concert, Alex had that bust up at the Brit awards. Trudy was in pieces. You could see the effects the drugs had on Alex. It was devastating for both of us. We loved those girls like our own. After that incident at the Brit Awards Alex dropped off the face of the Earth. Trudy tried to get in touch with her. We couldn't get anywhere near Alex because of her manager. He'd literally put up a wall around her. We spoke to him a few times, but he tell us the same old shit. Alex was recuperating and needed the time alone. We then asked about Abbey. He claimed Abbey was with her, helping Alex get back on her feet.' Freeman seemed to struggle with the next line. 'But it was all a lie, wasn't it, concerning Abbey? Around ten years ago, we were shown an article online. Abbey had committed suicide. Trudy was inconsolable. To her, she had lost a daughter. We tried to contact their dad, but he'd done a vanishing act. He'd sold the house in Monmouth. We didn't know where he was. Although we couldn't reach any of them, Trudy didn't give up. She'd write a letter to the studio every month. Even after Jordan had sold it.' Freeman paused. 'Then in 2005, we got a postcard from Spain.'

Fagan stared back at Freeman. 'By any chance, was it a place called Tarragona?'

'Yeah.' Freeman nodded. 'Every year for several years we'd get a postcard from Alex. Mainly saying the same thing over and over. That she was fine and had stepped back from the music industry. It was all too much for her. But the postcards stopped coming in 2012.'

'Did these postcards have an address?'

Freeman nodded.

'And you still have these postcards?'

'Yeah, Trudy keeps everything. She's got a massive collection of photographs from when we were bringing up the girls. Lots of little keepsakes. She gets them out now and then. It comforts her to remember the good old days.' Freeman inhaled. 'But every time she does it, Trudy ends up crying.'

Fagan reached into his pocket, pulling out a card. 'I'd like you to do me a favour, Mr Freeman. Is Trudy at home now?'

'Yeah, she's a retired nurse.'

'Text her my number. Ask her to dig out the postcards and text me the address in Spain.'

'Sure.' Freeman said, reading Fagan's contact details.

'What about Alex's dad? Did you ever see him again?'

'We did.' Freeman reminisced. 'We bumped into him in Chepstow. Must have been 2014. Trudy was over the moon when she clapped eyes on him. We were both happy to see him. We bombarded him with questions. How was Alex? Could we get to see her? Trudy then mentioned the postcards she'd received from Alex.'

'What happened?'

'Simon flew into a rage. *I don't want to talk about that. Just piss off and leave me alone.* Those were his exact words. I was too stunned to say anything. Trudy was really upset at what happened. I have a friend at the local council. I asked him to do a check on the electoral register. He told me where Simon

123

was living. So I went up to his house just outside Devauden to confront him regarding his behaviour. But he wasn't answering the door. That's the last time we bothered trying to get in contact with Alex. We just accepted that we're never going to see her again. Simon died in 2019. He collapsed in Waitrose in Monmouth. We only found out when the police knocked on our door. Said they'd forced entry to his house to look for information about close relatives. They found our contact details and came to see us. The funeral was three weeks later. He had all his affairs in order.'

'Did Alex attend the funeral?'

'No, it was just the three of us, which was odd. Me, Trudy, and a neighbour of Simon's. He told us that Simon was a very solitary man. Used to spend a lot of time at the back of his garden in the summer. The neighbour never got to see the garden up close. Simon wouldn't allow any visitors.'

Fagan snapped his notebook shut. 'Thanks for your time, Mr Freeman. You've been a great help.'

'Can I ask what this is about? If I text Trudy your details. She's going to have a lot of questions.'

'Unfortunately, I can't tell you anything at this moment. But it seems to me you really put yourselves out for Simon and those girls when they were struggling. So as soon as I am able, I will tell you as much as I can.'

Freeman nodded. 'Thank you DI Fagan.'

Fagan headed towards the door, stopping short. 'I forgot to mention. Did you know Andrea Jones?'

Freeman snorted. 'Yeah, bit of a leech. Her and Alex were old school friends. Me and Trudy didn't like her because she was from the wrong side of Newport. She was backstage at that concert we attended. Looked a right mess. Drugs and all that shit.'

'Thanks.' Fagan continued to walk towards the entrance.

'One more thing, DI Fagan.' Freeman called out. 'If you really want to know about Alex's early life, talk to her mother.'

Fagan froze on the spot, slowly turning. 'Their mother is still alive?'

Freeman nodded. 'Yeah, she's retired but volunteers in a charity shop in the centre of Newport. We bumped into her last year.'

'Can you remember which charity shop she volunteers at?' Fagan opened his notepad.

'The Homeless sanctuary. It's right in the centre of town. She even recognised us. And apologised for the grief she had caused all those years ago. Trudy looked her up on Facebook. She posts pictures of Alex now and then. The strange thing is, when we mentioned Abbey, she said. *We'll all have to sit down, and she tell us a story.* I thought she was full of it, so we never bothered. But it might be worth you asking her.'

'Thanks, I'll be in touch, I promise.'

Fagan tapped the speed dial. 'Sean, has Andrew been in contact with land registry about the property Simon Xavier owned just outside Devauden.'

'Yeah, I think so, boss.'

'Get your backside up to the property and ask the current owners if they know anything about the previous owner.'

'No worries, boss. What are you doing?'

'I may have tracked down Alex's and Abbey's mother.'

'Oh shit, no way.'

'I'm on my way to question her. I've a feeling the shit is about to hit the fan.'

'I'll let you know if I find anything, boss.'

CHAPTER 16

Newport Homeless Sanctuary – 11:37am

Fagan spotted a White haired woman serving a customer. He waited patiently until she was alone.

The woman smiled at Fagan as he approached the counter. 'Hi, how can I help?'

'I'm looking for Jan,' Fagan said as politely as he could muster.

The woman maintained her smile, despite her cheeks tightening. 'I'm Jan.'

'I'd like to talk to you about your daughter, Alex, if it's possible.'

The smiled vanished from the woman's face quickly. She looked over Fagan's shoulder at a woman who was sorting through a second hand clothes rack. 'See Helen, I said it wouldn't take long for the vultures to start circling. Let me guess, you're from the Sun, Daily Star or The Mirror?'

Fagan played his hand, showing his ID. 'Detective Inspector Fagan with Gwent police.'

The look of contempt dissolved into an expression of mild shock as Jan stared at Fagan's ID. 'Yeah, sure.'

Fagan placed a latte in front of Jan. They had found a deserted café a few doors down from the charity shop.

'Thanks.' Jan forced a smile. 'I'm sorry for the shitty attitude in the shop. But to be fair, you should have told me who you were.'

'I wanted to gage your response.' Fagan sipped from his cup.

'I was saying to Helen in the shop this morning. After the

126

announcement Alex made last night, it would only be a matter of time before someone tracked me down.'

'Have you had hassle from the press before?'

Jan nodded, savouring the latte. 'How far do you want to go back?'

'Right back to the beginning, if you don't mind.'

Jan composed herself. 'Me and Simon met in the late sixties. Two kids wanting to have a little fun. Only Simon wanted to get serious. His parents were from a very conservative background. They couldn't stand me. I was a rough Newport girl. Their precious son deserved better. But Simon was besotted with me.'

'What did you want?'

'Just a good time,' Jan sighed. 'Next thing I knew, I was pregnant with Alex. The sixties had ended. The age of free love quickly turned into austerity. We married in 1973. Simon got a job at the steel works in Llanwern. We set up house tried to play happy families throughout the seventies. But it never worked. Simon did his best. He was a hard worker. Double shifts, so that I could afford anything I wanted. When 1980 came, I finally had enough. I wanted out of our marriage. I didn't want to be trapped.'

'What changed your mind?'

'Being pregnant with Abbey.'

'You were still having sex with Simon? Although you weren't in love with him.'

'Yeah.' Jan admitted. 'He was a good-looking bloke, and he was great in bed.'

'Ok, so fast forward to when Simon had his accident.'

Jan stared into her latte. 'Not my finest moment. When Abbey was born, for some reason, and despite my best efforts, I couldn't connect with her. I suppose in this day and age, I'd be diagnosed with postnatal depression. Then Simon had that accident. I remember that morning like it was yesterday. We had one of our blazing rows. I said I was leaving. The last thing he said to me was that we'd be talking out our differences when he got home. I called him a stupid bastard for believing I was going to be there. I had a plan all figured out. I was seeing someone behind his back. The bloke I was seeing said I could stay at his place. Then around eleven in the morning as I was packing, I got the call.' Jan sipped from her mug. 'When I saw him badly burned in hospital, in so much agony, I realised I did love him.' Jan paused. 'But it was too much. I had to look after two girls. I was stuck at home all day with Abbey because she was only two years old. Whenever I managed to find a babysitter, I had to visit Simon in the hospital. I started to feel my life wasn't my own, and that I was just there to please other people. I phoned up a friend one day in Cwmbran and broke down. She said I could stay with her, you know, to sort my head out. Thing is, I didn't go back. A few months passed and social services tracked me down. I told them I couldn't cope with the girls and they should go into foster care. Until Simon got out of hospital and could work again. His mate from work turned up a few days later with his wife. They had a go at me. Called me all the names under the sun. I said if they were so concerned about the girls, then they should look after them. And apparently that's what they did.'

'Did you have any contact with your daughters?'

'Yeah, twice a year. At Christmas and in the summer. I was glad the girls lived with Paul and Trudy. They did a much better job bringing up those kids than I ever would.'

'When were you first aware that Alex was about to become famous?'

'Probably early 1990, March time maybe. I saw Alex on Wales Today with her music promoter. They were making out that she was about to become the biggest Welsh pop star since Tom Jones. I didn't even realise she could sing. Just goes to show what kind of mother I was. Anyway, Alex started churning out her greatest hits. And that's when my moment of weakness came. I was skint. Didn't have a job, and I was struggling on benefits. So I contacted Alex. Pretending to be the mother I should have been. Simon saw straight through me and slapped a restraining order on me for both Alex and Abbey.'

'How did you react?'

'I was fuming at first. But then I realised I was being selfish and didn't deserve to be part of their lives. It was probably the first time I realised what a shit mother I had been to those girls. But the restraining order wasn't enough for Simon. He had to take it one step further. The tabloids turned up at my door and hounded me. The stories came thick and fast. I was the mother who didn't care about her daughters. Who was out partying all the time. Kept leaving them in the house with no food. When the newspaper headlines became more intense, I noticed there were details about my private my that Simon would never have known about. That's when I discovered several of my close friends had been talking to the press. Selling their kiss and tell stories to the tabloids. Suddenly I was a cash cow to them. I was forced to move from where I was living because of what people thought of me. At one point the council put me in a place for battered wives. For about six months, I had to move several times. Eventually, the council found me a house in the sticks just outside Little Mill. I wasn't surrounded by people who would bang on my door and call me nasty names. I was a recluse for fifteen years. I couldn't get a job because people would quickly find out who I was.'

'Didn't you think about changing your name?'

'Why should I?' Jan questioned. 'I freely admit I wasn't cut out to be a mother. Especially now, after all that happened back then.'

Fagan recalled what Freeman had told him just before he left his office. 'When was the last time you actually had contact with Alex?'

Jan struggled with her next sentence. 'It was the night

129

she'd won that Brit award. The night she had that huge punch up with Charlotte and Dillon.'

Fagan tested a theory. 'Did you by any chance show up at the Agincourt hotel just outside Monmouth?'

Jan nodded.

'How did you know Alex was there?'

'I knew the studio where Alex recorded her songs. I also knew most of the popstars would use the hotel just down the road. I'd become friendly with this girl who worked at the hotel. She cleaned the rooms. All I wanted to do was have some sort of connection. This girl didn't know who I was. I told her I was a huge fan of Alex's. We'd meet up for a regular drink. And she'd tell me all the gossip she had heard or seen. A few months before the Brit Awards, this girl told me she had found Alex's sister sobbing her eyes out in the hotel's toilet. I already knew Alex was into the drugs. The papers had no problem spilling the beans about her private life. This girl asked Abbey if everything was ok and if she could help. Abbey told her that no one could help. She got up and stormed out of the toilet. I took action. I got hold of Simon and ask him if Abbey was ok. He told me to fuck off and stop pretending I cared about her.' Jan picked up her cup with a shaking hand. 'I wrote a letter to Abbey. I gave it to the girl at the hotel. And asked her to give it to Abbey the next time she was staying there. I knew it was a long shot, but I tried anyway.'

'What did you write in the letter?'

'I apologised for being a shit mother and that I should have been there when she was growing up. A week later, I got a phone call from the girl from the hotel. She told me she bumped into Abbey and gave her the letter. A few days went by, then Abbey turned up at my door. I was so happy to see her.' Jan inhaled. 'But she was a wreck.'

'Drugs?'

'No, it was something far worse.' Jan composed herself. 'By June 1992, Alex was topping the charts. Every single she released went straight to number one. Simon decided it would be a good idea to let Abbey go on tour with Alex to keep her company. It would be an adventure for Abbey. And she had a massive crush on Dillon.'

'What happened?' Fagan asked, knowing what was about to come.

'Abbey said she was besotted with Dillon. But she was old enough to know she was too young for a relationship. Plus, Dillon and Charlotte were already an item. Although rumours in the press were circulating about Dillon and Alex seeing each other behind Charlotte's back. In August 1992, when they were all at the studio, Dillon asked Abbey if she like to go for a walk with him. The studio was in the middle of nowhere, so there were loads of places you could go and no one would see you. Abbey told me they'd been walking about half an hour, well out of view of everyone. Dillon spun her a story about him not being in love Charlotte anymore and that he was falling in love with Abbey. She told me she was excited and terrified at the same time. Dillon then kissed her. Abbey thought she'd died and gone to heaven. Here was one of the biggest popstars of the nineties actually kissing her.' Jan sighed. 'And then his hands wandered.'

'What did Abbey do?'

'She pulled away from him straight away. Abbey was sensible enough to do that. She told me that Dillon apologised for his *wandering hands*. They walked back to the studio, hand in hand. A week later, when Abbey was at the hotel with Alex, Dillon knocked on Abbey's hotel room door.'

'Didn't she share a room with Alex?'

'No, Alex wouldn't allow it. Abbey told me it was because Alex was hooked on drugs. She didn't want Abbey watching her older sister snorting cocaine. Anyway, it was late at night when Dillon came calling. He was pissed as a fart. Claimed he'd had an argument with Charlotte and wanted someone to talk to, or a shoulder to cry on. He then started spouting a load of bullshit about how in love with Abbey he was. Abbey was too stunned to say anything.' Jan stopped talking.

Fagan plucked up the courage to say what Jan couldn't. 'Did he rape Abbey?'

Jan wiped a tear away, nodding. 'He, uh, raped her, twice.' She fought against her emotions. 'Abbey was only twelve. Dillon was twenty-five. But that was just the beginning. The next day, when Abbey was having breakfast in the restaurant, Charlotte came in. It was just the two of them there. Charlotte sat down opposite her. Dillon had told her what had happened the night before. Abbey said Charlotte got up and walked around to where she was sitting and whispered in her ear.'

'What did she say?'

It took a moment for Jan to respond. 'She said, *Dillon says, you've a tight little pussy*.'

Fagan almost choked on his latte.

'Charlotte stuck her tongue in Abbey's ear and said, *I can't wait to taste it for myself*.'

'Jesus.' Fagan gasped.

'The abuse and the rapes came thick and fast in the following months.' Jan revealed. 'Abbey said she kept track of her ordeals.'

'So Charlotte West was also abusing her?'

Jan nodded. 'Along with another woman.' She struggled to remember a name. 'Abbey said she was Alex's friend from school.'

'Andrea Jones?'

'I think so. We're talking thirty years ago.'

'When Abbey told you about the rape and abuse, what did you do?'

'I flew into a rage. I got hold of Simon on the phone. When I told him, he hit the roof.'

'He didn't know what was going on?'

Jan looked back at Fagan, nodding slowly. 'Simon didn't fly into a rage because of what I told him. He was pissed off

132

because Abbey had tracked me down. He ordered me to tell him where I lived so that he could send someone to pick her up. He also threatened that since I had broken the restraining order, he will make sure I do jail time.' Jan reflected. 'All of a sudden he was totally different from the man I had married. I slammed the phone down on him.'

'What happened next?'

An expression of grief etched across Jan's face. 'Over the next few days, Abbey told me everything. The abuse that went on behind the scenes. It wasn't just her, but there were loads of girls. She said it was like a revolving door.'

'Where did the abuse take place?'

'It would happen when they were out on the road, after concerts. Dillon would pick the girls. They'd be piled with alcohol. There was the Agincourt hotel just outside Monmouth. And also at the studio.'

'Was it just Dillon, Charlotte, and Andrea carrying out the abuse?'

'No, Abbey told me there were others at that studio, including Alex's manager. Abbey said he'd cop a feel, as he liked to call it, now and then. There was also a group there recording at the studio.' Jan stopped talking at looked around the deserted café.

'Are you ok?'

Jan nodded. 'Abbey said she wanted to stay with me. I asked why she didn't want to stay with Paul and Trudy. She said, although they were brilliant, she was afraid they'd call Simon, and he'd be there in a shot to drag her back to that life. The girl just wanted to be away from it all. I advised Abbey she should go to the police. We wrote a detailed statement of everything.'

'Do you still have it, by any chance?'

Jan nodded. 'I've kept all the original copies.'

'Good, because I'm going to want to see them.'

'We took the statement to the police. Abbey told them

133

everything. We thought they'd act immediately. But they didn't. Abbey became distraught. There was nothing I could do to comfort her. Then, one day, I had to go out for a few hours.' Jan sighed. 'When I came back to the house, Abbey wasn't sat in the living room. I called out to her, but there was no response. For a moment, I was terrified that Simon had tracked her down and dragged her out of the house. So I went upstairs to look for her.'

Fagan moved his chair, sitting beside Jan, who struggled with her next words. 'It's okay Jan, take your time.'

Jan sobbed. 'She'd uh, cut her wrists in the bath. God, there was so much blood.'

'I'm so sorry.'

Jan choked back her tears. 'The, uh, ambulance and police arrived straight away. The police took me away to give a statement. I didn't go back to the house for a few days. A day passed before I got hold of Simon. I told him what happened. I told him he needs to tell Alex that his younger sister had taken her own life because of what Dillon and Charlotte had done to her.'

'How did Simon take the news that his daughter was dead?'

'He said he couldn't tell Alex about Abbey, because she'd just been nominated for her first Brit award. And news like that would push her over the edge. Here was a man who threw me under the bus with the tabloids. Who made me out to be some kind of evil bitch towards Alex and Abbey. Yet, all Simon could think about was his eldest winning some fucking award. A month later, when it all kicked off at the Brits, I watched it all unfold on the telly. The girl from the hotel I'd become friendly with told me they we flying out there by helicopter. There was some big bash going on. So I jumped into my car and drove to the Agincourt. I told her I just wanted Alex's autograph. So she sneaked me in. When Alex arrived at the hotel, she looked a mess. I got past the minders and confronted her.'

'That's when you told her about her sister?'

Jan nodded. 'I told her about the abuse that Alex and Charlotte had subjected her to. I told her that her dad knew that Abbey had committed suicide weeks before and that he just shrugged it off. I also said to Alex, her best friend was involved in the abuse.'

'What was her reaction?'

'The drugs seemed to instantly wear off. But then security showed up. They chucked me out of the hotel. I wanted to have it out with Simon, but didn't get the chance.'

Fagan considered the story. 'Did you say Abbey documented everything?'

Jan nodded.

'How?'

'A few days after she committed suicide, I received a parcel in the post. Because of what happened, I didn't open it for months. When Abbey came to see me, she had a diary with her, but didn't tell me. I'm guessing she posted it the day she died. The parcel contained her diary. I haven't been able to read through it. I made a start, but it became too distressing.'

'And you still have the diary?'

'Yes. When Jimmy Savile died and all the allegations surfaced, I thought about handing it to the police. But I was afraid it would just disappear. Dillon and Charlotte were huge back in the nineties. I thought I'd come across as someone who was just out for money. I'd already been in the newspapers as a terrible mother.'

Fagan sensed his phone buzzing in his pocket. 'Excuse me a sec Jan.' He stood and headed for the café entrance.

'Boss, are you still in Newport?' Watkins asked.

'Yeah, and I've just found a massive piece of the puzzle. Why, what's up?'

'I'll ping you my location. You need to get up to Devauden right away.'

Fagan walked back into the café. 'Jan, I have to go, I'm afraid.' He placed a business card on the table. 'What I want you to do is put the diary in a sealed envelope and hand it into Newport central police station. Make sure my name is on the front of the envelope.'

Jan nodded. 'Does this mean you're going to do something?'

Fagan nodded slowly. 'I'm going to damn well try.'

Jan smiled. 'Thank you.'

CHAPTER 17

Devauden – Monmouthshire – 12:24pm

Watkins was waiting outside the front gate of the house, which was situated less than half a mile from the main village. The house that belonged to Simon Xavier was at the end of a long drive. Five acres of land surrounded the property.

Fagan surveyed the area, noting the house was partially visible from the main road. 'What have you got for me, Sean?'

'Andrew had a chat with land registry. Simon Xavier bought the house in 2003. He lived at the property until his death in 2019.'

'I'm guessing Alex inherited the house after his death,'

'No.'

'How come?'

'There was no will. So the property lay empty. All his funeral expenses were paid for. When covid hit, there was a survey to find all empty properties in the area that had no claimants.'

'So the property would have gone to the crown? I don't get it. Alex was the closest living relative. The house should have gone to her.'

'But it didn't.' Watkins said. 'It was auctioned off last year and snapped up straight away. The current owner is at home. He's a doctor. When I knocked on his door and asked for a brief history of this place, he took me out in the back garden.' Watkins waved his hand, analysing the surrounding countryside. 'Plenty of places you could hide secrets.' He glanced at the house. 'You're going to want to see this, boss.'

Both men walked through the enormous garden. Fagan

spotted a circular enclosure surrounded by a tall hedge.

A man was standing by the opening to the enclosure.

'DI Fagan.' He showed his ID to the property owner.

'The last thing I expected was a visit from the old bill.' The owner said.

'My colleague tells me you bought this property last year?'

'Yes, we got it for a steal at auction.' The owner looked back at the property. 'The house is in good shape. Haven't had to do much. When we moved in, the first thing my wife wanted to do was explore the garden. That's when we came across this.' The owner pointed at the entrance to the enclosure.

Fagan stepped into the enclosure. The hedge surrounding the area was approximately ten feet in height. The enclosure itself spanned roughly twenty feet. In the centre was a standard wooden bench. Like a wooden bench that would occupy a park. Fagan then cast his eyes on the distinctive shape of what appeared to be a headstone.

'My wife won't come near here. She's superstitious and all that. I have been tempted to clear away the weeds, but the wife goes ballistic when I mention doing it.'

Fagan circled the headstone. A thick layer of vine and moss covered the face, obscuring the engraving. Fagan glanced at Watkins, who was already slipping on a pair of gloves. He took a deep breath before giving the nod.

Watkins pulled away the vines that covered the headstone. After a few minutes he stood back.

Fagan stared at the inscription on the headstone. He read aloud. 'For Alex and Abbey. You will never be parted again.'

'Well, that's something we never expected.' Watkins remarked.

'What the hell is going on here?' Fagan sighed. 'We know Abbey committed suicide. But Alex is still very much alive. She released a single last night and is about to release her last album.'

'He could have been estranged from Alex. Which would explain why the house didn't pass to her.'

'That's what the argument was about,' Fagan suddenly realised.

'Boss?'

'I just spoke to Alex's mother. She was the mystery woman that turned up at the hotel. She told Alex that her little sister had committed suicide. According to our witness from the kitchen of the hotel, Alex was screaming at her father. She screamed, you knew, and you didn't fucking tell me. I'll bet any money that's what they were arguing about. Alex's mother told her everything.' He considered a way forward. 'Get on the blower to CSI. I want a full team up here digging this out.' He pointed at the headstone before glancing at the property owner. 'That's if it okay with you.'

The man nodded enthusiastically. 'I'm just as curious myself. You're more than welcome to look.'

'Get a couple of uniform to knock on doors in the village down the road. I want to know if anyone knew Xavier while he was living here. Instruct Brooks to double down on his research. We'll get together later this afternoon and hammer out more details on this case. Once CSI arrives, we'll head down Newport and have a chat to the journalist at the South Wales Argus.'

Watkins looked at the headstone. 'Strange to have a headstone in your back garden.'

'Hidden away from any curious eyes.' Fagan added, reading the inscription again in his head. 'We'll wait until CSI arrives. Then we'll head down to the Argus.'

139

C H A P T E R   1 8

South Wales Argus – Newport – 1:31pm

Terry Williams stared, mystified at Fagan's ID. 'I haven't done anything wrong have I?'

'Not all Mr Williams. Myself and DS Watkins, wish to know a little about an article you published in 2013. It was only a short piece regarding the arrest of Dillon Powell.'

Williams sensed a story. He grabbed a pen and paper.

'We're not going on record with this conversation, Mr Williams.' Watkins explained.

Williams frowned, placing his notepad on his desk. He leant back in his chair, clasping his hands behind his head. 'What do you want to know?'

'You released the article following a brief statement given out by Gwent police.' Fagan said. 'I would like to know if you heard any rumours about him, other than his arrest.'

'I wouldn't call them rumours. When news spread about the allegations made against Jimmy Savile after he died, six women contacted us regarding Powell.'

'I take it you advised them to get in touch with the police?' Watkins said.

Williams nodded. 'But not after hearing their accounts.'

Fagan glared back it him.

'We maybe just a small rag compared to the big leagues DI Fagan. But we're journalists all the same. So, naturally, any story that we feel is in the domain of public interest we have to listen.'

Fagan scribbled in his notepad. 'You just said six girls came forward with stories about Powell. Do you have any contact

140

details for these women?'

'Yes.'

'What allegations did they make?' Watkins asked.

'Three of the women who contacted the Argus were full of it. They just wanted to make up a load of shit to make a bit of money. I should imagine there were a few women like that during Operation Yewtree. But the three other women had genuine stories. One of them knew Dillon from the Gurnos estate in Merthyr. She said even in his teens he was dangerous.'

'Dangerous?'

'She came forward several months after Savile had died. Our abuse victim contacted us after we had published the brief article about Powell's arrest. She said she'd already been to the police, but they weren't interested.'

'She said that?' Watkins stated, glancing at Fagan.

'Yeah, she said that she walked into the police station in Merthyr and gave a full statement. A few months went by before she contacted the police again. I have a contact in South Wales police who said police took her story seriously and referred it to Operation Fallen Star.'

Fagan glanced at Watkins. 'I'm sorry, Operation Fallen Star?'

Williams stared back with a bemused expression. 'You've never heard of it?'

Fagan shook his head.

'It was an operation set up by South Wales police, in the wake of the Savile scandal.'

'Never heard of it.' Fagan stated.

A wry smile stretched across Williams' face. 'I'm surprised you've never heard of it. Operation Fallen Star was swallowed by Yewtree in the early days of its conception. But not before there were hundreds of claims. Made against popstars, rugby players, footballers, politicians and other people in the public eye. My contact told me there were claims made in literally every police force throughout Wales. It was too much for your boys to handle.'

'How did your contact hear about this Operation Fallen Star?' Watkins asked.

'He was part of the operation.' Williams answered. 'It was his job to collate all the information and statements.'

'What kind of information did he handle?' Fagan asked.

'Mainly statements from alleged victims. There were photographs of victims with the high profile suspects they made claims against. Nothing provocative or anything like that. The witnesses who sent photos in wanted to prove they had an encounter with their abuser.'

'When did you hear about this Operation Fallen Star?'

'It was probably in January 2013. A few months after ITV had screened their documentary, *The other side of Jimmy Savile*. South Wales police started to get a steady stream of women coming in. Claiming they had been the victims of sexual abuse. Many of the abuse claims were made against Dillon Powell. Ten women claimed both Dillon and Charlotte West had abused them. There were also three claims that another woman had been involved in abuse. A lot of the women that gave statements claimed the abuse took place at a hotel just outside Monmouth. Police arrested Dillon. Questioned him, but released him without charge.

'But some of these women said that Charlotte also took part in abuse allegations. Why wasn't she arrested?'

'I have no idea?' Williams replied. 'My contact at the time, told me none of the women could actually prove Dillon had abused them. Dillon denied having sex with any underage girls. Any relationships he had with women were entirely consensual. Dillon was massive back in the nineties. He had some very public relationships with some very famous women.'

'Do you know how long Operation Fallen Star ran for?'

'My contact informed me that Falling Star ran for about six

months before Yewtree swallowed it up. By then, police had received thousands of allegations from all over the UK. Not just Savile, but loads of celebrities. If you ask me, it was too big to put a lid on. The media only focussed on Savile because he was dead. But after a while, they lost interest.'

'Would you care to divulge who your contact is?'

Willams shook his head. 'I'm not going to land anyone in the shit, DI Fagan. I see Alex X has an album coming out at the end of the week.' He said, switching subjects.

'Were any allegations made against Alex?' Watkins asked.

'No, despite them being a bit of a trio, Alex seemed to be the normal one amongst them. Unless, of course, you factor in her drug addiction. She was definitely the biggest of the three stars. When she won that Brit award in 1993. Dillon and Charlotte were already growing unpopular with their fans. They didn't really go the distance like the other artists of the nineties. The Manic Street Preachers are still big. Saw them last year. Haven't lost their touch.'

'So Falling Star was merged with Yewtree?' Fagan said.

Williams nodded. 'But not before the files were tampered with.'

'How?'

'All information relating to Dillon Powell mysteriously disappeared?'

'Did your contact mention who gave the order to hand over the Fallen Star files to the Yewtree team?'

'The chief constable. But I forgot his name.'

Fagan jotted down some notes. 'Thanks for your time, Mr Williams. You've been a lot of help.'

'Every stone we kick over seems to reveal something new.' Watkins remarked as they headed back to Newport central police station.

'Williams mentioned the Chief Constable ordered all files relating to Fallen Star to be handed over to Yewtree. He also said that his contact claimed information relating to Dillon Powell vanished. Who was the chief constable of South Wales police back in 2013?'

Watkins fished his phone from his pocket and ran a search. 'Chief Constable Owain Lance. Highly decorated. Served over forty-five years in the police before retiring in 2015. Involved in several high-profile cases. In the early nineties, he was chief superintendent in the Swansea area. He led an investigation to bring down a grooming gang that operated in the South Wales valleys.'

Fagan sensed his heart skip a beat. 'Who was the chief constable of South Wales police at the time?'

'Chief Constable Bob Benson.' Watkins replied, glancing at Fagan.

'*Shit.*' Fagan swore under his breath. 'When we get back to the station, pull all the information relevant to that grooming case.'

'Now worries, boss.' Watkins stared at the screen. 'It says here that Chief Constable Lance was badly injured during an event called the battle of Six Bells. It was during the miners' strike of 1984. He was set upon by a gang of striking miners who were picketing the Six Bells colliery in Abertillery. Bob Benson also sustained injuries after pulling Lance out. He was awarded a commendation for bravery. He was also bumped up to the rank of Inspector.'

'Anything on Operation Falling Star?' Fagan asked, refocussing on the case.

Watkins stared at his phone screen. 'It's what the journalist said, boss. The operation was merged with Yewtree.in 2015.'

'He was right about one thing.'

Watkins looked at his superior. 'What?'

'Yewtree was too big for the police to handle. A similar thing happened in 2015 when scores of people were making claims about A list celebrities and footballers in Liverpool. A friend of mine was handling a lot of the allegations. Some celebrities being named were massive, and still are.'

'Why do you reckon Yewtree was just confined to a limited amount of famous people?'

'Because it would have turned more or less everyone against the entertainment industry. Some household names were on the list that I saw. People don't realise what a dark underbelly showbiz has. All we see is the glitzy side of things. The polished turd, which is light entertainment. Looking back, the likes of Savile and other celebrity paedophiles were massive. The women and girls used to throw themselves at them. It was all a normal part of the culture. No one questioned their behaviour because they were superstars. You have your popstars throughout the ages who have always been associated with hordes of women chasing after them.'

'Even the young ones.' Watkins pointed out.

Fagan sighed. 'Even the young ones.'

'It's suspicious that the files regarding Dillon Powell disappeared.'

'I was just thinking that.' Fagan clutched the steering wheel, staring at the road ahead. 'There were many people who knew what Savile was all about. But most of them were too afraid to come forward. Those who came forward were labelled as outcasts. The Sex Pistols saw right through Savile. But they were labelled as anti-establishment. Savile was part of the establishment. He knew everybody. Including popstars and celebrities who have since been convicted of sex offences. Yet while he was alive, no one had the guts to say anything. Dillon Powell has been arrested and questioned about sex offences. But he's not been convicted of anything. Then information regarding his alleged activities suddenly disappears.'

'You think he knew something about someone who had far more to lose?'

'It wouldn't surprise me.' Fagan flicked the indicator and spun the wheel to turn into the police station carpark.

CHAPTER 19

Newport central police station – 2:02pm
'Okay, so let's try to make sense of all this,' Fagan said, standing in front of the whiteboard. 'What have you got for me?'

Watkins looked at his screen. 'Both Frankie Jordan and Mickey Mercury will be in tomorrow for questioning.'

'It's a good bet they're probably talking at this moment. To get their story straight. Remember, all we have is a body at the back of the studio. It's not enough to accuse anyone of murder. We have to somehow prove they were at the scene of crime the night Andrea Jones was murdered.'

'I came across an interesting article regarding Jordan. It was an interview by Kerrang in 2012. The article was looking back on his career. He spoke extensively about Alex and her pop career. He also mentioned that she was in retirement and that he kept in contact with his from time to time. There's a line here that stands out. *Speaking from his luxury villa in Tamarit, just outside Tarragona.*'

'Shit.' Fagan cursed. 'So Jordan had a luxury villa in Spain near where Alex claimed to be living. The same location as the other magazine article mentioned. That's too much of a coincidence. This is a disjointed murder case.'

'What do you mean, sir?' Brooks asked

'Whoever was involved with the murder of Andrea Jones has had thirty years to cover their tracks. It's only because of the discovery of the body everything has been brought to light.' Fagan glanced at the whiteboard. 'We know everyone had signed the guestbook at the Agincourt Hotel the night

146

Andrea was murdered. There was a massive argument between Alex and the other members of the party. We now know the identity of the mystery woman who turned up at the hotel. It was Alex's mother. She tells Alex that her younger sister committed suicide a few weeks earlier. Alex's mam also told me that following Abbey's death, she contacted her father. He seemed more interested in Alex being nominated for a Brit award than his youngest daughter committing suicide. So, Jan finds out Alex is staying at the Agincourt hotel and confronts her with the news. Alex then goes after her dad and screams at him. An argument ensues in the kitchen.'

'The head chef then chucks them out of the kitchen.' Brooks continued. 'They were arguing for several minutes outside before disappearing.'

'They must have gone back to the music studio because they never returned to the hotel.' Fagan smiled, pulling his phone from his pocket.

'You just figured something out, boss?' Watkins enquired.

'Maybe.' Fagan tapped Evans' contact icon.

'Fagan, I haven't had time to search for that information yet.'

'Don't worry about it for now, Jamie. What I want to know is where you picked up Dillon, Charlotte, and the rest of the party.'

Evans took a few moments to answer. 'It was outside the Agincourt. And when I mean outside, it was on the main road. I remember because it was pissing down with rain. When I pulled up to the side of the road, they were all stood there, soaked through. Charlotte looked a right mess in her glitzy dress. Makeup running down her face.'

'Are you sure it was outside the Agincourt?'

'Positive mate,' Evans replied. 'I always make a note of where I pick up my fares. You've got to in this day and age.'

'Thanks Jamie.' Fagan hung up. 'Fuck.' He seethed, looking at Watkins and Brooks. 'They thought of everything. A taxi picked them up on the main road outside the gates of the Agincourt. If they would have been picked up at the studio, then we would have had a witness who saw them close to the scene of the crime.'

'The hotel isn't that far away from the studio, boss. Just over a mile.' Watkins pointed out.

'Yeah, it's still near the murder scene. Which is why we can pull all of them in as significant witnesses. But what we need to a witness that saw them walking from the hotel to the studio.'

'How are you going to get a witness?' Brooks enquired. 'We are talking thirty years ago. There were no CCTV cameras or dash-cams back then. And mobile phone technology was far from what it is now. I wasn't even born thirty years ago. Mam and dad sometimes talk about old mobile phones the size of bricks.'

'I've got an idea.' Fagan announced. 'We send out a press release. Just the basics. Body found at the back of Vine Road studios. It's enough to grab attention. And perhaps jog memories.'

'Jordan and Mercury will close ranks on us if we do that, boss.' Watkins said. 'All of them will. None of them are going to confess to anything. Not after thirty years of being able to cover their tracks. And not when they're about to make a shitload more money out of Alex's last album.'

Fagan nodded slowly. 'But we still let the media know. I've had loads of cases over the years where we've issued press releases and witnesses have come forward offering vital information.' Fagan glanced at the whiteboard. 'It's time to speculate on who murdered Andrea Jones. They leave the hotel and walk back to the music studio. They carry on arguing. Alex knows about Dillon raping Abbey. She also knows about Charlotte being involved with the sexual abuse. And finally, Andrea is also in the frame for abusing Abbey. According to Abbey's mother, her daughter kept a journal. She

148

going to hand it in to us. Abbey chronicled the abuse she endured. She names everyone, Dillon, Charlotte and Andrea. Along with Jordan, who groped her on several occasions.'

'The problem with that, boss, is that Abbey died thirty years ago. Any defence is going to dismiss the journal as fantasy. We need another witness. Otherwise we're dead in the water. At the moment everyone involved in this murder enquiry is just a significant witness, not a suspect. We've got a body, a Brit award belonging to Alex and a Rolex watch gifted to Andrea. But nothing significant to link them to the murder.'

'When Alex heard about Andrea abusing her younger sister, she must have been so pissed off with her. Think about it. They'd been friends since school. It was the ultimate betrayal. There was a fight at the music studio. In a fit of rage, Alex murdered Andrea. Didn't forensics mention there was blood on the award?'

'Yeah.' Watkins answered.

'How was it able to survive decomposition?'

'Remember what the owner said about the field where they're building? He said it used to be a peat bog. The council gave the new owner permission to drain it and build new studios. Peat bogs are low in oxygen, so they're great for preserving things. There's been several bodies found in peat bogs over the decades that are a few thousand years old. But are still remarkably intact. Which would explain why the body discovered has had a slow decomposition rate. Give it a few days and we'll have DNA ready to be tested.'

'We need to contact the pathologist. Find out if there are any distinguishing marks on the body that might help us confirm its Andrea. Have we tracked down any living relatives of Andrea's?' Fagan asked.

'Not yet, sir.' Brooks replied. 'She was born the same year as Alex. Her mother was single and died in 2007.'

'That makes it even more convenient, doesn't it? If there are no living relatives to give a DNA sample, we're stuck at square one. All we have to prove it's her, is the watch. Right then. So Alex flies at Andrea for being part of a sexual abuse trio. She kills Andrea. That's where Frankie and the rest come in. They're all witnesses to the murder. Alex is a superstar, so they won't want to give her up. Charlotte, Dillon, Jordan, Mercury, and Mitchell head down to London to cover their tracks. Alex stays with the body, along with her dad. According to a contact of mine, everyone who worked at the studio was fired the day after the Brit Awards. They closed the studio for two weeks before reopening and hiring all new staff.' Fagan stared at the whiteboard. 'We are dealing with more than just a murder here. Alex found out her sister was being sexually abused by Dillon. For the moment, let's concentrate on Dillon. We know South Wales police arrested him as part of Operation Falling Star, which later merged with Yewtree.'

'I found out something interesting about Powell back in the 90s, boss. And it has a link with that grooming gang in Swansea. I mentioned on the way back.' Watkins revealed.

'Go on.'

'In 1992, the police launched an investigation called Operation Sara. Following the discovery of a body in the Mount Pleasant area of Swansea. Number three Cromwell street to be exact. Detectives named the victim as 13-year-old Sara Weston. Two days before they found her body, Sara's mother reported her missing. Three hundred police officers aided in the search. They found her following a tipoff to south Wales police. DCI Owain Lance put out an appeal for any witnesses to come forward. That might help identify the murderer. A young girl contacted the police, revealing she knew Sara and that they'd been frequent visitors to Cromwell street. They had engaged in underage sex with several men. She also told police that one of these men claimed he knew Dillon Powell. And that he would introduce her and Sara. The girl identified one of her abusers. Forty-eight-year-old County Councillor Robert Norman was arrested in connection with the murder of Sara Weston.

'Was he charged with the murder?'

'No.' Watkins replied. 'Norman supplied a solid alibi. During his questioning Norman said that he knew of dozens of men throughout the South Wales valleys who were actively engaging in sex with underage girls. But didn't provide any names. Norman was charged on two counts of rape, including the rape of Sara Weston. He was handed a twelve year jail sentence. Following Norman's conviction a new crime imitative was launched to protect vulnerable young girls against grooming gangs. The Campaign was spearheaded by DCI Owain Lance. Dillon Powell was part of the campaign. The campaign was called, No Means No. Dillon even launched a single promoting the campaign.'

'Jesus, and all the while, he was abusing young girls.' Fagan shivered.

'It says here he toured all over Wales before the campaign went national. Charlotte performed with him at a lot of the venues.'

'And this was 1992?'

'Yeah.'

'Charlotte W was at the peak of her career.' Fagan said. 'They were a couple. The Welsh version of Kylie and Jason. Their manager was Mickey Mercury must have been rubbing his hands knowing all the money he was going to make.' Fagan's train of thought took a sharp turn. 'What about Lance? When did he join the police force?'

'According to his bio, 1970.' Watkins replied. 'Lance was born in Bristol in 1950 and moved to Monmouth when he was fifteen. Served in and around Abergavenny from 1975 to 1982, before he was bumped up to Sergeant. Then he served time in Swansea. He was fast tracked up to detective chief inspector by 1990. Bumped up to chief constable in 2008 until his retirement in 2015.'

Fagan mulled over the situation for a moment before

getting back on track. 'Andrew, write a summary regarding the discovery of the body at the back of Vine Road Music studios and email it to our press office for immediate release. Given that we have a body, it's enough to pull Jordan and Mercury in for questioning because they were the studio owners. We also have three witnesses that put Alex, Charlotte, Dillon and Alun Mitchell at the scene. Plus the murder victim, Andrea. That's also enough to pull the rest of them in for routine questioning.'

'But there is still nothing to connect them to the scene of the crime. Unless one of them confesses everything.'

'Fat chance of that.' Brooks let out a snort of derision.

'I think the press release in enough to rattle some cages.' Fagan explained. 'Alex has just released a new single and her last album is due out at the end of the week.'

'What are the chances of her manager telling us where Alex is, boss?'

'Zero.' Fagan replied. 'The single just released has topped the charts. There's no way her manager is going to reveal where she is.' He clapped his hands together, rubbing them. 'This is the plan for tomorrow. Me and Watkins will be the lead interviewers. Andrew, I need to you laying the groundwork. First thing in the morning, I want you to locate the sister of the murder victim from 1978. Interview her and find out if she has any suspicions that Mitchell may have had a hand in her sister's death. Sean, me and you will prepare our interviews and talk about how we're going to proceed with Jordan and the rest. What time are they in tomorrow?'

Watkins checked his phone. 'Jordan said he'll be in for nine thirty. Mercury will be her for eleven o'clock.'

'Remember, they've had thirty years to prepare for this' Fagan glanced at the clock on the wall. 'I suggest we all get a good night's sleep.

CHAPTER 20

Morrisons – Abergavenny – 6:23:pm

Fagan stared at the instructions on the back of the pasta meat feast microwave meal.

'Hello.' A woman greeted standing next to him.

Fagan maintained his stare on the packaging, throwing her a brief smile. 'Hi.'

'Marc, isn't it?'

Fagan looked away from his ready meal.

An attractive red-haired woman in her mid-fifties smiled back at Fagan.

'Uh, yeah.'

The woman maintained her inviting smile. 'I suppose age robs us of our memories. Melissa Knight. We were in school together.'

Fagan nodded. 'School, I barely remember it.'

Melissa giggled. 'I know what you mean. You asked me to the Pandy disco once. I dumped you at the disco, because a friend of mine said you'd only did it for a dare.'

Fagan laughed. 'I definitely deserved that.'

Melissa glanced at the ready meal Fagan was looking at. 'Home late, or cooking for one?'

'Both.' Fagan sighed.

'I'm sorry. I didn't mean to be nosy.' Melissa apologised.

'It's Okay,' Fagan said, waving the comment away. 'When I came back to Abergavenny, everyone expected me to have been divorced three times with loads of kids.'

'I know what you mean. I guess marriage and kids isn't for everyone one.' Melissa picked up a vegetarian ready meal. 'So where have you been living your life?'

'Liverpool.'

'I studied at university in Liverpool. Loved it. What have you been up to in Liverpool?'

'I'm a serving police officer. Decided to spend my remaining years in the force back in Abergavenny.'

'Well done.' Melissa praised. 'Wait, didn't you spend time in prison?'

'Yeah.' Fagan answered, feeling a little ashamed.

'Well, at least you redeemed yourself. I bumped into Sarah Trask the other day. We were best friends in school. I always thought she'd go to university. But she's got four grown-up children. And she's an alcoholic.'

'Yeah. Some people have done well for themselves and other have gone right off the rails. What about you Melissa? What have you been up to?'

'I studied criminal psychology before moving out to New York.'

'Wow, I bet that was an eye opener living in the States.'

Melissa nodded. 'Most of my work involved interviewing serial killers.'

'That must have taken a lot out of you.' Fagan remarked.

'It did.' Melissa sighed.

'Married with kids?'

'I was married for twenty-two years. Recently divorced. The pandemic made me realise how much I miss the simple things. When my divorce was finalised last year, it took me a further eight months to organise things. Then one day, I came across an article about the Abergavenny food festival.' Melissa smiled. 'That's when I decided to move back home.'

'Any kids?'

'No, unless you count my dogs.'

'So, are you enjoying being retired?'

'I'm not retired just yet. I teach criminal psychology at the University of South Wales. I just bought a house in Govilon on the banks of the canal.'

'Very mice, especially in the summer. I'm due to move up to the Mardy in Midway Lane. I see they've just revamped the Crown and Sceptre. I heard someone said the food is great.'

Melissa glanced at her ready meal and then looked at Fagan's before breaking out into a smile. 'You're on.'

'For what?'

'You can buy me dinner up at the Crown.'

Fagan was lost for words.

Melissa noticed his bemused expression. 'I'm just eager to reconnect with the people in this town. When I came back, it was wonderful to hear the Welsh accent against. Instead of the New York drivel I've had to endure for the past thirty years.'

Fagan pulled a business card out of his wallet and handed it to Melissa. 'I'm a regular at the Cantreff. Jackie Mills runs it.'

'I remember Jackie at school,' Melissa said, breaking out into an infectious laugh. 'She had an argument with our PE teacher, Mrs Stephens. I remember Jackie calling her a lesbo.'

'She hasn't changed. Jackie will still tell you to your face if you annoy her.'

Melissa tossed her ready meal into her shopping basket. 'I better go. The dogs are still getting used to their new home. If I'm gone too long, they'll tear the place apart.'

Fagan gently set his carrier bag into the boot.

'Well, well. If it isn't detective Inspector Marc Fagan.'

Fagan felt as if he'd been turned to stone by Medusa. He slowly turned to face Benny Nelson.

A man with an expensive camera walked towards Fagan.

'With all due respect Mr Nelson, you are invading my privacy.' Fagan stated calmly.

'So, it's Mr Nelson now, is it Fagan? You used to call me all kinds of things. Pervert, Benny the bender, Benny the kiddie fiddler.'

'All things that I regret.' Fagan tried to sound as diplomatic as possible.

'Don't make me laugh, Fagan. You may be a copper, but I can see the look on your face. You're dying to give me a good hammering.' Nelson taunted.

Fagan turned, walked around his car, and opened the door. The camera followed him.

Fagan put up his hand. 'Please, this is an invasion of my privacy.'

'You didn't give a shit about mine when you arrested me. Falsely accusing me of murdering Rebecca.'

'Your prints were all over Rebecca's phone case, Benny. You'd had an obsession with her for years. Following her everywhere she went.'

The man with the camera turned his attention to Nelson.

'Me and Rebecca could have had something special. If it weren't for the pricks of this town. Making my life a total misery for decades.'

'Is that what you tell yourself every time you go to bed at night, Benny?' Fagan questioned. 'Is that what you've been telling these guys?' He pointed to the man with the camera. 'Come to think of it, Benny. How is your wife these days? You know, the one you claimed to have loved. The one who is expecting your first child.'

The man with the camera focused on Nelson.

'You must be making a fortune. From your interviews.' Fagan glanced at the man standing beside Nelson. 'And now you've a documentary crew following you around.'

'The book I have coming out is already tipped to hit the number one spot on Amazon. Must get under your skin, knowing that in a few months I'll be rich.'

'Here's an idea Benny. If you get rich off that pack of lies you're about to publish. You'll do everyone a favour and leave Abergavenny for good.'

Nelson glared back at Fagan for a few moments before

156

approaching, standing face to face. 'I'm staying right here, Fagan. As a reminder to you and the other twats in this town that you're the ones who should be locked up.' Nelson looked at the cameraman. 'Come on, I'll show the spot where DI Fagan beat someone within an inch of their lives.'

Fagan watched as Nelson and the film crew walk through Morrisons carpark, toward where the Farmers used to be. He unclenched his fist.

The Cantreff Inn

Jackie placed a glass of coke down on the bar.

'What's this?' Fagan stared at the soft drink.

'It's called cutting back. From the look on your face when you just walked in, you look as if you've had another one of those days.'

Fagan picked up the glass. 'You could say that.'

'Benny?'

Fagan nodded, savouring the taste of the coke. 'Just bumped into him in Morrisons' carpark. He was armed with a documentary crew. I had to stop myself from planting my fist in his face. I don't know how much more I can take, Jacks. It's like he's knows what makes me tick.'

'Everyone wants that twat out-of-town.'

'That petition is gaining more signatures every day.'

'Have you ever considered the possibility that there is someone else who wants you booted out of the police?'

'Like who? I have no enemies. Sure, I've pissed my superiors off in the past. But not enough to want someone to get me kicked out.'

'You said it yourself, Fagan, when you were investigating Rebecca's murder. When you arrested Benny, it opened a can of worms. He had that stash of porn images in that shed at the allotment. He was pimping his wife out. God knows where she is now, poor cow. And like Evans said. You might have uncovered a paedophile ring that may have operated in

Abergavenny in the eighties. For all you know they could still be about. Nelson is. What about the old computers you found in the shed?'

'No good unless we find the missing hard drives, Jacks.'

'Well, you've certainly rattled someone's cage. By the way, Jamie said he was looking into something for you. He didn't want to speak with you personally because he thought he'd annoy you with one of his theories. He said he'd be in contact when he has something more *concrete*.'

'What's that supposed to mean?'

Jackie shrugged. 'You know what Jamie is like.'

Fagan drained the last of the coke from his glass. 'I need to move.'

'That was quick.'

'I just come in here to tell you about Nelson. You're one of the few people who I can rely on Jacks. You know, to keep me in check.'

Jackie smiled. 'I've always a shoulder you can cry on, Fagan.'

Fagan stepped away from the bar.

'Early night?'

'No, I just text George. I need a quick chat. I just remembered. Before I bumped into that prick Nelson, I met an old school friend, Melissa Knight.'

'Oh, yeah, I remember. Red-haired girl. Her family owned the Triley Court hotel just before you get to the Crown Pantygelli.'

Fagan smiled. 'She asked me out to dinner.'

'Wow, she's a fast mover. You going?'

'I'll think about it.' Fagan winked. 'See you later Jacks.'

Lower Monk street

Walker handed Fagan a glass of brandy. 'I just been on the Argus website. What's this about a body found at the back of Vine Road Music studios?'

158

Fagan sipped from his glass. 'Been in the ground about thirty years. A music award and an expensive watch were buried with the remains. Its opened another can of worms George.'

'How so?'

'Besides the body, we also discovered evidence of sexual abuse that took place at the music studio and the Agincourt hotel just down the road.'

Walker sat back in his chair. 'The Agincourt hotel is another place that had a reputation. I was called out there frequently. But that was decades ago. I know some rockers from the studio used to stay there. When they shut down the London Hotel, all the poofters had nowhere to go. So they all started going to the Agincourt. Including Bob Benson, Bill Nelson and the other filth.'

'Did you know a former chief constable called Owain Lance?'

Walker let out a snort of derision. 'I remember that arsehole.'

'I take it you didn't get on with him?'

'Lance joined the force in 1970. Bob Benson took a shine to him right away. After the London closed they used to spend a lot of time in the Agincourt.'

'Wasn't Benson married?'

'Oh, yeah. But that never stopped him from having more exotic tastes in partners. Both Benson and Lance would go out on patrol together.'

'Why didn't you like Lance?'

'Remember I told you when I was recruited into Operation Countrymen?'

Fagan nodded, taking another sip of brandy.

'Lance was the other copper who was recruited. I knew right away he was a bad egg. I even told my contacts in the Met. But they didn't want to know. Lance was feeding back information to Benson. Information I had been gathering.

159

Benson despised me for being part of Operation Countrymen. That's why he once said, no one likes a grass. He knew I was passing information on to countrymen about his activities.'

'But he wasn't arrested.'

'No.' Walker drank from his glass. 'Countrymen was a flawed operation. It got too big for the Met to handle. There were hundreds of bent coppers at all levels. In the end it came down to a few senior Met officers being arrested and charged. But even that fizzled out. I remember DCI Leslie Chapman telephoning me one day. He was irate they had closed the operation. He had so many bent coppers working under him, but there wasn't a thing he could do.'

'How long did Lance stay with Monmouthshire police?'

'Around twelve years. In 1982, they transferred him to Swansea. He was recruited into the Special Demonstration Squad. He infiltrated the national Union of Miners in the valleys, during the miners' strike of 1984. But he was found out and had the shit kicked out of him. They gave Benson a commendation for saving him from the miners who wanted to string him up.'

'They've just completed an enquiry into the Special Demonstration Squad.'

'Another whitewash.' Walker grumbled. 'Like Countrymen, the SDS would have brought the police to its knees. They infiltrated just about every movement you could think of. There was a story broke several years ago that several women who protested at Greenham Common got pregnant by undercover officers.'

'Owain Lance was a DCI when he cracked a grooming gang in Swansea. And Benson was Chief Constable of south Wales police.'

Walker savoured the taste of his brandy. 'It was all bent back then. You couldn't turn your head without bumping into a rotten apple. When I quit the force, I went through a period of deep depression. I remember the smug look on Benson's face when I handed him my letter.'

'You quit the force to save me, George. That's something I'll never forget. I'll keep my promise. I'll get Nelson because of what he did to Graham.'

'I know you will.' Walker managed a smile, glancing at a photo of his son.

CHAPTER 21

Day 4
Newport Central police station – 9:36am

'First, Mr Jordan, I'd like to thank you for coming to see us in today.'

'What is that supposed to mean, DI Fagan?' Frankie Jordan stated, frustration clear in his tone.

'It simply means we are grateful that you're helping us with our enquiry.'

'Let's get this over with, shall we, DI Fagan.' Jordan's solicitor grumbled. 'I'd like to remind you that Mr Jordan is here voluntarily and is not here to answer any questions other than those associated with your enquiry.'

'Which is the discovery of human remains at the back of Vine Road music studios. An establishment your client owned.' Watkins pointed out.

'Yes, my client did own Vine Road Studios.'

'When did you sell the studio?' Fagan asked, looking directly at Jordan.

'1995,' Jordan answered abruptly.

'Must have been hard for you to let go. You must have a lot of fond memories. Working with some of the world's top performers. You had some massive artists record albums at Vine Road studios, while you were the owner.'

Jordan clasped his hands behind his head. 'Yes. We helped many groups reach their potential when they recorded music there.' He managed a smile. 'We made a lot of fond memories at the studios.'

'We, as in Mickey Mercury?' Watkins asked.

'Yes, of course.'

'Mr Jordan. You've been asked to come in today because we found the remains of a woman at the back of Vine Road studios. Forensics have conformed the body has been in the ground for approximately thirty years. It was thirty years ago that you owned the studio.'

'I am aware of this, DI Fagan.' Jordan cut him off. 'I read that press release the police put out last night.' Jordan's frustration mounted. 'I have already had half a dozen phone calls from the press today accusing me of all kinds of things.'

'I'm sorry to hear that.'

'Are you? If that's the case, then why did you issue that press release?'

'We are appealing for witnesses to come forward. Who might help us explain how the body got there. How often were you at the studio?'

'Not every day. I was out on the road most of the time. I was promoting a lot of artists back then. This involved a lot of travelling back-and-forth London. Radio interviews, TV interviews and other press junkets. I had an office in the West End of London.'

'Artists, including Alexandria Xavier.'

'Yes. Alex was my biggest star.'

'Was, or still is?' Watkins picked up on what Jordan had just said.

Jordan stared at him. 'Still is, and was. I don't know whether the police actually watch the news. But Alex is in the final stages of cancer.'

'What cancer is she suffering from?' Fagan asked.

Jordon seemed thrown by the question. 'She has advanced bowel cancer. Her doctors have given her just weeks to live.'

'And where is she living these days?'

'Does it matter, DI Fagan? The fact is, the poor woman hasn't got long. She's trying to live life to the full in her last days.'

163

'She's doing that alright. Alex has just topped the charts with that single she's just released.' Watkins mentioned. 'She's probably making a lot of money for you.'

Jordan glared back at Watkins. 'Is that how you see me, DS Watkins? Some kind of money grabbing monster.'

'DS Watkins is right, Mr Jordan. Alex must be generating a lot of money from that single she released. Plus, she's releasing an album at the end of the week.'

'I don't believe this,' Jordan stated. 'How dare you drag me down here.'

'You volunteered to be questioned, remember, Mr Jordan?'

'My client is aware of this DI Fagan.' Jordan's solicitor countered.

'Let's get on, shall we,' Fagan said. 'Three days ago, a body was discovered at the back of a studio you and your partner, Mickey Mercury, owned. A Brit award with Alex's name was found with the remains.'

Jordan seemed rattled with what Fagan had just. 'I don't understand. Are you telling me Alex's Brit award was discovered with the body you found at the back of the studio?'

'Yes, that's exactly what we are saying. Police also found a watch with the body. A Rolex watch with an inscription baring the name Andrea. We believe this watch belonged to a woman called Andrea Jones, who we suspect is our victim.'

Jordan glanced at his solicitor.

Do you know who this Andrea Jones is, or was?'

'I vaguely recall the name, yes.'

'Do you have any information that might help us with our enquiry?'

'How should I know how that body ended up at the back of the studio? Like I just said DI Fagan. I wasn't at the studio all the time.'

'Tell us about the night that Alex won her Brit award.' Watkins said.

Jordan summoned a memory. 'She was ecstatic. She'd dreamt of winning that award ever since she won the talent competition.'

'This would be 1989?'

'Yes.'

'We have a witness who saw you arguing in the kitchen at the Agincourt hotel the night Alex won that Brit award.'

Jordan shifted in his chair. 'The night of the Brit Awards. We couldn't have been at the hotel that night when the Brit Awards were in London.'

'This was hours after the award ceremony. Between eleven o'clock and midnight several witnesses saw you in the kitchen at the hotel arguing with Alex. You arrived by helicopter and landed in a field at the back of the Agincourt.'

'Yes, I recall now.'

'How much do you remember about that night, exactly?'

'I remember it was a night to remember.' Jordan replied. 'Alex accepted her award before Charlotte invaded the stage and assaulted her.'

Fagan glanced down at his notes. 'After which Dillon Powell assaulted Charlotte.'

Jordan nodded slowly.

'Did Charlotte press charges against Dillan for assault?'

'Not to my knowledge.'

'What about Alex? Didn't she report being assaulted by Charlotte?'

'It was a lover's tiff, DI Fagan, that all.'

'Resulting in assault.' Watkins said.

'Jesus.' Jordan groaned. 'It was no secret Alex had been screwing Dillon behind Charlotte's back. There'd been rumours in the press for months. Charlotte jumped up on stage that evening because she was jealous of Alex. Her career was fading. She would have done anything to stay in the public eye.'

Fagan and Watkins exchanged glances.

165

'By the time we arrived at the hotel, they smoothed out their differences.'

'But you were still arguing. I've spoken to Alex's mother. She said she gained access to the hotel to confront Alex.'

Jordan rolled his eyes. 'Here we go. That money grabbing bitch has been stirring the shit again, has she? Making out that she was the perfect mother. She never gave a shit about those girls. When Alex became famous, she crawled out of the woodwork wanting to make money from her daughter.'

'Alex's mother informed her that Abbey, her younger sister, had committed suicide a few weeks before the award ceremony.'

Jordan folded his arms.

'Would you know anything about that, Mr Jordan?'

'I am aware of what happened to her sister. It was a tragic time for Alex. She had to deal with drug addiction and the stresses of being famous.'

Alex's mother also said she informed her father what had happened. But Simon Xavier withheld the information from Alex. Why was this?'

'How the fuck should I know? Look, if you're going to believe every word that lying bitch has to say, then this is going to be a quick interview.'

'Why were you arguing in the hotel kitchen?'

'Is this relevant to the case at hand, DI Fagan?' The solicitor grunted.

Fagan made eye contact with him. 'Yes, it's relevant.' He looked back at Jordan. 'We believe the victim found at the back of the studio was murdered on the night of the Brit Awards.'

'And how do you know that?' The solicitor asked.

A suitable answer escaped Fagan's mind.

'The body could have been dumped months, or even a year after that Brit Awards ceremony.'

'If that is the case, then why dump the Brit award and a

166

Rolex watch with the name of the murder victim etched onto the back? Plus, the date of the award ceremony was etched onto the brass plaque.' Fagan called up the magazine article on his tablet. 'According to Alex, in an interview she gave nine years ago, you booked her into rehab the day after the Brit Awards.'

'That's correct.' Jordan responded. 'She was under immense pressure. I thought it was best for her to take time out from the music industry.'

'Thirty years is a long time out session.'

'Alex didn't want to come back to the music industry. When she found out her sister had passed away, it was too much to take. She wanted out of the music industry completely.'

'What was the name of the rehab clinic?'

'It was thirty years ago. I cannot remember every tiny detail.'

'You provided a way out?' Watkins said.

Jordan nodded. 'It took a lot of organising. After she had recuperated in rehab, she settled in Spain.'

Fagan glanced at the tablet. 'Would that be Tarragona?'
'Yes.'

'Did she live in the town or on the outskirts?'

'In the town, I believe. On the beachfront.'

Fagan and Watkins exchanged another glance.

'Where is Alex now?' Fagan asked.

'She in palliative care.'

'Is she still in Spain?'

Jordan stalled on an answer.

'Mr Jordan, is Alex still in Spain?'

'No, she's in a palliative care centre in the UK.'

'Where in the UK?'

Jordan shook his head. 'I'm not going to tell you, DI Fagan. And I'll tell you why. She is at the end of her life. It would be pointless tracking her down and subjecting her to the same interrogation you are subjecting me to.'

'This isn't an interrogation, Mr Jordan,' Watkins said. 'We are trying to piece together the events of June 25th 1993. You and Alex's party returned to the Agincourt hotel after the award ceremony. There was an altercation in the hotel's kitchen. You were all thrown out of the kitchen. After which you were seen arguing at the back of the hotel. You then left and vanished for a few hours.'

Jordan chewed on his nail.

'You were then picked up in a minibus that drove from Abergavenny. You, along with your partner, Mickey Mercury, were driven down to London. In the minivan with you were Charlotte West and Dillon Powell. Alun Mitchell, Alex's minder, was also with you.' Fagan explained. 'What I would like to know is where Alex, her father and Andrea Jones were?'

'I don't know.' Jordan's voice quivered.

'Did you go back to the studio after the argument at the hotel?'

'We may have. It was thirty years ago, DI Fagan. My memory isn't what it used to be.'

'You must have gone back to the studio. It was pouring with rain that evening. You weren't going to stand at the back of the hotel getting soaked.'

'Yes, we went back to the studio.' Jordan confessed.

'What happened when you arrived at the studio?'

'I went to my office to sort out some paperwork.'

'Where did the others go?'

'I think they all went to one of the studios. I could hear them all arguing. The studio was quite close to the office.'

'And you didn't go to see why they were still arguing?'

'No, I wasn't particularly interested. I'd had a guts full of all the bickering. I wanted some peace and quiet.'

'Alex had just found out her sister had committed suicide. Don't you think you should have offered some comfort to the girl?'

168

'She had her father for that.'

'But Alex was seen screaming at her father.' Fagan checked his notes. 'She screamed, *you knew, and you didn't fucking tell me*. So she was obviously too distraught to get comfort from her father. You were the closest she had to a father.'

'I've turned up, haven't I?' Jordan argued. 'I have answered all your stupid questions. Sat here and had to fend off all your accusations.'

'With all due respect, Mr Jordan, we haven't accused you of anything. You have been invited here today relating to a body found at the back of Vine Road Studios that you owned in the early nineties. That makes you a significant witness.'

'But I didn't see any bloody murder.' Jordan raised his voice, wincing, rubbing his chest.

'DI Fagan. My client has a serious heart condition. As you can see, this interview is causing him anxiety. He has already stated he was at the hotel on the night in question. My client has also told you he went back to the music studio. Mr Jordan has said that he did not witness any events after going back to the studio because he was in his office. That, in my opinion, is a suitable explanation.' He stood. 'I am stopping this interview on the grounds of my client's failing health.'

'We haven't finished questioning him.'

'I suggest you make a further appointment.'

Jordan stood and followed his solicitor through the door.

Fagan stood and hurried after them. 'Mr Jordan.'

Jordan turned.

Fagan handed him a business card. 'These are my contact details. Should Alex decide to offer information that might help us with our enquiry.'

Jordan stared at the card for a moment before snatching it out of Fagan's hand.

Fagan walked back into the interview room. 'What a load of bollocks. That shithead is lying.'

Watkins' phone buzzed. 'Mickey Mercury has just arrived

at the station.'

'He'll be as evasive as Jordan. There's no way any of them will reveal anything significant.'

'You expecting more bullshit from Mercury, boss?'

'Definitely. They'll all try to squirm their way out of this.' Fagan looked at his tablet reading the magazine article. 'This article doesn't make sense.'

'How so?'

'According to this, Alex claims her sister committed suicide in August 1993. But when I spoke to her mother yesterday, she told me that Abbey had committed suicide in May 1993.' Fagan looked at Watkins. 'So who's telling the truth?'

Watkins shrugged.

'Right, we'll leave it an hour before talking to Mercury. If these twats want to lie through their teeth, that's fine by me. I want you to get on to the records office in the Usk. Find out exactly when Abbey died.'

'Will do.'

CHAPTER 22

10:39am

Fagan bit into a BBQ chicken wrap Brooks had bought from Greggs. 'Ok let's recap. We've just interviewed the first of our significant witnesses, Frankie Jordan. It looks like these arseholes are going to play the long game with us. Jordan wasn't very forthcoming with any relevant information. We should expect the same bullshit from the rest of them.'

Watkins was staring at his phone. 'According to the records office in Usk, boss, Alex's sister died on the 20rd May 1993.'

'I knew that twat was full of shit. Not only that, but Alex also lied in the magazine article. Hang a banger. What date did Abbey commit suicide?'

'20th May 1993.'

Fagan savoured the taste of his wrap. 'It's even more poignant because Alex's birthday is on the same day.' His phone rang. Falcon's name displayed on the screen. 'Eddie, how you doing, mate?'

'I just got off the phone to the magazine editor who wrote that article.' Falcon revealed. 'He said he didn't get to speak to Alex.'

'What do you mean, he didn't get to speak with her?'

'He said he contacted Alex's manager, Frankie Jordan, requesting an interview with Alex. Jordan e-mailed him back and said he had to prepare a set of questions for Alex to answer. The editor wrote some random questions and e-mailed them to Jordan. A few weeks later, Jordan e-mailed him back with a set of answers.'

'But he didn't get to speak with Alex?'

'No.'

'Okay, cheers Eddie, I owe you one.'

'What's the news, boss?' Watkins asked.

'That article is a load of bollocks. The magazine didn't even get to speak with Alex. None of it makes sense, does it? Since day one, we've been led from pillar to post. Alex lied in that interview, which puts her back on the top of our suspect list.' Fagan glanced at the whiteboard packed with information. 'Alex must have murdered Andrea because she found out her best mate had abused her sister. Along with Dillon and Charlotte. Abbey also committed suicide on Alex's birthday, which would have made it more traumatic for Alex.'

'But why lie about the date of her sister's suicide?' Watkin questioned.

'I don't think they've lied.' Fagan said. 'I think it's a case of their stories don't match up. We just mentioned Abbey's suicide to Jordan. He seemed to get a little twitchy when we asked about the mother turning up at the Agincourt hotel to tell Alex what had happened to Abbey. He also got anxious when I started quoting from that magazine article.' Fagan looked down at his tablet. 'It says here in Alex's own words. *But that was just the start of my nightmares. In August 1993, Frankie visited me at the rehab centre. He told me that my sister had taken her own life two days earlier.*' Fagan scrolled to the top of the screen. 'This article was published on the 25th June 2012. Twenty nine years after the Brit Awards. Memories always fade after time. However, certain memories like the death of a loved one always stay with you. My mam died on the 28th September 2019. It's something I'll never forget. I remember everything I did on that day. Right up until I got the phone call from her neighbour.' Fagan glanced down at his screen. 'According to this, Alex was told about her sister's suicide in August 1993. But she'd already been told about her sister's death on the night of the Brit Awards. Her mother told her.' A notion invaded Fagan's train of thought.

'You okay, boss?' Watkins asked, noting his expression.

Fagan shook off the idea. 'Yeah, I just had a silly thought, that's all. Where are we at regarding DNA from the body?'

'We can't find any living relatives of Andrea Jones?' Brooks revealed.

'She must have an aunt or uncle somewhere.'

'No. Like Andrea, her mother was an only child. There is no father's name on the birth certificate.'

'So all we have to identify the body is a watch with an inscription on the back.'

Watkins and Brooks nodded in unison.

'Bollocks.' Fagan swore. 'It's always back to square one with this. Everything points to Alex being the murderer. Let's assume for one moment she did murder Andrea. Alex found out Andrea was part of the abuse trio. She has an argument at the studio and the deed is done. Jordon says he didn't witness any arguments at the studio. He claimed he was in his office. So that leaves Alex, Mercury, Charlotte, Dillon and Mitchell. I'm betting, when we interview Mercury in less than an hour, he's going to throw Alex and the others under the bus.'

'You reckon he'll claim he wasn't part of the argument at the studio?' Watkins speculated.

'I'm certain of it. Which leaves Alex back in the frame for Andrea's murder. Think about it. She'll be dead within a few weeks. All they need to do is hold out until then. After she dies, they'll all change their story and blame everything on Alex. The Crown Prosecution Service will examine the evidence and probably decide that it's not in the public interest to go to trial. Because the primary suspect in the murder of Andrea Jones is deceased.'

'What about charging any witnesses with perverting the course of justice, boss?'

'Fat chance that'll happen. All they need to do is stick together on their story. Surround themselves with a wall of legal advisors. It could take months or even a few years to convince the CPS there's a case worth pursuing.' Another idea came into sharp focus. 'According to the current owner of the studio, the field in which they are building used to be a peat bog. I was doing a little research last night. Peat bogs are protected. Whoever murdered Andrea Jones buried her in the peat bog in 1993. Confident that no one would find her, because it was protected. The last thing they expected was for the current owner to get permission to build. Which puts Jordan and Mercury back in the frame for murder. Alex wouldn't have known the ins and outs of planning permission. But the studio owners would have known. The thing is, we're in a race against time. Alex is on her deathbed. Once she sheds her mortal coil, everyone who was at the Agincourt that night will make up whatever bullshit they want.'

'What are the chances of tracking Alex down before she dies?' Brooks asked.

'Zero chance,' Fagan answered. 'Until we have Mercury's statement, we won't be able to make any more assumptions.' Fagan's phone rang for the second time. 'Di Fagan.'

'Hello, you spoke to a friend of mine, Amy. She gave me your phone number. It's about Dillon Powell.'

'Yes,' Fagan said enthusiastically. 'Thank you for calling me. Is your name Vicky?'

'Yeah, Vicky James.'

'Where are you at, Vicky?'

'I live in Tredegar.'

'Do you think you could come in have a chat at Newport police HQ?'

'As long as it won't get me into trouble. I don't want money or anything like that.'

'I'll make sure you won't get into trouble, Vicky. When can you make it down here?'

'I'll be there as soon as I can.'

'Great, see you soon.' A smiled stretched across Fagan's

face. 'Finally, we have a breakthrough. That was a woman who claims Dillon Powell abused her in the 90s. It's a new witness, so we can arrest Powell.'

'What difference is that going to make, boss?' Watkins asked. 'We're trying to solve a murder, not drag up sexual abuse allegations.'

'Correct, but if we arrest Powell on suspicion of rape and sexual abuse, he may be a little more cooperative in helping us understand Andrea Jones' murder. Andrew, organise an arrest warrant for Powell.'

CHAPTER 23

11:17am

Fagan stood as Mercury entered the interview room. He smiled, offering his hand. 'Mr Mercury, thanks for taking time to speak with us today.'

Mercury gripped Fagan's hand. 'My Pleasure DI Fagan. I am at your service in helping you solve this perplexing mystery.'

Mercury's solicitor sat next to him furiously scribbling notes on a pad. She looked up, faking a smile.

'I take it your solicitor has briefed you on why we have invited you today?' Watkins opened the interview.

'Yes, something to do with a body at the back of Vine Road music studios.'

'That's correct.' Fagan said. 'Our forensic team believe the body has been in the ground for thirty years. You owned the studio thirty years ago with your partner. Frankie Jordon?'

'That would be correct, DI Fagan.' Mercury stated.

'A brit award and a Rolex watch were found with the remains.'

'Wait.' Mercury put his hand up, furrowing his brow. 'I'm sorry, but did you say a Brit award, DI Fagan?'

'Yes, I did.'

'A Brit award.' Mercury expressed a puzzled tone. 'How an earth did a Brit award end up with a murder victim?'

Fagan glanced at Watkins. 'We believe the *murder victim* was a woman called Andrea Jones. Would you know who this person is?'

'I might have known her. Alex had so many friends when she was famous, Inspector Fagan. Mostly people wanting to benefit.'

Fagan continued. 'A Rolex watch baring an inscription with Andrea's name on it was also with the remains. We have discovered Andrea was a close friend of Alex. We believe Andrea was murdered on the night of the Brit Awards.'

'Really.' Mercury said in a surprised tone. 'How did you come to that conclusion, DI Fagan?'

'We have witnesses who saw you at the Agincourt hotel on the night of the Brit Awards. Our witness said they saw you in the hotel's kitchen with Alex, Frankie Jordan, Dillon Powell, Charlotte West, Alun Mitchell and the victim, Andrea Jones.'

Mercury considered Fagan's words. 'Oh, yes, I recall. It was the night Charlotte had a fight with Alex in front of the TV cameras. I recall giving both Charlotte and Dillon a dressing down for their exploits.'

'Why did Charlotte assault Alex in front of the TV cameras?' asked Watkins.

'It was all for show. Charlotte was falling out of favour with her fans.'

'Why do you think she was becoming unpopular?'

'Charlotte was just a flash in the pan. I discovered her at a dreadful talent contest Frankie had convinced me to take part in. She, like many of those early nineties popstars, came and went in the blink of an eye.' Mercury relaxed in his chair. 'Charlotte had a few decent hits when she was on the pop scene, but in the end, she was more trouble than she was worth.'

'Why?' Fagan asked.

'For a start, she was common as muck. A girl from the wrong side of Swansea. Used to swear like a trooper. Smoked like a chimney. I'm surprised she could sing, considering how many cigarettes she used to get through every day. She was also a binge drinker. Whenever we used to do radio and TV interviews, I virtually had to lock her up for twenty-four hours so that she was sober. But that didn't stop her from dropping a few bloopers live on air. I lost count of how many times I had to apologise for her. We met Sarah Greene on Going live in 1992. Charlotte said something inappropriate live on air. I remember the producer going ballistic after the interview.'

'Do you recall what she said to her?'

'Not really, but Charlotte, being Charlotte, would have made a sexual reference. She was a bit of a nympho, if you catch my drift. Charlotte used to bat for both sides.' Mercury took a breath. 'She has a salacious appetite for sex.'

'Did she have many partners?'

'More than I could count, darling.' Mercury replied. 'She had an appetite that would have put a porn star to shame.'

'But she had a relationship with Dillon.'

'Oh yes.' Mercury nodded enthusiastically. 'Dillon was another star who couldn't keep his willy in his trousers, if you know what I mean.'

'Plenty of girls lining up wanting to meet him?'

'Definitely. Although Dillon was from the rough part of Merthyr, he was a very polite young boy. His mother installed him with manners.'

'Were there a lot of young girls interested in meeting Dillon?'

'Careful inspector Fagan.' Mercury's solicitor warned. 'You're drifting off topic.'

Mercury waved the comment away. 'I know where you're going with this DI Fagan. Yes, there were many young girls lining up to meet Dillon. He was gorgeous.' Mercury leant forward, interlocking his fingers. 'I even made several passes at him.' He sighed. 'But, unfortunately, Dillon was as straight as die. Pity, I bet he would have been spectacular between the sheets.' Mercury winked at Fagan.

Fagan refocussed. 'So it's the night of the Brit Awards and Charlotte has assaulted Alex. What happened directly after the award ceremony?'

'I gave the two of them a good bollocking. Charlotte

already knew Alex had been fucking Dillon behind her back for months.'

'According to the news media, Charlotte found out Dillon was having an affair with Dillon on the night of the Brit Awards.' Watkins remarked.

'Total nonsense darling.' Mercury laughed. 'Charlotte knew about Dillon and Alex months beforehand.'

'So why the theatrics on the night of the Brits?'

'I was planning to drop Charlotte. I'd already told the girl that her antics were getting out of hand. Her last hit was a total flop. And then her other hits tumbled down the charts. So, I thought it was time to cut the strings.'

'When did you tell her you were planning to drop her?' Fagan asked.

'On the day of the Brits.'

'That's why she lashed out at Alex in front of everyone.'

Mercury nodded. 'Thing is, DI Fagan. When you burn as brightly as Charlotte, you expect it to go on forever. There were loads of popstars with one-hit wonders back in the eighties and nineties. Look at Rick Astley. Never gonna give you up was massive back in the day. He's had a bit of a revival in recent years with that one song. Charlotte was no different. They still play her popular hits on the radio today. I still earn a decent income from royalties.'

'Does Charlotte?'

'Of course.' Mercury reflected. 'But in the end, she was too hot to handle. I tired pass her over to Jordan. But he was already raking it in with Alex. I guess it's the reason Charlotte did what she did that night. But it wasn't like she had no money. She made a fortune the brief time she was a star. She was a very good-looking girl. Like Dillon, she had blonde hair and blue eyes. When she wasn't singing, she was modelling. She had a figure most women would die for. She still has.'

'You still stay in contact?'

'Yes, we still meet up for lunch once or twice a year.'

179

'What about Dillon? Do you still have contact with him?'

'Not really.'

'When was the last time you met with him?'

'Around ten years ago.'

'Powell was arrested and questioned under Operation Yewtree, around ten years ago.'

Mercury let out a snort of derision. 'Again, Detective Inspector Fagan, I see right through you. If you think you are going to lump me in with the Savile perverts brigade, you can forget it. I can honestly say with my hand on a bible, any sexual relationships I had back then were all legitimate. It was all consensual. And my partners were of legal age.'

'Can I remind you, DI Fagan, you are not here to interview my client regarding his past. You are here to discuss matters relating to the discovery at the music studio.'

Fagan locked eyes with her. 'The body has been there since 1993, so that counts as the past.' Fagan glanced down at his notes. 'After the award ceremony, what happened?'

'There was a lot of arguing behind the scenes. Frankie was furious with me for allowing Charlotte to burst on to the stage like that in front of all the TV cameras.'

'Did you?'

Mercury smiled. '*Oh darling*, the music industry is all about the drama behind the scenes. All anyone gets to see is the polished turd, that is the star of the show.'

'So you freely admit encouraging Charlotte to storm the stage and assault Alex,' Watkins said.

Mercury folded his arms. 'I admit I was jealous of Frankie. Alex was massive. Her face was stamped on just about every bit of merchandise you could think of. She was an industry unto herself. I guess, in hindsight, I should have done the same with Charlotte and Dillon. But Frankie was the brains of the operation. When I first went into partnership with him, I didn't know all that much about the music industry. I loved music and wanted it to be my life. My dear old mother encouraged me to play piano. But Frankie had the brains.' Mercury looked at Fagan. 'Most of the time, I was just there for the sex.'

'After the Brits, you boarded a helicopter and flew to Monmouthshire.' Fagan continued.

'Yes, although I didn't want to go to the hotel. I wanted to stay in London. Elton was in town, you see.' He winked at Fagan again. 'He wanted to hook up. But there was a big bash at the Agincourt hotel. Charlotte and Dillon didn't want to stay in London because of their public display.'

'Who was waiting for you at the Agincourt?'

'A barrage of photographers. It was all over the news about Charlotte's little meltdown at the Brits. After we fought our way through the paparazzi, we went into the restaurant of the hotel. There were all kinds of people there. Showbusiness, local politicians, a few MPs, law enforcement.'

'What kind of law enforcement?' Fagan's curiosity peaked.

'I believe the Chief Constable of South Wales police was there. Along with his junior colleagues. Dillon had been promoting his No Means No campaign for young girls. It was following a successful conviction of a grooming gang in south Wales.'

'Bob Benson was the chief constable back then, wasn't he?' Fagan stated.

'You know Bob, do you?'

Fagan flashed a faint smile. 'I grew up in Abergavenny. Are you familiar with the London Hotel?'

'Ah yes, the good old days.' Mercury grinned.

'DI Fagan.' Mercury's solicitor sighed. 'Can we get back on track.'

'Of course.' Fagan responded. 'So you were in the restaurant and mingling with guests. Where was Alex?'

'I believe she was in the foyer. Apparently, some woman gate crashed and told Alex something that upset her.'

'Do you know what it was this woman told Alex?'

Mercury shifted in his chair. 'The leech of a woman was the

181

mother of Alex. Sad excuse for a woman, wanting to make money off a daughter she didn't care about. She told Alex her sister, Abbey had taken her own life a few weeks earlier.'

'So you knew Alex's sister, Abbey?'

Mercury stumbled over his next line. 'I did, well, kind of. Sweet young thing, very shy. Charlotte and Dillon took a liking to her. They took her under their wing, so to speak.'

'What happened to the woman?'

'Security threw her out.'

'After that?' Fagan pursued.

'And then, security came into the restaurant and told me that Alex was in the kitchen screaming at her father.'

'Security being Alun Mitchell.'

'Yes.' Mercury nodded.

'Where were Jordan, Dillon and Charlotte at the time?'

'They were in the restaurant with me. Totally oblivious to the commotion in the foyer. Mitchell came into the restaurant and told Frankie what was going on. I followed them, but the argument had moved to the kitchen. Dillon and Charlotte came with me.'

'Where was Andrea Jones?'

'Sorry, where was who?'

'Alex's best friend.' Fagan answered. 'The woman who was found at the back of the music studio.'

'Oh, yes, yes.' Mercury nodded. 'Your murder victim. Andrea was there.'

'Did you know Andrea?'

'Not really. I always thought she was a leech. I know she supplied Alex with drugs.'

Fagan glanced at his notes. 'You were arguing in the kitchen, after which you were thrown out and carried on arguing at the back of the hotel.'

Mercury shrugged, before yawning. 'Yes, they were arguing?'

'They were arguing?' Fagan quizzed.

'Yes, but I wanted no part of it.'

'Can you recall what they were arguing about?'

'Well, Alex's mother had just dropped a bombshell regarding her sister Abbey. So I'm guessing they were still arguing about that.'

'We have a witness that says Alex was arguing with her father.' Watkins revealed.

'With all due respect, DI Fagan, DS Watkins, it was over thirty years ago. I am no more capable of recollecting events back then than any of you.'

'But you went back to the studio after they'd been arguing for several minutes?'

'Yes, I did.'

'Where was Frankie Jordon?'

'I believe he retired to his office. Alex and the others were still bickering with each other, so I retired to my office. I used to keep it well stocked with alcohol.'

Fagan knew Mercury was going to attempt to wriggle out of being a witness to any murder. 'Was your office close to Jordan's office?'

'Yes.'

'So you could still hear the argument going on?'

'Yes.'

'Who did you hear arguing exactly?'

'Mostly Alun Mitchell. A nasty thug, if there ever was one. I don't know why Jordan hired him as security in the first place. Used to strut around thinking he owned the studio.'

'How long were they arguing for?'

'Another twenty minutes maybe.'

'And then?'

'And then Dillon and Charlotte wanted to go back to London. I called a taxi, and we all piled in.'

'All of you?'

'No.' Mercury replied. 'Alex, her dad and Andrea remained at the studio. Probably to sort out their differences.'

'Did you see Alex after that night?'

'No.' Mercury shook his head. 'The poor girl went straight into rehab the night after the Brit awards.'

'So you've not seen her in thirty years?'

'No one has seen Alex in thirty years, DI Fagan. Unless you count Frankie. He's the only one who has contact with her. I have asked over the years to see her, but Frankie has always brushed me off.'

'DI Fagan, my client has been very cooperative throughout this interview. I feel he has given you a reasonable story regarding Andrea Jones.'

Fagan nodded. 'Yes, thank you so much for coming down to speak with us.'

'Always happy to help the boys in blue, DI Fagan.' Mercury stood. 'I hope you get to the bottom of this mystery.'

'Can I ask what you do these days?'

'I run a visual effects studio in Cardiff.'

'Not in the music industry anymore?'

'Oh yes, I still keep my hand in. I worked with Taylor Swift last year on one of her videos. She appeared with Elvis. Very cutting edge stuff. We're working with the BBC this year. Creating the special effects for the sixtieth anniversary of Doctor Who.'

Fagan smiled. 'Again, thanks for coming in and speaking to us.'

Mercury and his solicitor left the interview room.

Fagan puffed out his cheeks. 'I knew he was going to spin us a bunch of bullshit. They're all going to deny everything. By the time we get any information Alex will be dead. They'll just blame it all on her.'

'He threw Mitchell under the bus.'

'He did, which means Mitchell is our next candidate for interviewing.'

Watkins checked his phone. 'Bad news boss. Mitchell won't be in until tomorrow morning now.'

'That doesn't surprise me.' Fagan remarked, checking his phone. 'Vicky James has just arrived at the station. I'll interview her alone. I want you doing groundwork with Brooks. Find out if he's made any progress with a headless corpse found in the Usk in the late seventies. If we can rattle Mitchell when we interview him tomorrow, then we might just get a result.'

C H A P T E R   2 4

12:59pm

Fagan smiled at Vicky James as he entered the interview room. 'Vicky, thanks for coming at such short notice. Glad you found the coffee machine.'

The duty solicitor was texting on her smartphone.

'I thought it would be appropriate for you to have someone else in the room while you give your statement.'

'I just want to get my side of the story across.'

Fagan nodded. 'And that's all I expect from you. If you get upset or anything like that, we can stop this interview any time you want.'

'I'm not out to make money or anything like that.' Vicky sounded nervous to the point of becoming upset.

'Vicky.' Fagan said calmly. 'I know you're nervous.' He glanced at the solicitor, who stared into her smartphone, smiling. 'Your *solicitor.*' He raised his voice.

She snapped out of her trance and looked up at Fagan.

'Will assist you should you get upset.'

The solicitor packed her smartphone away.

Fagan glanced at his phone and a notepad on the table. 'Would you be comfortable with me recording this conversation or would you prefer me writing your statement?'

'You can record it if you like.'

Fagan tapped on the record icon. 'Interview with Mrs Vicky James. Present in the room is myself, Detective Inspector Mark Fagan, and the duty solicitor. How old are you Vicky?'

'I am forty-two. I was born in December 1980.'

'Can you tell me when you first met Dillon Powell?'

'I entered a singing contest which was at my school. Dillon was there, judging. Looking back, he seemed more interested in the girls' singing ability than the boys. I didn't think I had a decent voice. I entered the competition on a dare. My friend from the home found out about the competition and dared me to enter.'

'Home?'

'I was bought up in a girls' home in Port Talbot.'

'If you don't mind me asking Vicky, what happened to your mam and dad?'

'My mam dumped me at birth. She left the hospital after she had given birth to me. I think she was very young herself. My mother's name isn't even on my birth certificate. As for my dad.' Vicky shrugged.

'Ok.' Fagan nodded. 'What happened at the singing competition?'

'Nothing.' Vicky replied. 'It all kicked off when he came to visit me at the children's' home in Port Talbot.'

'That's where you lived, yeah?'

Vicky nodded. 'Nuns and priests ran the place. They used to get up to all kinds of perverted things.'

'Did anything happen to you before you met Dillon?'

Vicky hesitated before nodding. 'Yes. There are loads of girls who were being abused. One priest in particular springs to mind. He'd prowl the dorms at night, and climb into bed with whomever he saw fit to abuse.'

'How many times did you encounter him?'

'More than I could count.' Vicky recalled reaching for a box of tissues.

'Are you okay with continuing?'

Vicky blew her nose. 'Yes, I need to say my piece.'

'What did this Priest used to do?'

'He'd climb into bed and spoon. He always used to have a hard on. Then he'd make me do other things.' Vicky blew her nose.

187

'How old were you when the abuse started?'

'I'd just turned seven years old. The other girls used to talk about how special he'd say they were to him. He told me god wanted him to love me. Whenever I'd refuse to do anything with him, the nuns punished me. They would make me kneel for hours on end and pray to god, begging for his forgiveness.'

'Do you recall the name of the priest?'

'Father Joseph Petro.' Vicky answered without hesitation.

'Did he ever engage in full on sex with you?'

'Yes.' Vicky blew hard on the tissue.

'Are you okay to carry on, Vicky?'

Vicky picked up a bottle of mineral water and drank. 'Yes. Um, it was just after my ninth birthday. A week before Christmas. Father Petro climbed into bed with me. I thought he just wanted me to do the usual thing. But, then he climbed on top of me. He said that it was a time of celebration. When Jesus was born. The three wise men gave the baby Jesus gifts. Father Petro said that I should offer the greatest gift to him.'

'What gift?'

'My virginity.'

Fagan swallowed hard.

Vicky wiped away tears. 'He said that the holy spirit had given the virgin Mary the greatest gift to man, the lord our Jesus. He told me that the holy spirit lived in him. And that he would give me the same gift.' Vicky took a deep breath. 'Then he raped me.'

Fagan scribbled Petro's name on his notepad. 'Moving on to when you first met Dillon. You said he visited you in the children's home. Do you recall when this was?'

'It was January 1991. I'd just turned eleven. Father Petro let us have his personal chambers. You know, so that Dillon could get to know me better. I knew as soon as that door shut what was about to happen. That bastard of a priest even locked the door to his chambers. Dillon seemed to know straight away I was sexually active. Dillon said that I was the most beautiful girl he had ever clapped eyes on. He'd just released his first number one hit. I was totally in awe of the man. As soon as he sat next to me, he his hands were all over me.'

'Did you fight him off?'

Vicky shook her head, tearing up again. 'There's one thing that no one ever understands. Especially when you've been abused.'

'What's that Vicky?'

'It's that after a while, it becomes normality for the victim. Father Petro had raped me more times that I could count before I met Dillon. Sometimes he would visit me twice in one night. A few years ago, I read a book about Fred and Rose West. It was written by one of their children. In it, she explains that the sexual abuse she had to endure from her father became a normal thing. He'd tell her it was his right to have sex with his daughter.'

In his mind's eye Fagan shuddered. 'Go on Vicky. You're very brave.'

'So when he locked the door and Dillon started groping me, I just did what I thought was normal. I stripped for him and led him to the bed.' Vicky sobbed. 'Jesus fucking Christ, I was just as bad as Father Petro and Dillon. I just spread my legs and let them do whatever they wanted.'

'Vicky, listen to me,' Fagan said calmly. 'None of what happened to you was your fault. You weren't in control, they were. Do you understand? You are nowhere near like the people who abused you.'

Vicky nodded. 'I keep telling myself that. But the more I think about it, the more I blame myself.'

'Have you ever talked to anyone about your experiences?'

'Only the chat group I found a few years ago.'

'This is what I am going to do. I am going to put you in contact with people who you can talk to freely, okay.'

Vicky nodded. 'I have been trying to wrap my head around

189

it for years.'

'You've obviously been through a lot. Do you want to stop?'

'No.' Vicky rumbled. 'I need to get this out.' She clenched her tissue, gritting her teeth.

'Did you ever meet Dillon away from the home?'

'Yes. After the first time he raped me, Dillon invited me to the studio to record some songs with him. He said he was going to make me as famous as him. I should have known he was full of shit. What I didn't realise is that the studio was full of perverts. As soon as I arrived, they swarmed around me. The producer who managed Alex X was one of the worst. He raped me within three days of me being at the studio. Said it was part of the music industry and that I should be grateful to be amongst show business royalty. About a month after I started going out to the studio Dillon introduced me to her, Charlotte West.' Vicky's expression turned to pure hatred. 'She was a right piece of work. The moment she found out I was from a children's home, she pounced on me. Charlotte had been in and out of foster care when she was younger. She said we had a connection. We'd hang out together at the studio. They'd send a taxi to the children's' home in Port Talbot to drive me out to the studio. Do you know what Alex's manager used to say every time I'd turn up?'

'What did he used to say?'

'Oh look, it's our *delicious* Port Talbot takeaway. Come to delight us with her treats.'

'Jesus.' Fagan gasped.

'When Charlotte wasn't recording her hits, we'd sing duets together. At the time I thought I'd died and gone to heaven. The rapes and abuse seemed like normal life. I convinced myself ordinary people used to do the same. But most of all, I was glad to be away from the home.' Vicky took a swig of water. 'In August 1991, when I was at the studio, Charlotte invited me back to the Agincourt hotel. She *claimed* she

190

wanted to buy me a meal to say thank you for my friendship, as we were both from similar backgrounds. What she didn't tell me, was that the meal was being delivered to her hotel room. When I arrived at her room, another woman was already there.' Vicky summoned up a name. 'Her name was Andrea.'

Fagan scribbled Andrea Jones' name.

'At first it seemed like a girls' sleepover. We ate the food, played songs and danced. Charlotte handed the alcohol around. I took it without hesitation. Then Charlotte and Andrea got on the bed. I was sat on the other side of the room.' Vicky inhaled. 'By that time I was pissed from all the cider they piled me with. Charlotte and Andrea started getting it on, you know. They stripped in front of me and do the things that lesbians do. After a few minutes Andrea got up from the bed and walked over to me. She took my hand and said, *it's time for you to become a real woman.* She then led me over to the bed, stripped me naked. Then Charlotte joined in.'

Fagan tapped stopped on his phone. 'Do you mind if we take a break?'

Vicky looked at him. 'Yeah sure.'

Fagan stood outside the police station, watching the traffic go by. The gentle breeze felt refreshing on his face.

The road was busy. Cars heading into Newport along George Street and in the opposite direction towards the Royal Gwent Hospital.'

'You okay, boss?' Watkins appeared out of the main entrance.

Fagan wrung the handrail. 'Not really.'

'How's the interview going?'

'Don't ask.'

'That bad, eh.' Watkins puffed on his vape.

'No, which is why I had to take a break.'

An Asda lorry roared by the police station.

When I was in Liverpool. After they had convicted those

bastards for murdering Aron Miller, I thought about quitting the force.'

'Why didn't you?'

'Because I thought moving away from a big city would change everything. I mean, this is South Wales. Nothing ever happens down at this end of the country.'

Watkins looked across the street at the buildings opposite. The ground floors of the buildings were a collection of restaurants, takeaways, and barbershops. The first floors were mostly residential flats. 'No one knows what goes behind closed doors. Until its exposed. It doesn't matter how many people you have come forward with sexual abuse allegations. There's always a thousand more waiting to be heard. And a thousand more behind them. It's endless. We as police officers just have to do the best we can.

Fagan looked at Watkins and patted him on the shoulder. 'You're a good copper, Sean. I better finish the interview.'

Vicky looked like she had been crying when Fagan walked back into the interview room. Her solicitor was on the phone to a counsellor making an appointment.

Fagan placed his phone on the table and tapped the record icon. 'Did you ever see Alex involved in any activity?'

'No.' Vicky answered. 'But I knew her sister, Abbey. And I knew she was being abused. Dillon, Charlotte, and Andrea would boast about what they used to do to her.' Vicky composed herself. 'On my twelfth birthday, I was driven to the studio. Dillon said he wanted to make me feel extra special. They invited me back to the hotel for a *special birthday treat*. Charlotte and Andrea were already there. Like before, they piled me with alcohol. Andrea and Charlotte were the first to pounce on me when I was unable to fend them off. Even though I was drunk, I remember every detail. After Andrea and Charlotte finished with me, it was Dillon's turn.' Vicky locked eyes with Fagan. 'Charlotte and Andrea held me down while Dillon raped me, twice.' She sobbed again. 'He raped me so hard I bled.'

Fagan felt utterly helpless as Vicky sobbed.

Vicky sniffed. 'After it was over Dillon said that it's was my birthday and Christmas present all in one.'

'Earlier on, when you mentioned Alex's manager. You said he was one of the worst. Besides him, Dillon Charlotte and Andrea, who else was there?'

'A band used to record at the studio. They were called the Paraphernalia. When I first met them, they were already into the early forties. Frankie loved them.'

'Did they do things to you?'

'Yes. They passed me around, like some kind of sex toy.' Vicky paused. 'But there was this other bloke there. I couldn't stand him. He always used to have a camera with him. He'd take nude pictures of me. Tell me I could be a supermodel and he'd send the pictures off a modelling agency.' Vicky shook her head. 'He never did any of what he promised. My guess is he used the images for himself. Horrid man. He once said to me he'd broken the virginity of most of the girls in his town. 'His name was Nelson, Benny Nelson. He didn't live very far from the studio. Abergavenny, I think.'

Fagan froze, hearing Nelson's name. 'You sure his name was Benny Nelson?'

Vicky nodded.

Fagan stopped recording. 'This is brilliant Vicky.'

'Are you going to arrest Dillon and Charlotte?'

'With this statement, we have enough to arrest them and bring them in for questioning. However, it's a long road. They will deny everything and they will have a legal team that will put you in the spotlight.'

Vicky nodded.

'If I may DI Fagan.' The duty solicitor spoke softly. 'I know a team that can help Vicky and others who are willing to come forward and talk about their experiences.'

'That would be great.' Fagan stood.

CHAPTER 25

2:03pm

Fagan gulped down a mug of lukewarm coffee. A package had arrived while he was interviewing Vicky. It was the journal Abbey's mother had spoken about. Fagan took half an hour to look through the diary. Abbey had documented the abuse she had endured. As he studied the entries, Fagan became uneasy at the detail she had chronicled.

'Police arrested Powell at his home just outside Llandovery, boss. About ten minutes ago. I just got off the blower with one of the arresting officers. A woman was with him at his house. She was in her early twenties.'

'Anyone from Dyfed Powys police have a moan?'

'No, they sent two officers. It will be another couple of hours before he's gets here and processed. His lawyer has also been in contact to tell us he in on his way.'

'That was quick.' Brooks remarked.

'Powell can afford a high-profile lawyer. Available at the drop of a hat. I bet Dillon phoned him the moment our boys arrested him.' Fagan glanced at the whiteboard. 'Right then, once again, it's looking as if Alex had a motive to murder Andrea Jones. I have just had a read through her sister's journal. And let me tell you, it makes for unpleasant reading. Not only did Abbey write about Dillon, Charlotte, and Andrea abusing her. She also mentioned other girls who were being abused, including Vicky, the woman I have just spoken to. She also names Alun Mitchell as one of her abusers, along with Frankie Jordan and the lead singer from the Protagonists.'

'That's the first time Mitchell has been implicated as being involved with sexual abuse that took place at the studio.' Brooks pointed out.

'Problem is, boss, that's just a diary.' Watkins said. 'Any decent solicitor our suspects hire will tear us a new one if we try to use it against them. You have the statement of Vicky, which is enough to arrest Powell. As for the diary. Powell's solicitor will dismiss it as fiction.'

'No, he won't.' Fagan shook his head, opening the diary. 'According to this, Powell made Abbey perform a sex act on Vicky at least three times. Mitchell also raped Abbey on several occasions.'

'Mercury dropped Mitchell in the shit earlier when he mentioned he heard Mitchell shouting. That should be enough to rattle his cage.'

'It should be. When he comes in for his interview tomorrow, we'll be able to throw quite a few things at him regarding what happened that night after the Brit awards. If he was witness to the murder of Andrea Jones, then it will be interesting to see if he drops anyone in the shit. This is all about solving the murder of Andrea Jones. Along the way we have uncovered a major abuse scandal that happened in the early nineties. If we can break open both crimes, then I reckon more women will come forward and reveal their experiences.'

'Do you reckon Powell will confess to witnessing the murder of Andrea Jones?' Brooks asked.

'Right now, we can't question him about that. We are bringing him on allegations of sexual assault and rape.'

'But if he doesn't want to spend the next ten years in prison, then he may confess to what happened that night. Jordan and Mercury state they were both in their offices at the time of the alleged murder. Jordan said he could still hear shouting from his office. Mercury goes one step closer by saying her could hear Mitchell shouting.'

'Strange how he couldn't hear anyone else,' Fagan pointed out. 'I mean, if they were all arguing, then surely Mercury would have been able to hear everyone.' He glanced at Watkins. 'Mercury didn't seem too fond of Mitchell, did he? He called him a thug.'

'You think Mercury wants to drop him in the shit, boss?'

'Yeah.'

'Why?'

Fagan tried to summon an answer. 'Shit.'

'Everything falls apart the moment we try to link any of them to the murder.'

'That reminds me sir, I got a result on the headless corpse you wanted me to look into.'

'Let's hear it.'

'Forensics identified the body as sixteen-year-old Dorothy Morris. She disappeared on March 14th 1978. Her sister Faye Morris and mother reported her missing. In 2017, Gwent police put out an appeal to the public. Asking members of the public to come forward regarding unsolved crimes. Faye Morris gave a DNA sample, which was a match for the headless body. Dorothy Morris was dragged from the Usk on the 23rd of March1978. An examination was carried out, revealing she was six months pregnant. According to records Mitchell was questioned in connection with her disappearance but released after providing an alibi.'

'Does it give a date of birth for Dorothy?'

Brooks stared at the screen. '4th January 1963.'

'Which means she was pregnant at fifteen years old.' Fagan considered the information. 'According to former boxer Richard Bishop, Mitchell confessed to a murder while he served time with him in Cardiff. Bishop states Mitchell claimed he buried the victim's head in a place where no one would find it, a back garden. Mitchell also revealed his victim was female.'

Brooks read from the screen. 'Because Dorothy was missing her head, the police assumed it was down to a serial killer. Between 1971 to 1978, eleven bodies had been pulled from the Usk. All the bodies were female. Our murderer had separated the head and hands. The case remains unsolved.'

'Where was Mitchell living when they questioned him about the disappearance of Dorothy?'

'Potter Street in Pill.'

'So Mitchell could have got away with murder because a serial killer was operating in Newport during the 70s. The MO is that he'd remove their victim's head.'

'Going off track again, aren't we, boss?' Watkins said.

'Yeah, I know.' Fagan sighed.

'There's no way we'll be able to get a search warrant based on a decades old confession that has nothing to back it up.'

'Is Dorothy's sister still alive?' Fagan looked at Brooks.

'Yep, and still living here in Newport.'

Fagan dismissed the notion. 'We'd have to get ground penetrating radar to search the property. That's just going to take too long. It's going to have to go on the back burner for now. Let's bet back to the murder of Andrea Jones.' Fagan rubbed his hands together. 'It's the night of the Brit Awards. There's a bit of a palaver in front of the TV cameras. They all fly back to the Agincourt by helicopter. There's already guests at the hotel, including local dignitaries and serving police officers. Alex's mother gains access and tells her daughter about Abbey being abused. She also tells her that her father knew about Abbey's suicide, but kept it from her. Alex flies into a rage at her dad for keeping secrets. They argue in the kitchen of the Agincourt. The others join in. The head chef then chucks them all out. They argue outside for several minutes before returning to the music studio. Jordan and Mercury retire to their offices, but can still hear them arguing.' Fagan paused. 'After that, it's a total blank. Until they call a taxi to pick them up outside the gates of the Agincourt. But it's just Dillon, Charlotte, in the minivan, along with Mercury, Jordan and Mitchell. We need a witness to the murder of Andrea.'

'Boss, we're going to interview Dillon in a few hours. Let's concentrate on a strategy for that.'

CHAPTER 26

Newport Central police station - 4:31pm

Fagan tapped the record icon on his phone before pressing the button on the digital recorder. 'For the record, could you confirm you name please?'

'Dillon Stephen Powell.'

'Dillon, you've been arrested today following allegations of sexual assault and rape.' Watkins explained. 'You do not have to say anything, but it may harm your defence if you do not mention, when questioned, something you later rely on in court. Anything you do say may be given in evidence. Do you understand?'

'Yes.' Powell nodded.

Fagan pressed his hand on the diary. 'How well did you know Abbey Xavier?'

'No comment.' Powell answered.

Fagan studied his expression. Powell looked nervous as he stared at the table. 'Do you know a woman by the name of Vicky James?'

Powell glanced at Fagan for a moment. 'No comment.'

'Vicky gave a detailed statement of how you engaged in sexual activity with her when she was eleven years old.' Watkins revealed. 'She said you raped her at a children's home in Port Talbot.' Watkins checked his notes. 'St Mary's orphanage for girls.'

'No comment.'

'Vicky also claimed you invited her to Vine Road music studios just outside Monmouth. You engaged in sexual activity with her at the Agincourt hotel, less than a mile from the studio.'

Powell's eyes darted around the room. 'No comment.'

Fagan opened up the diary. He'd already bookmarked a page. 'Abbey Xavier kept a detailed account of her experiences while she knew you. There are entries in this diary that stretch over a period of twelve months. She names you, Charlotte West and Andrea Jones, as being involved in sexual activity with her and several other young girls. This one diary entry is particularly disturbing.' Fagan stared at the page. 'Dillon made me go down on another girl. Her name was Vicky. He made us lie on the bed and do it. While he stood on the bed and wanked all over us. We both cried our eyes out when he left the room.'

Powell picked up an inhaler. He puffed on the device before wheezing. 'No comment.' He coughed.

'We have a guestbook from the Agincourt hotel that was signed by you the day this entry was written.' Fagan flicked through the pages of the diary. 'Abbey wrote all the dates she had engaged in sexual activity with you. It also gives accounts of Charlotte and Andrea being with you when other abuse took place.'

'No comment.' Powell stated defiantly.

'Do you mind if I ask a question, DI Fagan?' The solicitor requested.

'Go ahead.'

'You say you have signatures in a guestbook from the Agincourt hotel, is that correct?'

Fagan nodded. 'Abbey also signed the guestbook, along with Vicky.'

'Is there other information available in the guestbook, such as what room number my client was staying at?'

'No.' Fagan admitted. 'But the guestbooks have dates guests signed in.'

'All you have are signatures, nothing more. It doesn't matter if you have dates. If there is no specific evidence that my client was staying in a particular room at the hotel, then you have nothing more than a coincidence. For you know these alleged victims could have signed in and stayed in other rooms. It looks to me as if these so-called victims have just conjured up a story.'

'This diary gives a detailed account of sexual abuse that took place at the Agincourt and Vine Road music studios.'

'What you have, DI Fagan, is a fictional account by a delusional fan. Plus another statement by another star-struck fan. A jury could easily dismiss any accusations by these women.'

Fagan glared at the solicitor while pointing at the diary. 'This delusional *fan* who wrote this diary committed suicide.' He flicked to the last page. 'Abbey's last entry. Please god, no more, I want it all to go away. Only one way out of this hell.' Fagan looked at Powell. 'Did you know Abbey had committed suicide, Dillon?'

Powell stared back with a hollowed expression. 'Yes.'

'How did you find out?'

Powell shrugged. 'Her manager told me. No wait, it was Alex who told me, yeah.' He nodded.

'When was this exactly?'

'I dunno. It's a long time ago now.'

'Exactly Dillon.' His solicitor stated. 'As you can see, DI Fagan, my client has trouble remembering something that happened thirty years ago.'

Fagan shook his head dismissively. 'Something like that will stay with you for a while. So, I'll ask you again Dillon. When did Alex tell you her sister committed suicide?'

'I dunno.' Powell sounded frustrated. 'She may have told me a few months after it happened.'

'A few months after it happened.' Watkins said. 'Abbey committed suicide on the 20th of May, 1993. Alex was nominated for a Brit award in June 1993.'

'So.' Powell snorted.

'The day after she won the award, Alex was checked into rehab.' Fagan pointed out. 'Following that, she became a recluse and has rarely been seen since. You have just stated that she must have told you a few months after it happened, which would have been July or August 1993. Have you been in contact with Alex since that night at the Brit Awards?'

Powell shifted in his chair. He massaged his forehead. 'I might have found out Abbey committed suicide from someone else.'

'Who?'

'Jesus fucking Christ. You're expecting me to remember something that happened thirty years ago. I was off my face most of the time. The media knew I had a drug habit.'

'But it was a night to remember Dillon. Alex had been given her Brit award. Then Charlotte jumped on stage and gave her a smacking. A few moments after, you burst on to the stage and gave Charlotte a good belting.'

'You don't have to fucking remind me.' Powell barked. 'It was all over the news the next fucking day. The tabloids really went to work on me. Labelling me as some kind of violent thug.'

'What happened after the award ceremony?' Watkins asked.

'What do you mean?'

'Did you carry on arguing backstage?'

'For a while, then Alex's manager calmed us down. Me and Charlotte got a bollocking from our manager.'

Watkins looked down at his notes. 'You then went back to the Agincourt Hotel just outside Monmouth.'

Powell nodded. 'I remember that. We flew by helicopter. I was sick all over the place. Used hate flying back in the day. I used to get terrible air sickness.'

'When you arrived back at the Agincourt, where did you go?' Fagan asked.

'They were having a reception for us, so we went to join

201

them.'

'This would be the reception honouring you for your work on the No Means No campaign.'

'Yes.'

'Did all of you attend the reception?'

Powell hesitated. 'No, Alex wasn't with us. Ah, yeah, I remember now.'

'What do you remember, Dillon?'

'It was Alex's mother who told her about Abbey's suicide. Yeah, because she had sneaked into the hotel. That's when it all kicked off.'

'What kicked off?'

'The argument between Alex and her dad. Her mother had told Alex that her dad knew about Abbey committing suicide. But he had kept it secret. Alex went ballistic at him.'

'We have a witness statement saying that you were in the kitchen of the Agincourt. Together with your manager, Alex's manager, plus Charlotte, Andrea Jones and Alun Mitchell. Alex's father was also present. You were all seen arguing with Alex.'

'Alex was giving as good as she got. She was blaming all of us for Abbey's suicide.'

'DI Fagan.' Powell's solicitor interrupted. 'May I ask how all this connects to the allegations my client is supposed to be answering questions about?'

Fagan drew a breath. 'I have spoken to the mother of Alex and Abbey. Who said she gained access to the Agincourt for the sole purpose of telling Alex what had happened to her sister. She maintains she also told Alex about the sexual abuse that was going on at the Agincourt and at the music studio. In her diary, Abbey names you, Charlotte, Andrea, and Frankie Jordan as the main abusers. Is that why you were all arguing with Alex in the kitchen? Is that why she was kicking off?'

'No comment.' Powell had a look of defiance.

'Alex finally discovered the truth about what was

happening. So she threatened to expose you, didn't she?'

'No comment.'

'Inspector Fagan. Once again, you have an unreliable witness.'

Fagan looked at the solicitor. 'Why is that exactly?'

'The mother of Alex and Abbey Xavier abandoned her daughters when they were very young. She only came back on the scene when Abbey became famous. I understand there is a series of newspaper articles from the early nineties that highlight this. She abandoned her daughters before trying to reconnect for financial purposes. I find it more than a coincidence this woman has surfaced once more, following Alex's reappearance, and the release of new music. It seems obvious to me she is trying to connect for financial purposes, like she did before.'

Fagan felt as he had hit a stalemate. Powell wasn't about to admit to anything. He refocused. 'What happened when you left the Agincourt that night?'

Powell was caught off guard by the question. 'We, uh, left and went back to the studio. Leaving all the guests at the reception to carry on without us.'

'We've interviewed your manager, Mickey Mercury, and Alex's manager, Frankie Jordan. They maintain they both went back to their offices. Leaving Alex, you, Charlotte, Andrea and Alun Mitchell, plus Alex's father. Mercury also told us he heard Alun Mitchell shouting. What was he shouting about?'

'I dunno.' Powell responded hastily. 'I, uh, wanted no part of the argument they were having, so I went out for a walk.'

'In the pitch black? It would have been after midnight when you went for a stroll.' Watkins said.

'No, it was a full moon that night.'

Fagan smiled. 'No Dillon. On that night it was pissing it down with rain. We have a taxi driver to confirm this. He said he picked you up outside the gates of the Agincourt hotel on the road to Monmouth. He said you were all soaked through.'

Powell's solicitor released a snort of derision. 'So let me get this straight, DI Fagan. You're going on the word of a taxi driver for a weather report.'

'I'm sure it's only a case of checking with the Met Office to confirm this.'

'Frome thirty years ago?' The solicitor shook his head. 'You must be desperate if you think a jury is going to believe the twaddle you've presented us with this afternoon.'

Fagan ignored the solicitor. 'What was the argument about Dillon?'

Powell chewed on his lip.

'Did you see Andrea Jones arguing with Alex?'

'What?'

'You heard me Dillon. Did you see them having an argument?'

'Yeah, maybe.' Powell grabbed his inhaler again, shoving it into his mouth.

'Did Alex assault Andrea?'

'They were arguing.' Powell gasped.

'What about?'

'I can't remember. They were arguing about stuff.'

'Stuff?'

'Stop doing this, will you!' Powell shouted. 'I didn't fucking murder anyone, okay.'

Fagan and Watkins exchanged looks.

'Who said anything about murdering anyone, Dillon?' Fagan asked calmly. 'All I asked was if Alex and Andrea were arguing.'

Powell stared back like a terrified child. 'I mean, didn't see anything. Look, for the tenth fucking time, it was thirty years ago. Jesus, I was probably off my head that night on coke.' He clutched his inhaler, sucking the life out of it.

'As you can see, DI Fagan, this interrogation is clearly putting my client under unnecessary stress.' The solicitor complained.

Fagan sat back, folding his arms. Considering his next question. 'Very popular back in the nineties, weren't you, Dillon?'

Dillon put his inhaler down. 'Yeah, I suppose.'

'Three number one hits. You must have made a lot of money?'

He shrugged. 'I made a few quid.'

'They still play your songs on the radio. Which means you still get royalties.'

'It tides me over. I can still afford the little luxuries in life.'

'You used to have girls running after you. Isn't that what one of your pop videos depicts? You running down the road with a hoard of young girls behind you. What was the song called?'

'Screaming hearts?' Powell replied. 'And yes, I had an army of fans back then. And yes, many of them were very young. But that doesn't make me a pervert, Di Fagan. You think this is my first rodeo when it comes to this sort of thing? I get at least fifty letters a month from women who have accused me of all kinds of shit.'

'So it would seem.' Fagan said. 'In 2013, you were arrested under Operation Yewtree, which was set up following the Jimmy Savile scandal.'

'DI Fagan.' The solicitor said firmly. 'I needn't remind you that you cannot question my client regarding a past allegation. I will also point out that my client cooperated with Yewtree. He was questioned and released without charge. And now that you have raised a past allegation, I am stopping this interview.' The solicitor stood up.

Fagan studied Powell's expression, which was one of relief. They both left the interview room.

Watkins stared at Fagan. 'You fucked up, boss.'

'On purpose.'

'On purpose?' Watkins repeated, pointing towards the door. 'That twat of a solicitor will have our guts for garters because we mentioned a past allegation.'

'It was me that mentioned Yewtree, not you, Sean. I'm the lead interviewer. I will take full responsibility.'

'All the evidence we he have could have put him away. The diary, Vicky's statement, plus what Alex's mother said could have resulted in a conviction.'

'Sean, did you hear what Powell said?'

Watkins answered with a blank expression.

'He said I didn't murder anyone. Until he said that we didn't mention the murder of Andrea Jones. Which means he must have witnessed Andrea's murder. He's terrified the others might turn against him and blame the murder on him. Dillon is still very much in our sights for rape and sexual assault. All I have done is give him enough time.'

'To do what?'

'Contact the others and warn them.' Fagan stood up. 'Come on, we'll regroup and analyse the interviews given by Mercury, Jordan, and Powell. We should get a good idea of what bullshit yarn Charlotte is going to make up. And Mitchell, when we bring him in for questioning.'

CHAPTER 27

Newport Central Police Station – 5:24pm

'What are you doing?' Watkins asked.

Fagan scrubbed the whiteboard. 'Wiping the slate clean.' He scrawled three names. 'We now have statements from Jordan, Mercury, and Powell. I want to review them to see if we can use any of what they said against Charlotte and Mitchell when we interview them. Although their so-called memories are a little vague, Jordan, Mercury and Powell have all admitted to being at the studio. The night Andrea Jones was murdered. They have all stated that Alex, her dad, Andrea, Charlotte and Mitchell were also at the studio. But they're also saying they weren't present when it was kicking off. Mercury even threw Mitchell under the bus, stating he was shouting the loudest. All three interviewees have also stated they went back to London with Charlotte and Mitchell. Alex, her dad, and Andrea stayed at the studio. Let's concentrate on Jordan. In the interview he seemed to get frustrated. Until a certain point we don't mention the word murder. And then Jordan blurts out, *I didn't witness any bloody murder.*'

'That maybe so, boss. But we mentioned the fact that a body had been found. Jordan is not that stupid,' Watkins said.

'Fair enough. When we mentioned the mother turning up at the hotel, Jordan went on the attack. He ran her down, accusing her of wanting to profit from her daughter when she became famous. Yesterday, Alex's mother admitted that when Alex found fame, she tried to reconnect, hoping to cash in. But Alex's father put a restraining order on her. From what I gathered yesterday, she was a woman full of regret. She admitted to being a terrible mother. But when Abbey turned up at her door, she suddenly switched roles, becoming a concerned mother. Abbey told her everything about the sexual abuse she had endured. The maternal instinct kicked in and she swung into action. First, she contacts Alex's dad and tries to tell him what's been going on. He doesn't want to know, but he attacks the mother for having contact with Abbey. Jordan was trying to deflect everything we were throwing at him.'

'He wasn't too keen in revealing Alex's location.' Watkins pointed out.

'She's at the end of her life, plus she's about to release her last album later this week. A lot of money is involved there. One last money train before she dies.'

'It's all about profit, boss.'

Fagan nodded. 'If we can prove that one of them murdered Andrea Jones, then we can at least charge Jordan with perverting the course of justice. Despite the fact he says he wasn't at the scene of crime. Think about it. Jordan said he went back to his office, but could still hear them arguing. He didn't try to go and intervene. The next thing you know, Andrea Jones is dead. Jordan must have known what happened that night. Let's consider that Alex murdered Andrea in a fit of rage. One of the others ran to the office and told Jordan. He then comes to see what has happened. There's a body on the floor. That's when a plan was devised to get rid of the body. Andrea meant nothing to any of them. She wasn't a star. We have witnesses to say she was the one that supplied Alex with drugs. So it would have been a problem solved with her out of the way.'

'And since we have no living relatives of Andrea, it's impossible for us to make any kind of DNA match. Has Andrea Jones got form for anything?'

'I've checked on Andrea's background earlier. She was

arrested for shoplifting in 1984. But that's it. There's nothing else.'

'Okay, so moving onto Mercury. He seemed a little more engaging didn't he. His personality was the complete opposite of Jordan's. He was open with us. Within seconds of the interview starting, Mercury referrers to Andrea Jones as the murder victim. But like Jordan, he says he wasn't there when they carried on arguing at the studio. He went back to his office after they had left the Agincourt.'

'But he could still hear them shouting. And says Mitchell was shouting the loudest. It was almost like Mercury wanted to put Mercury in the frame.'

'He called him a nasty thug.' Fagan said. 'I had the distinct impression Mercury wasn't all that fond of Mitchell.' He glanced at the whiteboard. 'I'll tell you what struck me as odd about both interviews. It's when we mentioned the Brit award being found with the body. Both Jordan and Mercury expressed surprise and puzzlement when we mentioned this.'

'If it was Mitchell who disposed of Andrea Jones' body, he didn't' tell them the how and the where.' Watkins suggested.

'No, he didn't. They may have been present at the murder, but they weren't witness to the disposal of the body. I'm guessing whoever disposed of the body only gave them partial information. The studio was closed for two weeks and Jordan fired the staff who were working there at the time.'

'There were probably staff who may have known Andrea Jones, boss.'

Fagan nodded. 'And would have questioned her sudden disappearance. That's why Jordan fired everyone. We need a second interview with him. Find out the exact reason he closed the studio and fired everyone.'

'That's going to piss him off big time.'

'Exactly.' Fagan smiled. 'let's move on to Dillon. As with Jordan and Mercury we didn't mention anyone being murdered. But out of the blue, he denies murdering anyone.'

'He reckons he went for a walk to get away from the argument.'

'He claimed it was a full moon that night. But we know it was pissing it down with rain. He also admits they were all arguing with Alex in the kitchen of the Agincourt. But he sticks to the argument being about Abbey's suicide and nothing else.'

'He didn't mention the sexual abuse allegations made by Alex's mother when she gained access to the hotel.. Plus, his lawyer intervened every time we mentioned sexual abuse.'

Fagan recalled the interview. 'Powell said, *I didn't murder anyone, okay.* That indicates to me he's terrified the others will blame everything on him. So we have to consider he witnessed the murder, or he is the murderer. He was at the studio with the rest of them.'

'The problem we have here, boss, is they can all deny they were at the murder scene. Three of them have already have. I'm guessing Charlotte will do the same. Since Abbey and her father are dead, that leaves Alex and Mitchell the only witnesses. Alex is on her deathbed.'

'Which leaves Mitchell as our only suspect.' Fagan stared at Mitchell's name. 'Since the discovery of Andrea's body something has been gnawing at me.'

'What's that, boss?'

Fagan looked at Watkins. 'That's the trouble. I can't figure it out. We have a body found with a Brit award and a Rolex. We have witnesses to a to the murder of Andrea Jones. But none of them will admit to it. Any of them could have murdered her.' Fagan stopped in mid-stream. You know, we haven't considered the possibility that Alex's father could have snapped and murdered Andrea.'

Watkins nodded enthusiastically. 'He already knew that his youngest daughter committed suicide. He must have known Andrea was supplying with Alex drugs. It had been a traumatic night, starting with the Brit Awards.'

210

Brooks entered the incident room. 'I just spoken to CSI, sir. They've excavated the garden at the back of the house that Alex's father owned.' He shook his head, frowning. 'There's nothing there but a headstone.'

'That's another thing that's been bugging me.' Fagan said. 'The headstone with Alex and Abbey's name on it. We know Abbey's dead. But Alex is still alive. Why would he have a headstone with her name on it?'

'What did you make of Dillon's solicitor?' Watkins asked.

'Typical solicitor.' Fagan shrugged.

'But he mentioned several weaknesses in the case against Dillon. He said the diary that Abbey wrote could have been a fabrication. And that Vicky could have made the whole thing up. Then there's the signatures with dates, but no evidence to suggest that Dillon shared a hotel room with any of the girls. Why bring these up now during a suspect interview? Any decent solicitor would have presented this during the trial.'

Fagan thought about Watkins' theory. 'He doesn't want this to go to trial. So he'll try his best to dismantle any evidence we have in its early stages. He'll go to the crown prosecution service and demand the case to be dropped.' He puffed out his cheeks. 'I guess the next step now is to see what Charlotte has to say.' Fagan pulled his buzzing phone from his pocket, glancing at the screen.

UNKNOWN NUMBER

'Hello?'

'Is that Detective inspector Marc Fagan?' A woman's voice enquired.

'It is. Who am I speaking to?'

'It Alexandria Xavier.'

Fagan glanced across at Watkins, waving his free hand before pointing at the phone on Watkins' desk. He tapped the louder speaker icon on his phone. Before activating his voice

211

recorder app 'Hello Miss Xavier, thank you for calling.'

Watkins grabbed the phone handset and phoned through to the tech department, ordering a trace on Fagan's phone.

'I understand you have been trying to reach me.'

'We have indeed. Is there any chance you could come in for an interview?'

'I think you know what the answer is going to be, DI Fagan.'

'Can I call you Alex?'

'Yes, you may.'

'Alex, you need to come in to the station to talk to us. We need to find out what happened to Andrea Jones.'

'DI Fagan, I have just a few weeks left to live. I am bedridden. What do you hope to achieve by asking me to recall an event I have been trying to forget for the past thirty years?'

'And what event would that be?' Fagan asked back.

'Come on, DI Fagan. You've been trying to contact me because you believe I am responsible for the murder of Andrea Jones.'

Fagan looked across at Watkins, who was clutching the handset to his ear. 'No luck yet.' He mouthed before twirling his hand, encouraging Fagan to keep talking.

'Well, I guess I'll come out and say it, since you won't come in for an interview. Did you murder Andrea Jones on the night if the 25th June 1993?'

'Yes.' Alex answered.

'You're admitting you murdered her.'

'Yes.'

'Why?'

A moment of silence followed. 'I don't know why. There were many things that happened that night that led to her death. The Brit Awards were too much for me. I was at the top of my fame. Struggling to deal with the fame. The drugs became too much. Andrea would get me anything I wanted.'

'How long did you know Andrea?'

'We'd been friends since school.'

'Do you know if she had any family?'

'No, Andrea was an only child. Her mother died twenty years ago and was cremated. I paid for the funeral costs.'

'That's very kind of you.' Fagan looked across at Watkins.

'Keep her talking.' He whispered.

'It was the least I could do after what I did to her daughter.'

'Alex, tell me what happened that night.'

'It's impossible for me to remember everything, Inspector Fagan. I was already high from doing cocaine earlier on in the evening. I just about remember stumbling on stage and giving a slurred speech after they presented me with my Brit award.'

'That's when Charlotte burst onto the stage and assaulted you.'

'Yes.'

'Why didn't you press charges?'

'I was in a horrible place, DI Fagan. You could say I deserved it. I'd been seeing Dillon behind her back.'

'Surely, she must have known about it. The press had been speculating for months.'

'Yes, but Charlotte's career was taking a nosedive. She was jealous of me.'

'Ok, so moving forwards a few hours. You went back to the Agincourt hotel, did you not?'

'Yes.'

'Where you encountered your mother?'

'Yes, my mother snuck into the hotel.'

'What did she say to you?'

'She told me what had happened to Abbey. That she'd committed suicide.'

'The thing is Alex.' Fagan called up the magazine article on his laptop. 'According to an interview you gave nearly ten years ago. You claim you didn't find out your sister committed suicide until a few months after the Brit Awards.'

Several seconds of silence followed. 'DI Fagan, I cannot

remember every tiny detail. I didn't even want to be interviewed by that magazine. I wasn't particularly enthusiastic about the interview.'

'I spoke to your mother yesterday. She expressed regret abandoning you when you were young.'

'Of course she would. I have just released a single. I'm about to release a new album. It's obvious she wants to profit from this.'

'Your mother also told me she'd revealed to you the sexual abuse Abbey endured at the Agincourt Hotel and the studio. And that Dillon Powell, Charlotte West and Andrea Jones were all involved. Along with your manager, Frankie Jordon.'

Again, the line went silent for a considerable length of time. 'Abbey was a fantasist, DI Fagan.'

'A fantasist?' Fagan remarked. 'I have a detailed journal written in her own words that suggests otherwise.'

'Abbey was very jealous of me. The fame and the money. Even though I included her in my life, it wasn't enough for her. She wanted to be me. She begged me to let her go on tour with me when she was old enough. When I introduced her to Dillon, she became obsessed with him. She would talk for hours about how she was going to marry Dillon and live happily ever after.'

'But you were having an affair with Dillon. She was old enough to read the papers. She must have suspected something.'

'Dillon assured Abbey that there was nothing going on between us.'

Fagan looked across at Watkins, who shook his head.

'Still nothing, boss.'

Fagan sensed frustration mounting. 'Alex, this is all very confusing. You just said that you murdered Andrea Jones. Why?'

'I told you, DI Fagan, I cannot remember every little detail of that evening. You'll have to forgive me if my responses are limited.'

'Who was there when you murdered Andrea?'

'My father?' Alex replied.

'Just your father?'

'Yes, the others had left the studio and gone back to London. It was just me, Andrea, and my dad.'

'Why did you stay at the studio? Why didn't you go back to the hotel?'

'I was planning to.'

'But?'

'I got into an argument with Andrea. I just about remember hitting her with the Brit award I had been presented with.'

'Did Andrea fall straight away, or did she put up a fight?'

'DI Fagan, I have confessed to the murder of Andrea Jones. This is what you wanted, isn't it?'

'What I want, Alex, is for you to come in, or at least tell us where you are so that we can interview you properly. With a legal representative.'

'I'll be dead before any of that happens, DI Fagan. I suggest you take what I have said as my confession. The others weren't present when I murdered Andrea. I'm sorry, but that's all I'm prepared to say.' The line went dead.

Fagan gawped at the phone screen before looking at Watkins. 'Anything?'

'No.'

'What the fuck is going on? In all my years as a serving detective I have never heard such a bag of bollocks. She phones up, confesses to the murder of Andrea Jones, then just hangs up on us. Something isn't right.' Fagan called up Alex's Twitter page and played the video she released a few days earlier. He then played the recording on his phone.

'They sound the same.' Brooks said.

'Yeah, they do. But something still isn't right. Somehow we're having the wool pulled over our eyes. The lot of them

215

have lied through their arses. And now Alex phones up and delivers a half arsed confession she's expecting us to believe.'

Watkins' phone pinged. 'Charlotte West has just arrived.'

'We'll have to analyse the recording I just made later. In the meantime, let's see what bullshit story she's about to give us.'

CHAPTER 28

6:42pm

'For the recording, could you state your full name?'

'Charlotte Ann West.'

'The reason you've been today arrested Charlotte, is because of sexual abuse allegations made against you,' Fagan explained.

'No comment.' West replied before Fagan had the chance to say anything else.

'You do not have to say anything.'

'No comment.' West cut Fagan off in midstream.

'Charlotte, you need to listen to me. I need to finish your caution before the interview begins. Otherwise we won't be able to continue.'

West sat with her arms folded. She glanced at the ceiling before looking towards a mirrored observation window.

'You do not have to say anything. But, it may harm your defence if you do not mention, when questioned, something which you later rely on in court. Anything you do say may be given in evidence. Do you understand?'

West studied her manicured nails.

'Charlotte, do you understand the caution you've been given?' Watkins asked.

'Yes!' West shouted. 'let's fucking get on with it, can we.'

'Do you know a woman called Vicky James?'

'No fucking comment.' West seethed.

'Did you know Alex Xavier's younger sister, Abbey Xavier?'

West glared at Fagan for several moments. 'No comment.'

'I spoke to Vicky. She claimed that you and Dillon Powell

engaged in sexual activity with her when she was eleven years old.'

'No comment, no fucking comment.' West thundered. She repeated the phrase several times over.

Fagan put his hand up. 'Charlotte, stop this behaviour now.' He warned in a firm tone. 'Or I will be forced to stop this interview. You'll be rearrested in a few days when you've calmed down. It's your choice.'

West inhaled before nodding.

'Now I'll ask again. Do you know Vicky James?'

'Probably, if I saw her face. I take it you're talking about someone who I was supposed to have known years back. Don't tell me, someone who used to hang around the studio.'

'Vicky won a talent competition at her school. Dillon Powell was the judge. Vicky claimed he raped her at an orphanage before inviting her out to the studio. Vicky also states that you engaged in sexual activity with her. Another woman called Andrea Jones has also been named. A lot of the abuse took place at the Agincourt hotel.'

'Huh, that fucking druggie bitch.' West mocked. 'What has she been blabbering about now?'

For the first time in the investigation Fagan sensed a wind of change regarding the murder. 'Charlotte, we believe that Andrea Jones was murdered on the 25th June 1993 at Vine Road music studios.'

West stared back, looking confused. 'Ok, well, the fucking bitch deserved it, probably.'

'How do you mean?'

'She wasn't a singer or anything. She just hung around the studio. Used to get Alex drugs.'

'Did you know her well?'

'Fairly well, yes.'

'According to Vicky James, on one occasion you invited her up to your hotel room. She said you ate some food and listened to some songs. You also gave Vicky a large quantity of alcohol. You and Andrea Jones engaged in a sexual act in front of her. You then got up and led her over to the bed. Both you and Andrea jones sexually assaulted her.'

'She's a lying sack of shit.' West launched another rant. 'I never touched anyone. It's something I could never do. I know where are you're going with this. You're fucking trying to lump me in with that twat Jimmy Savile. Trying to make me out to be a pervert. Well, for your information, it's impossible for me to be like that.'

'Why is that, Charlotte?' Watkins asked.

'Because I'm a fucking woman, you cretin!'

'What's that got to do with anything?' Fagan asked.

'Women aren't capable of being paedophiles. It's not in our nature to do that kind of thing. Paedophilia is something only blokes are capable of. Us girls have a maternal instinct to protect children. Not to do them harm.'

'You ever heard or Aron Miller Charlotte.'

West took a few seconds to respond. 'Wasn't he the kid murdered during lockdown?'

Fagan nodded. 'I was part of the investigation involving Aron's disappearance. When police seized electronic devices belonging to Aron's stepmother and stepsister. They found video footage of both of them sexually abusing Aron. So you see, Charlotte, women are just as capable of doing the things men are capable of. In fact, there are a string of women who have taken part in the murder of young women and children. Rose West, Myra Hindley and most recently a nurse from Hereford convicted of murdering seven premature babies.'

'That's different.'

Fagan stared back, amazed at West's level of ignorance. 'Different, how?'

West summoned an answer. 'Because they weren't related to their victims.'

'And you weren't related to Vicky James, or Abbey Xavier.' Watkins added. 'So cut the wounded soldier act, Charlotte.

We have a detailed statement from Vicky saying that you, Dillon Powell and Andrea Jones took part in sexual activity on her twelfth birthday.'

'I didn't touch that bitch, okay. She's fucking lying to squeeze money from me. She's just like the rest of them.'

'The rest of them?' Fagan said.

'People have been crawling out of the woodwork over the years. Claiming all kinds of nasty shit. Ever since Jimmy Savile died, I have been hounded loads of times. From people expecting me to hand over compensation.'

'How many people have been in contact with you?'

'Loads.' West answered. 'So many I've lost fucking count.'

'Have you ever handed money over to anyone?'

West hesitated, unsure of how to respond.

'Charlotte, have you ever given money to anyone who's accused you of sexual abuse?'

'Yes, okay!' West exploded. 'Is that what you wanted to hear?'

West's solicitor looked at her before scribbling notes.

'Who did you give money to?'

'This fucking woman, don't ask me what her name was because I can't remember.'

'How long ago did you give her the money?'

West ran her hand through her long, blonde hair. 'I dunno. Must have been during lockdown. When the entire country came to a stop.'

'How much did you give this woman?'

West shrugged. 'Couple of grand, I can't remember.'

Fagan decided to change the tempo of the interview. 'Do you see anyone from the good old days anymore, Charlotte?'

'What do you mean?'

'Do you ever see Dillon or have contact with your old manager?'

'No, I haven't seen those twats in years.'

Fagan recalled what Mercury had claimed. 'Your manager

claimed he has lunch with you a couple of time a year.'

'That queer twat is lying. I haven't seen him in twenty years. He gets most of the royalties when they play my records on the radio. All I get is a shitty trickle of royalties every year.'

'Did you have a fallout with Mercury?'

'Yeah. Several years ago we had an argument about relaunching my career. Mickey said my music wasn't popular anymore. It would cost too much to relaunch my career.'

'You were best friends with Alex X for a while during the nineties?' Watkins remarked.

'Not really. Mickey and Frankie made us team up. They knew they'd make more money from duets. I wanted a solo career. And then they had us do a track with Dillon for Children in Need.'

'When did you find out Dillon was having an affair with Alex?'

'I knew about their little game for months.'

'Game?' Fagan said.

'You know. The way celebrities play games with the media. They started fucking each other because they both knew it would make them more popular. The newspapers loved that kind of thing back then. Every other week it was a case of was Alex screwing Dillon behind my back.'

'Made you very jealous.' Fagan suggested.

'Of course it did. Alex was topping the charts with her songs. Dillon was the perfect boy next door.'

'And you.'

West inhaled. 'I was a flash in the pan. At least that's what Mickey said I was. I released a couple of decent tracks on my own. But they weren't as popular as Alex or Dillon. Mind you, Dillon soon went off a cliff. I don't know why Mercury kept on promoting him. Perhaps it's was because he was obsessed with Dillon.'

'Obsessed, how?'

'Mickey was totally in love with Dillon. The amount of

times Dillon told me that Mickey had tried to get him into bed. In the end Dillon stopped making decent tracks and Mercury dumped him. The 90s were all about the boy bands. Take That, Oasis, Coldplay and the Manic Street Preachers had established themselves. Then along came Westlife. Dillon was outgunned and outnumbered. I remember him having a punch up with Robbie Williams in a Soho nightclub. Robbie told Dillon that his time was up and she should crawl back to the shithole of a housing estate he grew up on.'

'Tell us about the night you assaulted Alex.'

West grinned, recalling the moment. 'Bitch deserved a good slapping. Not only for shagging Dillon behind my back, but for also wasting her life away. She was so drugged up most of the time.'

'After the award ceremony, you all went back to the Agincourt hotel just outside Monmouth.'

'I didn't want to go back to that stupid hotel. But Mickey insisted on it. He said he had some new song lyrics for me to look over. I should have known he was full of it.'

'We have a witness that states you were seen arguing in the hotel's kitchen.'

West scratched the back of her head. 'If you say so.' She yawned. 'It was thirty years ago.'

'After which you went back to the studio.'

West shook her head. 'No, actually I went back to my room at the hotel.'

'Did anyone see you returning to your room?'

'I don't know.' West barked. 'Jesus fucking Christ, it was thirty years ago.'

'Dillon, Jordan and your former manager insist you went back to the studio with them. And that you were all arguing with Alex.'

'They're all fucking liars!' West screamed. 'I went back to my hotel room. I had fuck all to do with any murder. Ask Andrea if you don't believe me.'

222

'You mean Alex.'

West massaged her forehead. 'What?'

'You mean ask Alex,' Fagan said calmly.

'Yeah.' West stuttered.

Fagan stared at West for several seconds. 'Okay, I think we're done here. Interview ended.' Fagan stopped the digital recorder and tapped the stop icon on his phone screen.

'That's it.' West stated. 'You've fucking arrest me for something I haven't done and now you're chucking me out.'

'We need to investigate these allegations further to establish the truth.'

'Yes, you fucking do.' West sneered. 'These bastards are lying, and when I prove it, I'm suing all of you bastards for wrongful arrest and slander.'

'You're free to go, Miss West.'

West didn't hesitate in standing and marching out of the interview room.

'That is one bitter and twisted woman.'

'Why did you stop the interview?' Watkins asked.

Fagan looked at him. 'Remember, I said that something has been niggling me since the body was discovered.'

'Yeah.'

'Miss potty mouth West has just landed herself in the shit. Plus she said something that has totally thrown this investigation sidewards. When we first mentioned Andrea she said, what's that druggie bitch been saying now? Then she said, ask Andrea if you don't believe me.' Fagan smiled briefly. 'She the loose cannon in this investigation.'

'What do you think it means?'

'I don't know.' Fagan sighed. 'And that's the thing that's nagging me. Why hasn't the coroner been in touch?'

'Don't know, boss. I'll give them a bell and find out.'

Fagan checked his phone, that had just buzzed. He studied the message. 'I need to answer this text.' Fagan glanced at the clock on the wall. It's been a long day. 'Let's pick this up first thing.'

Watkins gathered his notes and left the interview room.

Fagan hit the speed dial and waited for an answer. 'Jamie, I just got your text. Thanks for sending me that taxi receipt.'

'No worries, mate. As you can see, I even got Charlotte and Dillon to autograph it for me. When we arrived in London, I asked politely. I think they just wanted rid of me, so they signed my receipt book.'

'What is this other shit you're babbling on about? I don't understand any of it.'

'Tyler has been analysing the video that Alex uploaded and the single she's just released. His company specialises trawling the internet for anomalies.'

'Jamie, I'm in the middle of a murder investigation. If this is some kind of scifi Star Wars bullshit, then I'll arrest you both for wasting police time.'

'Fagan, I wouldn't do this to you, mate. Tyler has been doing this for years. He knows his stuff. Remember when we were kids? Tyler was the one into computers.'

Fagan studied the text. 'Right, I'm trusting you now, Jamie. This is just between me, you and Tyler, okay?'

'Yeah, sure.'

'I'm sending you a recording of a conversation I had with Alex X.'

'No way. I thought she was on her deathbed. That's what the news has been going on about over the last few days.'

'I want you to send the audio recording to Tyler for him to listen to. Tell him to get back to me if he finds anything. Do not tell anyone about this, understand.'

'Yeah no worries mate. I won't tell a soul.'

CHAPTER   29

Day 5
Newport central police station – 9:43am

'Sit down please, DI Fagan.'

Fagan could sense straight away he was about to have another confrontation with his superior.

'When I told you to focus on investigating the body at the back of Vine Road Music studios, I meant just that. So, could you explain why you have gone off on a tangent?'

'I haven't gone off on a tangent, sir. While investigating the discovery, we have stumbled across several other crimes.'

'I've had to deal with Dillon Powell's solicitor threatening legal action. I have also had an unpleasant conversation with Charlotte West, also threatening legal action. Could you also tell me why you've had one of your officers looking into Operation Fallen Star and Yewtree?'

'Sir, I believe we have uncovered much more than a murder here. I have evidence that sexual abuse took place at Vine Road Music Studios and at the Agincourt hotel. I believe Alex Xavier was told her younger sister Abbey was raped by Dillon Powell and Charlotte West. A friend of Alex, Andrea Jones, was also complicit in the abuse of other girls at the studio.'

'Did you receive a phone call from Alex Xavier yesterday?'

'Yes.'

'And did she not confess to murdering Andrea Jones at the music studio in 1993?'

'I wouldn't call it a confession, sir. It was just a phone call. Alex wasn't exactly generous with the information she gave us. She wouldn't give a reason why she murdered Andrea Jones.'

'Why did you order one of your team to dig up files from Fallen Star and Yewtree?'

Fagan knew he had to lie to continue the conversation. 'When we contacted the press, we kept to the facts. We didn't expect someone was going to march in here and make sexual abuse allegations. What were we supposed to do, ignore this woman? My officers acted within the law. We also came across another police operation that Dillon was part of, operation Sara. I have been doing my own research before you dragged me in here. According to a statement given by a serving detective the police investigation was flawed. Many of the girls who came forward to give evidence were dismissed.' This detective believed several serving police officers may have been part of the grooming gang. But for some reason, the file on operation Sara has been restricted. Do you want to know whose signature is on the form? Chief Constable Bob Benson, your grandfather.'

Griffiths stared back

'When Vicky James came in, I had my team look into Operation Yewtree. That's when we came across Operation Falling Star. And that's when we discovered that Dillon Powell had been arrested in 2013.'

Griffiths hesitated before getting up and walking towards the window. 'I was with the London Met, when Savile died. We were inundated with allegations from hundreds of women. The public believe that there were around six hundred lines of enquiry regarding Savile.' Griffiths glanced at Fagan. 'There were close to two thousand lines of enquiry from all over the country. And that was just Savile.'

'We had a similar experience in Liverpool. Women coming forward, saying they'd been abused by many celebrities, both alive and dead.'

'Over the past ten years, there have been over fifteen

thousand allegations made against various celebrities. It's never ending. The BBC is still at the centre of many of these allegations. The recent scandal involving their top news reader has showed sexual abuse is still rife in the entertainment industry.'

'What about Operation Falling Star?'

'It was established after police from several constituencies across Wales received a mass of reports. Again, it was in the wake of Savile's death. There were accusation against footballers, rugby players, Assembly members and other celebrities.'

'Including Dillon Powell and Charlotte West.' Fagan added.

'You have to understand, DI Fagan. Yewtree was unprecedented. Allegations are still flooding in. The police are overwhelmed. We haven't got the resources to peruse every allegation. It would take an army of officers to look to everything. Hundreds of celebrities all taking action against the police. The system would just collapse.'

'So the solution is to brush everything under the carpet, is it, sir? Including sealing away files that may suggest police officers in the South Wales valleys were involved in the abuse of young girls. Pretend that nothing is going on.'

'What did I just say to you? It would take a bloody army to look into everything.'

'We have information that could put Powell away for over ten years. How can you sit there and justify all that's happened by saying we simply haven't got the men to pursue this?'

'And what if you're wrong, DI Fagan? Where does that put Gwent police? If the woman you interviewed is just another so-called victim out for money.'

'I interviewed this woman myself, sir. She didn't come across as a fraud. That's the problem Yewtree has created. I'm not saying that every accusation is genuine. But we can't ignore the ones that are. This isn't some ninety-year-old celebrity. This is someone who is still in control of his faculties.

Who knows full well the crimes he's committed.'

'Which is more important here, DI Fagan? The body at the back of the studio, or a woman who could be out for money. You are to proceed with the original investigation.'

'And drop the case against Dillon Powell. Is that what you're saying?'

Griffiths stared back.

'Here's an idea, sir. Why can't you have DI Saddler investigate the allegations made against Powell? At least we can get a result.'

'It could take hundreds of man hours just to get a conviction.'

'We can't just dismiss the allegations, for Christ's sake. We have to pursue this.'

DI Fagan, you cannot cherry pick your assignments.'

'Sir, it's you that's doing the cherry picking.'

'Do you or do you not have a confession from Alexandria Xavier regarding the murder of Andrea Jones?'

'We have a statement, but not enough for us to pursue a murder enquiry against her. Look at what we are dealing with. A body found at the back of a music studio. A Brit award was found with the remains, along with a Rolex watch. That has an inscription on the back with Andrea Jones' name. She is another person who's been named in allegations of sexual abuse. It first glance it looks as if Alex had a motive for murder.'

'Why is that?'

'Abbey's sister committed suicide in May 1993. Alex didn't find out about her suicide until a month after. Abbey also wrote a diary implicating Andrea Jones in sexual abuse. Until yesterday it was my belief that Alex may have murdered Andrea Jones. We have a witness that places several suspects at the Agincourt hotel the night of the murder. We have another significant witness. A man by the name of Alun Mitchell. He is due in for questioning today. He owns the company that manages security at the music studio. He was also Alex's former minder when she was famous. Mitchell has form for attempted murder over forty years ago. I also believe he could be a person of interest in another murder that took place in the late seventies.'

Griffiths scratched the back of his head.

'Can you see what I'm up against, sir? Whoever murdered the woman before removing her head and hands and dumping her at the back of the studio didn't expect her to be found. Until two years ago, the area at the back of the music studio had a protection order. Because the field was a peat bog, which is protected under law. However, the current owner got permission to drain the bog and build on it. We put out that press release asking for anyone to come forward regarding the body we found. Not because we were expecting other people to offer information on other crimes.'

'Very well, DI Fagan. This is how you are to proceed. You will carry on investigating the body at the back of the studio. However, should anyone else come in regarding allegations of sexual abuse at the studio, you are to log their name. And let Yewtree handle it.'

Fagan glared back at Griffiths. 'Yes, sir.'

'Don't forget, you are under investigation yourself. Regarding your conduct with Benny Nelson during the Rebecca Jenkins murder.' Griffiths paused. Dismissed, DI Fagan.'

CHAPTER 30

'Good morning Mr Mitchell.' Fagan shook Mitchell's hand. 'I'm DI Marc Fagan, this is Constable Andrew Brooks. We appreciate you coming down here to speak with us.'

'I'm here voluntarily, Inspector Fagan. Isn't that what you asked?'

Fagan nodded. 'Indeed, it is. Can I ask why you are here on your own?'

'What do you mean?'

'No legal representative.' Brooks mentioned.

'You invited me for an interview. Why would I need a legal representative?' Mitchell replied with a confident tone.

Fagan smiled back. 'You're right, Mr Mitchell, this is just an interview.'

Mitchell glanced at his Rolex watch. 'Let's get this over with. I have more important things to get on with.'

Yes, the celebratory function tonight at the Agincourt hotel. Celebrating the fiftieth anniversary of the studio. You must have a lot of fond memories.'

Mitchell cracked a smile. 'I've had some good times at the studio. If it wasn't for Frankie Jordan, I wouldn't have got where I am today.'

'What about Richard Bishop?' Fagan asked, to gauge a reaction.

Mitchell folded his arms, letting out a snort of derision. 'Why would that little shithead be connected with this interview, DI Fagan?'

'Didn't Bishop lend you ten thousand pounds so that you

230

could set up your security business?'

'Yes.'

'And you've yet to give him that money back.'

'Bishop made enough money in his day. He may cry poverty, but he's not exactly on the dole.'

'Wasn't it Bishop that introduced you to Frankie Jordan?'

Mitchell nodded. 'Yes, it was.'

'This was after you served time in prison with him.'

'Is this why you've invited me in today, Inspector Fagan? To interrogate me about my past. Yes, I served time in prison, and I deeply regret my actions.' Mitchell sounded agitated. 'Now why don't you skip the history lesson and get to why you have called me here today?'

'You're right. I apologise Mr Mitchell.' Fagan looked down at his notes. 'I'm sure you know by now police found a body at the back of Vine Road music studios.'

'I am aware of this, yes.'

'We believe the remains found is woman called Andrea Jones.'

Mitchell stared back, perplexed. 'Andrea Jones?'

'There seems to be a lot of mystery surrounding the body. Which was buried with a Brit Awara and a Rolex watch.' Fagan glanced at the Rolex Mitchell was wearing. 'The Brit award belonged to Alex X. What we don't understand is why the award was buried with the body. You were Alex's bodyguard during the time she was famous?'

'I was,' Mitchells stated.

'Tell us about Alex.' Brooks requested.

'She was a live wire. Full of life, at the time.'

'At the time?'

'Yes, when I first met her, she was clean. Wasn't into drugs. Her manager had just signed her up and was touting her all over the place. Promoting her to be the next big pop star. When I met Jordan, I explained to him that if Alex was going to be big on the music scene, then she was going to need a bodyguard.'

'Did you have any kind of experience as a minder?' Fagan asked.

Mitchell smiled. 'No, but I knew how to use my fists. It came in handy. Alex had more than her fair share of over the top fans. She was a good-looking girl. Loads of people wanting to meet her, to be part of her life.'

'Including Andrea Jones.'

'I knew she was trouble from the word go. I told Jordan that he should try to distance himself from her. But he wouldn't listen, so Andrea stayed with Alex. She would bring the drugs in and make sure Alex was kept happy and high.'

'What do you think Andrea got out of it?' Brooks asked.

'A life of luxury. Sex, drugs and rock and roll, take your pick.'

'What did Jordan think of her?'

'He never thought anything of her, besides the odd shag.'

'They were having a sexual relationship?' Fagan asked.

'Yeah. I suspect that's why Frankie kept her around. Andrea was a bit of a nympho. She was fucking everyone at the studio.'

'Did you ever have sex with her?'

'I was there as security Inspector Fagan, nothing else.' Mitchell paused. 'Yes, I have heard all the rumours.'

'Rumours?'

Mitchell grinned. 'Don't think I don't know why you've called me down here today. To find out about the rumours about that studio. For the record I would like to state that I never took part in any of that shit. I had a girlfriend.'

Fagan's curiosity kicked in. 'What shit would that be?'

'The underage sex that allegedly took place at the studio. Yes, there were loads of girls that used to visit. But I saw nothing. I already had a girlfriend.'

'What was your girlfriend's name?'

'Why did you need to know that?'

'You just said it yourself, Mr Mitchell. You weren't involved with any of the alleged underage sex. It would be useful for you if you could tell us the name of your girlfriend just in case we need to contact her.'

'I haven't seen her for decades. Jesus, we probably split up after a few months. I had a tonne of short-term relationships when I worked at the studio.'

'So this was just a short-term relationship. Where did you meet her?' Brooks asked.

Mitchell expressed frustration. 'In Monmouth somewhere. Probably at the Robin Hood, it used to be my local whenever I was at the studio.'

'So what was your girlfriend's name?' Fagan asked for a second time.

'Molly Lucas.' Mitchell replied.

Fagan jotted the name on his pad. 'And how long were you in a relationship with Molly?'

'Look, why have you dragged me down here today?'

'We haven't dragged you down here, Mr Mitchell. You just said you were here voluntarily.' Fagan glanced down at his notes. 'Let's talk about the night of the 25th of June, 1993. It was the night that Alex won the Brit award.'

'Huh, I remember that night very well,' Mitchell said.

'Why didn't you stop Charlotte West from assaulting Alex?'

'Because her manager, Mickey Mercury, told me not to intervene. He wanted it to happen.'

'He knew Charlotte was going to kick off?'

'Jordan and that queer, Mercury, knew Charlotte was going to give Alex a good belting. They set it up for the TV cameras.'

'So it was all staged.' Brooks said. 'Why?'

'Because Charlotte was on her way out. She pleaded with Mercury not to dump her. Charlotte hadn't had a number one in months. Both Alex and her were rivals. Even though they sang a few songs together, they hated each other's guts. Charlotte hated Alex because she was more popular. Alex hated Charlotte because she was common as muck. The moment Charlotte tumbled down the charts, Mercury wanted to dump her.'

'What happened after the award ceremony?' Fagan questioned.

'There was a lot of arguing backstage. Alex was off her face. I don't think she even felt the punch that Charlotte gave her. There was blood everywhere. She got it all over herself and her award. Frankie was sure Charlotte had broken her nose.'

'You all flew back to the Agincourt hotel by helicopter after the ceremony.'

'Yes.' Mitchell nodded. 'But Charlotte and Dillon Powell wanted to stay in London. Mercury had a go at Dillon. There was a load of people waiting for him back at the hotel reception room.'

'Why?'

'He was running a campaign about young girls being abused.' Mitchell thought for a moment. 'No means no.'

'We have a witness that saw you all in the kitchen of the Agincourt, arguing. Can you recall what the argument was about?'

'Alex's mother gained access to the hotel. She told Alex what had happened to her sister Abbey. Alex flew into a rage at her dad. I was in the reception hall watching a speech by the chief constable of South Wales police. He had just awarded Dillon a civilian commendation for his work on the No Means No campaign.'

'What happened?'

'The manager of the hotel came to me and said it was all kicking off in the kitchen. I followed him out and saw Alex fighting with her father.'

'Was Andrea Jones anywhere to be seen?'

Mitchell recalled the moment before nodding. 'Yeah, Andrea was there. The rest piled into the kitchen just after me.'

'This would be Charlotte, Powell, Mercury and Jordan?'

'Yes.'

'The head chef kicked you out of the kitchen and you carried on arguing outside.'

'Yeah, but it was pissing it down with rain. I didn't want a public show at the hotel, because the press were there. So I suggested we go back to the music studio and carry on with our conversation.'

'Mickey Mercury claims he went back to his office and could hear you shouting at Alex.'

'Huh, that fucking arse bandit would say that wouldn't he.' Mitchell gathered his thoughts. 'Yeah, I was shouting at them, but not for long. I went back to my office and call a taxi to take us back to London.'

'Why didn't Alex, her father or Andrea go back to London with you?'

'Alex's dad owned a house just outside Monmouth. He told me they were going back there.'

'So you left Alex, her dad, and Andrea at the studio. Who was locking up?'

'Alex's dad,' Mitchell answered.

Fagan looked down at his notes. 'Okay then, Mr Mitchell, thanks for coming in today.'

Mitchell stared back with a mildly shocked expression. 'That's it. You're not going to question me about anything else.'

'Should we?'

'No, of course not. I haven't done anything wrong.' Mitchell stood and marched out of the room.

Fagan stared at the whiteboard. 'This is all bollocks. None of them will confess to witnessing anything.'

'Course they're not, sir. It means a life term in prison for murder.' Brooks said.

'So we're back to square one.' Fagan glanced at the clock

235

on the wall. 'It's been another wasted morning on this. We'll have to wait on evidence to take this any further.'

A uniform entered the office. 'Sorry to bother you, sir. But there's a woman at the front desk claiming to have information about the body found at the back of the studio.'

Fagan peeled himself from his seat. 'Come on, I'll grab Sean. Let's see if this woman has anything interesting to say.' He looked at Brooks. 'Keep digging on this, Andrew. Something is bound to come up, eventually.'

A few minutes later, Fagan and Watkins were at the front desk. 'I'm DI Fagan, this is DS Watkins. You have information regarding the press release.'

A woman in her fifties stared back. 'Yes, I have something I wish to confess?'

Fagan glanced at Watkins. 'Confess?'

The woman nodded. 'I know what happened that night at the studio. I saw everything.'

'Could you tell us your name?'

'My name is Louise Kelly, but I have changed my name several times over the last thirty years.' The woman inhaled. 'My original name is Andrea Jones. I am her to tell you I witnessed the murder of Alexandria Xavier.'

Fagan stared back at the woman, too dumbfounded to speak.

CHAPTER 31

12:00pm

Fagan stared through the mirrored window of the interview room. The duty solicitor had taken over an hour to arrive. Fagan could tell they were both having an intense conversation.

'I don't get it, boss?' Watkins said in a bemused tone. 'How can she be Andrea Jones?'

'I don't know.' Fagan's tone was unemotional.

'All the evidence suggested it was Andrea Jones buried behind the studio. The Rolex watch was a major clue.'

'I know.' Fagan's expression could be described as a blank piece of paper as he stared at the woman who had arrived over an hour earlier.'

'And now she's claiming to have witnessed the murder of Alex in 1993.'

Fagan nodded slowly in response.

Watkins looked at Fagan wondering why he was so calm. 'But you spoke to Alex yesterday. She released new music a few days ago'

'I know.'

'She told you that she murdered Andrea Jones on the night of the Brit Awards.'

'I know.'

'So if it wasn't Alex on the phone yesterday then who the fuck was it?'

'We've been chasing shadows this whole time.' Fagan spoke evenly. 'Believing that it was Andrea Jones murdered that night. When in fact the clues have been right in front of us all along.'

'Clues?'

'First of all there's the body missing head and hands. It's like you said from the start, to prevent identification. But we've also asked, why do that to an unknown like Andrea? So it had to be Alex buried, not Andrea. Then there's that magazine article you came across. Its full of inconsistencies. The suicide of Abbey's sister happened in May 1993. But the magazine article stated that it happened in August. Then the article mentions in her early days Alex and the band she joined in 1986 toured universities and had a regular gig at Bristol university. When I spoke to Steve Wakeman the other day, he said they did none of those things. He even contacted the magazine editor and had a go at him. Then you have the gravestone at the back of where Simon Xavier used to live. He obviously put it there to remember both his daughters.'

Watkins nodded. 'Knowing full well they were both dead.'

Fagan nodded. 'There's the surprised reaction we got from Jordan, Mercury, Charlotte, Mitchell and Dillon. When we said we believed it was Andrea Jones buried at the back of the studio they all looked at us like we were stupid. Then there's the interview with Charlotte. When we mentioned Andrea jones she spoke about her in the context that suggested she's still alive.' Fagan glanced through the window. 'There have been loads more other clues screaming at us. Because the evidence suggests that it was Andrea Jones at the back of Vine Road. We've been chasing our tails for the past few days.'

'Let's back up here a sec, Boss. If the woman in that room is Andrea Jones, and if it is Alex who was murdered that night. Then how the fuck has she just released a video and new music?'

'It's another missing piece of this puzzle. For now I suggest we concentrate on the woman in that room.'

The solicitor looked towards the window and nodded.

Fagan and Watkins entered the interview room. Fagan ran

through the interview startup process. 'First of all, for the benefit of the recording, you say your name is Louise Kelly. But your original name is Andrea Jones. May I call you Andrea?'

The woman glanced at her solicitor, who nodded. 'Yes, Andrea is fine.'

'I guess my first question to you, Andrea, is where have you been for the past thirty years?'

'Hiding?'

'Do you want to tell us in your own words what happened that night? The night you claim Alex was murdered.'

'It was a total mess from the start. I was a mess, off my face on coke. So was Alex. We both did a few lines before the award ceremony. I'm surprised Alex stayed upright for the red carpet parade.'

'Did you supply her with the cocaine?'

Jones nodded. 'I was never into drugs in the early days. Before Alex signed with Frankie Jordan, we'd smoke a bit of weed, and that was it.' Jones smiled. 'Before Alex entered that talent contest, we used to have a lot of fun with her former band, Lead from the Back. Alex and Steve became an item. They were fantastic together. Looking back, I guess was always jealous of Alex.'

Fagan recalled his conversation with Alex's former boyfriend. 'When did you get into serious drugs?'

'After Alex signed with the studio. I was afraid I'd be tossed aside.'

'Tossed aside?'

'I didn't have any talent. Me and Alex had been friends since school. Once she hit the big time, I was afraid our friendship would end.'

'So you got her hooked on cocaine?'

'Not at in the beginning. When we first went to the studio regularly, I was allowed to tag along. Moral support and all that. Then Jordan dumped Lead from the Back. I was there when Steve punched Jordan. A few weeks after that, Jordon

239

wanted me gone from the studio. He just saw me as a leech who wanted to be part of Alex's fame.'

'What convinced him to let you stay?'

Jones hesitated before answering. 'I spread my legs for him.'

Fagan studied Jones' expression for a moment. 'Did he force himself on you?'

'Yes, and no. Jordan said he would let me hang around the studio if I let him fuck me.' Jones grimaced. 'He was a disgusting man. Heavy smoker and all that. I used to be sick after he had sex with me. That's when I got hooked on coke. It used to make it easier to tolerate him when I was high. After that I got Alex hooked, so that she always needed me.'

'Where did you get the coke from?'

'There were loads of bands recording at the studio that used to bring their own supply with them.'

Fagan glanced at his notes. 'After the award ceremony and Charlotte had assaulted Alex, what happened?'

'I knew the little drama on stage was all for the cameras. I remember Jordan arguing with Mickey Mercury about the stunt. Jordan was furious. Charlotte was only supposed to push Alex over. She wasn't supposed to punch her. Alex's nose exploded. She was covered in blood. I reckon Charlotte was desperate to stay relevant. That's why she did it. It was all over the newspapers the next day and the day after that.'

'Did they continue fighting when they left the stage?'

'No, Charlotte was in tears. For weeks, she'd been arguing with her manager. Mickey was going to dump Charlotte because she hadn't had a decent hit in months. Plus, she kept dropping F bombs every time she'd do an interview. Mickey said it wasn't good for the studio image. But I think what he was trying to say was that she wasn't good for his image. She drew the wrong attention from the press.'

'Can you confirm you returned to the Agincourt hotel by helicopter later that evening?'

Jones nodded. 'The award ceremony was over by nine. Dillon had to get back to the Agincourt hotel just outside Monmouth. They were presenting him with a commendation for his work on the police's No Means No campaign.'

'What happened when you arrived back at the hotel?'

'Dillon, Mickey, Charlotte and Jordan went into the reception room.'

'What about Alun Mitchell, Alex's bodyguard?'

'He also went in.'

'Why didn't you attend the reception?' Watkins asked.

'It wasn't my thing. I went to the bar.' Jones paused. 'But then I heard Alex and her dad arguing in the hotel's foyer. So I went to see what they were arguing about. That's when Alex had a go at me.'

'What was she angry about?' Fagan asked.

Jones inhaled. 'Alex had just seen her mother. She told Alex that her younger sister Abbey had committed suicide. Apparently, Abbey told her mother everything about what was going on at the studio.' Jones seemed uncomfortable with what she was saying. 'Anyway, she had a right go at me. Calling me every name under the sun. She was also having a go at her dad for not telling her what had happened.'

'So Alex's dad knew Abbey had taken her own life?'

Jones nodded. 'I had enough, so I returned to the bar. Alex chased me and we ended up in the kitchen. By this time there was no calming Alex down. Her dad couldn't even console her. He suggested we go back to the studio. That was when the rest of them came into the kitchen, but it only made matters worse. Alex's mum had obviously told her everything. Alex was screaming at everyone at this point. Accusing them of keeping secrets from her. That's when one of the kitchen staff chucked us out of the kitchen.'

'What happened when you were kicked out of the kitchen?'

'We continued arguing about what had happened to

Abbey. Alex was in full rage mode. Jordan tried to calm her down, but it didn't do any good.'

'Who suggested you go back to the studio?'

'That was Alex, and she didn't suggest it. She stormed off and headed back to the studio.'

'Was there anyone there that time of night?' Watkins questioned.

'No, there were just eight of us.'

'What happened when you got back to the studio?'

'Alex continued to have a go at us all.' Jones paused.

Fagan noted her expression. 'And then?'

'She attacked Dillon.'

'Verbally attacked, or physically attacked him?'

'She went to hit him with her Brit award. She held onto it all night.'

'What did Dillan do?'

'He fought her off and then snatched the statue away from her. Alex was screaming at him. Calling him a rapist cunt. She then had a go at me. Said that I'd betrayed her on so many levels. Pretending to be her best mate. While all the time taking part in the abuse of her sister. And then.' Jones took a moment to compose herself. 'That's when she threatened to go to the police and tell them everything that had happened to her sister. Everyone, including me, went into panic mode. Jordan screamed at her. He told her if she did that, then it would be the end of her career. It would be the end of all their careers. That's when he called her an ungrateful twat. And that Abbey's suicide was a small price to pay for fame. He said that she wasn't all that naïve. She knew young girls were being trafficked to the studio and handed out like sweets.'

'Those were his exact words.' Fagan queried.

'Yeah.' Jones nodded. 'Alex said she didn't give a shit about her career ending. She said she wished she hadn't had entered the talent contest. She said she wished she was still with her old band. Then she said she was going to the police.

She turned and headed towards the door.' Jones inhaled. 'Dillon chased after her. It all happened so fast.'

'What happened?'

'Dillon smashed her across the side of the head with the award. Alex went down immediately. Alex's dad was the first by her side. He picked her up and tried to revive her. But she wasn't responding. He was screaming at her. Alex sweetheart, please open your eyes. But she was gone. I guessed she still had a lot of coke in her system, which aided in her death.'

'What happened next?'

'Everyone was in shock. We all started screaming at each other. Blaming one another.'

'Why didn't you call the police?'

'I wanted to, but then Jordan said we'd all go to prison. Our lives would be over in a heartbeat.'

'What about Alex's dad? Surely, seeing his daughter lying dead on the floor would have persuaded him.'

'You have to understand, DI Fagan. Frankie Jordan was one of the most powerful people in the music industry. Jordan wasn't about to walk away. He had a lot of connections and could fix everything.'

'Including the murder of one of the biggest pop sensations of the nineties.'

Jones nodded. 'After we had all calmed down, we went back to Jordan's office. He said we had to act quick. Come up with a plan that could bail us out. He also said that we'd be set up for the rest of our lives if we kept silent. That's when they all headed back to London. But Alex's dad refused to go. He said he wasn't going to leave his daughter alone, dead in the studio.'

'Which studio Alex was murdered in?'

'Studio one,' Jones answered. 'Simon insisted on staying with his daughter. There was no changing his mind. So I stayed with him. I owed Alex that. They all jumped into a taxi and headed back to London.'

'So you and Simon Xavier stayed with Alex all night long?'

'Yes.'

'Must have been torture for the both of you.'

Jones nodded. 'It was. On several occasions we made up our minds to phone the police. But every time we would get up and walk towards the phone, we'd stop ourselves.'

'Who disposed of Alex's body?'

'It was Mitchell. The day after he returned to the studio.'

'Did you see him dispose of the body?'

'No, we assumed he took Alex somewhere else. When I read the article in the paper, I couldn't believe he buried her at the back of the studio. Jordan put his plan into action. He fired everyone who was working at the studio at the time. Told artists who were recording there, the studio was undergoing some sort of refit. He contacted the press and told them that Alex was in rehab. I know for a fact he put several gagging orders in place to stop people talking about the events following the Brit Awards. A few months after Alex was murdered, Jordan called me to the studio. He said that everything was in place and the press believed that Alex was living as a recluse out in Spain.'

'But you still could have gone to the police.'

'No.' Jones shook her head. 'By that time, Jordan had come up with a plan. He handed me fifty grand in cash and said I had a choice. Either I could take the money. Or I could go to the police and tell them everything. And then I'd go to prison for helping cover up Alex's murder.' Jones stared at Fagan. 'I didn't have a choice. I didn't want to go to prison. So I took the money. I bought a house for me and my mum. Back then, you could get a house for that kind of money. Jordan promised he would pay me twenty thousand pounds a year for the rest of my life. If I continued to keep my mouth shut. About two years after Alex's murder, mum was diagnosed with breast cancer. She died after a six-month battle.'

Fagan recalled what the woman had told him the day

before. 'Who paid for your mam's funeral?'

'I did.'

'Not Alex.'

Jones shook her head. 'I was beside myself. I had enough of everything. I couldn't stand living with so many secrets. That's when I went to Jordan and told him I couldn't live a lie anymore.'

'How did he react?'

'Jordan promised he'd up the payments to forty thousand a year. But I didn't want anymore money. I just wanted to get away from everything. At the time I was working in a supermarket in Newport. Then one day, Mitchell turned up as I was leaving work. He threatened that if I went to the police and told them about Alex, then I wouldn't live long enough to see the trial?'

'He threatened to kill you,' Fagan stated.

'Yes.' Jones replied. 'I was terrified. I was living in that house all alone. I brought new locks and everything. But it wasn't enough. So I decided it was time for me to disappear. I put the house on the market. Convinced the estate agent not to put a for sale sign outside my house. Just in case I was being watched. I spent several weeks selling everything I owned. I didn't want the hassle of a removal company. By the time I sold the house I didn't own one bit of furniture. A suitcase full of clothes, and that was it.'

'What about the Rolex watch Alex had given you? How did that end up with her body?'

Jones stared back. 'I didn't know Mitchell had buried my watch with Alex. When the morning came, Mitchell turned up at the studio. He said that he'd take care of everything and that we should leave. I remember taking off my watch and placing it in Alex's hand before saying my goodbyes. I then went back to Monmouth with Simon. We talked for hours about what we should do. Simon was inconsolable. He'd lost two daughters. We thought about going to the police again.

But at the end of the day we didn't want to go to prison. Simon said he was going to sell the house. He said there was nothing for him in Monmouth. I said my goodbyes and left'

'Did you ever see him again?'

'No. But I know Frankie offered him the same deal as he offered me. A lump sum and payments yearly after that.' Jones picked up a bottle of water she had bought. 'When I sold the house in Newport, I felt I was free to do whatever I wanted. So I moved to Surrey. I was afraid Mitchell would track me down, so I changed my name. I lived in a flat for ten years. Then I decided to move to Manchester. I changed my name again and lived In Manchester for another ten years before moving to Bristol. I thought moving closer to where I grew up would somehow ease the guilt.'

'But it didn't' Watkins guessed.

'No.'

'What about the money that Jordan said he would pay you?' Fagan asked.

'I haven't touched it,' Jones revealed.

'You still have the bank account, then?'

'Yes. It's in my name, so once the money goes in Jordan can't get at it. But I haven't touched a penny. There's over a million pounds in the account.'

Fagan considered the information that Jones had revealed. 'Why come forward now?'

'When I saw the video that Alex released, it broke me. I knew it wasn't her, and Jordan had somehow faked everything. He wanted to kill Alex again so he could cash in one more time. It just goes to show what an arrogant piece of shit he is.' Jones stared directly at Fagan. 'I've been a ghost for nearly thirty years, Inspector Fagan. Changing my identity so that Mitchell couldn't find me. When I moved away to Surrey, I kept myself to myself. I have wandered alone, carrying this burden. I've have lost count of how many times I have thought about taking my life. But every time I have thought about it,

Alex visits me in my dreams. Begging me to do the right thing. I can't live this life anymore. I will confess everything.'

'You have to understand Andrea. We will charge you with perverting the course of justice. The fact this has carried on for so long will add to your sentence. Not to mention the allegations that have been made regarding sexual abuse at the studio and the Agincourt Hotel. Abbey kept a diary. She has named you frequently.'

Jones nodded. 'I am aware of my actions, DI Fagan. In the beginning I wasn't a paedophile. And I know that's not an excuse. You have to realise, when you are trapped in an environment where everything is handed you on a plate, then it's hard to say no. That's the nature of the music industry. The public only gets to see the glitz and the glamour. They never get to see the dark underbelly of what it's really like.'

'How did it start?'

'When Dillon came to the studio he was eyeing anything with two legs. I was screwing Jordan just to stay relevant.'

'Did you have a relationship with Dillon?'

Jones nodded.

'How did it spiral into abuse Andrea?'

'Both Dillon and Charlotte had an appetite for that kind of thing, before they came to the studio. I joined in because I wanted to be part of that world.

'You'll be taken into custody for the time being Andrea.'

'I understand.'

'And you will be questioned more regarding the murder of Alex and the sexual abuse that went on at the studio.' Fagan paused. 'The only glimpse of hope I can offer you at this moment is that you have come in voluntarily. It may sway the jury.'

'I would like to end this interview DI Fagan.' The duty solicitor requested. 'I need to discuss the matter with my client.'

Fagan nodded.

247

Jones and the duty solicitor left the interview room.

'That was one hell of a confession.' Watkins said. 'It blows everything out of the water. At least we know why that headstone was at the back of that garden in Devauden. Alex's dad knew both his daughters were dead.'

'And he kept it silent for all those years.' Fagan said.

'I guess the first thing we need to do is rearrest Dillon for the murder of Alex.'

'Let's hold off a while. Andrea Jones, turning up and making a confession, is an unforeseen event. Not just for us, but for those who were involved in Alex's murder. Organise a warrant for the arrest of Dillon, Charlotte, Jordan, Mercury and Mitchell. We'll hold off until the bash at the Agincourt tonight. Then we'll do a bit of gatecrashing. They've had thirty years of hiding secrets. We owe to Alex and Abbey to air everyone's dirty laundry in public.'

'How do you reckon they faked the video and the music that Alex has just released?'

Fagan's phone rang. Dean Tyler's name appeared on the screen. He glanced at Watkins. 'We're about to find out. Organise those warrants. We'll grab Brooks and organise some extra bodies for an op.'

Watkins gathered his notes and left the room.

Fagan tapped the answer icon. 'Dean, what have you got for me mate?'

CHAPTER 32

Agincourt Hotel – 7:02pm

Simon Banks smiled at the assembled audience. 'Ladies and gentlemen, distinguished guests, musicians, and music lovers. I'd like to welcome you this evening to this amazing event. We are here to celebrate a momentous occasion. The fiftieth anniversary of Vine Road Music Studios. An iconic pillar of creativity and artistic expression in the heart of Monmouthshire, South Wales.'

Applauding resonated around the function room.

'Fifty years ago, a vision was born that would forever change the landscape of music production. And nurture the dreams of many artists. Founded by Frankie Jordan and Mickey Mercury. Vine Road Music Studios emerged as a sanctuary for those seeking to transform their musical visions and talents into reality.' Banks looked at Jordan and Mercury, who were sitting next to each other. 'This evening, we come together to celebrate this musical institution that has touched the lives of so many. Leaving an indelible mark on the music industry.'

More applause.

'In an era where music has the power to transcend borders and unite people of diverse cultures and backgrounds. Vine Road Music Studios has stood as a testament to the universal language of melody. For five decades, it has been a creative haven where melodies have danced and harmonies have sung. Where lyrics have woven stories and beats have ignited passions. Many artists have made their name at Vine Road studios. As the owner of that studio I'm looking forward to

249

welcoming future artists. Artists who want to turn their hopes and dreams into reality. Throughout its history, this remarkable studio has been the birthplace of timeless classics and modern masterpieces. Showcasing the immense talent of artists from all over the world. It has also touched the lives of those who live locally. Over the past fifty years, the studio has witnessed the evolution of music. From the warm analog sounds of vinyl records to the innovative digital production techniques of today. Vine Road Music Studios has embraced change and innovation, ensuring it remains a relevant and influential force in the music industry. And despite living in an age where AI is posing a threat to both jobs and creativity. Vine Roads Studios stands tall, ready to meet the challenges that artificial intelligence presents.'

Audience members rose to their feet, clapping loudly and whistling.

Banks smiled as the audience continued to applause his speech. 'Beyond the tangible achievements and impressive technology. What truly sets this studio apart is the people who have walked through its doors. The artists who have poured their hearts and souls into their craft. The producers and engineers who have crafted sonic landscapes. And let's not forget the dedicated staff who have nurtured dreams and supported creativity at every step.'

The audience fixed their eyes on Banks, hypnotised by his mesmerising speech.

'As we reflect on the legacy of Vine Road Music Studios. Let us remember the countless stories of resilience, passion, and determination that have unfolded within those walls. It is a place where songs of love and heartache, joy and sorrow, dreams and aspirations, have been given life and shared with the world. Each note, each chord, each lyric has resonated far beyond the studio. Touching the lives of millions of music lovers across the globe. Today, we celebrate fifty years of this remarkable journey. We pay tribute to the spirit that has driven Vine Road Music Studios to thrive and endure. We honour the visionaries who planted the seeds of inspiration. Visionaries like the two men who founded this studio back in 1973. Frankie Jordan and Mickey Mercury.' Banks clapped. The audience followed suit.

Jordan and Mercury stood, taking a bow.

'As we embark on the next fifty years, let us carry forward the torch of creativity, innovation, and collaboration. This has been the hallmark of Vine Road Music Studios. May this institution continue to be a beacon of artistic excellence, a place where the music of today and tomorrow is moulded with passion and precision.' Banks picked up a glass of champagne and held it up. 'To the staff, past and present. Who have poured their hearts into preserving this musical heaven. We thank you for your dedication and unwavering commitment. To the artists who have graced these studios with their talent, we salute you for sharing your gifts with the world and enriching our lives with your music. And to you Frankie Jordan and Mickey Mercury, we thank you for turning your dreams into the music we have come to love today. Here's to you, cheers.' Banks drank from his glass.

The audience stood and toasted the former studio owners.

'And finally, to the community of Monmouthshire and music lovers everywhere. We invite you to join us in celebrating the fiftieth anniversary of Vine Road Music Studios. A place where melodies have soared, where dreams have found wings, and where the power of music has touched our souls. Thank you, and here's to the next fifty years of harmonious creativity and boundless inspiration!

The room seemed to pulsate with excitement as the audience applauded. Camera flashes exploded around the room.

'I would like to hand things over to Frankie Jordan who will now say a few words about the history of this studio.'

Again, the audience stood and applauded Jordon as he

251

took his place behind the microphone.

Jordan smiled. 'Thank you, Simon, for that incredible opening speech. I don't think there is much more I can add to that. But I'll do my best.' Jordan reached into his inside pocket and unfolded a speech he had prepared. 'Back in 1973, the world was a different place. The music industry was undergoing a revolution of its own. It was during this time that two passionate souls, myself and my good friend Mickey Mercury, dared to dream the impossible. We envisioned a place where creativity would have no boundaries. where melodies would be born and where musical aspirations would be nurtured. In the heart of Monmouthshire, South Wales, Vine Road Music Studios became a sanctuary for all those who sought to weave their musical magic. Myself and Mickey's belief in the power of music, our dedication, and unyielding spirit shaped the studio into what it is today.'

More applause.

'Our journey was not without challenges. We spent countless hours fine-tuning the studio's acoustics, carefully selecting cutting-edge equipment, and recruiting a team of passionate sound engineers who shared our vision. With each hurdle, our determination only grew stronger. Over the years, the walls of Vine Road Music Studios echoed with the sounds of laughter, tears, and applause. Countless melodies were born within these walls, and many artists found their voice under our guidance. Artists like Alexandria Xavier, who I am so happy can join us tonight.' Frankie pointed to a large TV behind him. An image of Alex lying in a hospital bed appeared on the screen.

The sound of gasps rippled through the audience.

'Hi Alex,' Jordan greeted.

'Hi Frankie, thanks for inviting me here tonight.'

Jordan smiled, glancing at the piece of paper. 'Tell us about your time at Vine Road Music Studios, Alex.'

'First and foremost, I want to express my deepest gratitude

252

to the team at Vine Road Music Studios. Especially to you, Frankie Jordan and Mickey Mercury. I remember stepping into the studio for the first time, nervous yet exhilarated. Knowing that I was standing on the threshold of something magical. Your guidance and expertise sculpted my songs, turning my dreams into melodies that touched the hearts of millions. I am so grateful for that.'

Jordan glanced at his speech again. 'Would you like to share a special memory with our audience this evening?'

Alex smiled. 'I have so many wonderful memories of working at the studio. With you, Frankie and Mickey. Late nights spent perfecting every note. The joyous laughter that echoed through these walls, and the camaraderie we shared as a creative family.'

'It was an absolute pleasure working with you all those years ago, Alex.'

'I recall one particular day when inspiration struck like lightning. I sat at the piano, fingers dancing across the keys, and the melody for my breakthrough hit flowed effortlessly. The energy in this studio that day was electric, and I could feel the music enveloping me, taking me to places I had never imagined. It was as if Vine Road itself had become the heartbeat of that song.'

'What wonderful words.' Jordan wiped a tear away.

'Beyond the music, Vine Road Music Studios was a sanctuary for me during my journey as a popstar. In moments of doubt and vulnerability, Frankie and Mickey, you were my pillars of strength, reminding me of the power of my voice and the impact of my music. Your belief in me gave me the courage to keep pushing boundaries, to explore new sounds, and to grow as an artist.'

The audience exploded into a rapturous applause. Jordan held his hand up and the applause faded away.

'To my incredible fans, thank you for being the driving force behind my career. Your unwavering support and love has given me the strength to face every challenge and embrace every triumph. You have made my songs a part of your lives, and for that, I am forever humbled and grateful. As I find myself in the last moments of my life, I am filled with peace, knowing that my music will live on. I hope the songs that were born within Vine Road will continue to resonate with generations to come, carrying a piece of my spirit with them. In closing, I want to leave you all with a message of hope and gratitude. For all of you who have recorded their music at Vine Road studios. Cherish every moment, seize every opportunity, and let the music in your heart guide you to places beyond your wildest dreams. Life is a symphony, and we are all composing our own unique melodies. Thank you, Frankie and Mickey. And thank you to Vine Road Music Studios, for being the canvas upon which I painted my musical legacy. Thank you, my dear fans, for being the colours that brought my songs to life. As I bid farewell, know that I will carry the memories of this place, and all of you, in my heart until the last note fades away.' The screen went black.

A sombre silence enveloped the room.

'That was incredible.' Jordan struggled with his emotions. He held his glass up. 'To Alex, thank you for the joy your music has brought to millions around the world.'

The audience stood and held their glasses up.

Jordan wasn't finished. 'To the musicians and artists who have graced these studios with their talent.' He read from the piece of paper. 'Whose melodies have danced across these walls. And whose songs have found their way into the hearts of millions. Thank you for sharing your gifts and enriching our lives with your music.'

'Here, here.' Members of the audience cheered.

Jordan smiled. 'Here's to the hours of hard work and collaboration that have birthed musical masterpieces. From the earliest analog recordings to the innovative digital productions of today, Vine Road studios has embraced innovation and evolved with the times. Leaving an indomitable imprint on the music industry. To the dedicated staff and engineers who have worked tirelessly behind the scenes, ensuring that every chord, every note, and every beat was brought to life with precision and care. Your dedication and expertise have been the backbone of this enduring legacy.'

More cheers and applause from the audience.

'Let us also raise our glasses to the fans and supporters who have stood by Vine Road Music Studios. Cheering on the artists and embracing the magic of music that resonates within the studio walls. Your unwavering enthusiasm and love for music have been the driving force behind the success of this studio. And finally, let us raise our glasses to the future. To the next fifty years and beyond, as Vine Road Music Studios continues to be a centre for inspiration for generations to come. May it remain a place where creativity knows no bounds, where melodies find their voice, and where the power of music continues to unite hearts and souls. So, here's to the enduring legacy of Vine Road Music Studios. A place where dreams take flight and where the magic of music will forever live on. Cheers.'

The room erupted into applause for a few minutes. Audience members cheered and whistled. Eventually, the din faded. However, one person kept on clapping loudly and slowly.

Jordan felt his heart leap in his mouth, spotting DI Fagan, who stood up and approached him.

CHAPTER 33

Fagan slowly strolled to where Jordan was standing continuing to clap loudly and slowly.

The audience watched Fagan as he walked towards the music producer.

'Detective Inspector Fagan. I don't recall you being on the guest list this evening.' Jordan locked eyes with Mitchell, who stood up and signalled to a man standing at the entrance to the function room.

Fagan glanced at the security guard, who remained where he was. 'We've given your man orders to stay where he is.'

'Nevertheless, you were not invited to this event this evening.'

Fagan reached into his pocket and pulled out a piece of paper, holding it up for the room to see. 'I have a warrant, so I thought I'd pop along to witness this charade.'

Whispers resonated around the room. Some of the audience stared at Jordan. A journalist with a camera stood and snapped a picture of a concerned-looking Jordan.

'The only charade here, Inspector Fagan, is you.'

'I wouldn't be so sure about that.' Fagan halted his approach. He glanced around the room. 'I have to admit, it was a stroke of genius pulling off your little act over the past several days. Creating this illusion. Convincing everyone that Alex had just released a new single, and that you had just spoken to her via zoom.' Fagan looked at Mercury. 'With the help of your old partner, who conveniently owns a special effects studio.'

Mercury glared back. 'I suggest you give your solicitor a ring, DI Fagan.'

'It's you who will need a solicitor, Mickey.'

Mercury stared back. Not daring to answer.

Fagan smiled, looking back at Jordan. He shoved his hands into his coat pockets. 'You've had the wool pulled over our eyes for several days. Until earlier today the evidence was overwhelming.'

'Evidence?'

'That it was Andrea Jones buried at the back of the studio. The watch was a nice touch, by the way.' Fagan made eye contact with Mitchell. 'After all, it belonged to Andrea. So there was no reason to suspect the body could have been anyone other than Andrea.'

More camera flashes exploded.

'Who would have believed it was Alexandria Xavier in that grave, and not Andrea?'

'Preposterous.' Jordan snorted. 'We have just had a conversation with Alex. So I suggest DI Fagan, you show a little respect towards this poor woman who is in the last weeks of her life.'

'It's you who has shown disrespect, Frankie, not me. You see, something has been nagging me ever since the body was found.' Fagan glanced at Mitchell. 'Removing the head and the hands was necessary to prevent identification. It wouldn't have really mattered if it was Andrea that was murdered. She was a nobody. Her mother is long dead and Andrea didn't have any other relatives. So DNA evidence would have proved difficult for us. That's why I had to prove that it was someone else. That someone else was Alex.'

A photographer stood in front of Fagan and snapped a picture.

'Even though we've just had a conversation with Alex, you believe it was her body that was found at the back of the music studio. I have never heard such fantasy.'

'Alex's mother gave a DNA sample earlier today. We fast tracked the results. It's a perfect match.'

The colour drained from Jordan's face.

Fagan looked around the room. 'You see, all you good folks here tonight have been conned. I'm not much of a techie, but I have a friend who owns a company in London. This company specialises in analysing music, sound and video that has been created by artificial intelligence.'

Shocked expressions focused on Jordon.

'I've had quite the education about artificial intelligence this afternoon. I have seen it mentioned on the news from time to time. But never really took notice of it. I'm not particularly fond of modern technology. It's made us a little backward.'

Mercury stood. 'What exactly are you implying, Inspector Fagan?'

'Don't play naïve, Mickey. You are the one who has made all this possible. Your special effects company in Cardiff is responsible for all this.'

'Responsible for what?'

'For faking all this.'

Whispers from the audience turned to low murmured conversation.

'Do you honestly expect us to believe this nonsense you're spouting?'

'The other day, when you volunteered for an interview. You told me that your effects company was capable of bringing dead actors back to life. You mentioned that you'd worked on a project where Taylor swift appeared with Elvis. So I did a little research earlier. Your company owns the rights to software called Infinity AI. It was created during the pandemic. You did an interview for a technology magazine. It was under the radar stuff. Only those die hard techie enthusiasts would have read it. What you didn't know was that the magazine you had the interview with is owned by my friend who runs the company I just mentioned. The Magazine specialises in the development of AI technology. My friend

258

sent me a copy of the article. You boasted, if another catastrophe brought the world to its knees. Your software could create content with near photo realistic quality.'

'My software will revolutionise the entertainment industry.' Mercury boasted.

'Yeah, but what you didn't count on was your software coming under heavy fire over the past twelve months. Especially regarding the war in Ukraine.'

'I don't know what you are waffling on about.' Fear was clear in Mercury's tone.

'My friend has contacts in the intelligence community. He told me you made a trip out to Ukraine last year.'

'That's public knowledge, DI Fagan. I even had Wales Today cover the journey. I was out there writing a story about the LGBT soldiers fighting on the front line.'

'But what you didn't mention is that you met with Ukrainian intelligence and handed over a series of deep fake videos. Which depicted the Ukrainian president ordering Russian troops to surrender. And also the people of Russia to rebel against their leaders.'

Mercury smirked. 'You think I'm the only company doing that? There's an AI information war being fought across the globe at the moment, DI Fagan. People have no idea what's going on behind the scenes.'

'I've no doubt about this,' Fagan said. 'You've also come under criticism over the past several weeks. From the actors and writer's guild. I scrolled through your Twitter feed earlier today. A year ago you boasted about creating a series of streaming shows for Netflix, Amazon and Disney plus.' Fagan looked at Simon Banks. 'Why do you think they all contacted you about building new recording studios?' Fagan pointed at Mercury. 'It was Mr Mercury who pointed them in the direction of Vine Road studios because he had already signed deals with all three streaming giants to create AI content for various streaming platforms.' He smiled at Mercury. 'It's

259

amazing what you find out from Companies house in Cardiff.'

'I'm about to transform the entertainment industry, DI Fagan. No more ungrateful whinging writers and actors moaning about how much they are being paid. Actors have signed away so many of their image rights. The studios can do whatever they want. Intellectual property will be raided. Imagine a Star Wars film with Kirk Douglas wielding a light sabre. Or James Cameron's aliens going up against a younger Bruce Willis or Arnold Schwarzenegger. Or Bruce Lee in a modern day action film. All this is now possible. And my company will lead the way.'

Fagan waved the warrant. 'Not for a while, I'm afraid.' He turned his attention to Jordan. 'Was it your idea?'

'Was it my idea to do what, DI Fagan?'

'To resurrect Alex from the dead.'

Audience murmurs grew louder.

'She's the one popstar that has sold the most songs for you, wasn't she? Over one hundred and fifty million songs sold worldwide over the past thirty years. She was your primary source of income. Until you signed Alex up, you'd had moderate success in the music industry.' Fagan paused. 'You own the right to Alex's music library, do you not?'

Jordan swallowed hard. 'Yes, I own the rights.'

'And the rights to use her image, since she'd dead and there's no one to contest your claim. Alex's father is dead. And her mother wouldn't be a problem for you. You'll just use your media contacts to warn her off. Together with the help of Mercury's special effects company and AI software, you resurrected Alex. But the only problem was, Alex was already dead. She had been murdered in 1993.'

'You have witnesses to prove this, do you, DI Fagan?' Mitchell asked in a confident tone.

Fagan ignored the question. 'Both you and your former partner came up with a plan. The media and fans have always believed that Alex was a recluse. Living off the grid somewhere. In order for your plan to work, you had to kill Alex off for a second time. So you invented the cancer story. You'd already created new music using Alex's voice. You were eager to test it on the world. But you panicked. Your original plan was to release new music after the new studios had been built. However, the discovery of a body at the back of the original studios forced you to accelerate your plans. And this was because you didn't know that Alex was buried at the back of the music studio.' Fagan caught Mercury flashing Mitchell an angry look. 'You assumed that whoever disposed of her body took her somewhere else.'

'Your imagination is really running away with you, Inspector Fagan.' Jordan said. 'I already told you. I was not party to any murder.'

'Yes, you told me you were in your office. But because of what happened over the past few days at the studio, you and Mercury accelerated your plans. And released AI generated music using Alex's voice. It went viral straight away. Seven million downloads in the space of twenty-four hours. Not bad. Made you a lot of money in a short space of time. And now you've just uploaded her album. I'm sure it will make you even more money. I bet you have loads of record labels lining up to use your software. Former dead popstars being brought back to life. Releasing new music. I mean, who wouldn't love to hear new music from Whitney Houston, or Amy Winehouse, or the recently deceased Sinead O'Conner. The potential to make millions is alluring. And it can all be done using your software.' Fagan made eye contact with Mercury.

The room plunged into shocked silence.

'There is only one person in this room who knew that Alex was buried at the back of the studio. And that is the person who disposed of the body. But let us focus on the murder of Alex, for the moment.' Fagan looked across to where Dillon Powell was sitting.

Powell glared back at him.

'Why did Alex deserve a death sentence? How far would someone go to protect their reputation and their career? And let's not forget, remain free to carry on with their lives. Knowing full well the crime they committed.' Fagan strolled towards Powell's table. Charlotte West was sitting beside him. A look of terror etched across her. Fagan locked eyes with Powell. 'You must have been terrified when Alex threatened to reveal the truth.'

'I made it quite clear during my interview, DI Fagan. I wasn't there when Alex was murdered.' Powell suddenly realised what he just said.

Fagan smiled. 'Not very good at lying, are we Dillon?'

Powell's eyes darted around the room.

'You've all claimed that you weren't there when Alex was murdered. Following her death you all travelled back to London. This part is true. But Andrea and her dad stayed at the studio with Alex's body. Someone had to return the next day to dispose of Alex's body.' Fagan locked eyes with Mitchell, who was sitting at an adjacent table. 'Someone had to do the dirty work. Getting rid of Alex's body.'

'Enough DI Fagan!' Jordan shouted. 'How dare you interrupt this celebration and spin a pack of lies.'

Fagan turned to face him. 'No Frankie, I haven't been spinning a pack of lies. You see, there is one element you have all forgotten. And that is Andrea Jones.'

Jordan stared back.

'You thought she vanished with the money you paid her to keep silent about what happened that night. Andrea Jones is currently talking to detectives. She has confessed to being a witness to the murder of Alexandria Xavier. She has told me you all witnessed the murder.' Fagan looked at Powell. 'She's told us who murdered her. How Alex had threatened to go to the police after finding out her sister had committed suicide a month earlier. And that her sister had committed suicide because of the sexual abuse she had endured. The abuse you and Charlotte had subjected her and other girls to.'

Springing to her feet, Charlotte aimed an accusing finger at Powell. 'It's all his fault. He forced me to do everything,' She declared before sinking back into her chair, succumbing to sobs.

Fagan nodded at the man positioned by the function room door, prompting him to open the door. Following the signal, Watkins ushered several officers into the room.

Fagan approached Powell. 'Dillon Powell, I am arresting you for the murder of Alexandria Xavier in June 1993. You do not have to say anything. But, it may harm your defence if you do not mention, when questioned, something which you later rely on in court. Anything you do say may be given in evidence.'

A uniform yanked Powell to his feet and cuffed him.

Charlotte held up her hands, sobbing hysterically. A uniform cuffed her before cautioning her.

Walkins strolled up to Jordan, accompanied by Brooks and another uniform. 'Frankie Jordan. I am arresting you for perverting the course of justice. You do not have to say anything. But, it may harm your defence if you do not mention, when questioned, something which you later rely on in court. Anything you do say may be given in evidence.'

Other officers cuffed Mercury and Jordan, reading a caution. They were all marched out of the room. A symphony of camera flashes erupted in every direction.

Fagan trailed the procession towards the exit. He turned to confront an audience, frozen in astonishment. 'Apologies for disrupting your evening, ladies and gentlemen.'

CHAPTER 3 4

Newport Central Police station
Two days later.

Fagan began the interview start up procedure. 'Interview with Dillon Powell in relation to the murder of Alexandria Xavier on the night of the 25th June 1993. Present in the room are Mr Powell and his solicitor, James Morcombe. Interviewing detectives are Detective Inspector Marc Fagan and Detective Seargeant Sean Watkins. Mr Powell, I need to remind you at this point. You do not have to say anything. But, it may harm your defence if you do not mention when questioned something which you later rely on in court. Anything you do say may be given in evidence. Do you understand what I have just said to you?'

Powell remained motionless.

'Mr Powell, do you understand the caution?' Watkins asked.

Powell nodded.

Fagan studied Powell's expression. One that spoke volumes, revealing the undeniable truth. Powell realising his life was now over, and a lengthy prison sentence awaited him. 'Tell us about the night you murdered Alex?'

'No comment.'

'Andrea Jones has given more information relation the night of June 25th 1993. She said that you fought with Alex. She attacked you in the kitchen of the Agincourt hotel. This was following a conversation she had with her mother. A conversation that revealed her sister Abbey had committed suicide. We have spoken to Alex's mother, Dillon. She told us everything. She told us you raped Abbey repeatedly over several months. Andrea Jones has admitted taking part, along with Charlotte. Is this true?'

'No comment.' Powell made brief eye contact with Fagan.

'When Alex discovered what had happened to her sister, she went on the warpath, didn't she? Her dad knew Abbey had killed herself. But his only concern was Alex winning the Brit award the night she was murdered. That's why Alex had a go at him first. She then flew at Andrea for her part in all this. Andrea has stated that she fled to the kitchen of the hotel. Someone then alerted Jordan while you were in the function room, being honoured for your work on the No Means No campaign. You followed Jordan into the kitchen. Charlotte, Mitchell and your manager Mickey Mercury also entered the kitchen to see why Alex was kicking off.'

'No comment.'

'She must have been particularly angry with you. After all, you and Alex were having an affair behind Charlotte's back. It made headlines in the media. You were really popular with the girls back then, weren't you Dillon? You had the boy next door look. Alex must have thought it was the ultimate betrayal when she discovered what you'd been doing to her thirteen-year-old sister. Not only that, but Charlotte and Alex's best friend Andrea Jones were involved in the abuse.'

Powell rubbed his sweaty hands together. He glanced at his solicitor, who was scribbling notes. 'No comment.'

'Did she threaten to go to the police?'

'No comment.'

Fagan relaxed. He knew Powell wasn't going to be very helpful in the interview. 'Is that why you snapped and lashed out at her? You were terrified your pop career was going to be over. What choice did you have but to murder Alex? She could have ended all your careers.'

'Careful DI Fagan, you're speculating.' Powell's solicitor warned.

'No comment.'

'Come on Dillon. We already have Andrea Jones' statement. You think the others are going to cover for you. They'll fall like dominoes and throw you under the bus.'

A tear rolled down Powell's face. 'No comment.'

'Did you know Alex was buried at the back of the music studio?'

Powell's expression answered Fagan's question.

'Must have been quite a shock when we arrested you the other day. You probably thought that Mitchell had disposed of Alex's body far away somewhere. Or even hacked her to pieces before cremating her. Never in a million years did you think her remains would be found. I mean, it's been thirty years since the events that night. You've had thirty years of freedom. Allowed to carry on with your life. But now, it's all about to come crashing down around you. Still you've made your money over the years haven't you?' Fagan looked down at a piece of paper. 'Earned plenty in royalties. Even did a stint in several West End Shows from 2001 – 2005. You played the leading role in Jospeh and his Technicoloured dream coat in 2004. I went to see that show when Jason Donavon was in it.' Fagan sang the opening line. '*I close my eyes, draw back the curtain.*' Fagan smiled. 'Love that song.' He stooped over and plucked a diary out of an evidence box he had brought with him. 'I am showing Mr Powell a dairy that Abbey Xavier kept.'

Dillon stared at the diary.

Fagan read an entry. 'This account is dated August 17th 1992. Abbey writes she was staying at the Agincourt hotel. We have obtained guest registers from the early nineties. The time when you stayed at the hotel regularly.' He fished a register out of the evidence box and opened it. 'I'm showing Mr Powell a guest register.' Fagan opened a page that had been booked marked, pointing at his signature. As you can see, you signed the guest register on the date Abbey wrote her entry.' Fagan looked at Abbey's entry and started to read.

266

'Dillon showed up at my door tonight. He was pissed again. He's always pissed these days. I'm on my period at for fuck's sake. Andrea and Charlotte were with him. They brought another girl. She was terrified. Dillon made her eat me out. She was sick all over the bed. Dillon didn't care. After it was over he raped the girl. She was crying out for her mam. Dillon said if she told anyone, then he knew someone who would kill her.' Fagan locked a stare on Powell. 'Who was the other girl, Dillon?'

'No comment.' Powell fired back.

Fagan flicked through the diary pages. 'Abbey writes about other girls that stayed at the hotel. Other girls who you forced to engage in sexual acts with her. By all accounts there were dozens according to Abbey.' Fagan gestured toward the guestbook. 'We have dozens of these guestbooks with your signature Dillon. Along with Charlotte's and Andrea Jones.'

'Fuck off.' Powell exploded. 'I know what you're trying to do. It's written all over your faces.'

'What are we trying to do, Dillon?' Watkins asked.

'You're trying to make out that I was the only one at that studio who was abusing the girls there.'

'Haven't mentioned the studio yet, Dillon.' Fagan remarked.

Powell crossed his arms and leant back in his chair. He glanced at his solicitor.

'So what, you're saying that besides you, Charlotte and Andrea, there were others who were taking part in abuse at the hotel?'

'I want amnesty.' Powell demanded.

'Amnesty, Dillon.' Watkins smirked. 'You're being charged with murder. We have a witness to Alex's murder.'

'I mean, the other stuff you are accusing me of.'

'If you say we are accusing you Dillon, then there's no need to ask for amnesty, is there?'

'Ok then, I want protection.'

'Protection from what, Dillon, or who?' Fagan asked.

'You have no idea the can of worms you've opened up here.'

'Really.' Fagan responded.

'Why do you think most of the focus was on Savile? It was to hide the fact that there were hundreds of celebrities, politicians and other prominent people who visited that hotel. Who visited the studios. Most were there for a gander, you know. Massive artists have come and gone over the years. But there were others who visited the studio and the hotel for one specific reason. It was an endless production line of young girls and boys.'

'Tell us about the night you murdered Alex, Dillon?' Watkins asked.

Powell responded with the silent treatment.

'You realise you're stuck between a rock and a hard place here, Dillon. On one hand we have you on the murder of Alex. On the other hand, we have evidence to convict you of rape and sexual abuse.'

'Piss off.' Powell seethed. 'Those girls knew what it was all about. Yeah sure, they come forward now, claiming to be victims. Buts it's for one purpose. To profit.'

'The night you murdered Alex, Dillon, what happened?' Fagan pursued.

'The situation spiralled out of control. It happened in the blink of an eye. She swung that Brit award at me, catching me off guard and leaving a deep gash on the side of my head. Reacting instinctively, I grabbed it away from her. As she made another aggressive move towards me, I couldn't help but lash out in self-defence. I was not like I was aiming for her head or anything. Thing is, Alex was off her face on coke. It probably quickened her death.'

'What did you do next?'

Powell inhaled. 'As soon as she dropped to the floor, I rushed to help her. I'd realised what I had done. It was pandemonium. Everyone was shouting or either screaming.'

'What was her dad's reaction?'

'He was furious with me. Simon rushed over and pushed me away. He was shaking Alex, begging her to open her eyes. I knew as soon as she hit the floor, she was dead. Mercury dragged me out of the studio. He was petrified. It took a few minutes to calm me down. We then went back into the studio. They found something to cover Alex's body. Her dad was sat on the floor sobbing his eyes out. He was saying over and over. They're both dead. Both my girls are gone. Then Andrea said that we should at least call the police. Simon agreed. But Jordan went ballistic. So did his thug of a security guard, Mitchell. Frankie said there'd be too many questions asked. It would bring a lot of unwanted attention to the studio. He knew what the media was like back then. They would have finished him. There was nothing better than the News of the Worl liked better than to bring people down. Especially when they were at their lowest. You only had to look at what they did to Princess Diana.'

'Whose idea was it to go back to London?' Watkins asked.

'Frankie's.' Powell replied. 'He said we need to regroup and come up with a plan. That's when he went back to his office and phoned everyone who was working at the studio, telling them not to come in the next day.'

'He told you that himself, did he?'

Dillon nodded. 'Yeah. When he got back from his office, he told us he'd phoned all the staff. He said he was giving them a day off to celebrate Alex winning her Brit award. We called a taxi to take us back to London. The taxi driver recognised me and Charlotte as soon as we got in the minibus. He'd obviously seen the Brit Awards on the telly earlier that night. He wouldn't shut up for the first twenty miles. Mitchell told him to shut his mouth and just drive. When we got back to London, he pestered me and Charlotte for an autograph.'

'What happened in the days that followed?' Fagan asked.

269

'We met up at my flat about a week after the events at the studio.'

'All of you?'

Powell shook his head. 'No, it was me, Charlotte Jordan and Mickey. Jordan explained that he had taken care of everything. As far as anyone was aware, Alex was in rehab. Jordan was a master at telling stories.'

'Did you ever see Alex's dad or Andrea jones after the incident at the studio?'

'No.' Powell sighed.

Fagan glanced at Abbey's diary. 'How many girls were there, Dillon?'

'I lost count. But I wasn't the only one who had a taste for that kind of thing. Jordan was just as bad. Near enough, every time I was at the studio, I'd see young girls there. There was a band recording there, the Paraphernalia. They used to supply Jordan with the girls.'

'Did you help yourself to any of these girls?'

Powell hesitated before nodding.

Fagan opened the diary. 'Abbey mentioned someone called Ben or Benny frequently. She said he used to take photos of the girls, naked photos.'

Powell's face bore the unmistakable expression of terror. He shook his head rigorously. 'No, I'm not giving any names other than the ones I have already given.'

'What was his second name?' Fagan persisted.

'I've given you enough already. If I give you any more names, then I won't last five minutes.' Powell glanced at his solicitor. 'I want to end this interview right now.'

Fagan stopped the recording.

'What do you reckon that was all about, boss?'

'He's terrified.' Fagan answered.

'Of what?'

Fagan flicked through the diary. 'That's what I intend to find out. We'll break for an hour then hammer Jordan.'

CHAPTER 35

Fagan started the interview process by reminding Jordan of his rights. Upon asking if he understood the reason for his arrest, Jordan nodded in response. Fagan observed Jordan's expression for a moment. Trying to determine if the interview would yield valuable information.

Jordan's solicitor stared at Fagan. Looking like a man who was engaged in a mental standoff. His pen poised over a notebook.

Fagan opened with a question. 'How did you manage it?'

A long silence followed.

'How did you convince millions of fans and the media that Alex had gone into rehab? And following her time in rehab, she retired to Spain. Living in seclusion. You being her only contact with the outside world. It must have taken a lot of planning to pull a stunt like that off. And a lot of balls. Surely you must have known that people would have gone looking for her. Obsessive fans, or a journalist wanting to dish the dirt on her lifestyle. She was massive in the early nineties. Eclipsing every other female popstar, even Madonna. They still play her songs on the radio and all the music channels on Sky. Towards the end Alex was constantly in the tabloids. If it wasn't her affair with Dillon Powell, it was her struggle with drug addiction making the headlines. It takes a lot of planning to cover up a murder. But to cover up the murder of one of the most iconic popstars of the nineties. So much evidence to get rid of. In this case, a lot of witnesses to silence. But then again, you all had a reason to keep silent, didn't you? None of you wanted to be exposed for who you really were. The only other victim there that night was Alex's dad. He wanted to call the police. Simon wanted to tell them what had happened. But you silenced him as well. How did you do that?'

Jordan remained silent.

'Alex must have terrified you when she threatened to expose Dillon and Charlotte.' Fagan paused. 'And you. When she threatened to go to the police after learning what happened to her sister.' He looked at the diary Abbey had written. 'There's a lot more in this diary than accounts of abuse that Abbey had to endure. What a brave girl she was. Despite being preyed upon by Powell, Charlotte, and Andrea. She talked to loads of girls at the studio. Who had been abused by so many popstars.' Fagan paused making eye contact with Jordan. 'And you.'

Jordan cleared his throat. 'No comment.'

'Must be hard for you. Sitting there, wondering where your future is going. It's all out in the open now. Your arrest at the Agincourt has triggered a tsunami of media interest. There are journalists camped on the doorstep of this police station at this very moment. There are journalists at Vine Road Music Studios. And there are journalists at the Agincourt Hotel. It's all over the news. Your life is being picked apart by social media. So far, Gwent police have received over seventy calls from people claiming to have experienced sexual abuse at the studio and the hotel. I'm expecting those numbers to skyrocket over the next few days. So do yourself a favour, Frankie. Tell us how you convinced the world that Alex has been alive for the past thirty years.'

Jordan smirked at Fagan.

'Find this whole affair funny, do you?'

'Do you have any idea how fickle people are, DI Fagan? The nineties gave birth to the internet, and production line pop stars.'

'So, what you're saying is that Alex was just a product to you?'

'They all were back then. It was all about profit, nothing else. These days its different. More artists wanting to be independent. Choosing their own paths. It's pathetic.'

Fagan smiled.

'Why do you find that funny, DI Fagan?'

'Because men like you who have had power in the past are realising how weak you actually are. As you just stated. Many of the stars of today are independent. Not needing anyone like you to promote them.'

'I was never weak.' Jordan sneered. 'I had the power to make or break an artist. They flocked to the studio, begging me to make them famous.'

'Why don't we return to the night that Alex was murdered? Why did you claim to me the other day that you didn't witness her murder? And that you went back to your office.' Watkins said.

'No comment.'

'When you saw Alex lying dead on the floor, you must have thought your world was about to end.'

'No.' Jordan shook his head. 'I merely saw it as an opportunity.'

'An opportunity?'

'To make more money, of course. Alex was a unique phenomenon. I knew this when I discovered her at that talent competition. I knew straight away she was special.'

'Special, how?'

'Over the years, Alex has become a cultural icon. Just like Marylin Monroe. Her image has been immortalised. Alex had the looks, the talent, the persona. She was the darling of the music industry. She even passed my wildest expectations. The media loved her. Her fans adored her.' Jordan paused for thought. 'In the beginning she was a shy girl, not realising the raw talent ready to burst out of her. Just like Monroe when she first started out. All it took was the right person to come along and channel that raw energy.'

'Still, to keep her memory alive and making everyone belive she was still alive must have taken a lot of planning.'

'It was easier than you think.' Jordan boasted. 'I knew a lot of powerful people back then, DI Fagan. People who had secrets they needed to keep. I admit it was hard for the first year. I would have fans and press hounding me every day. Asking when Alex was going to be back on her feet. When was she going to be releasing her next record? I almost came close to breaking. But then, 1994 came along.'

'What happened in 1994?'

'Spice Girls mania, of course. The moment those girls burst onto the scene, it became easier to manage. There were so many girl groups around back then. All jostling for attention. The fan interest died down. The media interest stopped overnight. It was a relief. All I had to do was keep Alex's memory alive. That was simple enough.'

'And the others, how much did you pay them to keep their mouths shut?'

'It didn't take any convincing. They were party to the murder. They all knew that if it ever came out that Alex was dead, they'd all be in the frame.'

'How come you didn't keep track of Andrea Jones?'

'I thought that silly cow was dead.' Jordan had an air of resentment in his voice. 'It's been a minor inconvenience. But nothing I cannot deal with.'

'Andrea claims Mitchell threatened her.'

'Wouldn't surprise me. It was a mistake taking him on in the beginning. But he wasn't the kind of man to take no for an answer.'

'You were frightened of him?'

'We all were. Just his stare was enough to put the fear of god into everybody.'

'So here's one of my key questions. Who did I speak to the other day on the phone? It wasn't Alex. She'd been dead for thirty years.'

Jordan smirked. 'That was Mickey and his toys.'

'Toys?'

'He has software capable of mimicking someone else's voice. He can create all kinds of voices, including Alex's. When you gave me your business card, I simply supplied him with your phone number.'

Fagan glanced at the diary. 'Abbey Xavier names you as one of the main abusers at Vine Road studios.'

'No comment.'

'Frankie, we already have you on a charge of perverting the course of justice. And given the nature of the crime, you will spend the next twenty years in prison. The fact that you witnessed Alex murder, plus covered it up, will not sit well with a jury. You not only covered up her murder, but you have spent the last thirty years perpetuating a lie. Your career is over, you've no future. You are all over the news. Your former partner is all over the news. You've nothing more to lose.'

Jordan stared at the diary. 'Alex's father came to me a few days before Alex won her brit award and told me what had happened to Abbey. I confronted Dillon and Charlotte about the truth. Why she committed suicide.'

'What was their response?' Watkins asked.

'They blamed everything on Andrea. They said she provided the girls.'

'What about the group the Paraphernalia?'

'What about them?'

'We have several people claiming they supplied the girls. They would pick them up on gigs and bring them to the studio.'

'No comment.'

'We'll eventually talk to them, Frankie. The more people offer information, the more dominoes will fall.'

Jordan grinned. 'Do you really think I will go to jail, DI Fagan?'

'You covered up the murder of an iconic popstar. I know

you'll do time for that.'

'What did I just say to you? The public is fickle. They tire of things so quickly now. The Jimmy Savile scandal sparked a nationwide outcry. But the focus was entirely on him.'

'You were arrested as part of Operation Yewtree.' Watkins pointed out.

'And released.' Jordan replied smugly. 'You see, what few people knew at the time was there was a surge of celebrities coming forward to confess their sins. Especially those who knew Savile had the secrets he kept. Everyone from popstars, TV stars, and politicians came forward to offer any help they could regarding Savile and his actions. Myself included, Along with Dillon Powell.'

'Why? Did you decide to grow a conscience?' Fagan asked.

'It wasn't about growing a conscience, DI Fagan. It was a get out of jail free card. Savile knew everyone who had dirty little secrets to keep. They even arrested him before anyone knew about these allegations. But Savile knew how to play the game. He knew others just like him in the world of show business who shared similar tastes. Far more powerful people who had the means to make any allegation disappear.'

'Such as?'

'DI Fagan. Do you honestly think I'm going to spill my guts?'

'If it would help reduce your jail sentence.'

Jordan smiled back. 'You simply don't understand, DI Fagan. You think because it's plastered all over the news, the law will punish me. I have had thirty years to plan for this. Like Savile, I have made preparations. Dillon will take the fall. He has known this for the past thirty years. It will probably be a manslaughter charge, not murder. We all saw how Alex was that night. How she found out about what happened to her sister. How she became violent. Attacking Dillon with her Brit award. How he snatched it out of her hands and accidentally lashed out. It will be just another media circus showcase.'

'What about disposal of her body?'

Jordan hesitated. 'I know nothing about that.'

'Who disposed of the body?' Watkins asked.

'I assumed it was Mitchell. He was the only person who could carry out a depravity like that.'

'Did you speak to him about where he disposed of Alex's body?'

Jordan seemed uncomfortable with the question. 'No.'

Fagan smiled. 'You didn't expect him to dump Alex's body at the back of the music studio, did you?.'

'No, I did not.' Jordan sighed.

'That must have upset your plans.'

Jordan didn't respond.

'Whose idea was it to bring Alex back to life?'

'That was all down to Mickey. At first I thought he was a bit barmy even suggesting the idea. But then he came to me with a demo tape. I was blown away. It was like listening to Alex all over again. I told Mickey it would be impossible for us to bring Alex back from the dead without raising suspicion. That's when he showed me a demo reel of Alex laying in a hospital bed.'

'Are you saying the cancer story was Mickey's idea?'

'Yes.'

'Still, you must have had your reservations.'

'I wanted to shine again.' Jordan confessed. 'I have been living as a recluse myself over the past ten years, DI Fagan.'

Fagan looked down at his notes. 'We've run a financial background check on you, Frankie. It says here you've over half a million in debt. I would have thought given how popular Alex was. And the fact they're always playing her songs on the radio, you'd be living a comfortable life. She had a Christmas number one in 1992. That's enough to support you for the rest of your life. Didn't you write the lyrics to Christmas Time spent with You? They play that song more time than they play Mariah Carey's All I want for Christmas. So where's all the money going, Frankie?'

Jordan shifted in his chair.

'Dillon and Charlotte must be milking you dry. Not to mention Mitchell and your former partner.'

'Mickey knew how much debt I was in. I hadn't promoted anyone in years. The royalties from Alex's songs were still coming in. But it wasn't enough. Alex was a pop icon. But it costs money to maintain the façade of keeping Alex alive.'

'So Mickey offered you a way out?'

Jordan nodded. 'Mickey first approached me last year about Bringing Alex back to life. He knew how much I was struggling. We had a meeting about what would happen if we were able to pull Mickey's plan off. It was agreed that we'd all go our separate ways if the plan worked. We'd split the initial earnings, then part company. I would get to keep any further royalties from Alex's music.'

'That all depended on how much money you made of Alex's new songs.'

Jordan nodded.

'DI Fagan, I think we're finished here for the time being. My client has been very cooperative.'

Fagan stared at Jordan for several seconds before ending the interview.

'What do you reckon, boss?'

Fagan studied his notes. 'I think he will walk.'

'Why?'

'Because of what he just said. He's right, the media interest will die down. Yewtree will deal with this and the information will just sit there. It will be a trial behind closed doors.' Fagan looked at the clock on the wall. 'We'll take an hour's break, then interview Mitchell. DI Saddler and DS Shaw are interviewing Charlotte and Mercury later on.'

278

'We'd like to ask you some questions about an incident that happened on the 22nd June 1993.' Watkins explained after running through the interview process.

Mitchell didn't respond.

'We've already spoken with Powell and Jordan. Frankie seemed more than willing to place all the blame on you,' Fagan stated.

'No comment.' Mitchell growled.

'Andrea Jones said you turned up at the studio the morning after Alex was murdered. She said you told her and Alex's father to leave the studio. And that you would take care of everything.'

'No comment.'

Fagan drew a breath. 'Why remove the head and hands, and not the whole body? You could have taken her anywhere. But you dumped the rest in a peat bog at the back of the studio. Wouldn't it have been a lot easier just to get rid of Alex elsewhere instead of risking her body being discovered?'

'No comment.'

'You must have had a bit of knowledge about the peat bogs. They're protected by law.' Fagan looked down at his notes. 'I've been doing a bit of research into the history of the studio. According to local planning records Frankie Jordan applied for planning permission in March 1990. It was a request to extend the studio beyond its current boundary. Which would have meant having to drain the peat bog. The council turned the application down.'

'You were in charge of security back in 1990, were you

not?' Watkins asked.

Mitchell nodded. 'Yes.'

'You would have had access to information relating to Jordan's plans to extend the studio.'

'It was thirty years ago, for Christ's sake. You seriously expect me to remember some vague planning application.'

'Were you not head of security back in 1990?'

''I just told you, didn't I. Yes,' Mitchell sneered.

'Let's discuss your whereabouts on the night of June 25th 1993. Can you recall what you were doing?' Fagan asked.

'Course I bloody well can. It was the night of the Brit Awards.'

'You organised security that night for Alex.'

Mitchell rolled his eyes. 'I was head of security, so yes, I organised everything.'

'Then how was Charlotte able to storm the stage and assault Alex?'

'That was all for the fucking cameras. I knew she was going to do that.'

'Not much of a minder, were you? Allowing Charlotte to assault Alex.'

'I was fantastic at my job, DI Fagan. Mercury had a word with me earlier on in the evening. He told me what was going to happen.'

'Moving forward to when you arrived at the Agincourt hotel following the Brit Awards. Where were you when Alex's mother gained access to the hotel?'

'I was at the reception. Watching Dillon receive his award.'

'His would be for the campaign he spearheaded. No Means No?'

'Yes.'

'How many security staff did you have that evening?'

'I can't remember. It was thirty fucking years ago.'

'Don't you keep records of the staff you hire?'

'I do now. But thirty years ago, it was a different matter.

Yeah, once Alex had taken off, I had to ask Jordan for more funding so I could hire a couple of extra bodies.'

'Yet you don't remember how many people you hired that night.'

'No, probably a couple of doormen to make sure no one gained access to the hotel. Fat lot it did, considering Alex's mother gaining access to the hotel. Look, haven't we been over all this when you interviewed me yesterday?'

'But Alex's mother gained access to the hotel.' Watkins pointed out. 'She spoke to Alex and told her that her sister had committed suicide. Which is what led to her murder.'

'Why didn't you break up the fight between Alex and her father?' Fagan asked.

'I tired, but then Alex got aggressive with me.'

'Surely you would have known how to handle her.'

'She's had tantrums before, if that is what you are asking. I used to let her get on with it. Alex had a temper, but she'd burn out after a while.'

'We have a witness that saw you, and the others having an argument at the back of the hotel.'

'Again, we've been over this.' Mitchell drew breath. 'Everything was getting out of hand. Alex was off her rocker that night. Jesus, she'd snorted enough cocaine at the Brit Awards.'

'You went back to the studio where you carried on arguing. Dillon has already confessed to assaulting Alex with the Brit award. Our labs are going over the statue. We believe there are traces of blood still on the statue.'

'So.' Mitchell shrugged. 'If Dillon has already confessed, then it's an open and shut case for you.'

'Is it?' Fagan said.

'Yeah.'

'You claimed in your interview that you went back to the office to phone a taxi to take you all back to London.'

'That's exactly what I did.'

'Andrea Jones said that you were all witness to the murder of Alex.'

'That lying bitch is just trying to land us all in the shit.'

'She has also stated she was involved in a sexual relationship with you. Along with Dillon and Jordan.'

'That slut was fucking everyone who came to the studio. It's the only reason Jordan kept her around. She was entertainment for the various artists that visited the studio. We are talking thirty years ago. It was chaos at that studio. There were so many people coming and going, it was hard to keep track of anyone.'

'Including young girls.'

Mitchell hesitated. 'Yeah, including young girls. Look, I know where you are going with this.'

'And where is that?' Watkins asked.

'You're about to lump me in with the Jimmy Savile scandal.'

Fagan and Watkins made eye contact. 'Why would we do that?'

'Because I know Dillon Powell and Frankie Jordan were both questioned in the wake of what happened with Savile.'

'Were you aware of abuse at the studio?'

'There were many girls that visited the studio and the hotel.'

'That not what I asked Alun.'

'Ok, yes, there were loads of girls who used to go to the studios. And there were stories floating around.'

'So there were rumours floating around about what was going on at the studio?'

'I'm not a grass. If that's why you've dragged me down here.'

'You know why we've *dragged* down here. I will ask you again. Andrea Jones said you turned up at the studio the morning after. She has claimed in a detailed interview, she and Alex's father stayed with Alex's body all night. You turned up at eight o'clock in the morning. You told Andrea Jones and

Simon Xavier that you would take care of everything.'

'No comment.'

'Right now we have forensics going over studio one with ultraviolet light. They are looking for blood samples. Blood can survive for decades, Alun. If there are traces of Alex's blood in studio one, then we'll find them.'

'What's that got to do with anything?'

'Last year, the owner of the studio finally got the go ahead for planning permission. You are still in charge of security for Vine Road Music studios. Shortly after planning permission was approved, there was a break in at the studio. I take it you are aware of this incident?'

'Yeah, it was brought to my attention.'

'Can I ask why the studio wasn't permanently manned by security?'

'Before the pandemic hit, it was. But when the country went into lockdown, it was pointless keeping anyone there. Anything of value was taken away from the studio.'

'According to our police records, studio one was stripped bare. All but the floor and skirting boards.'

'No comment.'

Fagan switched subjects. 'Tell us about Dorothy Morris.'

Mitchell stared back, wide eyed.

Fagan observed the fear in his expression.

'Who?' Mitchell's voice seemed to quiver.

'Dorothy Morris. She was an ex-girlfriend of yours, was she not?'

Mitchell took several seconds to answer. 'Dorothy Morris.' He said her name slowly.

'Dorothy Morris went missing on the 14th of March 1978. Her mother and sister reported her missing.'

'And I was fucking questioned about that.' Mitchell barked. 'I'll tell you what I told the police forty-five years ago. I had no idea where she went that night. I was in the pub with a mate, who backed up my story.'

'You've been living in London since 1995?' Watkins stated.

'Yeah.'

'Ever get back to Newport over the years?'

'Occasionally, when I have had a job on.'

'Ever call in on old friends?'

'No. After I became Alex's minder, I never looked back. Sure, I have been back to Wales plenty of times. But always on business.'

'Ten years ago, South Wales police opened up their cold case files. Dorothy Morris' remains were found washed up on the banks of the Usk in 1978. Just down from the transporter bridge. Her head and hands had been removed. The police of that era couldn't identify the body. But they kept samples. When police reopened into Dorothy's disappearance, her sister came forward and provided a DNA sample. It was a perfect match. Her sister also said that you were living with Dorothy at the time of her disappearance.'

Mitchell glanced at his solicitor, who was frantically scribbling notes. 'I just said didn't I, police questioned me about that and released me. I had no idea where the bloody girl went.' Mitchell's temper rose.

'We have been to visit Dorothy's sister. She claims you had a turbulent relationship with Dorothy. And that you frequently beat her. Dorothy confided in her sister Faye just before she disappeared. She said she was pregnant, and that you and her had a blazing row about it. The autopsy carried out on her body in 1978 confirms that she was pregnant at the time of her death.'

'Jesus fucking Christ, that woman and her poxy mother bloody hated me going out with Dotty. She's probably made up a pack of lies.'

Fagan checked his notes. 'You served time for attempted murder from 1979 to 1988?'

'Yes, I fucking did.' Mitchell scowled. 'Why are you dredging up my past suddenly? I thought I was here in

284

connection with the murder of Alex Xavier.'

Fagan glanced up from his notes momentarily. 'You shared a cell with Richard Bishop.'

Mitchell sat back and folded his arms. 'Fuck, here we go. Another ghost from my past. He's still pissed off. I owe him money, I suppose. Well, he's not getting shit from me now. He can forget it.'

'You claimed to Bishop once that you had murdered someone.'

Mitchell shook his head, grinning. He glanced at the ceiling, clasping his hands behind his head. 'I can't believe I'm hearing this bullshit?'

Fagan looked directly at him. 'You shared a house In Potter Street in Newport with Dorothy? This would have been at the time of her disappearance. Dorothy's sister provided the address.'

Fear streaked across Mitchell's face again.

'Early yesterday morning, Gwent Police got a warrant to search the back of a property in Potter Street. The property you lived in with Dorothy. They used ground penetrating radar to look for anything unusual. Yesterday afternoon police excavated under the patio. They came across a skull and other bones that CSI identified as being the remains of two hands. Would you know anything about that?'

Mitchell glanced at his solicitor. 'No comment.'

'We have also tracked down the witness you say was your alibi from that night. Unfortunately, they died during the pandemic.'

Mitchell tapped his foot nervously on the floor. 'No comment.'

'You're stuck between a rock and a hard place, Alun. Officers will question you about the disappearance of Dorothy Morris. Detectives are piecing together her last movements.' Fagan's voice dropped even lower. His words dripping with gravity. 'You told someone, Alun. Someone you thought you could trust. Richard Bishop. You told him about the murder of Dorothy Morris in chilling detail. Details that only the killer would know.'

Mitchel's face drained of colour, his eyes widening with realisation. The memories surged back. The hushed conversations, the weight of his secrets. He thought he was clever, that he could escape, But now, facing Fagan's unwavering scrutiny, he understood the gravity of his situation.

Fagan allowed silence to linger. 'Alun, it's time to come clean. We have evidence that points to your involvement in the murder of Dorothy Morris and Alexandria Xavier. We have witnesses who will testify. Don't you understand Alun? No one is afraid of you anymore.'

Mitchell's shoulders slumped, defeated. He finally saw the walls closing in. The realisation hit him like a physical blow. He looked at Fagan. His expression resembling a terrified child. Then he began to talk. 'I never expected anyone to find her.'

'Who Alex or Dorothy?' Watkins asked.

Mitchell looked at him. 'Alex.'

'What happened that night at the music studio?'

'Dillon smashed Alex over the head with the Brit award.'

'Was it an accidental blow, or did he kill her intentionally?'

'It was deliberate. Alex was screaming at him about her sister Abbey. She threatened she would tell the police about him. She smacked him first with the award. I thought she'd taken his eye out. There was blood everywhere. Everything happened so fast. Dillon flew into a rage and just went at her. He grabbed the award, screaming at her. Before anyone could stop him, Alex was on the floor in a pool of blood. Her dad was hysterical. He turned and went to find the nearest telephone to phone the police.'

'Did you stop him?'

Mitchell nodded. 'Not by choice. On the orders of Jordan.'

'Frankie ordered you to stop him from phoning the police?'

Fagan said.

Mitchell nodded. 'Jordan was terrified. He knew if the police would have turned up, then it would all be over for him. It was me who suggested heading back to London. The initial plan was to leave Alex let a member of staff discover her when they turned up the next day.'

'There were staff who had spare keys to the studio?'

'Yeah, but Frankie phoned them and told them not to go into work. I turned up at their house the following day to get the spare key to the studio.'

'If the original plan was for you all to head back to London, why didn't it happen?'

'Alex's dad didn't want to go anywhere. Despite Frankie literally getting on his knees. That's when I stepped in and said I'll sort things out the next day. Everyone except for Adrea and Simon headed back to London. We had to hire a taxi. The taxi driver wouldn't stop yapping until I told him to.'

'What happened when you got back to London?'

'We talked about the events for a few hours. Then Frankie said he had to make a few phone calls. I headed back up to Monmouthshire, grabbing a few tools. When I got back to the studio, Andrea and Simon were in Jordan's office. I told them to clear out, and I'd take care of things.'

'Did Alex's dad put up any kind of resistance?'

'No. I think he'd finally realised he had lost both his daughters. We went back into studio one. They said their goodbyes to Alex and left.'

'And that when you went to work.'

'Yeah.' Mitchell's tone was no longer threatening, but timid. 'I knew the peat bog at the back of the studio had a protection order on it. A few months earlier Frankie moaned that the local council refused planning permission to expand the studio.'

'When the council gave permission to build on the peat bog, why didn't you go back and remove Alex's remains?'

Mitchel; took a deep breath. 'Honestly, I don't know. I had plenty of opportunity. None of it seemed real to me. It was so long ago I didn't think she would be found.'

'But you dumped the award and Andrea's watch with Andrea's body. Why did you do that?'

Mitchell shrugged. 'I dunno. I suppose her body would have been discovered eventually and it would create a mystery. But I thought that wouldn't happen until long after we're gone. I have read stories about bodies being found in peat bogs. Perfectly preserved, hundreds or thousands of years after they ended up there.'

'DI Fagan. I feel my client has been very cooperative during this interview. I suggest we end so that I can talk to my client.' The solicitor requested.

Fagan looked at Mitchell before nodding and ending the interview.

CHAPTER 37

The Cantreff Inn - Two weeks later

'Fagan!' Evans called out.

Fagan grabbed his pint and walked towards his friends.

Dean Tyler was sat Jackie and Evans, huddled around a tablet.

A copy of the Monmouthshire Beacon was one the table.

Fagan glanced at the headline.

End of an era: Famous studio closes its doors following Alex X murder

Fagan sensed guilt tug at his emotions. 'Poor sod who bought that studio in 2019 has lost a fortune.'

'Tyler has something to show you Fagan.' Evan's handed him the tablet. 'It's Mickey Mercury at a seminar on AI last week.'

Fagan tapped the play icon on the screen.

'Ladies and gentlemen, esteemed members of the music industry, and my dear colleagues. Thank you for gathering here today as we embark on a revolutionary journey that will forever change the landscape of music.'

'I can't believe his arrogance.' Fagan stated.

'Today, I present to you a concept that will push the boundaries of creativity and captivate the hearts of millions across the globe. Allow me to introduce you to the legacy of the late and great pop sensation, Alexandria Xavier. Her untimely departure from our world left an immense void that can never be filled. But fear not, for I have a solution that will not only honour her memory but also generate unimaginable profits. Members of the audience, I bring you the future of music production. AI-generated Alexandria Xavier hits.'

Music began to play.

'Have to admit, it is catchy.' Tyler said.

Mercury continued. 'Imagine reliving the magic of Alex's voice, her style, her charisma. All channelled through state-of-the-art artificial intelligence. We've gathered an unparalleled team of AI experts, music producers, and data analysts to meticulously analyse every aspect of Alexandria's musical journey. We've dissected her melodies, studied her vocal nuances, and even delved into the emotional undercurrents that made her music resonate so deeply with her fans.'

'Well I won't being buying any of that crap.' Jackie said. 'I love her old stuff.'

The video played on. 'With this data in hand, we've harnessed the power of AI to recreate Alexandria Xavier's essence. Our advanced algorithms can now craft original compositions that echo her unique sound, the infectious hooks, the soul-stirring ballads. These AI-generated songs are not mere imitations; they are the evolution of Alex's artistry. A continuation of the legacy she left behind. I understand that there may be concerns about the ethics of using AI in this manner. Let me assure you, our intent is not to replace genuine human creativity but to complement it. Our AI tools will work hand in hand with talented artists and producers, breathing new life into Alexandria's musical legacy while fostering fresh collaborations that bridge the past and the future. I say to those who fear what AI can do. Let us not fear it. But let us embrace what AI can do. Imagine a world where the music doesn't end. Imagine listening to new tracks by David Bowie, George Michael, Prince and many other artists that have given us so much in the past. I say let them keep producing the music for current and future generations. This is not about ethics. It's about the music.' The video ended.

Jackie looked at the newspaper. 'Can't believe Dillon killed her.' Jackie stated. 'I was madly in love with that bloke when he was a popstar. He had the looks and the personality. All us girls from town fancied him.'

'But underneath Jacks, Dillon was a sexual predator.'

'Looks like you've uncovered another shit storm, Fagan.' Evans remarked.

'Tell me about it. In the past two weeks alone, there've been over two hundred people contact Gwent police. Regarding certain activities at the studios over the decades.'

'But the news has lost interest in this already.' Jackie pointed out.

Fagan gulped down his pint and nodded. 'Of course they have. That's because the entertainment industry doesn't want to be embroiled another sexual abuse scandal. And the police don't want another criminal investigation that's going to cost more man hours than they can afford.'

'I tell you what, it took a lot of balls to pull this off.' Evans said. 'Dillon murdered Alex in 1993. That's thirty years ago. I was looking on the net the other day. There've been loads of conspiracy theories about Alex's whereabouts over the years. There's even been a few saying that she was dead.'

'But try proving it. Her manager, Frankie Jordan, pulled the wool over everyone's eyes. Making everyone believe she was alive all this time.'

'What's going to happen to them?' Jackie asked.

'Dillon has been charged with murder. Although given that there were several witnesses to the crime, he'll probably convicted of manslaughter. Everyone who was there that night at the studio claims Alex attacked Dillon first. Which means his defence will ask the jury to consider a plea of manslaughter. It's all about having a shit hot defence team these days.'

'But what about the others?'

'I couldn't tell you, Jacks. It's in the hands of Yewtree now.

Alex's former minder has been charged with the murder of a woman in 1978. There's a massive amount of evidence that points to sexual abuse at the Agincourt hotel and the music studio. Charlotte West and Frankie Jordan are in the frame for that. We have a diary written by Alex's sister Abbey. She chronicled what was going on at the hotel and the studio. There are loads of popstars she mentioned who were into all kinds of shit. I've read the diary. It's really harrowing in parts. I had to stop reading on a number of occasions.'

'Bloody hell, that was brave of the girl.'

'It was, but in the end, she committed suicide. That will play into the trial when that happens.'

'Well, I hope they all go to prison for what they did to that poor girl and other who were abused.'

Evans was staring at his smart phone. 'Even though the song that was released a few weeks ago was created by AI, it's still topping the music charts.'

'I thought it would have been taken off the net by now, considering it's not her.' Jackie said.

'But it is her Jackie. That's what makes this AI so scary. It can create a perfect match of anyone's voice and recreate it. There are loads of websites that can record your voice and turn you into a singing sensation. I was talking to Tyler last night about it. He says there's a growing trend in people having their voices digitised. Many people are getting twitchy about AI. It's got a lot of actors and writers worried. That's why there's a strike in America. By the end of the year, there'll be nothing decent to watch on the streaming services. *Stranger Things, the Last of Us* and *Star Trek Strange New worlds* are going to be affected. Along with other TV shows.'

'You know, it would be nice if everyone turned off their smartphones for a while and just stepped back. I never got into technology and it hasn't done me any harm.'

'Yeah, but every time you get stuck with something tech, you always call me.'

'That's because Tyler lives in London.' Fagan smiled winking at Tyler.

Jackie looked towards the entrance. 'Hey Nigel. Never thought I'd see you stepping through my door.'

'I'm not much of a drinker, I'm afraid Jackie.' Thomas looked at Fagan, holding up a tablet. 'I have something to show you. It relates to the incident at the music studio a few weeks back.' He placed the tablet on the bar.

Evans, Tyler and Jackie huddled around Fagan and Thomas.

'I have been trawling through the pictures from the Abergavenny Tribune archive. There are hundreds of pictures that have been taken in the Agincourt Hotel over the decades. That place has had loads of celebrities stay there. Mainly from the music industry.'

'I was looking through the register they keep purely for celebrities.' Fagan revealed. 'Tom Cruise was there a few months back.'

'Piss off.' Evans moaned. 'And you didn't tell me.'

'I was in the middle of a police investigation, remember Jamie? I can't tell you everything.'

'How come they haven't shut that place? Considering all the things that went on there?' Jackie asked.

'The hotel has been around since the thirteenth century. It's survived a lot of historical upheaval over the years.' Thomas explained. 'It's owned by a big chain of posh hotels throughout the country.' Thomas located the picture. 'Here we go.'

Fagan stared at the picture.

'This was taken in June 1993. Dillon Powell was part of something called No Mean No.'

Fagan nodded. 'Yeah, it was a campaign to raise awareness of grooming gangs and sexual predators. From 1990 to 1993, a police investigation called Operation Julie ran. It ended up in the arrest of twenty-three men who were grooming young girls. Mainly concentrated around the Swansea area. But there were a few arrested from up the valleys. During our investigation into Alex's murder, we kicked over a real hornets' nest.'

Jackie pointed at the tablet, glancing at Fagan. 'So what you're saying is that Dillon was campaigning against the abuse of young girls. While all the time he was an abuser himself.'

Fagan nodded.

'Oh my god, that just makes me sick to my stomach. I hope he gets life for what he did to Alex and all those other young girls he abused.'

Thomas pointed at the photograph on the tablet. 'I've enhanced this photo.'

'That's Dillon in the Middle.' Fagan said. 'Next to him is the Chief Constable of south Wales police at the time, Bob Benson.' He glanced at Evans and Jackie. 'We all know him. Stood next to him is Detective Chief Inspector Owen Lance. Who later became Chief Constable after Bob retired.'

'Look at the group standing behind.' Thomas instructed. 'Just standing behind Benson. At first I didn't notice, but when I enhanced this picture.' Thomas zoomed in on the person standing several feet behind Benson. The man was staring at the camera, smiling.

'Holy fuck!' Evans said with an excited tone. 'That's fucking Benny the perv.'

Jackie let out a snort of derision. 'Urh! That twat was in the South Wales Argus tonight, going on about his fucking book. Plus, he was on Wales Today earlier. He was at a book signing in Cardiff. There must have been two hundred people queuing outside Waterstones just to get him to sign a book. All probably perverts themselves.'

Fagan stared at the image of Nelson. 'Eddie Falcon mentioned that Benny used to hang around the music studio when he worked there. I was doing time in Usk prison when Eddie worked there. He said that Benny was always hanging around this group called the Paraphernalia. They were rounded up last week and questioned about their activities at the studio. We've also got statements from other girls who said that Benny used to take nude photos of them.'

'Come to think of it,' Evans said. 'I always used to see Benny with a camera around his neck I saw a group of girls having a go at him once in the Shire. He was taking pictures of them.'

'Jesus, I just remembered something.' 'When police raided Benny's shed up at the allotment, CSI found a shit load of old computers. Their hard drives were missing.'

'So where are the missing hard drives?'

Fagan stared at the photo. 'That's what I intend to find out.' He glanced at his friends. 'I owe it to everyone who has suffered at the hands of that prick. Graham, Justin Pike's sister, Michelle. All the other girls he's abused. The other boys from Forest Coalpit dorms. From now on, I'm going to make it my mission to nail that bastard, once and for all. Even if it costs me my career.'

Evans put his hand on Fagan's shoulder. 'You won't be alone, Fagan. All of us will stand by you.'

The end

Detective Inspector Marc Fagan will return in, The Dead Remember.

Help an independent author.

Many thanks for buying a copy of Melody from the dead.

Before you take to Amazon and hammer me about grammar, please stop to pause.

Please e-mail and tell me if there are any problems with the book.

If you have enjoyed what you have read, then please spread the word to other avid readers.

I don't have an e-mail list. I don't enjoy spamming people and cluttering up their e-mail boxes. If you would like to know when the next book will be available, then please drop me a line. You can look me up on Facebook or go on my Amazon page to see if there are any more DI Fagan books to read. You can also click on the follow button.

Many thanks.
Jason Chapman

Jasonchapman-author@hotmail.com

Other books by Jason Chapman

The UFO Chronicles
The fallen
Codename Angel
The Angel Conspiracy
The Angel Prophecy

Detective Sergeant Samantha Drake
Dystopia
Avalon Rising
Signals
Project Genesis

Detective inspector Mark Fagan
The dead will beckon
The Dead and the Buried

Quality declaration

Please note, this book has been written in UK English. US English and UK English differ slightly.

I have taken every care to produce a quality item. As an independent author, it is hard to find people who will edit for a fair price. With the cost-of-living crisis biting down, it gets harder with every passing day. Most editors and proof-readers cost thousands of pounds. Way beyond the budget of struggling indie authors. As a result, independent authors are often criticised for producing sloppy work. Packed with mistakes and a poor use of grammar. It can be an uphill struggle against reviewers who ignore the storylines and concentrate on missing full stops or speech marks. I am constantly updating my books, reading through them. Making sure you, the reader, enjoy the stories I write. I use the latest AI editing software to help me with my writing and editing. It's not perfect, but it's better than just giving up.

Mainstream publishers label independent authors as desperate, inexperienced, self-published cry-babies. There are many indie authors who work hard to perfect their craft. Producing exciting stories for an ever-hungry reading public. Often writing better stories than many of the top bestselling authors. It comes down to two choices. Chase the dream, or give up because you simply can't afford it.

OFFWORLD
PUBLICATIONS